THE TIDEWAY GIRLS

By Pamela Evans and available from Headline

A Barrow in the Broadway
Lamplight on the Thames
Maggie of Moss Street
Star Quality
Diamonds in Danby Walk
A Fashionable Address
Tea-Blender's Daughter
The Willow Girls
Part of the Family
Town Belles
Yesterday's Friends
Near and Dear
A Song in Your Heart
The Carousel Keeps Turning
A Smile for all Seasons
Where We Belong
Close to Home
Always There
The Pride of Park Street
Second Chance of Sunshine
The Sparrows of Sycamore Road
In the Dark Streets Shining
When the Boys Come Home
Under an Amber Sky
The Tideway Girls

THE TIDEWAY GIRLS

Pamela Evans

headline

First published in 2009 by
HEADLINE PUBLISHING GROUP

1

Cataloguing in Publication Data is available from the British Library

ISBN 978 0 7553 4542 7

Typeset in Bembo by Palimpsest Book Production Limited,
Grangemouth, Stirlingshire

Printed and bound in Great Britain by
Clays Ltd, St Ives plc

HEADLINE PUBLISHING GROUP
An Hachette Livre UK Company
338 Euston Road
London NW1 3BH

www.headline.co.uk
www.hachettelivre.co.uk

Acknowledgements

A big thank-you to all the team at Headline, in particular Sherise Hobbs for her brilliant editorial guidance and general support, and the design department for creating such gorgeous jackets time after time.

Warmest thanks to my agent Barbara Levy, who 'discovered' me some twenty years ago and has been there for me ever since.

Thanks also to historical researcher Ruth Boreham, who burrowed into various archieves and found for me invaluable information about photography around 1912. I must also mention Bob Mason, who lives in the village on which Tideway is based and who has educated me on certain geographical and maritime details.

Chapter One

'Ta-ta, Mum, see you tonight,' chorused the Bow sisters as they stepped lightly out of the cottage door, lifted their skirts, put on their hats and tore down the hill to catch the ferry to work.

'You're late this morning, gels,' observed a local woman who was a regular in the gathering at the landing stage waiting for the boat to take them across the river to the larger village. 'That isn't like you. A few more minutes and you'd have missed the ferry.'

'May's fault,' joshed Bessie, her blue eyes sparkling with fun as she grinned towards her sister, a lock of golden hair escaping from the knot it was woven into at the back of her head. 'It was her turn to go and get the milk from the farm for our breakfast, and she was so busy flirting with the dairy lad she lost track of the time and put us all behind. I had to go and fetch her in the end. You should have seen her there; giggling and making eyes at him as though she had all the time in the world.'

'Ooh, May, you naughty gel,' teased the woman in the strong Essex accent that was still prevalent among the older residents here in the village of Tideway. 'I bet your ma gave you a bit of a ticking-off about that.'

'She was none too happy about it,' confirmed dark-eyed May, omitting to add that she was used to being out of favour with her mother at the moment. 'I wasn't all that long really. Anyway, it's rude not to pass the time of day with the person who's serving you with the milk.'

'You were doing more than just passing the time of day with him, and you shouldn't hang about when people are waiting for you,' chided Bessie, who was eighteen and generally considered to be the more sensible of the two sisters. A year younger, vivacious, fun-loving May tended to be rather too impulsive at times.

'All right, sis, I'm sorry,' May sighed ruefully. 'I wouldn't want you to lose your job for bad timekeeping because of me.'

'I'm not likely to do that because my boss is very tolerant, but I'm not so sure about yours.'

1

'Old Mother Misery Guts wouldn't get rid of me, don't worry,' her sister responded jovially. She was referring to Mrs March, the owner of the haberdashery shop where she worked. 'I'm popular with the customers so she wouldn't want to lose all that goodwill, since she creates precious little of it herself.'

'Modest little thing, isn't she?' said Bessie with irony, and everyone smiled, enjoying the youthful banter. The Bow family went back generations in the Essex village of Tideway and was very much respected. Everyone knew Bessie and May and their two brothers. Children of a fisherman, they weren't well off, but their mother was strait-laced and strict so they knew how to behave.

It was a cold November morning in 1912 with a raw mist hanging moistly over everything, occasional shafts of hazy sunlight breaking through and catching the gently undulating waters of the river Colne, edged on the banks by fishing boats. There were also yachts – mostly owned by rich non-locals – laid up here for the winter. They often needed work, which provided gainful employment for the boatyard, from which the sound of hammering and sawing could be heard from a very early hour.

Local fishermen, back from the sea, worked on their boats or stood about in groups on the quay smoking and talking. Heaps of silver sprats and small whiting had been discharged on to one of the designated quays, to be sold for a pittance as manure to farmers by those fishermen whose luck was against them and who were too late getting their catch into Brightlingsea in time for the fresh fish market or the railway quay for transportation. A few local people were sorting through the slippery piles with buckets, helping themselves for the family supper. Traditionally no charge would be made to them, so it was most unprofitable for a fisherman to miss the market.

The ferry crowd were stamping their feet and hugging themselves to keep warm, their voices echoing into the damp morning air as they chatted among themselves, the subject having moved on to the forthcoming Guy Fawkes celebrations, which were made much of in Tideway.

Looking towards the river, Bessie could see the ferry boat approaching through the mist. The service was as reliable as the seasons and operated no matter how extreme the elements, being the essential link between the maritime village of Tideway and the slightly larger settlement of Haverley on the opposite bank. At Haverley there was a small amount of industry, a few more shops and a train station with a direct link to London. The nearest other place to cross the river was at Colchester three miles away, so the social classes sat side by side to cross the water. Boatbuilders, businessmen, shop workers and skivvies, housewives, the doctor, vicar and undertaker all travelled to and fro on the ferry at one time or another.

Tideway was a tight-knit, clean-living, God-fearing community, the majority of its male residents earning an uncertain living from fishing, situated as it was just a few miles from where the tidal Colne – saltwater at Tideway – flowed into the open sea.

A good-humoured cheer went up when the ferry arrived and the ferryman shipped the oars for landing.

'Ooh come on, mate,' whispered May under her breath as the courteous ferryman – dignified in dark clothes and a bowler hat – carefully helped his alighting passengers on to dry land. 'He'll have to scrape us off the ground if he doesn't hurry up, 'cause we'll have turned to ice in this weather.'

'He's being as quick as he can,' her sister pointed out. 'He does a good job.'

'I know; it's just me being impatient as usual,' said May, her velvety brown eyes shining against her olive skin, her dark hair swept up and piled on top of her head under her wide-brimmed hat. 'Bless him.'

At last he was ready for customers to board, and the sisters waited their turn. Lifting their ankle-length skirts, they stepped in and sat down on the wooden bench, shawls drawn tight around them and hats pulled down against the weather, as the flat-bottomed boat moved smoothly across the narrow stretch of water. Bessie would then head for the photographic shop and studio where she was an all-round assistant and general dogsbody, and May to Mrs March's haberdashery emporium, where she worked as a shop girl.

The mist had cleared and Bessie was out on the cobbles cleaning the bowed shop window in the row of whitewashed shops in Haverley's main street when she saw the first customers approaching: a couple well into middle age whom she recognised from when they had booked their appointment. Swiftly lifting her skirt and nipping down the stepladder, she went inside, smoothed her high-necked white blouse into place over her long black skirt and took her place behind the reception desk.

Greeting them with a mixture of warmth and efficiency, she checked their appointment and settled them in the waiting area – a comfortably furnished room with a few high-backed chairs and a table with a selection of magazines for clients to browse. As well as displaying his work in the shop window, her employer also had examples placed around the shop in a variety of sizes and frames. Not too many; he was particular about that. He liked things kept tasteful.

3

'I'll go and tell Mr Parsons that you're here,' Bessie told the couple with a polite smile. 'He won't keep you waiting long.'

'I thought you'd be busier than this,' remarked the man, who was plump and bearded. 'Photographs are so popular these days.'

'We are careful not to overbook,' Bessie explained. 'But I expect it will be a bit hectic later on.'

Bessie had worked here since leaving school at thirteen, originally employed as a cleaner and errand girl. But the role had quickly developed into studio assistant, receptionist, occasional dark-room helper, cleaner, tea-maker, bookkeeper and any other task that needed doing. She enjoyed the job enormously, especially helping in the studio, something that she was often asked to do when the sitting involved a female. Her employer had noticed that women were more accepting of any tactful suggestion as regarded adjustment to hair or clothes if it came from a member of their own sex rather than from a man. Bessie knew she was lucky to have the job, since nearly all employment for women in the area was domestic. She and May were both fortunate in that respect, though the wages in each case were meagre.

'Your first appointment is here, Mr Parsons,' she announced, going into the studio, a room flooded with light from the huge window and the partly glazed ceiling. Unlike Tideway, which still didn't have piped gas, the service had recently come to Haverley, and there were gas lamps in here. However, Digby Parsons – being a traditionalist – preferred to work with natural light whenever possible. 'It's Mr and Mrs Brown for a silver-wedding portrait.'

A widower of middle years, Digby Parsons was a kind-hearted dome of a man; short and plump, bald on top, with curly ginger hair at the sides peppered with grey and creeping towards his straggly beard. His round, somewhat protuberant blue eyes often had a preoccupied look about them, usually because he was thinking about some aspect of his work. He had a slight stoop and walked in an odd shuffling manner. Passionate about his work, he was inclined to take far more interest in achieving the best possible results from an artistic point of view rather than the commercial aspect.

'Bring them in then, please, Bessie, and I'd like you to stay in the studio for a while if you wouldn't mind; just until we get them relaxed and settled.'

'Certainly.' Most unusually for an employer, Mr Parsons was so considerate of her, she sometimes wondered if he needed reminding that she was actually paid by him to do whatever task he asked of her.

A few minutes later, having titivated in the mirror in the dressing room, the couple were seated on an ornate bench with mock potted plants at the side and a plain canvas behind, Mrs Brown looking as though she was in the advanced stages of paralysis. Rigidly corseted and dressed in a high-necked brown dress and an elaborate matching hat, she was upright and stiff, staring at the camera wide eyed and worried. Mr Brown was looking ahead of him, his mouth fixed in a false, unconvincing smile. The two were at such a distance from one another, one might have thought they were in the middle of a row rather than celebrating an important anniversary.

It was Bessie's job to help put them at their ease. She wondered how she was going to do that with this pair, since they didn't administer laudanum here.

'Maybe if you could try to loosen up a little, Mrs Brown,' suggested Digby gingerly with a cautious chuckle. 'You are only having your photograph taken, not going to the gallows.'

The woman didn't appreciate his attempt at humour. 'I am perfectly relaxed, Mr Parsons, thank you,' she said tartly. 'And I'll thank you not to be personal.'

'Sorry,' he said, colouring up.

'Mr Parsons was only trying to help, Mrs Brown,' put in Bessie, hoping to gloss things over, ever mindful of the fact that the customer must be pandered to at all times. 'But I can see that you are a little more at ease now that you are getting used to us. A silver wedding anniversary is a very special celebration. You must both be feeling very happy.'

'Humph,' muttered her husband through his forced grin.

Mrs Brown just stared ahead, looking about as much at ease as someone about to have major surgery. 'We're not of an age to think much about feelings,' she said at last. 'That sort of indulgence is for the youngsters.'

'Do you have a family?' Bessie enquired, seizing the opportunity to move the conversation forward.

'I should hope so after twenty-five years,' snorted Mrs Brown. 'It would be a funny to-do if we hadn't.'

'We have five children, all grown up and married,' put in Mr Brown helpfully. 'It's for them we're having this portrait done.'

'How lovely!' enthused the indomitable Bessie. 'I'm sure they'll be delighted to have such a thing on show in their homes.'

'They'd better be,' said Mr Brown. Bessie guessed he was in trade in some way, though if he was really wealthy he would have gone to one of the larger, more expensive Colchester studios. 'Seeing as it will be costing me enough.'

5

'Get on with you. You can afford it,' declared his wife, keen to make their financial position clear and seeming a little less tense as her attention was distracted from the camera.

'I wonder,' began Bessie, deciding it was time to get this job under way, 'if you could get just a tiny bit closer together to make a warmer image . . . That's better, move up a little and lean towards each other . . . just a tad more. Thank you very much. Would you mind, Mrs Brown, if we were to show a little more of your hair for the picture? Just to soften it up.'

Mrs Brown nodded.

Bessie made a small adjustment to the position of the woman's hat. 'That's lovely. Now, could you look up please?' She raised her hand. 'Look towards my hand . . . er, without moving your head if you can. Just your eyes, please. That's perfect. You both look very handsome.'

'Indeed you do,' added Digby, who had his head down in position by the camera, which was on a stand. The black body of the apparatus consisted of symmetrical bellows that served as a dark chamber. Being a perfectionist, Digby threw an opaque black cloth over his head as extra security against light, even though the apparatus was guaranteed by the manufacturer to be light-tight. 'All we need now is a nice natural smile. That's the stuff. Hold it there.'

Bessie slipped quietly from the room, satisfied that the session would run more smoothly now that the ice was broken between sitters and photographer. Some people were so anxious to look their best for the camera that they actually looked their worst unless they had a little professional guidance.

Oh well, she'd just about have time to finish cleaning the windows before the shop got busy, she thought, getting her cloth from under the counter and heading for the door, where she almost collided with a young woman on the way in.

'Morning, Joan,' greeted Bessie.

'I've come to see my father,' announced Joan Parsons, ignoring Bessie's welcome. Joan was the only child of Digby and a similar age to Bessie, though the two had never hit it off.

'He's busy in the studio doing a sitting at the moment,' replied Bessie, bracing herself for some sort of altercation because, unlike her father, Joan was habitually hateful. 'Would you like to take a seat while you're waiting?'

'Waiting! I'm not waiting!' Joan stated categorically, her bluish-grey eyes resting on Bessie coldly. 'I need to see him now; this instant. And that's what I intend to do.'

Bessie bit her lip. 'He won't want to be disturbed,' she made clear. 'I'm sure you must realise that. If the shots are ruined by an interruption that upsets the mood, the customers won't be satisfied when they see the proofs so won't bother to have the finished photographs done. Even if your father can talk them round, the sitting will have to be done again free of charge.'

'They pay in advance, don't they?' Joan said casually, illustrating how little interest she took in her father's work.

'Only a deposit to cover the cost of the sitting and the proofs,' Bessie explained. 'If they aren't satisfied and don't give us an order, we don't make any profit.'

'Oh.' A thin, sharp-featured redhead, Joan was a striking figure in a smart blue coat with a fur trim and a matching hat; she was attractive in a contrived and harsh sort of way. 'Well, I'm sure he won't mind being disturbed by me.'

As it was part of her duties to protect her employer from any such interruptions, Bessie took a step back so that she was standing between Joan and the door of the studio.

'Get out of my way this minute,' Joan demanded. 'Don't you dare try to stop me going in to see my own father.'

'Not so loud; they'll hear you in there and it'll upset things,' hissed Bessie. 'Why don't you just sit down and read a magazine until your dad is free to see you. He'll be engrossed in what he's doing. You know what a stickler he is as regards his work and how hard it is to get people to relax during a sitting. If he has to do the sitting and proofs all over again free of charge, that's an expensive business, the cost of materials being as it is. Not to mention his time and reputation. The customers pay for his wholehearted attention and are entitled to complain if they don't have it.'

'I think you must have forgotten your place,' Joan warned coldly. 'You're just the hired help around here.'

Bessie met her stare. 'Yes, I realise that. But part of my duties is to organise your father's time and make sure he is allowed to get on with the job uninterrupted.'

'I'm his daughter, which makes me immune to rules that apply to other people, you stupid girl.'

'It's a pity you didn't inherit some of his good nature,' Bessie blurted out.

Joan stared at her father's assistant, her eyes smouldering with pure malice, cheeks flaming. Bessie knew that this need to assert her authority wasn't only Joan establishing her superior status in the pecking order, though that was part of it. Her easily aroused temper was inflamed because she hated the fact that her father seemed to like Bessie, even though Joan herself had no time for him. 'Don't get above yourself just because Dad seems to have some sort of misplaced regard for you. You're of no importance whatsoever. So do as I say this very instant and get out of the way.'

'I work for your father, not for you,' Bessie reminded her. 'I take my orders from him. He isn't to be disturbed when he's doing a sitting; that's the rule.'

'We'll soon see about that,' Joan said, stepping forward. 'Now move aside and let me get by.'

Bessie stayed where she was.

'I shall see to it that you are dismissed,' threatened Joan through tight lips. 'We don't want the likes of you working in the family business. A business that will be all mine one day.'

'This photographic practice would cease to exist without your father,' Bessie pointed out. 'It's his expertise that people come here for. Without that there is nothing.'

Taking Bessie unawares, Joan lunged towards her and gave her a forceful shove that sent her staggering across the room. Then, without a word, she marched into her father's studio without even knocking and slammed the door behind her, leaving a stunned Bessie recovering her balance.

Whatever it was she wanted from her father, Bessie knew he would give it to her, as he never denied her anything. Joan's mother had died giving birth to her and her father had brought her up alone. Perhaps to compensate for the lack of a maternal influence, he indulged her excessively, and in return she treated him with such contempt Bessie could hardly bear to see it. She belittled him in public, her manner towards him scathingly humiliating.

Digby visibly smarted from it but never retaliated. Bessie longed for him to show some spirit and stand up to his daughter, but he was no match for her bullying personality. As far as Bessie could see, Joan grabbed the good life he bestowed upon her without so much as a smidgen of appreciation. She never helped in the shop and they had a full-time house-keeper at home, so she was free for a life of idleness and enjoyment. Bessie assumed that her employer must have money beyond the income from his business, because that was unlikely to be enough to support Joan's expensive tastes on its own.

Now Joan emerged from the studio, smiling victoriously.

'My father was delighted to see me, as I knew he would be, so keep your nose out of our family business in future,' she ordered. 'Know your place and stay in it.'

'How dare you speak to me like that,' Bessie ground out. 'You've no right and I won't put up with it.'

'You don't have a choice because you need this job,' Joan retorted haughtily. 'I'm sure your fisherman daddy doesn't earn enough to support you.'

'You leave my father out of this. He's a hard-working and decent man.'

'Now, now, Bessie Bow, mind your temper,' Joan taunted with a brittle laugh. 'Jobs like this one are few and far between for girls like you. I'm sure you'd rather work here than go into domestic service, cleaning the grates and the privies of the better-off and waiting hand and foot on people who are your superiors, which is all that will be on offer if you were to be forced to leave here. One word from me to my father about your attitude towards me, and you'll be joining the queue for a job as a skivvy.'

'You won't utter that word, though, will you, Joan?' This was actually more bravado than conviction on Bessie's part so as to stand her ground in front of this bully. 'Because with me out of the way, your father will be looking for a replacement, and he might look in your direction.'

'Don't be ridiculous. He wouldn't put his daughter to work,' Joan stated confidently.

Unfortunately, that was probably true, but Bessie wasn't about to admit it. 'It isn't a good idea to underestimate anyone. One of these days he's going to put his foot down and you will really notice the difference.'

'I'll enjoy myself while I'm waiting for that time to come then,' Joan returned lightly. 'Meanwhile you can get on with the work you are well paid to do while I go to the dressmaker for a fitting for my new winter outfit.'

Bessie said nothing. What could she say to someone whose values were so different to her own? Although Joan appeared to have everything, she had very little compared to Bessie in terms of real blessings. Her childhood must have been lonely with just her father for company, whereas Bessie had grown up with three siblings and both parents, who meant the world to her.

After Joan had headed for her dressmaker, Bessie went outside into the cold air and finished cleaning the shop window, her breath turning to steam as she exerted herself polishing the glass. She felt a sense of pride when she'd finished and it was gleaming and showing off the examples of Digby's work inside.

Thinking back on Joan's visit, she felt a pang of empathy for her employer. Just an occasional kind word from his daughter would mean the world to Digby. Sadly, she doubted if he would ever hear such a thing. She finished the job and went back into the shop.

Although she was still only seventeen, May Bow already had definite opinions and a strong sense of justice, which meant that deference didn't come easily to her. She knew her place, of course; that had been drummed into her for as long as she could remember. The premise was, according to her mother, that as the daughter of a poor fishing family she must be humble towards her betters, who, in her mother's opinion, included all and sundry. But May didn't have that sort of subservience in her.

Willingly she would defer to the doctor, the vicar, the local policeman, and anyone else of that ilk who deserved reverence. She even held the ferryman in high esteem for his courtesy and diligence. But Mrs March was another matter altogether. Her only qualification for respect was the fact that she paid May's wages, an important factor admittedly. But the woman was entirely without heart or manners, and at the current moment it was as much as May could do not to throttle her, or at least throw the drawer of embroidery silks at her. In full view of a customer, the harridan with the physique of a small oak tree had just made a showy performance of falsely accusing May of putting the drawer back in the wrong place, when in fact it had been Mrs March herself who was the culprit.

'Staff aren't what they used to be,' complained Mrs March to the customer as though May, her only employee, wasn't standing right next to her. 'The quality just isn't there these days. Time was when you could rely on your shop girl completely.' She shrugged her shoulders in a gesture of despair, her mouth turned down at the corners. 'Nowadays you're lucky to get half a day's work out of them when they've been paid for a full day. They can't be bothered to do the job properly, and that's how things get put in the wrong places so that the customer has to wait while we find them.'

'I speak as I find and I must say that May has always seemed very conscientious to me, Mrs March,' ventured the customer, obviously feeling awkward.

'That's because you don't know what goes on this side of the counter and how hard it is for me to get any work out of her. I searched high and low for the embroidery silks this morning and couldn't find them anywhere,' went on the unstoppable witch, a formidable figure dressed entirely in black, her greying brown hair dragged severely back into a bun. She was a widow and had inherited the shop from her late husband. 'It turned out she'd put them where the elastic goes on the other side of the shop. Honestly, that's the sort of carelessness I have to put up with.'

May's temper was hanging together by a thread. There was no excuse for lies, blatant rudeness and injustice. She opened her mouth to deny the allegations, then remembered how difficult it was for her father to earn a decent living in the winter and managed to hold her tongue. She couldn't afford to be unemployed for so much as one day at this time of the year. In the summer her father and elder brother hung up their fishing nets and crewed for the wealthy yacht owners during the racing and regatta season. The money they earned then helped the family through the winter, but cash was tight even so, and each family member had to make a contribution to the household budget. Even her younger brother Sam, who was still at school, ran errands for the butcher in Tideway in the evenings and on a Saturday to earn a few extra coppers.

With this in mind, she managed to stay silent. When the shop closed for dinner, as soon as she'd eaten her sandwiches in the bitterly cold room at the back of the shop – Mrs Marsh considered heating unnecessary in there, she herself eating upstairs in her private accommodation – she put on her shawl and hat and left the shop to walk off some of her temper.

Incandescent with rage, she set off to the other end of the main street to see Bessie at the photographer's and tell her all about it. Her sister would be equally outraged on her behalf and it would be a welcome release for May to have a good grumble.

'Good afternoon, Miss Bow,' said a male voice, startling May, who was so immersed in her own fury as to be barely aware of her surroundings.

Looking up, she found herself staring at William Marriot, the son of the owner of the yacht her father and brother usually worked on in the summer. She judged William to be about twenty; he was wonderfully good looking, with shandy-coloured eyes, a charming smile and a clear complexion. He was wearing a fashionable tweed coat of the type the well heeled favoured for casual occasions and a cap worn at a jaunty angle, which he had raised politely on meeting her.

'Good afternoon, Mr Marriot,' she responded absently, her lovely eyes somewhat distant.

'How are you?'

'Er, fine, thank you.'

'You don't sound too sure.'

'Sorry. I was miles away.' She gave a wry grin and her face lit up prettily. 'But don't ask me to tell you what I was thinking about, because my thoughts at the moment are not fit for the ears of decent people. I am so angry it's a wonder I haven't exploded.'

'Someone has upset you, then?'

11

'Good and proper. I don't mind being talked down to now and again, but when people unfairly make a laughing stock of you just because they're employing you, it isn't right.' She heaved an eloquent sigh. 'Still, it's all in a day's work, I suppose.'

'Where do you work?'

She told him. 'Of course someone like you wouldn't have to worry about such things.'

'On the contrary,' he corrected. 'I work for a living. And yes, I do get talked down to at times. I have my superiors too.'

'Really! I thought your sort spent all your days in a round of pleasure. Drinks at the club, afternoon tea, parties and all that sort of thing.'

'Not at all,' he told her. 'I don't work with my hands, building boats or fishing for a living, but I do have to show up in my father's bank on a regular basis and make a decent contribution to the company. I have to justify my existence. My father is a stickler for that sort of thing. He worked hard to get where he is and he doesn't see why I shouldn't do the same.'

'Good for him.' She looked at him. 'But what are you doing around here at this time of the year? We don't usually see you yachting types much outside of the season.'

'I'm on my way to Tideway to see the boatbuilder to discuss what needs doing to the yacht during the winter; she needs a spot of refitting,' he explained. 'I took the day off and got the train down from London.'

'I have an aunt and uncle who live in London,' May mentioned. 'I've been there to visit a few times.'

'What did you think of it?'

'Grey, dusty and crowded, it seemed to a country girl like me,' she said. 'But I loved the buzz of so much going on. It was thrilling and so different to Tideway.'

'Indeed.' Smiling at her and seeming to want to prolong the conversation, he added, 'So, how are your family?'

'They are all very well, thank you for asking,' she replied politely.

'Where are you off to now?' he enquired.

'I'm going to see my sister to let off some steam,' she told him. 'She works in the photographer's and will be on her dinner hour, so I can bend her ear and calm down before going back to work. It might just stop me from murdering my employer.' She paused. 'In fact, I'd better be on my way or I'll be late back and be in more trouble over that.'

'I'll let you get on then,' he responded. 'It was very nice to see you again. Give my regards to your family.' He paused. 'Oh, and tell your father and brother we shall need them again next season, so I hope they'll be available.'

'I'll tell them. They'll be pleased, I'm sure.'

'Goodbye, then.'

'Ta-ta,' she said, hurrying away down the cobbled street.

Unbeknown to her, William stood looking after her admiringly until she disappeared into the photographer's.

As it happened, Bessie was also looking for a sympathetic ear when May arrived, as she was still seething from the incident with Joan Parsons. The two girls sat in the back room of the shop, which was closed for the dinner hour, and exchanged grumbles and support in equal measure. They always shared their troubles.

'These stuck-up folk want to learn some manners from people who really do have money and breeding,' remarked May.

'Some of those are even worse.'

'Not the one I've just been talking to.'

'Oh yeah, and who is that?' asked Bessie.

'William Marriot, son of the yacht-owner Dad and Henry crew for in the summer.'

'Ooh, I say. You are mixing with the toffs now.'

'Give over. I met him in the street on my way here and we talked for about two minutes,' May explained. 'What a gentleman he is! He made a point of stopping to pass the time of day with me and ask about the family. He's got lovely manners, not to mention being absolutely gorgeous!'

'Don't get any ideas about him,' warned Bessie lightly. 'He's way out of our league.'

'I'm not daft. I know that,' May came back at her. 'But a girl can dream, can't she?' She didn't add anything about hope.

'Course she can,' confirmed her sister. 'As long as that's all she does.'

'William is the most courteous chap you could ever wish to meet. Honestly, Bessie, he's charming.'

'Mmm.' Bessie looked at the clock. 'Be that as it may, it's time I opened up for the afternoon session,' she said, rising.

'Oh Lor, Mrs March will give me a right trouncing if I'm late back,' May said, looking worried. 'See you later.'

And she hurried from the shop and ran down the street.

13

Chapter Two

The Bow family lived in a small whitewashed dwelling called Berry Cottage in Albert Street, a short walk from the waterfront. The cottage was in a row of similar properties and had a large parlour downstairs that was used for eating as well as rest and recreation. There was also a small sitting room at the front, which was only used on special occasions. Fresh water was drawn from a well in the back garden, where there was also a privy. The father of the family, George Bow, owned a fishing smack in which he and his elder son Henry earned their living, in the North Sea and all around the British coast.

That same evening the family was gathered around the table in the parlour, enjoying mutton stew with dumplings. There was a fire glowing in the hearth and candles emitting a soft glow over the room, and a black spaniel called Whistler sat quietly by the table hoping for some scraps.

'Can I have some more stew, please, Mum?' asked Henry, who was nineteen and the eldest child, a strapping young man with a hearty appetite.

'Course you can, son. I'll go and get you some,' said his mother Edie, putting down her knife and fork.

'I'll get it, Mum,' offered sweet-natured Henry, rising and heading towards the range in the kitchen that led off the parlour. 'You stay where you are and finish your meal.'

'That's kind of you, son. Ta very much.'

'Does anyone else want more?' called Henry from the kitchen. 'There's only one dumpling left, though, and that'll be Dad's. Dad, are you ready for some more?'

'Yeah, please, son,' replied his father George, 'but your mother will get it. You come and sit back down. You don't want to be doing woman's work.'

'He doesn't mind doing it, so why not let him get on with it to save Mum's legs?' put in the outspoken May, who disliked the assumption of male superiority over women as a matter of course, especially as the latter seemed to her to be equally intelligent and hard working. As well as the daily cooking and the family wash, which took her all day on a Monday and most of Tuesday for the ironing and starching, Edie Bow spent her life cleaning, polishing, mending, and waiting hand and foot on the men. The white lace curtains at the windows were always beautifully laundered; a vital symbol of respectability here. But neither she nor any other woman in the village had a say in anything outside of the domestic routine; they weren't even allowed to vote in public elections.

May personally knew of no one else who shared her views, since every woman around here accepted the status quo without question. But she was aware that there were women further afield who did more than just question it, because she'd read about them in her father's newspaper. Known as the suffragettes, they were always in trouble because of their controversial beliefs.

'Don't be silly, May. Your father is quite right. It's my job,' Edie said now, getting up obediently. She was a tall, thin-faced woman with fair greying hair drawn back severely into a knot. 'You go and sit down, Henry. Is anyone else ready for some more? What about you, Sam?' She paused. 'Bessie and May, obviously you can get yourselves some if there's any left when the others have had theirs.'

There was an unspoken law in the Bow household that father George came first; next in line were the sons of the house, then the mother, with the daughters – who were expected to do their share of the chores when they were at home – in last place.

It was generally accepted in the family that Edie's firstborn son was her favourite. Her adoration for him exuded from every pore, Bessie observed, as Edie walked to the kitchen, a pinafore over her clothes, the skirts sweeping the floor. Henry could do no wrong in her eyes, but his siblings didn't resent it because they all loved him that little bit extra too. At least that was the way Bessie perceived it to be.

Naturally there was a certain amount of banter about it but never any acrimony, probably because Henry did nothing to court special attention from his mother. The firstborn child was often closer to the mother's heart than the rest, so they said, and it was certainly true in the case of Henry.

He must surely be the most handsome young man in the whole of Essex, Bessie thought, looking at him proudly across the table, and the best natured: kind, funny and genuinely interested in other people. The house was a warmer place when he was at home. Tall and fair haired, he was muscular and strong and had a tanned complexion from being at sea. But there wasn't an ounce of conceit in him and he was a very caring person.

16

'How's school going lately, Sam?' Henry asked now of his twelve-year-old brother, a slim, blond-haired boy similar in colouring to Henry and Bessie.

'All right, I s'pose,' replied Sam. 'Except for arithmetic. I really 'ate that.'

'Sounds familiar,' remarked Henry. 'I seem to remember feeling that way about it too.'

'School is wasted on our sort,' opined their father, a big, burly man with a mop of curly grey hair and a ruddy complexion from years of exposure to weather on the ocean. 'They should never have made it compulsory.'

'Surely everyone has the right to be educated, Dad,' Bessie pointed out.

'Having the right is one thing, being forced into it is quite another,' he preached. 'They don't teach you about the wind and the tides in the classroom. That's what you need to know when you're earning your living on the sea.'

'I don't want to be a fisherman, Dad,' announced Sam bravely, causing a hushed silence.

'*Don't want to be a fisherman!*' exploded George. 'Of course you'll be a fisherman, the same as your brother and me and practically every other man in this village.'

'I 'ate being on the water,' admitted Sam. 'It makes me feel sick; and as for gutting the fish . . .' He gave an expressive shudder. 'That really turns my stomach.'

'In that case we'll have to take you out with us more often, to get you used to it and toughen you up,' stated his father. 'Yes, that's what we need to do.'

'If he doesn't want to be a fisherman, surely he should be allowed to explore other possibilities,' suggested Bessie. 'Not everyone can take to being a seafarer.'

'Hear, hear,' agreed May.

'They can in this family,' roared George. 'Why do you think I sweated and slaved to get our own smack? So that my sons would have a future, that's why.'

'And very well you've done too,' put in Henry with his usual gift for diplomacy. 'I enjoy the life at sea and I wouldn't want to do anything else. But it isn't right for everyone.'

'It's right for any son of mine,' stated the immovable George.

'You'd have your daughters out there too if you could, wouldn't you, Dad?' said May cheekily.

'No I would not,' he denied, for it was unheard of for respectable

Tideway women to go out to sea. 'The only time women go on a boat is on the ferry and an occasional outing in the summer. Dry land is the place for the females of the village.'

'Good job too,' said Edie, now back at the table. 'I wouldn't want to go out there in the wind and the rain.'

'There's nothing like it, Mum,' enthused Henry. 'It gets right into your blood.'

'Exactly,' she came back at him. 'It makes my blood run cold at the thought of it.'

'And mine,' said Sam.

'You'll be at school until you're thirteen, Sam, so you've no need to worry about it for another year,' put in Bessie soothingly. She was very fond of her younger brother, and protective of him. If he could find employment other than seafaring when the time came, so much the better as far as she was concerned. She had lived too long with the dominance of the sea in their lives; the constant worry for her father's life, and later for her brother's. Friends of hers had lost fathers, brothers, uncles. Worst of all was the agony her mother went through when the two men in her life were out at sea in stormy weather. You could feel her fear despite her stoicism. Edie rarely displayed emotion of any kind. She had never been demonstrably affectionate towards her children, but she'd raised them well, albeit with a very firm hand. Proper to the point of primness and a worshipper of respectability, she had taught them how to live as decent human beings. 'In the meantime, you've got the Guy Fawkes celebrations to look forward to,' Bessie added. 'We all have. It's a cracking bonfire you boys have built this year down by the waterfront.'

'Yeah, I noticed that,' said Edie, grateful for the change of subject. 'Bessie, I'm putting you in charge of the baked potatoes, and you'll do the sausage rolls, May. I shall do the parkin as always.'

'Your parkin is the best part of Bonfire Night,' declared Bessie, 'and that's a view shared by the whole village. No one makes it like you do. My mouth is watering just thinking about it.'

'I've been asked to make more this year as it's so popular,' Edie said proudly.

All entertainment was local and English traditions were staunchly upheld in Tideway. The women of the village organised the events and most of the residents turned out, especially those involved with the church, around which the village revolved.

'Meanwhile, as you've all finished, collect the plates up and take them to the kitchen, please, girls, while I get the pudding,' commanded Edie. 'Quickly now.'

'What is for afters, Mum?' asked Sam.

'Stewed apples and custard,' she replied.

No surprise there then, thought May. Cooked apple was on the menu most days in the Bow household with a variety of accompaniments, such as custard, semolina, tapioca or rice. The apple tree in the back garden was fruitful in the autumn, and the women of the family wrapped each apple individually in newspaper and stored them so that they lasted for the best part of the winter.

The sisters got up and collected the empty plates and took them into the kitchen as they did every night. Routine was of the essence in this household. Sometimes Bessie found it slightly irritating and longed for variation and excitement; other times it soothed her. Tonight it was the latter. Maybe she was still smarting from the altercation with Joan Parsons and needed the security of home and family. Whatever the reason, she felt a warm feeling inside as she and May piled the plates into the sink.

'How much longer are you going to be with the iron?' asked May later that evening as Bessie pressed the creases out of the skirt she was ironing on the kitchen table.

'As long as it takes.'

'Get a move on then, will you, sis?' urged May lightly. 'I don't want to be ironing my clothes for work tomorrow at midnight.'

'You won't be,' Bessie assured her, holding the flat iron down on a stubborn crease. 'But don't nag me. I'm doing it as quickly as I can.'

As well as being raised to believe that cleanliness was next to godliness, the Bow sisters had also been trained to be fastidious about their appearance, and neither went out with so much as a wrinkle in their clothes if at all possible. Edie had taught them at an early age how to iron as well as how to cook and clean, knit and sew; all essential skills for any young woman, who would need them especially when she found a husband.

'Are only girls allowed in here?' joked Henry, entering the room and heading for the larder. 'Or can anyone join in?'

'Anyone can't, but we might let you stay, if you're nice to us,' said May jokingly.

'When am I not nice to you?' he asked.

'That's a point,' she conceded.

Henry took a loaf of bread out of the pantry and cut himself a thick chunk, which he spread with dripping and munched into with enthusiasm.

'You ought to be the size of a whale, the amount of food that goes into your mouth,' commented May.

'I'm a growing lad.' He grinned. 'Anyway, this is supper and an early breakfast rolled into one.'

'Are you going to bed then?' Depending on the weather and the tide, Henry and George often left very early in the morning so on working days weren't late to bed.

'Soon,' he replied. 'Roll on the weekend. Ooh, I love that Sunday-morning lie-in.'

'Shall I make you a cup of cocoa?' offered Bessie, finishing her ironing and hanging the skirt over the back of a chair.

'That's all right. I'll make one for myself when I've eaten this, thanks,' he told her.

'Ooh, don't let Mum know that you can do it yourself,' May said with a giggle as she picked up the iron. 'It would break her heart if she thought she wasn't essential to your well-being over every little thing.'

'She means well, bless her,' he said.

'I know she does,' May returned. 'But she spoils you something rotten.'

'It makes her happy, so why should I stop her?'

'It's a wonder she hasn't made you into a lazy good-for-nothing,' May told him.

'With two sisters to keep me on my toes, there's no chance of that.' Henry smiled.

'Oh, by the way, I've got a message for you from William Marriot,' said May, remembering. 'He said he hopes that you and Dad will sign up to crew for them next season.'

Henry looked pleased. 'We'll be there to register when the time comes. It's good news that he mentioned it to you, though; must mean he's pleased with us. There's plenty of competition for the summer jobs on the yachts.'

'She's been gooey-eyed ever since she saw that William,' remarked Bessie, teasing her sister. 'She's got a real crush on him.'

'Don't listen to her,' responded May, blushing furiously. 'I've got no so such thing. I just happened to mention that he seemed rather nice, that's all.'

'I've always found him to be a really good bloke, but don't you go getting designs on him or anyone from that side of the fence,' warned Henry. 'They live in a different world to us, so as nice as he is, he's not for you.'

'Honestly, I don't know what you two take me for,' objected May with good humour. 'I do have a brain in my head. Of course he isn't for me.

I know how the system works. That doesn't mean I can't speak to him if he starts up a conversation, does it?'

'Of course not,' returned Henry. 'Just don't go fluttering those flirty eyes at him like you do at the village boys.'

'I do not do that,' she denied.

'Ooh, May, don't tell such porky pies,' warned Bessie, smiling.

'Well, maybe I do, just a little,' admitted May. 'But it's only a bit of fun.'

Bessie decided on a change of subject, turning her attention to her brother. 'Luckily the Guy Fawkes celebrations start early tomorrow evening so you can have some fun before bedtime.'

'That's right.'

'Roll on tomorrow night then,' said Bessie.

'Hear, hear,' chorused the others.

The waterfront was lined with oil-lit lanterns emitting a yellowish glow that reflected on the dark river. The crowds were out in force for the celebrations and gathered around the bonfire, which had been lit as soon as it was dusk so that the small children could enjoy the party before they got too tired. It was now in full flow, with the flames leaping and crackling, the guy almost a cinder.

The landlord of one of the waterfront pubs was in charge of the fireworks, and the villagers cheered and clapped to see the rockets shoot to the sky, leaving a shower of coloured sparks, the kiddies clinging to their mothers' skirts when the bangers went off.

There had been a dramatic change in the weather since yesterday, when all was still with a hazy sunshine after the mist cleared. Now the air was crystal clear and a bitter wind howled through the village, pulling at the flames, blowing the fallen leaves and causing craft to creak at their moorings. But the elements didn't spoil the enjoyment of the crowds. Except, that is, for the members of the Bow family. Every gust and passing moment plunged them deeper into worry and despair, because their men hadn't yet returned from the fishing trip they had departed on in the early hours of this morning. Every second that ticked by made their absence more concerning.

Being the sort of people they were, they were determined not to spoil the party for others because of their own personal fears. After all, there could be a perfectly reasonable explanation: the men could have run aground down the coast and could be making their way back; or the boat could have been damaged in a storm and the men were waiting for some passing ship to bring them back. So it wasn't fair to put the mockers on the celebrations for everyone else. Word got round in a small village like this, though, and some of the men had gone to look for the Bows in their own boats, despite the weather.

Wearing two sets of warm underwear, two thick jumpers and her shawl around her head against the cutting wind, Bessie moved among the revellers, handing out potatoes baked in the fire, with a fixed smile on her face, her head turning almost of its own volition towards the river. While the women distributed the food and hot drink, the men looked after the fire and let off the fireworks, guzzling beer from the waterside pub as they worked.

Nerves sensitised to a punishing degree, every sound was magnified to Bessie, and the laughter, the crackle of the bonfire and the pop, fizz and bang of the fireworks pierced through her.

'They'll be back,' she said, seeking out her mother, who was putting on a brave face, though she was pale with worry as she handed round her freshly made parkin. Sam, usually so robust and full of fun, wasn't straying far from her side.

'Course they will, Mum,' added May, appearing at her sister's side. Usually at an event like this May would be off with her friends at the first opportunity, playing up to the local boys. But as things were tonight she wanted to be with her family and she knew they needed her. 'Any minute now they'll turn up as large as life and twice as ugly. They've been late back before and they've always got here in the end.'

Not this late, thought Bessie. But she said, 'May's right, Mum. They'll come striding over at any moment.' Her eyes were drawn towards the quays as they had been all evening and her breath caught in her throat as, in the far-reaching glow from the fire, she could just make out the dark figure of a man in a sou'wester and oilskins heading their way.

'Dad, it's Dad,' she cried. 'They're back, Mum, they're back here. It's all right.'

'Oh thank God,' said her mother, and she and her children moved as one person towards him.

It was only as they drew nearer and saw that he was alone that they began to feel uneasy. That empty space spoke volumes.

'We've been worried about you,' Edie said thickly. 'We heard there was a storm at sea.'

George nodded.

'Where's Henry?' asked May.

'Seeing to the nets?' suggested her mother hopefully.

'I'll go and tell him to hurry up,' offered May.

'No, don't do that,' said George quickly, his voice trembling. 'He isn't there.'

In that split second Bessie knew that this was one of those moments that would change everything, like the first blood on the handkerchief of an undiagnosed consumptive, or the policeman at the door when a child had gone missing.

'I'm so sorry,' he said, looking at Edie, the words torn from him. 'It was the storm. The gale was so violent he was swept overboard. I went in after him but he'd gone; swept away. There was nothing more I could do.'

Edie stood perfectly still, almost as though she had been turned to stone. Then, without a word, she turned and walked in the direction of the house, still carrying the plate of parkin.

Bessie's hands were shaking as she drew water from the bucket with a jug and poured it into the kettle to make tea. She hung the kettle over the fire in the stove and went into the parlour, where May was sitting on a chair sobbing and ashen-faced Sam was standing fiddling nervously with his fingernails. She watched as their father tried to comfort his wife, who was sitting stiffly on the sofa.

'Would a drop o' brandy help?' he coaxed, his voice deep and guttural with anguish. 'I can pop down the pub and get some for you if you like.'

Edie didn't reply; she just sat very still, staring into space, her face the colour of chalk.

'She's in shock, Dad,' said Bessie shakily. 'Sweet tea is supposed to be good for that. The kettle won't be long.'

Suddenly Edie turned to her husband and laid into him. As he stood up and moved back, she went after him with fists clenched, striking blow after blow, which he took without making any effort to defend himself.

'I don't want brandy or tea or anything else. I want my son back,' she shrieked hysterically in an outburst the likes of which had never before been witnessed by her children, who had rarely seen their mother lose the slightest composure. 'You shouldn't have let him drown. You've taken my son from me.'

'Edie, love . . .'

'Don't speak to me,' she ground out, her voice unrecognisable, her face contorted with grief, eyes staring madly. 'Just go and bring my son back.'

'I can't, Edie,' he said thickly. 'He's gone.'

Then she started to scream, while her grief-stricken children watched in horror. Acting on impulse, Bessie did the only thing she could think of, the thing she had heard you should do in such cases: she stepped forward and slapped her mother's face, shocked that she had done such a thing to a woman she held in such high esteem.

Edie stopped instantly, looked bewildered for a moment, and then fell to her knees with her head down, her body shaking as she cried, making raw, ugly noises.

'Mum,' said Bessie, kneeling down and putting her arm around her mother's shoulder, unable to find words of comfort because there weren't any. 'There, there.'

'All right, Bessie, you look after the others,' commanded her father firmly. 'Take them into the kitchen and shut the door. I'll take care of your mother.'

'But . . .'

'Do as you're told,' he ordered gruffly, and Bessie could feel his pain. She'd seen the way her mother had looked at him; she blamed him for Henry's drowning.

Gently Bessie led the others into the kitchen. They would support each other and Dad would comfort Mum, but who did he have to turn to? He certainly wouldn't allow his children to help him because he would see that as a sign of weakness. The pure hatred in her mother's eyes when she'd looked at him would not be easily erased from Bessie's memory. It was undoubtedly the result of shock, but it had been very real.

Standing by the range, the kettle beginning to sing, Bessie gathered her siblings in her arms and they wept together. How could they live with the knowledge that they would never see their lovely brother again? He'd never been just a mother's boy. He'd been everyone's favourite. A strong young man with his life ahead of him was as nothing against the cruel ocean. Bessie knew one thing for sure: when Sam's turn came, if he still didn't want to go to sea she would support him one hundred per cent in his decision, whatever the opposition from their father.

There was a knock on the back door: the first of the neighbours to arrive offering kindness and support. Bessie welcomed them in but explained that their mother wasn't quite up to seeing visitors just at the moment.

Edie lay in bed staring into the shadowy darkness, the trees outside swaying in the wind and making lacy patterns on the wall in the pale moonlight through the window. She was physically exhausted from the shock and extensive weeping but mentally alert and feeling as though she would never sleep again. It was late, but George was still downstairs. Good job too. She didn't want him anywhere near her. She was too full of rage towards him. If one of them had to die it should have been him who drowned, not her dear Henry.

They were wicked thoughts, she knew, but she couldn't stop them coming. She'd sooner be without George than her firstborn son. Her husband must have seen it in her eyes. Had she really attacked him downstairs? It was all a bit of a blur. All she could remember was the terrible pain of knowing she would never see her eldest child again. But yes, she had aimed blows at George and she wanted to again. She wanted to hurt him as she herself was hurting. For George's pain she could feel nothing, overcome as she was with her own grief.

What of the other children? She had been too immersed in her own feelings to comfort them. Being a good Christian woman, guilt consumed her as she recalled her behaviour. That was no way for a wife and mother to behave. She got out of bed and felt for her woollen dressing gown on the chair. She put it on over her long flannelette nightdress and made her way across the room and out on to the creaky landing, lit by a candle. Intending to offer some consolation to her children, she was on her way to the boys' room when she heard a noise downstairs.

She crept down the stairs, through the parlour and into the kitchen, where her husband was sitting at the wooden table with his head in his hands, sobbing. It was something she had never seen before. To George and his sort, weeping was strictly for women, and any man who succumbed wasn't fit to call himself a man. Obviously unaware that she had entered the room, he emitted deep moaning noises.

'There, there, George,' she said, forcing herself to put her hand on his shoulder. 'It will do you good to let it out. There's no shame in shedding tears at a time like this.'

'I'm sorry, Edie,' he wept. 'I'm so very sorry for losing our boy. It should have been me; at least I've seen something of life. He wasn't much more than a lad.'

'The Lord saw fit to take Henry, so who are we to question it?' The words were dragged from her. 'It isn't for us to say who stays and who goes.'

'That doesn't seem to help.'

'I'll make you a hot drink,' she offered.

'I'll have some of that brandy that Frank from the pub brought over,' he said. 'A drop of that won't do you any harm either.'

Edie wasn't normally a drinker, but she needed something to get her through this moment. This man was her husband and it was her duty to care for him under all circumstances. But it was no longer easy, because she hated him for being alive when her son wasn't. George should have died, not Henry, and despite all her Christian beliefs, that feeling persisted. Somehow she was going to have to live with and care for a man she now despised.

Pouring two glasses of brandy and handing one to George, she took a sip from the other and forced her mind to the practicalities in an effort to ease her pain. There were things to be done after a death; arrangements to be made and relatives to be told. Most of them were local to Tideway, but a telegram would have to be sent to her sister in London. Edie took another mouthful of the bitter liquid and prayed for the strength to do what was required of her.

Winnie Trent and her husband Albert lived in Hammersmith in west London and ran a stall in a local street market selling serviceable under-wear for men and women, plain knitwear and a few other cheap clothes. Albert ran the stall, bought the stock and worked a full day, while Winnie helped out part time. It was an arrangement that suited them both and they enjoyed market life, both being gregarious, outgoing types. Albert was in his forties; older than his wife, who was still only in her early thirties. Never having had any children, they were closer than many married couples and totally devoted to each other.

'It's on days like today I wish we had an indoor job,' remarked Winnie to her husband at breakfast as the wind whistled around the house, rattling the windows and sending icy draughts through every nook and cranny.

'Me too. It's a vicious wind all right,' he said, finishing his porridge and tucking into a doorstep of bread and jam. 'Make sure you wrap up well before you go out.'

'Don't worry, I shall have two pairs of me warmest drawers on when I come down to the market,' she said, her warm brown eyes full of fun. 'And as many vests as will fit under my clothes.'

A big man with a face like a bruiser, though he was the gentlest of souls, Albert looked across the table at his wife. 'Look, why don't you give it a miss today, love?' he suggested. 'I can manage on my own for one day. You stay home and keep warm.'

'And leave you to freeze to death all by yourself? No fear.' Albert's welfare was more important to Winnie than her own. 'I wouldn't dream of it. It's too much for one person all day on that stall. You need me by your side for part of the time at least.'

He shook his head, his pale blue eyes full of concern. 'I don't like the idea of you standing about in the cold. It's no weather for a woman to

26

be out, and one of the other stallholders will cover for me while I go to get a cup o' tea to keep me going.'

Winnie leaned her head back and gave a hearty laugh, her dark hair falling away from her face. 'Oh, what rubbish you talk sometimes, Albert Trent, about women being the weaker sex. It won't be any colder for me than it is for you just because I'm a woman. The temperature is the same for everyone.'

'Men are stronger.'

'Oh, get away with you,' she disagreed laughingly. 'That's a myth and must have been thought up by a man. Anyway, you know me: I'm a tough old bird.'

Not quite as tough as she pretended, he thought. She was always the life and soul of the party, the person everyone turned to with their troubles, but there was a vulnerable side to her that only he knew about. Her life hadn't always been easy; she'd had her share of trauma. She was a wonderful woman and he felt privileged to be married to her. Even after all these years he could still hardly believe that a handsome woman like her had chosen to marry a dull bloke like himself.

'Well, don't stay as long as usual then,' he suggested.

'I'll see how it goes,' she told him casually.

The conversation was interrupted by a knock at the door.

'Someone's early,' Winnie said, getting up and going to answer it. 'One of the neighbours on the borrow, I expect.'

When she opened the door to see the telegram boy standing there, her legs buckled and her breath was short. 'Oh my giddy aunt, what terrible thing has happened?' she said, taking the envelope from him with a trembling hand. 'Thank you, son.'

She walked slowly back to the kitchen, clutching the telegram unopened.

'Who was it?' Albert looked at what she was holding. 'Oh my good Gawd! Not one of those.'

'Yeah, one of those.'

'It might not be bad news,' he said without much conviction. They both knew that nothing good ever came out of a telegram; not for people like them. 'Do you want me to open it?'

She took a deep breath. 'No, I'll do it. It's just that these things give me the creeps.'

'Me an' all.'

He waited, watching her as she tore open the envelope, her hands shaking so much she could hardly keep hold of the paper.

'Oh no,' she gasped at last, a scarlet flush suffusing her face and neck before she turned ashen. 'It's my sister Edie's eldest.' She looked at Albert, her face crumpling. 'He's dead; drowned at sea.' Her voice broke as she added, 'That's so tragic. He was just a boy. Oh Albert! What a terrible thing!'

He was on his feet in an instant with his arms around her as her body was racked with sobs.

'I must go to Essex to be with Edie at once,' she said thickly through her tears. 'She'll be heartbroken. She doted on that boy. They all did. Oh Albert, I will have to leave you to do the stall on your own today after all. I must go at once. I'll have to stay overnight as well. You don't mind, do you?'

'Of course you must go, love. Don't you worry about me or the stall,' he assured her. 'I'll manage.'

'Thank you ever so much, dear,' she said tearfully. 'Oh what a terrible thing.'

The kindness of the people of Tideway towards the Bow family knew no bounds. Streams of people came to the cottage to offer their condolences. Many came bearing prepared food just in case the family didn't feel like cooking; some of them had lost loved ones at sea themselves. The person Bessie and her siblings were most glad to see was Aunt Winnie from London, who stayed with them for a week immediately after the tragedy, then returned to London before coming back as soon as she could. Her cheery manner and warm heart were just what they needed, though their mother didn't seem to approve of her younger sister's outgoing personality. In fact, she seemed to disagree with every single word Winnie uttered.

Because of the circumstances of Henry's death there could be no funeral, but they had a memorial service at the village church a few weeks later. The lovely old church was packed to the doors and banks of people stood outside. Neither Edie nor George felt able to speak to the congregation, but each of the children took part. Bessie spoke about her cherished memories of her brother and read a poem; even Sam did one of the readings, and May – who had a very good singing voice – sang one of the hymns as a solo. It was a beautiful service and Bessie was very moved by it. At least the occasion had enabled them to say a proper farewell to dear Henry.

When the family came out, there was a mass of people all dressed in black filling the churchyard and beyond, everyone keen to pay their respects but not wishing to intrude on the family's grief.

'May I offer you my most sincere condolences, George and Mrs Bow.

I was shocked when I heard about your loss through the people at the boatyard,' said William Marriot, who appeared unexpectedly out of the crowd. He shook George's hand and lifted his hat to Edie respectfully. 'Henry was a fine young man and a great yachtsman; he will be sorely missed by a great many people, I am sure. The yachting season won't ever be the same again for us.'

'Thank you for coming today,' responded Edie, pale and dignified in black with a veil over her face, which she lifted while speaking to him. She was managing to hang on to her composure by a thread. 'Especially as you had to travel to be here.'

'The very least I could do, Mrs Bow. When I heard from my contacts in the village about the service I wanted to pay my respects so I hopped on the train.'

'It's very good of you.'

William turned to May. 'Your singing was beautiful. Your brother would be proud.'

'Thank you,' said May, moist eyed but calm, her skin smooth and pale against her black hat and shawl. Their eyes met for a few special seconds. It wasn't just a look but a gesture of support, almost an embrace. This wasn't the time, a sad family occasion, but she knew at that moment that William Marriot would seek her out at some time in the future. His eyes said it all. Despite the solemnity of the occasion and her own grief, she felt a thrill and was immediately ashamed.

William Marriot spoke to the other members of the family in turn, then moved away, and the group, including Aunt Winnie and Uncle Albert, walked out of the churchyard and began the trek back to the cottage.

'Nice of him to come, wasn't it?' said George. 'Especially him being a toff and all.'

'Says something for young Henry,' put in Aunt Winnie. 'To bring the gentry out.'

'Aye, that's a fact,' agreed Albert.

'A lovely service,' said Winnie.

'Beautiful,' added Albert.

'Well, I reckon we all deserve a good strong drink to steady our nerves,' suggested Aunt Winnie. 'Let's stop off and have a quick one at the pub, shall we?'

Edie was outraged at the suggestion. 'There's plenty of food and drink back at the house, Winnie,' she said cuttingly.

'I know, it's just that—'

'Decent women don't go into public houses,' declared Edie scathingly. 'Public houses are for men.'

'Mostly they are, of course, but women can go in on special occasions as long as they are accompanied by a man,' Winnie pointed out. 'In our local, women usually go in the snug bar at the back and leave the men to talk among themselves.'

'Decent women never go in, and I don't know how you can even suggest it on such a serious occasion,' Edie cut in. 'It's nothing short of disgusting and an insult to Henry's memory.'

'I thought we all needed cheering up,' explained Winnie lamely, 'and a pub can do that somehow . . . temporarily anyway.'

'Trust you to get the wrong end of the stick,' reproved Edie sternly. 'Cheering ourselves up isn't what today is all about. Today is all about quiet contemplation. A day when we remember Henry.'

Henry had been the jolliest of lads and would have hated his family to go about with their chins on the ground all day on his account, Winnie thought. Personally she preferred to remember the happy times and could see no disrespect in that. You didn't have to have a poker face to grieve for someone. She'd been extremely fond of Henry, as she was of all Edie's children. Not having any of her own made them even more special to her. But she said, 'All right, Edie dear. I'm sorry I suggested it, I really am, because I don't want to upset you today of all days.' A well-meaning soul, she was keen to placate her sister while she was in this delicate state. 'I suppose I must have got used to the way people do things in London.'

'This is Tideway,' stated Edie unnecessarily. 'We do things differently here, as you very well know.'

'She didn't mean any harm,' put in Albert, making his allegiance perfectly clear. 'She only suggested a quick one, not a party. It's hardly a crime.'

A tense silence ensued, and Bessie noticed, as she had on other occasions during her aunt's visits, how her mother talked down to Winnie and how the latter let her get away with it, which was surprising for a spirited woman like Winnie, who was not the sort to be bullied. Perhaps it had something to do with the fact that Winnie was the younger sister by a good few years. Bessie couldn't imagine ever treating May that way, or May allowing her to.

Walking behind her parents, and seeing even from behind the helpless droop of her mother's shoulders, it occurred to her that the anxiety didn't end here. After this they would all be even more worried when Dad went out to sea. They could no longer tell themselves that it wouldn't happen to them, because it had. And it could again.

30

One thing Bessie did know for sure was that she would never, ever marry a seagoing man. She had seen what it had done to her mother's life, and to that of her family. She didn't want to put any children of hers through this. The cruel sea dominated their lives, a constant threat. If she ever received a marriage proposal from a man of the sea, no matter what her feelings for him, were the answer would be a resounding no.

Chapter Three

Despite the tragedy that had devastated them all, somehow life went on for the Bow family and some sort of normality returned; as far as it ever could without Henry. The cottage on the hill ached with his absence and they all hurt along with it, particularly Edie, whose sadness was overwhelming and manifest in her entire being. She attended to her duties with even more diligence than usual but was much quieter and more withdrawn. She looked older and emaciated, her hair almost white now, her pallor emphasised by the severity of her black mourning clothes.

How could a mother ever come to terms with outliving her child? Bessie wondered. It also occurred to her that while the rest of them were out of the house during the day, which helped to distract them from their grief, their mother was at home on her own. Not that Edie sat around brooding. Quite the opposite. The cottage shone brighter than ever as she grew increasingly manic in her work around the house: cooking, cleaning and caring for her family. Even in the evenings she would find some cupboard to clear out or brass to polish.

The church was her only outside interest and she took on more duties there, doing extra turns on the cleaning rota and arranging flowers for the Sunday services. It was as though she was on the run from the awful thing that had happened; as though keeping busy would deaden the pain. The excessive physical exertion left her drained and exhausted, but anyone who suggested that she should take things easier did so at their peril. So the family accepted that this was her way of coping and didn't intrude.

Then one day in February of the following year, she made an astonishing announcement.

'We shall be taking a lodger,' she declared at supper.

'A lodger?' responded Bessie in surprise. Theirs was only a small cottage and they were a very close family.

'That's right,' Edie confirmed in a manner to suggest that her mind was made up. 'We need the extra income now that we don't have Henry's contribution to the household budget and your father has to pay someone from outside the family to help him on the boat. I shall be looking for a single man of good habits.'

'Why a man in particular?' May enquired.

'There are more men looking for lodgings than women,' Edie informed her. 'Anyway, men are simpler. We don't want some fussy spinster about the place, wanting to wash her smalls outside of wash day.'

'But where will this man sleep, Mum?' asked May.

Edie's gaze turned towards her youngest child. 'I'm afraid you'll have to move into the box room in the attic, Sam,' she told him. 'I know it's small, but your father and I will clear it out and make it comfortable for you. I shall have to give our paying guest a room of a decent size, so he will have yours. You don't need such a big room now that you no longer have to share it.'

'That's all right with me,' said Sam cooperatively.

'Sam can come in with us if he wants, can't he, Bessie?' suggested the soft-hearted May. 'Rather than being stuck up in the attic all on his own.'

'Course he can,' agreed her sister.

'That would be most improper,' Edie informed them primly. 'He's growing up and shouldn't be sleeping in the same room as his older sisters.'

'It's all right really, about the box room,' stressed the obliging Sam. 'It's not been the same in our . . . I mean my room since . . .' His words tailed off.

'Since we lost Henry,' Bessie finished for him. She didn't agree with the ban on mentioning her late brother's name that their mother had imposed on the family by severely rebuking anyone who spoke about him.

'Bessie,' reproached Edie predictably.

'Sorry if I've upset you, Mum, but I think we should speak about Henry whenever we want to,' responded Bessie. 'It isn't right to act as though he was never here. He was a part of this family and he will always be in our hearts. We should keep his memory alive, and that means mentioning him whenever it feels natural to do so.'

'The girl is right, Edie,' supported George.

Edie threw her husband a withering look. 'You don't have to talk about someone to remember them,' she stated tartly.

'Neither should you make his name taboo,' he came back at her.

She looked annoyed but moved on swiftly.

'Getting back to our paying guest,' she continued, addressing her children, having already discussed the matter with her husband, 'I know it isn't very pleasant for us to have to share our home with a stranger, but there isn't any other alternative at the moment, I'm afraid. So I hope you will all make him feel at home. It goes without saying that he will have preference when it comes to second helpings at meals and use of the . . . er, facilities.'

'You mean the privy,' said May.

'Really, May, do you have to spell everything out?'

'The lavatory is a fact of life, Mum.'

Edie tutted. 'That doesn't mean we have to be vulgar when referring to it. Honestly, you girls are getting to be so outspoken lately,' she said disapprovingly. 'You'll get to be like your Aunt Winnie if you're not careful.'

'I can't see anything wrong with Aunt Winnie,' defended Bessie strongly. 'She's got a lovely warm heart and is always very nice to us. I like her a lot.'

'She can be coarse and unladylike,' Edie blurted out. 'Not an example I would like you to follow.'

'Just because she likes a bit of a laugh and a joke, that doesn't make her bad,' opined May. 'I think she's a lovely person. I always have.'

'Me too,' added Sam.

Edie seemed to be lost in her own thoughts for a few moments, before she said, 'Anyway, as regards us having a lodger . . . As soon as we've got the room ready, I shall put an advertisement in the local shop windows here and over at Haverley, and hopefully it won't take long to find someone suitable.'

'Where will he wash himself and bath?' wondered May.

'I shall put a washstand with a jug and bowl in his bedroom for washing and he'll bath in the kitchen in the tin bath the same as us, of course,' her mother replied.

'Ooh, blimey, we'll have to stay well clear of the kitchen on his bath night, won't we, or we might get the shock of our lives,' May blurted out, her words tailing off into a giggle that set her siblings off, the three of them in fits.

'Have some respect, if you please,' admonished their mother, frowning darkly.

'You can't expect them never to laugh again because they've lost their brother, Edie,' their father put in. 'It's the last thing Henry would want. They're young people. They need fun and laughter in their lives, just as he did. It's been more than three months now. That's a long time for healthy youngsters to keep a straight face.'

The look Edie gave him was enough to turn the fire instantly to ashes. 'Respect, George, that's all I ask,' she said. 'Respect for the fact that we are still in mourning.'

'All right, dear,' was George's response. He liked a quiet life and there-fore would only oppose his wife up to a certain point. He turned to his children. 'Just remember what your mother said.' His manner implied that they should be more careful in front of Edie and keep any tendency towards laughter out of her hearing. 'We are still a family in mourning.'

'I wonder what he'll be like, this lodger,' said May thoughtfully. 'I hope he isn't peculiar or creepy.'

'Why on earth should he be?' asked Edie.

May shrugged. 'You never know with strangers what they'll be like,' she said. 'He might have odd habits.'

'Don't be silly. He'll be highly respectable; that much I can promise you. I won't take anyone who I suspect has the slightest stain on their character,' pronounced Edie. 'I shall ask for references and will study them carefully.'

'Very wise,' approved George.

'You girls will have to make sure that you are more careful around the house with a strange man living here, especially as regards being fully dressed at all times outside of your bedroom,' lectured Edie. 'Not so much as an ankle must be showing. Is that clear?'

'Yes, Mum,' the sisters chorused.

'A teacher! At my school!' exclaimed Sam in horror a few weeks later when a suitable lodger had been found. 'We can't have a teacher living in this house.'

'Why on earth not?' his mother wanted to know.

'I'll never be able to relax with his beady eyes on me. I like to get away from school when I come home, not have a flamin' teacher in the house. Besides, my pals will think I'm getting special privileges because he lives here and they won't want anything to do with me,' he explained emphatic-ally. 'I'll lose all my mates.'

'I'm sure that won't happen,' expressed Edie. 'It could be that the others will want to stay on the right side of you because of it.'

'I know exactly what Sam means, Mum,' said May. 'I don't think I would have liked having one of the teachers living here when I was at school.'

'Nor me,' added Bessie.

'But he'll be off duty when he's here,' Edie pointed out.

'Teachers are never off duty,' said Sam miserably. 'He'll have his horrid teacher's eyes on me all the time.'

'At school he'll be in charge; at home I will make the rules, and I won't allow him to mix the two, I promise you,' Edie tried to assure her youngest. 'Anyway, he hasn't even started at your school yet, so you can't be sure that he has horrid teacher's eyes.'

'They all have; they can't help it.'

'Well I'm sorry that you're not happy about it, Sam, but we need the extra money until you are old enough to leave school and work for a living,' she explained. 'I'd have a long way to go to find anyone as suitable as this man is. He's highly respectable, clean, polite and in a steady job.'

'Why can't we have a fisherman or someone who works at the boat-yard?' said the downhearted Sam. 'Anyone except a teacher at my school.'

'Because no one of that type answered my advertisement,' Edie explained.

'They might do given a bit more time,' he suggested. 'Can't you leave the advert in and see who else replies?'

'We don't have time. We need the income right away,' she told him. 'Anyway, it's all arranged and the agreement has been made between myself and Mr Minter. So you'll have to get used to the idea because he's moving in on Sunday, ready to start his new job at the school on Monday.' Edie was delighted to have bagged a teacher as a lodger. Having someone from the professional classes eased the shame of having to take a paying guest. 'I'm sure you'll like him when you meet him. I thought he was very nice indeed.'

'He'll be a bald-headed old bath bun with mean eyes and a loud shouting voice,' wailed Sam.

Jim Minter arrived with his suitcase in time for Sunday lunch and was neither bald, beady eyed nor loud voiced. He was an amiable young man of slim proportions with warm brown eyes and wavy chestnut-coloured hair combed tidily into place. Quietly attractive, he was well turned out in a dark suit and nicely spoken with a natural gentility about him.

'Well, this is very nice indeed, Mrs Bow,' he complimented when they were enjoying a roast meal, having all been introduced. 'I can see that I shall be bursting out of my clothes if the meals are all going to be as delicious as this one.'

May's imagination ran riot and she collapsed into fits of nervous laughter before being slapped on the leg by her sister and ordered away from the table by her mother. Sam stared at the visitor with blatant apprehension and Bessie said, 'We are all very pleased to welcome you to our home, Mr Minter. I do hope you're going to be happy staying with us.'

'I'm sure I will, Miss Bow,' he said with a friendly smile. 'I hope my being here won't inconvenience you in any way. I should hate to interfere with your family life.'

Bessie couldn't imagine him putting anybody out. From what she'd seen so far, he was an absolute sweetheart. 'Please feel free to call me Bessie, and you won't interfere with us in the least. I'm sure you'll fit in perfectly.'

'Hear, hear,' agreed Edie. Turning to Sam she added, 'Will you go and tell your sister she can come back in now, please, if she's going to behave.'

Sam did as she asked and May returned suitably shamefaced. 'Sorry, everybody,' she said.

'So what particular subject do you teach, Mr Minter?' enquired Bessie.

'Games and English are my special subjects,' he told her. 'But as I shall be working in a small school, I shall probably be required to help out all round at times; if they are short staffed or anything.'

Sam brightened considerably. Having a teacher in the house might not be quite so bad after all if he was the games master, especially when it came to choosing the football or cricket team. Surely this would give Sam an advantage over the others?

'Most interesting,' remarked Edie, obviously delighted at having such a refined house guest.

'I've never seen much need for education for people of our sort who earn their living on the sea,' said George bluntly. 'I don't think they should have made schooling compulsory for everyone. It's a waste of time and government money, if you ask me.'

An uncomfortable silence ensued. Bessie and May squirmed with embarrassment, while their mother threw their father a warning look. They needn't have worried, though, because Jim Minter was more than able to hold his own.

'I respect your views, Mr Bow,' he said politely. 'So perhaps we had better agree to differ on this one.'

George shrugged.

Jim turned his attention to Sam. 'Do you like games, Sam?' he asked pleasantly.

'I'll say I do, sir,' he replied with gusto. 'Football and cricket especially.'

'That what I like to hear,' approved the teacher. 'Plenty of enthusiasm for healthy exercise and sportsmanship.'

The conversation didn't exactly flow after that – it would take time for the lodger and the family to get used to each other – but it managed to limp along until the end of the meal.

'Perhaps you girls would like to take Mr Minter for a walk when we've done the dishes,' suggested Edie. 'You could show him around the village.' She paused, looking at him. 'Unless you have something else to do, of course.'

'I do have some preparation to do for tomorrow's lessons, Mrs Bow,' he explained. 'But I can do that a bit later on. A walk would be just the thing.'

May said she was meeting some friends, so Bessie accompanied Jim on a tour of the village.

'We'll have to step out a bit lively to keep warm in this weather,' said Bessie as they walked down the hill to the waterfront. She was dressed in her Sunday best, in a red coat with a black bereavement band on the arm, a woolly hat and her hands enclosed in a muff. The whole family had been to church that morning, as always, and she would keep her best clothes on all day, as was customary.

'So what do you think of our village so far?' she enquired.

'Lovely,' Jim replied. 'I must admit, I'd never heard of it until the job came up.'

'I don't suppose many people have heard of us outside the area. We are very out of the way here. It's a busy enough place, though, in its own way. Being a maritime village, there's always lots going on along the waterfront.'

He nodded.

'It's rather bleak at the moment, but in a couple of months everything will be out,' she told him. 'It will be really beautiful then.'

'Bleakness has its own beauty, especially in a place as quaint as this,' he opined. 'It's very different to my home town of Ipswich, which is much more built up.'

His comments inspired Bessie to look around and see the village with a fresh eye. On this cold February day, the low winter sun spread its heatless glow over everything, brightening the whitewashed cottages and creating splinters of light on the river at high tide, the fishing boats creaking at their moorings. The clear blue sky sweeping down to the horizon was etched here and there with greyish-white streaks of cloud, moving and changing shape.

They walked along the waterfront and across the heath and woodland surrounding the village. Bessie took Jim on a tour through the narrow cobbled streets, where children played and neighbours gossiped, showing him the village church and the little shops, including the grocer, the butcher, the sweet shop, the drapery store and the toy shop, all shut and silent on a Sunday afternoon.

'We're pretty self-contained, but you have to go across on the ferry to Haverley for various things not available here: the doctor and apothecary, for instance.'

'I'm one of these healthy types, so with a bit of luck I won't need them,' he said. 'But the ferry seems reliable should I need anything outside of Tideway.'

'Have you been teaching long?'

'Three years as a qualified teacher, but I worked in different schools when I was training,' he replied.

'Plenty of experience, then?'

'Mm, though starting a new job is always an ordeal, so I'm slightly apprehensive about tomorrow. It's a big change for me. I'm used to working in a large town school.'

'You'll be all right,' she said reassuringly. 'A man like yourself with all the proper qualifications.'

'Qualifications count for nothing if you don't have the thick skin necessary to control a class of children. The kids can make your life a misery if you can't hold your own with them, no matter how well qualified you are,' he told her. 'One colleague of mine ended up in an asylum because he couldn't keep order in the classroom. His nerves were in shreds, the poor man. You have to keep one step ahead of the kids the whole time. If they spot so much as a sign of weakness they'll seize the chance to give you hell.'

'On the other hand, you don't want them to hate you for being too strict, I suppose,' she suggested.

'Exactly! You have to strike a balance,' he said. 'You need to be friend and mentor but all the time making sure they know that you are in charge. Above all you have to make your lessons interesting. I think that's paramount. A bored child is a rebel in the making. It's all about communication, really. It's no good knowing the stuff you want to teach if you can't get it across to a classroom full of kids who'd much rather be out in the school yard playing.'

'I'm sure you'll get along just fine in Tideway. You seem like quite an authoritative type.'

'Oh dear, do I seem like a stereotypical teacher with accusing eyes and my cane at the ready?'

She laughed, enjoying his company enormously. 'Of course not. I meant that you seem quite confident; not afraid to speak up for yourself, but diplomatic too.'

'With your father, you mean?'

'Yes, I thought you handled it really well,' she told him. 'Dad can be intransigent on certain issues. He's had a hard life, and for him the world begins and ends with the sea.'

'Hard, courageous work, and all so that we can have fresh fish on our plate.'

She nodded, not about to confide in him at this early stage about her feelings on being a fisherman's daughter. 'Perhaps we'd better make our way back home soon,' she suggested after a while. 'It's freezing out here and I don't want you to catch your death of cold before you've even started your new job.'

He laughed and she joined him. He was so easy to be with, she knew she was going to enjoy having him around. He told her he was twenty-two and the only child of a bank clerk. She gave him a few details about herself and filled him in on the rest of the family. She put him in the picture about their bereavement to avoid any awkward moments, and he listened compassionately.

'Just one thing I ought to mention before we get home,' she began as they made their way back. 'I'd better warn you that my young brother is more than a little apprehensive about having a teacher in the house. Among other reservations, he thinks his mates will give him a hard time about it.'

'Don't worry, I shall make sure I am not a teacher when I'm at home, and I'll see to it that he doesn't get any special privileges that will make him unpopular with the others,' he assured her. 'I shall also keep an eye out for him, just in case there's any trouble with the other kids. In a discreet way, of course.'

'Thank you.'

As they reached Albert Street and made their way up the hill, Jim stopped for a moment and turned to Bessie. 'Thank you for the guided tour. I think I'm really going to enjoy living here.'

I'm certainly going to enjoy having you around, thought Bessie, but she said politely, 'I do hope so.'

'Good grief, girl. You didn't waste any time, did you?' remarked May later on when the girls were in their bedroom with the door closed, having returned from seeing her friends. 'Talk about starry eyed. He's only been here five minutes and you're trying to nab him already.'

'I went for a walk with him, that's all,' Bessie pointed out haughtily, 'and you were invited to come along.'

'Just as well I didn't by the look of you,' May joshed. 'Flushed cheeks, a great big smile on your chops.'

'I was trying to make him feel welcome here, that's all,' Bessie defended hotly.

'Pull the other one; it's got bells on.'

'Trust you to think the worst.'

'I'm thinking the best, not the worst,' May put in, smiling. 'He wouldn't be a bad catch for you. Teachers don't earn much but they do have steady employment; they get paid holidays and they work on dry land. None of this going-to-sea malarkey and scaring us all half to death.' She paused. 'Just think how pleased Mum would be to have a nice respectable teacher in the family. Someone from the educated classes but not so much a cut above as to be out of reach or to make us feel inferior.'

'If he's got so much going for him, why don't you go after him?' Bessie asked lightly.

'Not my type,' May replied. 'Too serious for me. I'd be out of my depth with one of those clever types.'

'He's been here half a day,' Bessie pointed out. 'How on earth can you tell what he's like?'

'He can't be thick or he wouldn't have the job.'

'That's true, but it's too early for us to form an opinion about him as a person.'

'First impressions are all you need for the sort of feelings I'm talking about,' May said with a wicked laugh.

'May!' Bessie cried in a tone of admonition.

'I'm only being truthful. He seems a nice bloke, though, so if you want him, he's all yours.'

'Oh yeah, just like that,' Bessie said with a wry grin, though she did think Jim was very special. 'He might not be interested in me. I'm not educated like he is.'

'What's that got to do with it?' May wanted to know. 'Anyway, you're intelligent. We both are. It isn't our fault that Mum and Dad needed us to go out to work as soon as it was legal for us to leave school so that we only learned the basics.'

'He might already be spoken for,' suggested Bessie. 'He could have someone in his home town.'

'There can't be anyone serious or he wouldn't have moved away, and we know he isn't married because Mum wouldn't have taken him if he was,' May reminded her. 'She said she didn't want a married man in case his wife and kids turned up on the doorstep and she was forced to put them up. She only wanted someone without complications. So there you are, sis. He's young and single and there for the taking.'

'I think we'd better let the poor man settle in before we start planning the wedding,' laughed Bessie. 'And don't you dare embarrass me by making remarks about any of this.'

'As if I would. Anyway, I've got other things on my mind besides you, you know,' May said, pulling her nightgown over her head.

'Such as?'

May grinned mischievously. 'The weather, the meaning of life, how to make my pocket money last . . . Who knows what I might be thinking about?' She paused. 'Anyway, I've got to go down to the lav now, so I hope your Mr Minter isn't about. We have to be careful of things like that with a stranger in the house.'

'He isn't *my* Mr Minter and I think you'll be quite safe with him,' said Bessie getting into bed. She giggled and added, 'Especially while you're wearing that hideous nightdress.'

In reply, May threw a pillow at her.

When May came out of the shop for a breath of air one lunchtime a week or two later and saw William Marriot hovering on the other side of the road, she was delighted but not surprised.

'Hello there,' she said with the warmest of smiles. 'I knew you'd come.'

'Oh really, and how is that?'

'I didn't know when or where, but I knew you would seek me out at some point.'

'You're no shrinking violet, then,' he said.

'No. I must admit I am not. But I knew you would come after me in the same way as you knew I would want you to,' she told him in a tone so confident it belied her youth.

'Good gracious me, aren't you the cheeky one?'

'If being honest makes me cheeky, then I plead guilty as charged,' she returned.

He smiled at her and she melted. 'There's no point in my denying it,' he confessed, his deep, cultured voice thrilling her. 'I haven't been able to stop thinking about you.'

'Same here.'

He looked at her as though he never, ever wanted to take his eyes off her.

'Have you had lunch?' he asked.

'We call it dinner at this time of day, but yeah, I ate my sandwiches in the shop.'

'So would you like to take a walk with me, Miss Bow, so that we can get better acquainted?'

It was madness, she knew. They didn't even express themselves in the same version of English. But she was young and he was handsome and she was driven by the passion he aroused in her. 'I don't have long because I'm on my dinner break, but yes, I'd love to.'

'Good. Let's go, then.'

'I think it's time we got on to Christian-name terms, don't you, William?' she suggested.

'Yes, May, I do,' he said. 'So take my arm.'

'Not here with so many people about,' she said in a whisper, brushing his gloved hand away from her. 'If my sister gets to hear that I've been seen out walking with you, she'll give me a real roasting.'

'Is my reputation that bad?' he asked.

'Now you're just being kind,' she told him. 'You know very well what I mean.'

'It's just a walk.'

But they both knew it was more than that. It could be the beginning of something that would have no future. However, this ebullient and warm-hearted girl wasn't at an age to dwell too much on the problems of tomorrow. Today was for living and discovering. But she did have the prudence to wait until they got out of sight of the main street before she took his arm.

'Can we have the parents of the bride and groom in the picture with the happy couple, please? No . . . not the bridesmaids in this shot, darlin',' said Bessie, gently taking the hand of an excited little girl decked out in a pink satin dress and a floral headdress who had wandered into the shot. 'You'll be having your photograph taken again later on, I promise, when I call for the bridesmaids.' She handed the child over to one of the older brides-maids and turned to the gathering outside the church. 'Parents of the happy couple, please,'

No one took the slightest notice of her. They were all far too busy chattering among themselves. Wedding photographs could be hellish to do, and this one wasn't proving easy, thought Bessie. Clients wanted the pictures of their special day to be perfect, but everyone was too happy and excited to pay much attention to the instructions of the photographer.

Digby always wanted her with him when they did out-of-studio jobs such as weddings, christenings, school photographs and civic occasions because the participants were so difficult to arrange into a group, being far more interested in whatever it was they had assembled for than the actual photographs. Being a perfectionist in his work, the frustration of organising wedding guests made him irritable, especially as he also had the vagaries of the weather to contend with. This morning, too, his daughter Joan had called at the shop and treated him with her usual disdain.

At last Bessie established the identity of those required and ushered them patiently into a group, ruined several times by people walking in front of the camera. Digby went under the black cloth and clicked away.

'Say cheese, everyone,' urged Bessie. 'Come on, you can do better than that. A nice wide smile. Good. That's it. Lovely. Now, can we have the bridesmaids, please?'

And so it went on until every possible group combination had been taken care of. Having assured the happy couple that the proofs would be sent to them within two weeks, unless they cared to call into the shop before then to view them, Digby and Bessie piled the equipment into the pony and trap and made their way back to the shop.

It was a fine sunny afternoon in late spring and the countryside was lush with new life, the cows back grazing in the fields after winter and wild flowers adorning the hedgerows. Looking back on the last couple of months, Bessie recalled how quickly Jim Minter had settled into their home, the school and the village in general.

Having someone else to look after had been good for her mother in her time of grief, too. A paying guest gave her something else to think about, especially someone as different from the family as Jim was. Although wary at first, even Dad seemed to like him. They were poles apart as regarded many things, particularly politics – Jim was a supporter of the Labour Party, which was gaining ground and beginning to be a challenge to the two major parties and which was far too progressive for George – but they seemed to enjoy each other's company. One of Jim's most endearing qualities was his ability to pay attention to other people's interests, in Dad's case all things nautical. George found an audience in Jim, who listened intently to his sea stories.

Jim's quiet courtesy won the hearts of the locals, and his enthusiasm for his work gained him popularity at the school, though Sam had told Bessie that he didn't put up with bad behaviour. From what she could gather, Jim put much more time into the job than he was paid for. He always seemed to be organising some sort of extracurricular activity or giving slow learners lessons after school. He put his heart and soul into the job, and with the approach of summer he was currently getting together a cricket team and thinking in terms of the sports day.

He confided in Bessie about all of this at odd times in the house as well as when she joined him for a stroll of an evening, which she did at every possible opportunity, using the family spaniel as her excuse and taking him with her.

'You'll get yourself talked about, Bessie Bow,' her sister could be heard to tease her. 'Being seen out on your own with Mr Minter in public every night. Tut-tut, you naughty gel.'

'Don't be so silly, May. He's like one of the family,' Bessie would retort defensively. 'I just go with him because Whistler needs his walk; nothing more.'

'Give over. You'll be telling me next that it's like going for a walk with your brother.'

'I wouldn't dream of insulting your intelligence by saying that because it isn't like that at all,' she admitted. 'Anyway, you're welcome to come along too when you're not working late. He always asks if anyone wants to join him in a stroll.'

'Mm . . . I think I might take you up on that the next time I'm in when he asks,' teased May.

'Don't you dare,' Bessie said and they had a good laugh. 'At least, not until he's asked me to walk out with him in the real sense of the word. I'm sure he wants to, but he seems a bit shy about that sort of thing.'

'He won't rush it with Mum and Dad's hawk eyes on him and him not wanting to lose his lodgings,' May pointed out.

'There is that,' agreed Bessie. 'So I'll spend as much time as I can with him away from them to get to know him a bit better, in the hope that he'll ask me out properly. All open and above board, you understand.'

'If he doesn't, you could always ask him,' suggested the incorrigible May.

'Don't be so ridiculous,' gasped Bessie.

'What's ridiculous about it?' May wanted to know. 'Why would it be such a terrible thing?'

'You know why: because it isn't done,' Bessie reminded her. 'A lady waits to be asked.'

'There's a first time for everything,' May responded. 'It isn't actually illegal for a girl to make the first move, you know. You can't get put in prison for it. Sometimes you have to break the rules if you want to get anywhere in life.'

'Considering you're only seventeen, you think you know an awful lot.'

'Just my opinions I'm giving you the benefit of, sis,' May said, laughing. 'I can't see any point in being all coy and ladylike if it gets you nowhere.'

Now Bessie was recalled to the present because Digby was speaking to her.

'Come on, Bessie,' he was saying. 'Let's get this stuff back inside and get the shop ready for the afternoon appointments. I'll need your help in the dark room later on too.'

'Yes, Mr Parsons,' she said, pushing the adorable Jim Minter from her mind and concentrating on the task in hand.

While Bessie indulged openly in a chaste, slowly developing friendship with Jim Minter, May was involved in a passionate, clandestine love affair with William Marriot. He would wait for her after work and they would steal away into the countryside and find a private place. He told her he loved her and she left him in no doubt that it was most definitely reciprocated. She was absolutely besotted.

'This is going to get a lot more difficult as the nights get lighter,' she mentioned to him one evening as they were lying on the grass in a wooded area just outside Haverley while the sun slipped under the horizon. 'It used to be fully dark by this time when we first started seeing each other. Now it's barely even dusk.'

'Yes, I know. It's going to get difficult in more ways than one,' he told her.

'How do you mean?'

'All this leaving the office early to travel down to Essex is going to get back to my father and he will smell a rat. I tell them at the office that I'm going to see clients. Father is going to want to know who these non-existent clients are before long.'

'My folks are going to get suspicious too about my coming home late from work. I'm getting plenty of earache about it already,' May told him.

'Really?'

'Oh yeah. My mum is very strict about us being home on time,' she said. 'I tell them I'm working later because of stocktaking, but I can't keep that up for ever. I'm dreading that she will call into the shop and mention it to Mrs March. The cat will be out of the bag good and proper then. Luckily I usually get Mum anything she needs from Haverley while I'm at work to save her bothering. She would have forty fits if she ever found out what I was really doing when I'm supposed to be working late.'

'It's what mothers of daughters do, I think.'

'Mine sets great store by respectability; it's almost a religion with her. My sister and I have had it drummed into us all our lives, more than most girls probably.'

47

'She's right to look out for you and we shouldn't be doing this,' said William, sitting up suddenly and looping his arms around his knees. 'It's all wrong.'

'Are you saying that you want to stop seeing me?' Just the thought of that caused May unbearable pain.

'Of course not; that's the last thing I want, my dearest May,' he assured her. 'But you're a beautiful young girl. You deserve more than just a romp in a field, and having to tell lies to your parents on a regular basis.'

'Give me more, then,' suggested May, to whom all things were possible and who didn't have the guile to hide her feelings. 'We are young and in love with the world at our feet. We can do anything we want to.'

'If only it was that simple.' He gave a wry grin. 'Unfortunately the real world doesn't work like that,' he pointed out.

'Because you are posh and I'm not, you mean,' she suggested bluntly.

'No, don't be silly.'

'It is because you are wealthy and I'm not, though, isn't?' she persisted. 'My sister and brother warned me about you toffs using girls like me and then discarding them.'

'I am not using you, May.'

'You'd be ashamed to be with me in front of your family and friends, though, wouldn't you?' she said, unable to hide the rising panic in her tone.

'No,' he stated in a categorical tone. 'I would never, ever be ashamed of you. How could any man be ashamed of being with such a beautiful girl? You are lovely and good and funny. You are everything any man could want. I'd be very proud to have you on my arm, and the envy of all my friends.'

'Why don't we come out into the open with this wonderful thing we have, then?' she suggested. 'You know the sort of thing: you come calling for me in the normal way of a courting couple, and I eventually get to meet your folks . . . when you're ready, of course.'

'You're a bright girl; you know that our situation is more complicated than that,' he said.

'You *are* ashamed of me,' she accused.

'You don't really believe that, surely,' he said, slipping his arm around her. 'We will do what you want, I promise. I want it to be all above board too.'

'When?'

'Just give me some time to do a little groundwork,' he urged softly.

'I hope you are not stringing me along, William Marriot,' she said, keeping her tone light with some difficulty.

'Of course I'm not.'

'You'd better not be.'

'Trust me, May,' he said softly. 'Now, don't let's waste any more time arguing. Time is far too precious for us.'

Brimming over with love for him, she melted into his arms as he lowered her on to the grass.

Chapter Four

'They're a damned disgrace,' declared George Bow one evening, looking up from the newspaper he was reading. 'An absolute blight on society.'

'Who are you talking about, dear?' asked Edie absently. She was in her armchair, working her way meticulously through a pile of socks that needed darning.

'That Pankhrust woman and her cronies, of course,' he replied heatedly. 'Lock 'em up and throw away the key, I say, and if they want to starve themselves to death for their ridiculous cause, let 'em get on with it. Hunger strikes, forced feeding, bah!'

'That's a wicked thing to say, Dad,' reproved Bessie, who was busy with a needle and thread finishing the new pinafore she was making. 'You're being very harsh. Those poor women are suffering for their cause. Forced feeding is a brutal practice. They put a rubber tube down into their stomach and pump in liquid food. Can you imagine how painful that must be?'

'You're calling me harsh?' he exploded, completely disregarding the rest of Bessie's comments. 'And what they're doing *isn't* harsh, I suppose? Good grief, girl, do you not know that they are violent people? Have you not read about them in the paper? Smashing shop windows in London's Oxford Street; setting off firebombs. They even bombed Lloyd George's country house earlier this year. They're mad, the lot of 'em; dangerous too.'

'There are some militant suffragettes, I admit,' Bessie was forced to concede. 'But it's only because no one will give them a proper hearing. They've been driven to violence because of the way they are treated. They are fighting for a worthy cause.'

'Are you saying you support them?'

'Not actively, of course,' she was quick to point out, for fear of enraging him further. 'But I do think they are courageous in trying to win the legal right for women to vote in public elections, and they are suffering for it. I admire their guts. The law is totally unfair in excluding us.'

'Thank God there are none of them around here,' pronounced George, ignoring Bessie's valid points on the subject. 'I wouldn't like to tell you what I would do if one of you gels were to get mixed up with them.'

Jim made a timely intervention to defuse the rising tension. 'The headmaster was saying that he saw one of the new motor cars made in William Morris's factory near Oxford when he went to a conference in London the other day. Morris Oxford, I believe the new car is called,' he said in a swift and complete change of subject. 'Very smart, according to him.'

'We won't see any of them round here,' said Bessie, throwing Jim a grateful look.

'I'd love to see one,' put in Sam.

'You'll see plenty of cars before long, Sam,' Jim told him. 'One day in the not-too-distant future, they'll be everywhere; even in Tideway, eventually.'

'What makes you say that, Mr Minter?' Edie enquired.

'It's progress, Mrs Bow. Once they invented the combustion engine, there was no turning back.'

'It will be a while before we see them around here, I expect.' She looked at the clock. 'It's time you were in bed, Sam,' she said. 'Go and get washed and get yourself into bed. I'll come up later to tuck you in.'

'Mu-um,' he said, embarrassed. 'I'm much too old for that sort of thing.'

'I shall come anyway.'

'I must go to my room, too,' said Jim. 'I've still got some marking to finish.'

'I'll be making cocoa later on,' Edie informed him. 'Shall I bring you one up?'

'It's very kind of you to offer, Mrs Bow, but there's no need,' he said. 'I'll come down here for it when I'm ready. I can make it myself if you've gone to bed.'

Wonderful, thought Bessie. With a bit of luck, Mum and Dad will take their cocoa up to bed, so I'll have him to myself.

When Jim and Sam had left the room, Edie said in a low voice, 'I don't know what on earth has happened to May. It's nearly nine o'clock and still no sign of her. She should be home by this time. Surely Mrs March wouldn't keep her as late as this to do the stocktaking?'

'Perhaps she met a friend on the way home and has stopped to have a chat,' suggested Bessie.

'Could be,' Edie agreed. 'I gave her some extra sandwiches to keep her going if she had to work late again, so at least she won't be too hungry.'

'Do you want me to go out looking for her?' offered George. 'I'll go down to the ferry if you like.'

Before she could reply, Whistler started barking and bounded off to the back door with his tail wagging, which meant a member of the household had arrived.

'Hello, Whistler; it's all right, boy, I'm pleased to see you too, you daft thing,' they heard May say, and she came into the room looking flushed and happy, with the dog at her heels.

'About time too,' admonished her mother. 'I was beginning to get worried about you. Stocktaking again, I suppose?'

May nodded.

'That Mrs March is really pushing her luck now, making you do all these extra hours for no additional pay,' Edie said disapprovingly. 'I shall have words with her if it goes on much longer.'

'It's all part of the job, Mum,' said May quickly. 'I'd rather you didn't say anything. Mrs March doesn't take kindly to criticism and she'll take it out on me.'

'We'll see. Anyway, I kept some supper for you,' Edie informed her. 'Toad in the hole. It's in the oven. I've put a plate over it, so it should still be all right.'

May bit her lip. 'Sorry, Mum, but I'm not hungry,' she confessed ruefully. 'You gave me so many sandwiches, I can't eat another thing. Sorry.'

'It won't go begging around here, don't worry,' said her father. 'I'll polish it off later if Sam doesn't want it.'

'Good.' May yawned. 'Ooh, I'm so tired, I think I'll head towards bed.' She gave her sister a look, indicating that she wanted to talk to her. 'Is that all right, Mum?'

'Course it is. You need all the sleep you can get, the long hours you're working.'

'I'll be all right. G'night all,' she said and hurried from the room.

'You little fibber,' accused Bessie lightly, perching on the edge of her bed looking at her sister as she unlaced her stays. 'Stocktaking, my Aunt Fanny. You've been with a boy.' She sniffed. 'You've been drinking alcohol too. I can smell it on your breath.'

'I've had champagne,' May announced proudly.

'No!' her sister gasped. 'No one we know ever has that. Who gave it to you? None of the boys from around here even know what it is, let alone can afford to buy it.'

'It wasn't anyone from round here,' May confirmed, putting her stays over the chair. 'Oh Bessie, I've wanted to tell you about it so much. You and I always tell each other everything.'

'Whoever it is, you'd better tell me now, then, before I die of curiosity,' Bessie urged her.

'I've been seeing someone regular.'

'I gathered that much,' she responded, smiling. 'I didn't think Mrs March would ply you with champagne and make you look that happy. So who's the lucky man?'

May hesitated for only a moment, then gave a beaming smile and said, 'William Marriot.'

'Oh, May,' Bessie blurted out, unable to hide her concern.

'I knew you would react like that,' she said, looking disappointed. 'That's why I haven't told you before. I was afraid you'd go and spoil it for me.'

'I wouldn't want to spoil anything for you, you know that. But William Marriot . . .'

'To be honest, I don't think anyone could spoil it anyway, not even you. Because it's all so lovely.' May sighed. 'Oh Bessie, I'm so happy I'm floating.'

'No wonder, if you've been guzzling champagne.'

'You don't guzzle champagne; you sip it daintily. Anyway, it's nothing to do with that,' she made clear. 'It's William. There are no words to describe how wonderful he makes me feel. I'm flying and glad to be alive.'

'So this explains all these extra hours you've supposedly been working.'

May gave a wry grin. 'I've been meeting up with him after work several times a week, and tonight he brought a hamper and we found a quiet stretch of the river and had a picnic. Champagne and lovely little sandwiches; fruit tarts and chocolate éclairs for afters. It was great fun and so romantic. Oh do be pleased for me, sis. It would mean a lot. You and I have always been so close.'

Bessie wanted to be pleased for her, she really did, but the whole thing had disaster written all over it. William Marriot did seem very nice and was from a good family, but that in itself was a problem. May would never be accepted into his circles, and he would be fully aware of that even if she wouldn't face up to it. But Bessie couldn't bring herself to crush her sister while she was so ecstatic. It would be too cruel.

'Come here,' she said, hugging her. 'Of course I'm pleased for you. If you're happy, so am I.'

'I know you think that posh blokes just use girls like us then drop them when they feel like it, but William isn't like that,' May told her. 'He really loves me. He's gonna tell his people about me and we can have a proper courtship.'

'That's wonderful,' uttered Bessie, struggling to sound positive. 'Are you going to tell Mum and Dad, and invite him to tea?'

'That's the plan, but not just yet,' May replied. 'I'll let him tell his people first. Mum will go into a complete tizzy and I don't want all of that at this stage; things are too good as they are.'

'I'll be here to back you up when you do tell them,' Bessie assured her.

'Thanks, sis. Oh, I can't believe all of this is happening to me. My whole life has changed because of William.'

Bessie smiled affectionately. It was no wonder that William Marriot had noticed May; she really was the prettiest thing, with her round brown eyes, rosebud mouth and thick chestnut hair currently flowing loosely to her shoulders ready for bed. She was vulnerable, though, for all her outward confidence. Maybe fate would defy tradition and have things work out well for her and William. Bessie hoped so with all her heart, because May was obviously infatuated.

Jim was going through some papers on his desk in the classroom during afternoon break when he happened to glance up and saw through the window a fight break out between two of the boys outside in the playground. One of them was Sam Bow. He was rolling around on the ground with Johnny Willis, one of the school's most notorious troublemakers. Jim tore outside, hoping to end the hostilities before the headmaster got to hear about it. Fighting was a punishable offence and the culprits were caned as a matter of course. Although this was standard procedure in most schools, Jim instinctively recoiled from violence towards children and tried to find other ways to enforce discipline whenever possible.

'All right, the show is over, so scram,' he said now to the crowd of spectators, having dragged the two brawlers apart.

Some of the children hung back, enjoying the diversion.

'Go on, off you go – skedaddle,' he said more forcefully, and the gathering eventually broke up.

The transgressors went to follow the others.

'Oh no. Not you two,' Jim said forcefully. 'You're not going anywhere until I've found out what all this is about.'

The boys looked at him, Sam decidedly sheepish, the other boy blatantly arrogant.

'None of your business,' said Johnny Willis, a tall, skinny lad who Jim guessed was the instigator.

'Don't you dare speak to me like that, Willis,' Jim warned fiercely. 'As you well know, anything that happens in this school is very much my business. So tell me why the two of you were fighting in the yard like a couple of hooligans.'

Silence.

The headmaster strode on to the scene. 'Trouble, Mr Minter?' he enquired.

'All under control, Headmaster,' replied Jim with an air of confidence. 'Nothing you need concern yourself with; just a slight misunderstanding.'

'I'll leave it to you then,' the headmaster said and walked away

The bell rang for the end of playtime.

'We'll continue this discussion after school,' Jim told the boys. 'You will both stay in when the others have gone home. By then I will have thought of a suitable punishment for you.'

'Yes, sir,' said Sam.

Willis replied with a look of contempt.

'Do you have anything to add, Willis?'

He shrugged. 'Yeah, sir, all right, sir,' he replied with an air of lazy indifference.

'I would have preferred you to say it with more sincerity but it will have to do for now. I will see you both after school,' Jim told them in a firm tone. 'Off you go, back to the classroom.'

At that particular moment the headmaster's policy of caning seemed an attractive option in the case of Johnny Willis, but that wasn't Jim's way, at least only as a last resort.

As the boys joined the stream of ingoing children, a straggler, a little girl called Alice, approached the teacher.

'It wasn't Sam's fault, sir,' she said. 'He only hit Johnny Willis because he said things about Sam's sister Bessie.'

Jim's eyes widened with interest. 'Oh, and what things might they be?' he asked.

'He said that she is sweet on you and she hangs around with you a lot,' she informed him. 'He said that Sam's sister must be cheap because she is always with you of an evening and you're not even walking out together. He said that Sam's sister is a tart. He said that—'

Jim stopped her in full flow. 'All right, Alice. I think I get the picture. But it isn't good idea to tell tales, I'm sure you know that. Now run along.'

He was shocked. He had no time for tale-tellers but was grateful in this particular instance. Things must be being said in the village or this wouldn't have got back to him. He found himself in a fury in Bessie's defence. How dare anyone cast aspersions on her reputation? She was the sweetest, loveliest girl he had ever met and he felt ashamed for being to blame for causing gossip in her direction. How stupid of him not to realise. He wasn't used to village life, where the smallest thing was noted and magnified.

The rumours had to be stopped once and for all, and there was only one way to do that. He would deal with it this very evening. Meanwhile, he had a class to teach in English grammar, followed by two boys to discipline.

'Fighting isn't tolerated in this school, as you very well know,' lectured Jim later when the rest of the class had gone home. 'There is nothing that can't be put right in a peaceful manner. You are both old enough to know better and are a thoroughly bad example to the younger members of this school.' He paused, looking from one to the other. 'Well . . . have you anything to say for yourselves?'

'Sorry, sir,' said Sam.

The other boy just scowled, his deep-set grey eyes filled with mockery.

'You will both write "I must not fight" one hundred times. You will stay after school tomorrow to do it, so you must tell your parents that you will be late home.'

They both nodded. Johnny Willis made as if to go.

'Not so fast, boy,' roared Jim. 'I haven't finished with you yet. That isn't your only punishment. Sam, you are banned from after-school cricket practice this week.'

'Oh.' Sam looked crestfallen at having been deprived of the highlight of his week.

'You, Johnny Willis, *will* attend cricket practice this week,' Jim announced.

The boy's eyes widened and he coloured up with anger. 'But I don't like games and I never go to cricket practice,' he protested. 'I 'ate anythin' like that.'

'Exactly,' said Jim smoothly. 'It wouldn't be a punishment if you enjoyed it, would it?'

Johnny Willis's eyes were bright with fury, his mouth drawn tight in defiance as he stared at Jim.

'You can go now, Sam Bow,' said the teacher. 'You stay where you are, Willis.'

When the door closed behind Sam, Jim said to the remaining boy, 'If I hear that you've been discussing Sam's sister in a derogatory manner ever again, or in any way at all come to that, you will know what real punishment feels like.' He took the boy's arm in a firm grip and stared into his face. 'I can promise you that you won't enjoy it. Now get out of here and stay out of trouble.'

Jim watched from the classroom window as Johnny Willis swaggered across the playground towards the gates. He was one of life's aggressors. An enforced period on the games field after school might make him a little less eager to cause trouble in future. If nothing else, he would get some exercise.

William was waiting for May after work at the end of the road, standing under a large black umbrella, which he held over her as they headed for privacy in the countryside.

'No riverside picnic for us tonight then,' she said. 'The grass will be like a mud bath.'

'As long as we have some time together, that's all that matters to me,' he said, warming her heart,

'Rain or shine makes no difference to me either, but I mustn't be too late home or my mum really will get suspicious. She's not daft. She knows that stocktaking doesn't go on indefinitely.'

He laughed. 'I'm sure she does. I won't keep you out late, I promise, but I just had to see you.'

'Aah, that's nice.' She was brimming over with joy at his words. 'Mind you, the sooner we get this thing out in the open, the better. I hate telling lies at home.'

'It isn't nice, I must admit.'

'Have you said anything to your folks?'

'Not yet, but I will do.'

'I can't wait.' May paused. 'I have told my sister, I just couldn't help it, but she won't say anything until I've told Mum and Dad. I'll do that as soon as you give me the word.'

They had reached the end of the built-up area and headed along a lane towards some woodland. As soon as they were out of range of any prying eyes, William took her in his arms, the umbrella falling to the ground, other people and wisdom forgotten by them both in the joy of each other.

Jim followed Bessie into the back garden that evening when she went to get some washing off the line. It had been raining earlier and the clothes would have to be dried indoors on the clothes horse.

Without further ado he told her what had happened at school that day.

'The last thing I want to do is taint your reputation in any way,' he assured her. 'I'm not yet wise in the ways of village life so I didn't realise how something so innocent could be misconstrued.'

'Don't worry about it. It's just the talk of a sulky schoolkid,' she said. 'Anyone who matters wouldn't think ill of me.'

'Just the same, though,' he insisted, 'I don't want to do anything to harm your good name.'

She unpegged a cotton frock, added it to the washing she was holding and turned towards him slowly, her heart like lead. 'So you'd rather I didn't go with you when you go out for a stroll, is that what you're saying?' she suggested. 'You don't want to be seen out with me on our own.'

'It isn't that—'

'It's your reputation you're worried about, isn't it?' she cut in.

'No, not at all.'

'As a school teacher you don't want to be seen doing anything inappropriate, though what's wrong with two people going out for a walk together, I can't imagine,' she blurted out. 'But it's all right, Jim, I quite understand your position.'

'I don't think you do,' he said, shifting uneasily from foot to foot.

'Tell me about it then.'

'I was wondering . . . that is, I was hoping . . .'

'Yes? Get on with it, Jim, for goodness' sake.'

'I was thinking perhaps we could put things on a more proper footing,' he suggested. 'The thing is, Bessie, I like you. Well, actually, I mean I *really* like you a lot, and I wondered if you might consider walking out with me . . . er, properly.'

Her face was lit with a smile that came right from her heart. 'I would like that, Jim, very much indeed,' she said.

He was smiling too as he drew her towards him and they had their first kiss, neither even noticing the damp washing Bessie was holding pressed between them.

A few weeks later, Bessie spread the proofs of a set of wedding photographs Digby had taken recently on the shop counter to cries of approval from the bride and her mother. Bessie was happy for them. Marriage didn't seem to be just a distant dream for her now that she had a boyfriend. It was still early days, but she and Jim were good together and a girl couldn't help hoping.

She smiled as she recalled how delighted her mother had been when

Jim had asked for her parents' approval to walk out with her formally. Since she considered him the epitome of respectability, Edie couldn't have wished for a better suitor for her daughter, and she had finally stopped calling him Mr Minter.

'Take your time in choosing which ones you want for the wedding album and any individual copies you might need for family and friends,' said Bessie, adding, 'You can take them home with you if you wish to show them around so that people can make their own selections.'

While she was speaking, an extremely elegant woman of middle years stepped into the shop. Seeing the photographs spread out, she spoke instinctively. 'Oh, how lovely!' she enthused in a cultured accent. 'They really are excellent photographs indeed and just the recommendation I need, as I am here with a view to making a booking.'

'I won't keep you a minute, madam,' said Bessie politely. 'Please take a seat.'

'Thank you.'

Bessie finished with the business in hand then paid attention to the waiting customer. 'So, you'd like to make an appointment, then,' she said with a smile, opening the appointments book. 'Is it for a studio portrait of yourself?'

'No, no, my dear; it's for a wedding,' she replied, getting up and going over to the counter. 'I wonder if it would it be possible for me to have a chat with the photographer about it before I make a definite booking.'

'He has someone with him at the moment,' explained Bessie. 'But I'm sure he'll be happy to see you as soon as he's free.'

'I want to make sure that everything goes to plan, you see,' the woman went on chattily. 'The bride's people have most of the responsibility for the wedding arrangements, as is customary, so I want to make sure that our small part in the proceedings is as good as it possibly can be. We've agreed to look after the photographs, the wedding cars and a few other bits and pieces. We can't be too pushy about it for fear of causing offence.'

'It's your son's wedding, then?'

'That's right.' She nodded. 'But the young lady he is marrying I hope will become like a daughter to us. She's a most charming girl. My husband and I are very fond of her. Her father is a business associate of my husband, which is how the couple met.'

'You won't lose a son but will gain a daughter, as they say,' Bessie said lightly.

'I do hope so, because he is our only child,' she said. 'Our pride and joy.'

'When is the wedding?' enquired Bessie. 'Only Mr Parsons gets booked up a long time in advance.'

'Which is why I've come to see him now, though the wedding isn't until the autumn.'

Bessie flicked through the book. 'We already have a few bookings for September, so it's just as well you did come along now.'

'I was amazed at how far ahead these things have to be arranged,' she said. 'We booked the church ages ago.'

'May I take a few details, please?' asked Bessie. 'So that I can have them on record.'

'Certainly. I am Mrs Marriot,' the woman informed her, 'and it's the wedding of my son William at the end of September. At the very least we shall want a sizeable album for the happy couple and one for both sets of parents, as well as some framed photographs to have on display around the house.'

Bessie barely heard the second sentence after the shock of the first. Could it be the same William Marriot that May thought she was going to marry?

'Do you live locally, Mrs Marriot?' she asked. 'I haven't seen you around here before.'

'No, we live in London but my son's fiancée lives in Colchester, so the wedding will be there. Mr Parsons was personally recommended. He is very highly regarded, which is why I want him to take care of the photographs,' she explained.

'London to Colchester is quite a distance for an engaged couple to be from each other,' Bessie said, digging for more information.

'William has connections around here, over at Tideway mostly. He and his father are great yachting enthusiasts and keep the boat in the boatyard over there. They had an open invitation to stay at his fiancée's parents' home when they were down here, which is how the young couple got so friendly.'

'I see.'

'So it will be rather nice to use a business near to where the happy couple have done their courting, don't you think?'

'Oh yes, that will be lovely,' replied Bessie, managing to sound normal, though her spirits had taken another dive because there was no doubt now about the identity of the soon-to-be bridegroom. 'I'm sure Mr Parsons will be most flattered that you have chosen him.'

It was just as well she had, thought Bessie, or May could have ended up having an affair with a married man, if he hadn't discarded her before the deed was done.

'Are you all right, my dear?' asked Mrs Marriot. 'You seem a little flushed suddenly.'

'I'm quite well, but thank you for asking,' Bessie responded politely.

In fact she was incandescent with rage towards this congenial woman's son, sad on May's behalf and dreading being the one to break the news to her. But no matter how painful, it had to be done. She felt quite ill at the prospect of hurting May in this way.

'What do you want me to do then?' asked a sulky Johnny Willis of Jim on the school playing field. 'I don't know anything about the stupid game of cricket.'

'You should have paid attention in games lessons then, shouldn't you?' Jim pointed out. 'You will be fielding, so stand over there and recover the ball as quickly as you can after the batsman has hit it; that is the aim. Catch him out if you possibly can.'

'Fat chance of that,' grumbled Willis.

'Stop complaining and get on with it,' said Jim with authority. 'This will be a team effort, so don't spoil it for the others. You are not here to enjoy yourself.'

The ball was bowled, then whacked, and it came soaring towards Willis, who missed it by a long way. The other boys on his side jeered at him. Willis wasn't a popular pupil.

'That isn't the spirit of the game of cricket, boys. You do not criticise your team mates on the field,' admonished Jim in his grey flannels and open-necked shirt. 'Just do your best and get a move on, Willis. The idea is to stop him getting runs, not to let him get more while you hang about feeling sorry for yourself.'

Willis was angry and humiliated. He might be top dog in the play-ground, but it was different here with people getting so het up about the game they were good at and he didn't have much of a clue about. He put on a spurt to get the ball and threw it back to one of the other fielders. Much to his surprise, his aim was good and the fielder caught it.

Again the ball was bowled and hit and came hurtling towards him like a ghastly retribution. With some sort of survival instinct he leapt in the air, threw his arms up, caught it and held on to it.

'Out!' he heard the cry go up. *He'd caught someone out.* Well, that was a turn-up for the books. In fact it was nothing short of a bloomin' miracle.

'Well caught,' the other boys were saying.

Inspired by this small success, Johnny put his all into it and began to enjoy himself; he even managed to hit the ball when it was his turn to bat. Well, this cricket lark wasn't so bad after all. Who would have thought he would be able to keep up? He hadn't shone early in his schooling during games lessons so had made a point of putting in as little effort as possible and sneering at anyone who took an interest, especially those who stayed behind after school to take part.

But at the end of the session he asked, 'Can I come again next week, sir?'

'Well, well! I can see that I shall have to find a new way to punish you for your misdeeds, Willis, if you're going to start enjoying sport,' was Jim's reply.

'I did do the lines, sir,' the boy reminded him, fearful of another penalty.

'Yes, I know you did, and this was meant to be a punishment too, so that wipes the slate clean even though you enjoyed it.' He looked at Willis, observing that for once he wasn't scowling. 'You did very well. I didn't know you had it in you.'

'Neither did I,' said the boy.

Jim experienced one of those rare moments that made teaching worthwhile and for which, in this instance, he could take no credit. Quite by accident he had caused the boy to find something in himself that might give him pleasure and possibly make him less aggressive in the future.

There was never a right time to shatter someone's dreams. But after worrying about it all day, Bessie decided that bedtime would probably be her best bet to break the news to May. At least her sister would have the night to get used to the idea before work in the morning and Bessie would be on hand to give support. So after being on edge all evening, her heart heavy with the task ahead, spirits sinking even more when May came home even later than usual looking pink cheeked and glowing with happiness, she finally told her about the meeting with William's mother when they were both about to get into bed.

'You're lying,' was May's initial reaction. 'That is just filthy lies. You're jealous because I'm happy with a gorgeous, well-off man and you're stuck with a stuffy schoolteacher who earns a pittance and isn't even good looking.'

'I wish that was true, I really do, but we both know it isn't,' Bessie said. 'William Marriot is engaged to be married and in a few months' time he will be a married man.'

'How could you do this to me, Bessie?' demanded May through dry lips, her eyes bright with rage.

'How could I not tell you?' her sister replied. 'I couldn't let you go on seeing him knowing that you were going to be humiliated and have your heart broken. That would have been wrong.'

'It must have been another Marriot family who have a son called William,' May suggested, clutching at straws. 'It couldn't have been my William because he loves me. He's not engaged to someone else. I'd know about it if he was.'

'How would you know? You don't mix in his world. In fact you know nothing about him except that his family has a yacht they keep in Tideway and he works in his father's bank,' Bessie pointed out. 'I know it must be painful for you, May, and my heart goes out to you, but once you face up to it, it can begin to heal.'

Bessie, who had been perched on the edge of May's bed and speaking in hushed tones, suddenly found herself under attack.

'You spiteful cow,' roared May, her voice contorted with emotion, slapping her sister's face and pulling her hair. 'You're a nasty vindictive bitch.'

A scream was torn from Bessie's lips as her hair was almost dragged from its roots, causing her intense pain.

'Get off me,' she yelled, pushing her sister away and trying to escape. 'Calm down, May, for heaven's sake.'

The noise had attracted attention in other parts of the house and someone was knocking on their door.

'What's going on in there?' their mother wanted to know.

'Nothing, Mum,' replied Bessie, trying not to sound too shaky.

'Well do nothing more quietly if you please,' Edie ordered in low tones. 'Or you'll have the whole house awake. We do have a paying guest, remember, and he's entitled to a decent night's sleep.'

'Sorry, Mum,' said Bessie.

May drew away from her sister and Bessie sat on the edge of her own bed.

'You say another word against William,' hissed May, 'and I'll make sure I do more than just pull your hair. I'll have the bloody lot out. Now get to your own bed and leave me alone. I want nothing more to do with you, you evil witch.'

'Please, May . . .'

'Shut up.'

'But I had to tell you.'

May got out of bed and, putting her face close to Bessie's, said in a harsh whisper, 'Did you not hear what I said? I want nothing more to do with you, so keep your filthy lies to yourself.'

'May . . .'

'Are you deaf or something?' she rasped. 'I don't want to see you or hear your voice ever again. I'll be glad when I get married and out of this house.'

As painful as it was, Bessie knew that she must accept what May said for the moment. She watched her sister get into bed and turn on her side with her back towards Bessie, who then blew out the candle and got into bed herself. The room throbbed with silent tension as both girls began a sleepless night.

'Pink ribbon, dear,' the customer pointed out as May put the pink button drawer on the counter. 'I asked for ribbons, not buttons.'

'Oh yes, I'm sorry,' she apologised, taking the ribbon drawer away and replacing it with the correct one.

Mrs March's darting little eyes were on May, who followed that first error with a second when she gave the customer the wrong change. As soon as the woman left the shop, her employer turned on May.

'What on earth is the matter with you, girl?' she demanded. 'You'll lose us every customer we've got if you carry on like this. You've been making mistakes all day.'

'Sorry.'

'Are you ill?'

'No, I'm not ill.'

'Well pull yourself together and do your work properly, then,' she ordered.

'Yes, Mrs March.'

May's manner was very subdued. She was barely aware of what she was saying or doing. Her mind was full of thoughts of the altercation with Bessie last night. She would not believe what her sister had said; she couldn't believe it because it hurt too much. William wouldn't do that to her. *He wouldn't*. He loved her and she trusted him.

But the nagging doubts persisted. Bessie had always been a good and caring sister; she wasn't the type to make things up, especially a hurtful thing like that. It must just be some sort of a mistake. Please God let it be that.

Somehow May struggled through the rest of the day, longing to see William to have her mind put at rest. When she was with him the doubts would disappear and all would be well, she was sure. She did hope he would be waiting for her when she finished work.

He was. He was standing in the evening sunshine in his usual spot just out of sight of the shop, and he was carrying a hamper. The sight of him was bittersweet.

'I thought you might like some light refreshments,' he said.

'Lovely.'

They went to one of their favourite secluded spots by the river and sat on the grass, sheltered from prying eyes by weeping willow trees on one side and horse chestnuts on the other.

'Is anything the matter, May?' William asked as he popped the champagne cork and filled her glass. 'You're looking a bit tired. I do hope all these secret meetings aren't wearing you out.'

'I didn't sleep well last night,' she told him.

'Oh my poor love,' he responded sympathetically. 'Was it anything in particular keeping you awake?'

She wanted to forget Bessie's allegations about him. She wanted to lie in his arms and let the world disappear. But the honesty in her nature refused to let it go.

'As much as I enjoy our secret meetings,' she began, not quite able to put the question directly and hoping it wouldn't be necessary, depending on his response, 'I must admit that I am getting very fed up with all this hole-and-corner carry-on. It makes me feel a bit cheap, to tell you the truth.'

'Oh May, you must never feel cheap. That's the last thing you are.'

There was a brief hiatus, then she asked, 'Do you really intend to tell your family about me so that we can carry on like normal decent people?'

She watched him closely as he took rather a large swallow of his drink. 'Of course I am,' he replied smoothly. 'I've told you I will and I'm a man of my word.'

Every line and angle of his face registered with intense clarity as she stared at him: his fine features, straight nose, beautiful pale brown eyes that so entranced her. She fixed her gaze on him to study his reaction as she said, 'Are you engaged to be married to someone else?'

'What!' was his seemingly shocked reaction. 'What sort of a question is that? Where on earth did you get that idea from?'

'Are you?' she persisted.

'No, of course I'm not,' he denied quickly. 'Would I be here with you now if I was?'

His words were convincing but the momentary bulging of his eyes and the stiffening of his face muscles in reaction to her question gave her the answer she didn't want to have.

'Apparently, yes,' she said. 'One woman isn't enough for you. You like a bit on the side too!'

'Why are you saying these terrible things, May, when you know they aren't true?' he asked her.

'Your mother called at the photographer's where my sister works to arrange your wedding photographs, so don't insult me with any more denials.'

'Oh. Oh, I see.' At least he had the decency to look sheepish now that the game was up. 'It isn't like it seems, I promise you,' he said. 'I don't love my fiancée, I love you.'

'Oh, please . . . don't give me that old toffee.'

'It's true, May, honestly,' he insisted. 'This wedding will be good for the two families from a business point of view, and I thought I could go through with it until I met you.'

'And now you're going to break it off with her to be with me, are you?' she challenged cynically.

'I'm trying to,' he told her lamely. 'That's what I want, but I need a little time. It isn't easy for me to hurt someone.'

'You don't seem to have much trouble hurting me,' she said coldly. 'The lies have just rolled off your tongue.'

'I know what it must seem like . . .'

'I know what it *is* like.'

'All right, everything you say is true. I've behaved despicably,' he finally admitted. 'But despite all that, it is you I love.'

His words felt like a balm; she wanted to hear them so much and longed for them to be true. But she couldn't allow herself to be so charmed by him that she lost her common sense. Words came easily to a man like him; a man who was a liar and a cheat. May put her champagne down and stood up as though to go.

He scrambled to his feet too. 'Please, May . . .'

'Go home to your family and your fiancée, William,' she said. 'Don't you ever come near me again. Do you understand? I want nothing more to do with you, so don't come to me for your bit of rough.' She bent down and picked up the champagne bottle and threw the contents into his face. 'You disgust me.'

She marched towards the path along the river bank to walk back to the town to catch the ferry. He followed her. 'May, I know it looks bad, but it isn't—'

His sentence was cut short as all the pain and disappointment culminated in a flash of violence and she turned to him and gave him a hefty shove towards the river, where he landed with a splash.

'Perhaps that will cool your ardour,' she said as a parting shot as he struggled to his feet in the waist-high water.

'May,' he called, coughing and spluttering.

'Go to hell,' she shouted back at him. 'I never want to see you again, so keep away from me.'

And she hurried along the river bank weeping uncontrollably, her bright new world plunged into darkness.

'Sorry I said those awful things to you last night,' May said later when the sisters were in the privacy of their bedroom and she'd told Bessie what had happened with William.

'That's all right,' Bessie assured her. 'I knew you didn't mean what you were saying. You were hurt, and we all say things we later regret at times like that.'

'I couldn't bear for what you'd told me to be true, but I suppose I knew all along it was, deep down inside.' May was pale and exhausted, her eyes swollen from crying. 'I'm just a daft girl falling for the first real man to take an interest. It was a silly dream; the old story of the rich using the poor, wasn't it?'

'Something like that,' said Bessie.

'But I loved him so much. I still do and I think I always will. Those feelings don't go away just because I've found out that they weren't reciprocated. It's like an awful ache in the pit of my stomach, a real physical pain. Just the thought of him made me happy, and being with him felt as though I was touching heaven.' She filled up again. 'All that's over now.'

'You'll meet someone else,' Bessie tried to soothe, 'someone with serious intentions.'

'I suppose I will at some point. But there will never be anyone like William,' she said with passion. 'Never, ever.'

'Maybe not, but there will be someone else who can make you happy in a different way. There's sure to be.'

'Anyone else will be second best, but I'm not ready to consider anything like that at the moment,' May told her.

Their mother was calling from downstairs. 'Cocoa is made, girls. Come on down.'

'I can't face going down there and having Mum ask me again why I've been crying, and having to make out that I haven't been,' confessed May.

'I'll bring your cocoa up and I'll have mine here with you,' suggested Bessie warmly. 'I'll be here for you all night if you want to talk.'

'What about your delectable Mr Minter?' said May with an effort at a watery smile. 'Won't he want you to go down for a spot of canoodling later on when Mum and Dad have gone up?'

'He won't mind,' Bessie assured her. 'He is very easy going is my delectable Mr Minter, as you call him. And you need me more than he does tonight.' She paused, giving her sister a look of mock admonition. 'And not so much of the canoodling, if you don't mind. A good-night kiss, maybe.'

May wished that she had limited her contact with William to that. Maybe if she had she wouldn't feel so used and abused now. Oh well, hindsight was a wonderful thing for future reference, but it didn't make her feel any better at this moment.

Chapter Five

As the evenings lengthened and the sun grew warmer, cottage gardens throughout the village burst into floral glory along with plump vegetables and crisp green lettuces. The riverside at Tideway was buzzing with activity, the sails of the freshly painted yachts billowing in the breeze ready for the racing season.

Many Tideway fishermen hung up their nets, put their fishing smacks on to the hard for the high summer and signed up with the yacht-owners. Being an experienced mariner, George Bow registered with the Marriot crew as usual, with the idea of making some decent money to help when the winter storms raged and fishing was poor, and sailed away to distant waters.

Accustomed to their men being away during the yachting season, the Tideway women had plenty to occupy them, looking after their homes and families and taking part in village summer activities: picnics with the children by the river, and helping to organise such annual events as the fête, the Sunday-school outing and the flower show.

There was added excitement in the air just lately, created by the arrival of piped gas to the village, which meant proper street lighting, and gas for cooking for those who could afford to buy one of the new cookers.

The women of the Bow family, however, were far too preoccupied with a serious family matter to take their usual keen interest in events outside the home. Berry Cottage was fraught with whispers behind doors closed to Jim and Sam. There were tears and tantrums, furrowed brows, nerves on edge and tempers fraying.

'What's goin' on in this house?' Sam asked his sisters one day. 'Why do you two keep whispering with Mum? I want to know what it's all about.'

May and Bessie looked at each other.

'There's nothing going on, Sam,' fibbed Bessie.

'Why is Mum in such a bad mood all the time, then, if nothing's wrong?' he wanted to know. 'She keeps snapping my head off for no reason at all, and you two are being peculiar. I'm bloomin' well fed up with it, I can tell you. There's a secret in this house and I don't see why I should be left out of it, seeing as I am a part of this family.'

'It's nothing you need bother your head about,' Bessie told him. 'Everything will be back to normal before very long and Mum will be her usual self again.'

'In other words you're not gonna tell me.'

'It's nothing that would interest you.'

'Honestly,' he huffed. 'It's no fun living here lately. Dad's lucky to be out of it.'

As it happened it was, indeed, very fortunate for them all that their father was away, thought Bessie. Heaven only knew what would happen if he ever got to know what trouble had befallen his family.

'Oh Lor . . . oh my good Gawd. Good heavens above, that poor child,' cried Winnie emotionally, looking up from a letter that had just come in the morning post.

'Whatever's the matter?' asked Albert, peering at her over his breakfast teacup.

'It's Edie's girl May. She's only gone and got herself up the duff,' Winnie explained, scarlet anxiety blotches suffusing her face and neck.

'Blimey, that's torn it,' exclaimed her husband. 'Is the chap gonna do the decent thing by her?'

'Is he, my Aunt Fanny,' she replied. 'May won't even tell her mother who put her in this predicament.'

'I bet she's had a right good rollicking from her dad,' guessed Albert.

'George knows nothing about it, thank the Lord. He's away crewing on a yacht, and by the time he gets back the problem will be solved, with a bit o' luck, so he won't ever have to know,' Winnie told him. 'Edie wants me to get it seen to for her. She doesn't know of anyone down Essex way who does that sort of thing but there's a couple round here who earn a few extra quid that way. There's a woman on the pie stall down the market who knows a friend of a friend. I heard 'em talking about it when the grocer's daughter was in trouble a few months back.'

Albert didn't look happy. 'I don't like the idea of you getting involved in that sort of thing, Winnie,' he told her.

'What else can I do?' she asked, shrugging her shoulders in a helpless gesture, her dark eyes clouded with worry. 'Edie's been good to me and I owe her. Anyway, I'm very fond of young May, as you know, and someone's got to help the poor girl. Her mother will be giving her hell; you can bet your sweet life on it. You know how strict Edie is about the straight and narrow, and Gawd help anyone who strays from it.'

'Even apart from the fact that abortion is against the law, you hate the idea of it,' he reminded her. 'You know how much it upsets you when you hear of someone doing it.'

'I do know, but needs must when the devil drives, Albert. I can't let them down, can I?' she said, biting her lip. 'May's coming here on Saturday for the weekend. I'll have to get something arranged before then.'

'Oh well, if you're determined to help out, I don't suppose there's any point in my trying to talk you out of it, is there?'

'Not really, no, love,' she confirmed. 'Our feelings on the subject don't matter in this particular instance. I have to do what I can to help.'

'If I knew who it was who did this to young May, I'd sort him out good and proper,' declared Albert, his voice rising. 'He wouldn't do it again in a hurry. Not after I'd finished with him.'

'Well we don't know who he is, so all we can do is support the poor girl through the wretched business.' Winnie sighed. 'Men, eh! Why can't they behave?'

'We're not all tarred with the same brush, you know,' Albert pointed out.

'I know, love.'

'That's all right then,' he said, finishing his tea and rising. 'It's time I was off to work.'

'All right. I'll see you down the stall later.'

He pecked her on the cheek and left the house, donning his cap on the way.

Winnie cleared the table, put some soda crystals in the bowl and got busy with the dishcloth. Her stomach was churning from the news about May. She felt sad and worried for her and already dreading what she was being forced to do.

'I wish I could come with you, May,' said Bessie on the station platform waiting for the train to London on Saturday. 'But Mum is dead set against it and she's in enough of a state, I don't want to make her even worse.'

'She wouldn't want to make things any easier for her disgraceful daughter by letting her have her sister's support,' opined May. 'And I'll be all right with Auntie and Uncle. So don't worry.'

'I didn't expect Mum to be pleased, obviously, but I didn't think she'd be quite so angry,' mentioned Bessie. 'She's almost beside herself.'

'I've committed the worst sin in the book, in her eyes,' commented May. 'I doubt if she would have been as upset if I'd murdered someone.'

'But you are her daughter, after all. I don't think it's necessary for her to be quite so hard.' Bessie paused. 'She's still grieving for Henry, so perhaps that has something to do with it.'

'Yeah, she's had a hard time and I feel terrible for adding to her troubles,' confessed May. 'I wish I didn't have to get rid of the baby, though. I really do. It makes me feel sick every time I think about it.'

'Aah, it must be awful for you,' Bessie sympathised.

'Mum is adamant about it,' May went on. 'She won't even consider the idea of my keeping it, so there's nothing else I can do.'

'It's the disgrace she can't take,' said Bessie. 'It would bring shame on the family and Mum couldn't bear that. Dad wouldn't have an illegitimate child in the house anyway. So I suppose there isn't any other way.'

Bessie's heart lurched when the train came in.

'Ta-ta, sis,' she said, hugging May. 'Good luck. I'll be thinking of you all the time you're away. See you in a day or two.'

May boarded the train, a small, forlorn figure. Bessie waved until the train was out of sight, then made her along the stony path to the ferry, her eyes moist with tears.

That evening, May and her aunt walked through the back streets of west London in the gas-lit dusk. Winnie had her niece's arm tucked into hers companionably.

'I'll be with you all the time, love, and there to look after you while you recover,' she said gently. 'You'll be all right with me and Uncle Albert. By the time you go home you'll be as right as rain and no one in Tideway will be any the wiser.'

'I wish I could keep the baby, Auntie,' May told her.

'Yeah, me too. But your mother is immovable on the subject. She wants it gone.'

'I feel so powerless against her,' confessed May. 'I wish I had the courage to go off and have it anyway.'

'It isn't a question of courage; it's more about facing up to reality,' said Winnie. 'You and the little one would have a terrible life if you were to do that.' She paused, looking at the houses. 'It must be along here somewhere. Here we are, number twenty-four.'

'Oh, it looks so ordinary,' said May with surprise.

'What were you expecting, something from the Chamber of Horrors?' her aunt responded.

'It's such an awful thing to do, I was expecting something gruesome.'

'The woman is probably just an ordinary housewife making a few extra quid by helping young girls out of trouble. There are plenty of women doing the same thing.'

The door was answered by a little girl. Winnie asked to see the person whose name she had written down on a scrap of paper given to her by the woman on the pie stall.

'Mum,' the girl shouted. 'Someone for you.'

A small woman appeared. She poked her head out of the door furtively and said, 'No one saw you coming, did they?'

'No,' replied Winnie.

'You didn't tell anyone anything, I hope.'

'Only Florrie from the pie stall who arranged it for us,' Winnie told her.

'Come in then,' she said and ushered them inside and straight upstairs.

They were taken into a room with a high bed in it. The woman asked May how far gone she was, then whipped the eiderdown off and told May to remove her lower undergarments, raise her skirt and lie down on the bed.

'Before we start, I have to tell you that if there are any complications later on and you have to consult a doctor, you were never here,' she said forcefully. 'You have never heard of me or this address. Understand? I have to be very careful. I could go to prison for what I am about to do.'

'We understand,' Winnie assured her.

'I'd rather you waited outside if you don't mind,' the woman said to Winnie.

'I'd like to stay to give my niece some moral support,' Winnie told her.

'I prefer to have no one else in the room, if you please,' she insisted in a tone that warned against argument.

'Al right, I'll go.' Winnie squeezed May's hand. 'I'll only be outside the door waiting for you, darlin',' she told her and slipped quietly from the room.

'It won't take very long,' said the woman, who was wearing an apron over her long dark skirt, her hair taken back off her face with greasy strands escaping and falling untidily on to her cheeks. 'Now just relax, dearie, or you'll make it harder for me and yourself. When all this is over you can get on with your life as free as a bird. And don't be such a silly girl in the future. You must learn to say no. Now up with your skirt so I can get at you.'

As May did as she was asked, she had never felt more degraded and disgusting in her life. She was about to let this woman kill her baby; a child she would love. But she herself was the murderer for allowing the woman to violate her body and end a life, a child conceived out of love, on her party anyway.

As the woman leaned towards her with a sharp instrument about the size of a knitting needle, May was galvanised into action. 'No, no, stop this right away. I've changed my mind.' She pushed her away, shot up and off the bed and pulled her skirt down.

'Don't mess me about, you little cow,' objected the woman, trying to force May back on to the bed roughly. 'I've started the job and I'll finish it. I'm not losing my earnings just because you want to play games.'

'You'll get paid,' said May, struggling to get free. 'But leave me alone. I'm keeping my baby.'

Retrieving her underclothes from a chair, she ran from the room, pursued by the woman rattling on about her money. 'I put time aside for you. I'm entitled to be paid.'

May told her aunt what had happened and Winnie handed the woman an envelope that May had been given by her mother. 'Here's your money.'

'Oh. Oh well, that's all right then,' said the woman, instantly appeased.

'All we need now is a few minutes while my niece gets herself properly dressed and we'll be on our way,' Winnie told her while May struggled into her knickers. 'I'm so sorry that you've been troubled in this way.'

'That's all right,' said the woman, happy now that she had been paid. 'It isn't the first time a girl has changed her mind, and it won't be the last.' She looked at May. 'But I'm warning you, my girl. You'll regret it a few months down the road. Your life won't be worth living. Your baby won't be with you if you end up in the workhouse. They split families up and send kids to a different institution. You won't get your child back till it's fourteen, and it'll have a hell of a life at school, jeered at by the other kids for being a workhouse kid. It's wicked how they treat people there. So you know where I am if you have second thoughts.'

'I won't,' May stated firmly, 'and that's definite.'

Outside in the street, May collapsed into tears.

'I'm so sorry, Auntie. I just couldn't do it,' she sobbed. 'I *wouldn't* do it. I know that my baby and I will be outcasts, but I couldn't rob it of life. I want it so much, you see. Somehow I'll bring it up; somehow my baby will have a chance. I'll do everything I possibly can to keep us out of the workhouse.'

Winnie put her arms around her. 'I'm proud of you, love, you're a brave girl.'

'Mum will kill me,' she wept. 'I've spent her money and not got the job done. That money was from her rainy-day fund. She can't afford to lose it, Auntie.'

'You let me worry about your mother,' Winnie tried to pacify her.

'I'll pay back every penny somehow,' May went on. 'It might take a while but I'll do it. It isn't fair to rob Mum and Dad of money just because I've got myself into a mess.'

'I'll pay your mother and you can pay me when you've got it,' Winnie offered.

'I can't let you do that, Auntie. It wouldn't be right.'

'Of course you can,' she insisted. 'Uncle and I don't do too badly on the stall and we don't have any kids to spend our money on. Your mother has a hard time as a fisherman's wife, so you let me and your uncle help you out. We are family after all. There'll be no need for your mother to know anything about it.'

'I'll pay you back.'

'If you want to, in your own time, I won't stop you, but I won't be chasing you for it,' she said kindly. 'For the moment you must concentrate on looking after yourself now that you've got a nipper on the way.'

The dire consequences of May's action hit her suddenly.

'Mum won't let me stay at home unless I get rid of the baby,' she said. 'So I don't know what I'm gonna do.'

'She might change her mind with a bit of persuasion,' Winnie suggested. 'Stay with us for the rest of the weekend and try to calm down after that nasty experience, then I'll go home with you and we'll talk to your mum together.'

'Thank you, Auntie,' said May, wiping her eyes. 'You are so good to me.'

Winnie held her tight.

Edie's eyes were like slits of ice as she stared at Winnie and May across the parlour table on Monday, the envelope containing the money in front of her.

'Are you telling me that you didn't get it seen to?' she said in disbelief. 'That the problem is still there?'

'Yes, I'm afraid we are,' confirmed Winnie, meeting her sister's cold, accusing eyes. 'Young May couldn't go through with it and I can't say I blame her.'

'Can't I trust you to do anything right, Winnie?' Edie blasted at her. 'All you had to do was go with her and make sure she got it seen to. Heaven knows, it wasn't much to ask. Surely you could have done that without messing it up.'

'It wasn't her fault, Mum,' May put in. 'I refused to have it done and she couldn't make me.'

'I *wouldn't* make her,' corrected Winnie. 'It's her baby so the decision must be hers.'

Edie's face was bloodless, save for two red stains on her cheeks. 'What world are you living in?' she demanded of her sister. 'She's a seventeen-year-old girl in the family way with no husband or even a boyfriend. She doesn't have the right to decide. She needs to get the problem sorted.' She transferred her steely gaze to her daughter. 'You'll have to go back. I don't care how much that upsets you; we are removing this blight from our lives. I know it's wrong in the eyes of the Lord, but it has to be done.'

'I can't do it, Mum, I'm sorry.'

'You *won't* do it, you mean.'

'If you want to put it that way, yes.'

'You've always been a selfish little madam,' Edie rasped. 'Never mind other people as long as you get your own way. You've always been the same.'

'Oh Mum.' May was crying now. 'Please don't say these awful things. I know I've been a disappointment to you and I'm so sorry for that.'

'Make up for it then by doing the right thing by your family now,' insisted her unrelenting mother harshly. 'You're the one who has done wrong but we will all suffer from it. So it's no more than your duty to spare us from the disgrace.'

'I would do anything in the world for you, Mum, but I just can't kill my baby.'

'In that case you relinquish all rights to this family,' Edie informed her through tight lips. 'I refuse to let you bring shame on us all. Not only will it disgrace your father and me, it will also rub off on your sister and brother. With a bastard in the house we'll all be tainted.'

'What about family solidarity, Edie?' put in Winnie. 'What about looking after your own in times of trouble?'

'If she does as she's told she will be looked after, which is more than many mothers would do in these circumstances. Some would have thrown her out at the first sign of morning sickness. But I'm giving her the chance to stay a part of this family. If she chooses not to take that opportunity, that's her lookout.' She gave May a withering look. 'If you're not prepared to go back and get the job done, you can pack your things and get out.'

'What!' May couldn't believe her mother would go to such lengths.

'You heard, and if you do go you won't be welcome in this house ever again. The door will be closed to you and your illegitimate child for good.'

Although May had expected a negative reaction from her mother, she wasn't prepared for quite such a verbal lashing. She felt utterly alone and rejected. But she knew she couldn't change her mind about her baby.

'I'd better pack my things then,' she said.

'And make it sharpish too,' returned Edie cruelly. 'I want you out of here before your sister gets back from work because I don't want a lot of sloppy sentimentality and arguments. My mind is made up and I won't change it. Sam has gone with Jim for football practice. They'll be home soon, so get your things together and get out.'

'Mum, I can't believe you're being so hard,' cried May.

'And I can't believe you'd bring this trouble home after the care I've taken in bringing you up to know the difference between right and wrong. What a fine way to pay anyone back.'

'You are being extremely callous, Edie, and it isn't right,' admonished Winnie.

'You would say that, wouldn't you?'

'What do you mean by that?' asked May.

There was a brief hiatus. The two sisters looked at each other.

'I mean that your aunt has never been any good at behaving herself either.' Edie paused. 'But don't waste time nattering. I want you out of here.'

'I'll come and help you get your things together, love,' offered Winnie kindly.

'That's right, you take her side,' said Edie scathingly. 'You'd do anything to upset me.'

'That just isn't true, Edie,' denied Winnie. 'Someone has to look out for the girl. You don't seem to care what happens to her as long as she's away from here.'

'She's brought this on herself.'

'That is irrelevant.' Winnie was shouting now. 'You don't cast someone out just because they've made a mistake. You're a spiteful woman, Edie Bow. You call yourself a Christian, but all that churchgoing hasn't made a good person out of you. Quite the opposite.'

'Don't you dare speak to me like that.'

'I'll speak to you how I wish. If you are prepared to throw a young girl out on the street, you don't deserve respect, not as far as I'm concerned.'

'Stop it, you two,' interrupted May, her voice ragged with emotion. 'Please don't fall out over me. I feel bad enough already without being responsible for that as well.'

'And so you should,' said Edie tartly.

'Sorry, love,' Winnie apologised. 'Now let's go and get your things together and be on our way. The sooner we get away from here, the better.'

'Where will I go?' asked May.

'Home with me, of course,' replied Winnie. 'Me and your uncle Albert will give you a home for as long as you want it; you and the baby.' She turned to Edie. 'As much as you might wish it on her as a punishment, May won't be destined for the workhouse because I shall make damned sure she isn't.'

And with that she ushered May upstairs to pack her things. When they came down again, Edie was waiting by the door ready to show them out.

'Please, Mum, don't let's part like this,' begged May. 'I know I've let you down and I'm sorry.'

'Sorry isn't any good to me,' Edie responded. 'It's far too late for that.'

'Maybe when you've calmed down I can come and see you; see how you and Dad are.'

'I have just told you: you won't be welcome in this house ever again, so keep away,' declared Edie. 'You had your chance to get the problem sorted and you chose not to. You defied me, so as far as I'm concerned you no longer exist.'

May felt completely crushed, but a spark of spirit rose above her dejection. 'Fair enough,' she said defiantly. 'I'll make sure that you don't see me or your first grandchild. I hope that will make you happy.'

And she walked through the door carrying her case with her head held high.

Winnie stopped by her sister. 'You wicked bitch,' she hissed. 'I've always known you were hard; now I know it's more than that. You are downright evil.'

'And you have no sense of decency,' the other woman retorted. 'You have taken her side against mine so you have betrayed me. I never want to see you again.'

'That's fine with me,' said Winnie, and she marched out of the house and down the street to catch up with her niece.

'Give me that bag, love,' she said, taking the suitcase from May. 'You shouldn't be carrying anything heavy; not for the first three months anyway.'

'What about Uncle Albert?' May asked tearfully. 'How's he going to feel about having me and a baby born the wrong side of the blanket in his house?'

'If I'm happy with something, then so is he,' Winnie replied. 'So stop worrying.'

Bessie was disappointed when she got home from work to find that May wasn't there.

'I thought she would have come home today; still, I suppose it's a bit too soon,' she said to her mother, who was in the kitchen at the range. Jim was in his room and Sam was down in the village with his pals. 'I hope everything is all right. It can be dangerous, so I've heard.' She bit her lip anxiously. 'You don't think anything went wrong, do you?'

'Nothing went wrong because she didn't have it done,' her mother informed her sharply. 'She has been back and taken her things and gone; she doesn't live here any more,' she added, stirring some gravy in a saucepan with extra vigour. 'She's gone to live with your aunt Winnie.'

'What? Permanently?'

'Yes.'

'Why?'

'She has gone against my wishes and is keeping the baby, so I told her to leave,' explained Edie, keeping her eyes fixed rigidly on the saucepan. 'She will be living in London from now on, but as far as Sam and anyone outside this family is concerned, and that includes Jim Minter, she's got a job in London and that's why she's left. I shall have to tell your father the truth when he comes home, of course, but no one else must know. For my part, May and her brat don't exist. She is not welcome in this house and I have told her so.'

Bessie was shattered by this news. 'They exist for me, Mum, very much so,' she said, her eyes filled with tears. 'May is my friend as well as my sister and I love her. I can't banish her from my life. I would never do that.'

'What you do about that is up to you,' said Edie. 'If you wish to keep in touch with her after what she's done, even though it will be disloyal to me, I can't stop you. But don't mention her name to me because I don't want to hear it.'

Bessie could hardly believe that her mother had taken such extreme action. She'd always been a stickler for right and wrong, of course, and it was a terrible disgrace May would bring on the family, but Bessie had expected Edie to stand by her offspring through thick and thin. She couldn't bear the idea of not having her sister around. She'd thought they would always live in close proximity to one another even after they had left home and gone their separate ways. London was a long way away and the train fare was expensive so she wouldn't be able to visit very often, and May obviously wouldn't come back to the village again. Her sister must be feeling terrible. Thank goodness she had dear Aunt Winnie. Bessie couldn't imagine that lady being unkind to anyone.

'Couldn't she have stayed here, Mum?' she asked. 'She's our flesh and blood and so will the baby be . . . we could have helped them.'

'No, she could *not* have stayed here,' Edie cut in, her voice rising angrily. 'I will not have the reputation of my family ruined by the selfishness of that girl. Now I don't want to hear another word about it. The subject is closed. Lay the table, please.'

Sadly, Bessie did as she was asked, planning to write a letter to May immediately after supper offering to support her in any way she could.

Edie was stirring the gravy through a blur of tears. Why did she feel as though she was in the wrong when May was the transgressor? Honestly, the way Winnie and Bessie spoke, you'd think May's predicament was nothing much to be ashamed of, when everyone knew it was the worst disgrace that could befall any family.

Because of May's self-indulgence there would be another empty chair at the table. First it was her dear Henry; now May. She'd always been a wild and reckless child, never able to do what she was told. So why did Edie herself feel so guilty when she'd done nothing wrong? All her life she'd been a good, clean-living woman. She'd made sure she kept to the rules and raised her family to do the same. May had not only let her down but she had refused to save the family from shame as well by not getting the problem seen to. So Edie had had no choice but to turn her out. There were other people besides May in this family to be considered, all of whom would be tainted by such a scandal.

So she would not be driven by some misplaced sense of compunction to change her mind. No! Not ever! That girl had done wrong; now she had to pay the price. She couldn't break the rules and expect to get away with it. Anyway, Winnie would see that she was properly looked after. Edie's sister had a different attitude towards such things, which wasn't really surprising considering the irresponsible sort of woman she was. No self-discipline at all, that one. She just threw herself into life with no thought of the problems lurking ahead.

The whole wretched business had been very upsetting, though, and Edie would be glad when George came home; at least he would see her point of view. She wiped a tear from her eye and removed the pan from the heat.

Dear Bessie,

I'm missing you so much and was very glad to get your letter. I was especially pleased to receive it as I was afraid that Mum might turn you against me for keeping the baby. I just couldn't do what Mum wanted and I'm sorry if any of this rubs off on you, though as I'm away from there there's no reason for anyone to know. I'm really sad about that because I'll always think of Tideway as home and would want people there to know my baby and watch it grow up.

Sorry I didn't call in at the shop on the way to the station to tell you what had happened but I was feeling so wretched I wasn't thinking straight. I'm very hurt by what Mum's done. I've always known I wasn't her favourite child but I didn't expect quite such a hostile reaction. Still, it's my own fault. I knew what happened to girls who got themselves into this situation so I shouldn't have been so reckless. I loved him so much, you see.

What with being cast out of the family and betrayed by William I'm not exactly on top of the world. But Auntie and Uncle are very good to me and I enjoy helping out on their stall. It's a lot more fun than Mrs March's shop and the market people are ever so friendly. There's a young chap called Archie who works on the fruit and veg stall and has been very kind to me. He's a bit of a comic with the Londoner's gift of the gab and he makes me laugh, which I didn't think I ever would again.

It'll be cold working on the stall in the winter but Auntie says as long as you wrap up well and keep moving you get used to it. It's a very busy market so they are glad of my help. I don't know what I'll do to pay my way after the baby comes as I'll have a child to look after so working won't be easy. I'll find a way, though. I shall have to. I can't expect to sponge on Auntie and Uncle. Nobody here, apart from them, knows about my condition yet. I don't know if they'll all be so friendly when they do. Only time will tell.

It's a different world here, Bessie. So many people everywhere and a surprising number of motor cars; motor buses too. There are quite a few of those suffragettes about, selling their newspaper on the streets. It seems funny actually seeing them instead of just reading about them in Dad's paper. They are very unpopular with most people

— especially men, naturally — but I think they're brave to fight for their cause; our cause too as we're women.

Auntie and I went to the cinematograph the other night. It was great fun watching the moving pictures. You sit in rows and watch a screen and there is a woman playing the piano at the front in time with the action. I thoroughly enjoyed it.

As well as that, Uncle and Auntie are taking me to the music hall on Saturday. Auntie says I need some fun to keep my spirits up. She's such a lovely person; so kind and thoughtful and has such a zest for life. I've no idea why Mum never seemed to like her much. I really don't know what I would have done without her. I would have been in a real pickle, that's for sure.

Living here with them, I'm getting to know them better and love them both. Uncle is a real sweetheart. They are a lot more outwardly caring of each other than our mum and dad, probably because they haven't got any kids to worry about. I know that Mum thinks Uncle Albert is a bit rough and ready but I think he's lovely. He's very popular with the other market traders.

Auntie is very excited about the baby. As they have never had any children of their own and she loves kids, she can't wait to have a little one about the place. She makes a real fuss of the nippers who come shopping with their mums down the market and they love her. So I expect she'll spoil mine rotten when it comes. I feel so sad that you won't see much of it. I'd always thought our children would grow up together.

Which reminds me to say that I hope all is well between you and the delectable Mr Minter. Give him my best regards. Also give my love to Sam and tell him I'm thinking of him.

I know you won't be able to visit me much but I would love it if you could at some point as I miss you something awful. It will be best if I stay away from Tideway altogether. Mum wouldn't want me anywhere near the place so I'd better not come down and meet you somewhere in case we are seen.

Hope to hear from you soon.

Love,

May

Bessie dried her eyes and put the letter in her dressing-table drawer to read again in the evening after work. Ever since May's departure she had been looking out for the postman, and when she was rewarded this morning

84

with a letter, she slipped the precious missive into her pocket without her mother noticing. It was such a relief to hear that May was all right. Bessie had been so worried about her. She would go to London to see her at the very first opportunity.

There was a distressing conflict underway in her mind, an awful sense that by staying friends with her sister she was somehow betraying her mother, who had done her best for them all as they were growing up. But she could never cut May out of her life, whatever the circumstances. Never, ever! She meant too much to her.

Mulling over the rift between her sister and her mother, Bessie knew in her heart that nothing would ever be as bad for Edie as losing Henry; the loss of any of her other children or even her husband would not have the same impact as losing her adored firstborn. It had taken all the heart out of her, even though she plodded on day after day with her characteristic stoicism.

Even so, she had been affected by May's going; you could see it in her eyes. Was it sorrow, though? Or was it resentment at being let down? Surely it couldn't just be the latter, although there was a hard glint there sometimes. She must miss her daughter, the same as any mother would.

Whatever the truth of the matter, it was hard for Bessie to bear. She wished she could talk to Jim about it, but she daren't defy her mother as far as that was concerned. Bessie didn't believe there was one iota of disapproval in Jim's nature; he took people for what they were with all their faults and weaknesses.

That wasn't to say that he didn't get angry about things and people; he was sometimes beside himself with rage about incidents that happened at school, but that was usually because of the pompous headmaster, who was set in his ways and not open to new ideas as regarded education. As far as Jim was concerned, there was always an answer to any problem that arose. He usually tried to work out why things had happened rather than just condemn.

It would be a relief to share this burden with him, Bessie was sure of that. But Mum wouldn't want him to know, so she would keep it to herself. It wasn't as if Jim was family, even though it sometimes felt like it with him being so much at home at Berry Cottage and such a part of all their lives, especially hers, now that they were walking out.

He was a very calming presence about the place; so pleasant to have around with his quiet humour and his kind heart. Bessie was very fond of him; well, more than just fond really. They had become quite close lately, in the most respectable way, of course. Jim would never take liberties with her. She was pleased that he felt able to confide in her about his work at the school; she enjoyed hearing about it. It gave her a whole new insight into the world behind the staff-room door.

Sadly, though, May's plight was one piece of Bow family business she couldn't share with him.

Chapter Six

'Get your lovely red apples here, folks; the best in town today.' The young fruit and vegetable seller held up a specimen for potential customers to inspect. 'Just look at that. Have you ever seen a healthier russet? I've been up all night picking 'em from the orchards of Kent myself, so you won't get fresher anywhere in London.' He grinned broadly. 'And if you believe that, you'll believe anything.'

'Enough of your old toffee, Archie Mott,' smiled a regular customer, Mrs Brown, a hearty woman the wrong side of fifty with a big family and a sense of humour to match. 'Just get on with your work and give me some service.'

'Any time, Mrs B,' he grinned, teasing her. 'Just let me know when your ole man isn't at home and I'll be round your place like a shot.'

'Ooh, you cheeky young article,' she said in a tone of feigned outrage but obviously enjoying the joke. She'd known Archie all his life and had watched him grow up. 'It's a good job we know you around here.'

'I might say the same thing about you, Mrs B,' he joshed. 'Fluttering your eyes and making a young fella blush.'

She loved that and emitted a raucous laugh.

'So, joking apart, what can I do for you this fine morning?' he asked in a pleasant manner.

'A pound of carrots and a marrow, please.' She studied the display of the latter and pointed to a healthy specimen. 'That one there'll do for me.'

'Certainly,' he said. 'Any apples for you today, Mrs B? An apple a day keeps the doctor away, so they say.'

'You're very keen to get shot of your apples, aren't you, son?' she observed with a wry grin. 'Did you buy too many or something? You're overstocked, I bet.'

'Would I use such devious tactics?' he asked her, replying to his own question immediately. 'Course I wouldn't because I look after our customers. Truth is, the little beauties looked so nice at the wholesale market we took plenty, and I want to make sure our regulars get some before they sell out.'

'Go on then, give us a couple of pound.'

'Coming up,' he said, weighing the goods, taking her shopping basket and emptying her purchases into it.

'Thanks, Archie,' she said, handing him the money. 'You're a good lad.'

'I do my best,' he responded, rummaging in the money bag he wore around his waist and handing her her change. 'You look after yourself now and enjoy those lovely apples. See you tomorrow.' He watched her go, then turned his attention to the queue that had now formed. 'Right now, ladies. Who's next?'

It was a month since May had left home, a sunny Saturday morning in late August, and she was working with her aunt on their stall opposite the Motts', admiring the way Archie handled his customers. There were market stalls the length of the street and a sea of people lapping over the pavements into the road, seemingly uncaring of the traffic: bicycles, horse-drawn carts, a few motor vehicles.

It made a colourful sight: women with their summer frocks being held up above the street dirt, and little girls in pinafores, some well dressed, others ragged and barefoot. The market was mainly the haunt of the proletariat but their circumstances varied. The roar of human voices sounded almost deafening to a country girl like May; even now she found it strange, though exciting too. There were traders calling out their spiel, punters bargaining, motor horns tooting, children laughing, dogs barking and babies crying. A complete contrast to the quieter ambience of Tideway.

Also observing events opposite, Winnie mirrored May's thoughts. 'It's a treat to watch young Archie work,' she said. 'He's a market trader through and through. I reckon he could sell saucy knickers to nuns, that one.'

'Perhaps we should borrow him then,' May joked, 'as business is a bit slow this morning.'

'It'll pick up later,' Winnie assured her. 'Saturday afternoon is always busier for us. People concentrate on the day's essentials in the morning, food and the like. Anything to wear – even if it is only a new vest or a pair of long johns for the old man – is bought at their leisure in the afternoon.'

'Yeah, I suppose so,' said May, unable to stifle a yawn. Her aunt had told her that the tiredness she was experiencing at the moment would lessen later on in the pregnancy.

'You can go to the café for a cup o' tea and a bun while it isn't busy, if you like,' suggested Winnie, and when May made a face because tea was repellent to her at the moment, she added, 'Get 'em to give you a glass of milk then, or a cup of Oxo. You need to take the weight off your feet every so often in your condition.'

'Thanks, Auntie, I think I will,' May said gratefully and made her way across the street to the café used mostly by market people.

She had just sat down with a glass of milk and a bun when she saw Archie come in. He spotted her and came over since they were neighbours on the market and already acquainted. 'Mind if I join you?' he asked with a smile.

'Not at all.'

He got himself a mug of tea and a cheese roll and sat down opposite her.

'Dad's just come back from an errand so I took the chance of a break while I can,' he explained. 'It's always busy on a Saturday morning for us so we sometimes don't get one and I'm starving.'

'My aunt reckons you could sell saucy smalls to nuns,' May told him, smiling.

Archie laughed. 'I don't know about that, but I'd have a go and that's a fact. I ought to able to shift the stock the length of time I've been at it. I used to work with my dad on the market when I was too little to see over the stall. I love it.' He bit into his cheese roll and chewed it with relish 'So what about you?' he asked between bites. 'Are you getting used to market life?'

She nodded and told him about her job in Mrs March's emporium and how different it was to what she was doing now.

'You've had a lucky escape by the sound of it. That sort of work would kill me,' he confessed. 'I couldn't stand being stuck inside a shop having some stranger watching my every move; not after working with my dad since I was in short pants.'

'You've certainly got all the chat with the customers, I notice,' she mentioned.

'Some like a bit of a joke, others don't. You learn to judge the situation and make sure you never step over the line. Our customers know we would never sell 'em anything less than the best we can get. Never second best at Mott's stall, that's our slogan.' He took a healthy swallow of tea, looking at May. 'Are you planning on staying around here permanently?' he asked casually.

She nodded. 'I don't have any plans to go home at the moment,' she replied.

'Good news for us then,' he remarked lightly. 'But you sound a bit sad about it.'

Moving away from the family had been a wrench and she still suffered from periods of homesickness. 'It was a big change and now and again it hits me,' she explained.

'You might get to like it here if you stick around a bit longer,' he suggested.

'I like it already and everyone's been really friendly,' she made clear. 'I'm beginning to get used to London, though it was a bit of a shock to the system at first for a village girl like me. The noise and the crowds; the air of confidence everywhere.'

'I s'pose it would seem strange if you're not used to it,' he agreed. 'I've never lived anywhere else so I wouldn't really know.' He paused and added in a gentle tone, 'You'll be missing your folks too, I expect.'

'Exactly, especially my sister; we're good pals as well as sisters,' May told him. 'Still, I'll get to see her occasionally, I hope. She'll visit when she can.'

'Do you fancy coming out one night?' Archie asked suddenly. 'We could go to see a film if you like, or just for a walk by the river if you'd rather. A night out might make you feel less homesick.'

Because of her condition, she was instinctively on her guard so didn't reply at once. He certainly wouldn't be inviting her if he knew the truth.

'It's all right,' he said quickly, misunderstanding her hesitation. 'Don't feel obliged. I only suggested it because I thought you might like some company of your own age.'

Archie was a nice-looking bloke, though not stunningly handsome. May guessed he was about nineteen or twenty. He was tall and well built with mid-brown wavy hair and even features. His complexion was fresh and clear, his eyes of the warmest brown and he had the most beaming smile.

'Forget I said it,' he said, and the reddening of his ears tugged at May's heart strings. 'I know I'm no oil painting and a girl like you could have anyone.'

'No, no, that isn't the reason I didn't jump at the chance,' she tried to explain.

'It's all right, there's no need to be polite. I can take it,' he cut in with a cheery smile. 'It was only a casual suggestion.'

She desperately needed a friendship with someone of a similar age to herself and she didn't want to miss the chance of Archie's. She would probably lose it anyway when her condition became apparent, but she most certainly wouldn't gain it by turning his invitation down, because he would feel rejected and embarrassed and give her a wide berth. He had such honest, compelling eyes, she trusted him instinctively.

She looked around to make sure that they were out of earshot, then leaned forward and said in a confidential manner, 'I'm not free to go out with anyone.'

'Oh, I understand. I should have guessed there would be someone else,' he said. 'A girl like you.'

'There's no one else in that way,' she hissed. 'It's just that I'm er . . . er . . .'

'What? Spit it out, for Gawd's sake,' he urged. 'You're getting me worried now.'

She bit her lip, then burst out in a whisper, 'I'm pregnant . . . and, er, single.'

'Ooh, bloody 'ell,' he blurted out.

She stared at him. 'Not such an attractive proposition now, am I?' she said.

He put his half-eaten cheese roll down as though he had lost his appetite. He could hear his father saying, 'Steer well clear – she'll be looking for a husband to give her kid a name.' But Archie said, 'It isn't that. It came as a bit of a surprise, that's all. It was the last thing I was expecting.'

'You're quite safe,' she assured him hastily, anticipating his fears. 'I'm not looking for a husband to save my reputation. I'm prepared to go it alone and that's what I'm going to do, with the help of my aunt and uncle.'

'Oh . . .' He seemed lost for words.

'It would be nice if you and I could be friends but I'll understand if you'd rather not,' she told him. 'I'm going to be the talk of the town around here once I start to show, so you might not want to be seen with me.'

He nodded vaguely, seeming preoccupied.

Not wanting her drink suddenly she said, 'Please don't tell anybody, Archie. I want to keep it dark for as long as I can.'

'No one will hear about it from me.'

'Anyway, I'd better go back to work.' She got up. 'See you around.'

He put a restraining hand on her arm. 'Don't go off like that, May,' he urged her. 'Please sit down. I didn't mean any offence. I was just getting used to the idea.'

'I don't want to make you feel awkward, that's why I was going,' she explained.

'These things happen and it would take more than something like that to make me feel awkward,' he told her, back to his usual self, smiling his enormous smile, which lit up his whole being. 'It seems to me that you're going to need a friend, so if you fancy coming for a walk tonight with me, I'd be the happiest man on the market.'

'Just friends, though,' she said, keen to make the point.

'Oh yeah, just friends,' he agreed.

That evening they walked through evil-smelling alleyways between factories, sheds and brewery oasthouses, then crossed the high bridge over the creek outlet, crowded with sailing barges on their way to the Thames. Reaching the towpath and the open air of the riverside, May felt a sudden pang of nostalgia for Tideway. Her head was filled with images of Bessie walking by the Colne with Jim, holding hands and with Whistler at their heels.

Although it was still only August, incipient autumn already spiced the evening air, though the weather was warm and humid, the setting sun splashing its orange rays on to the undulating surface of the river near Hammersmith Bridge. Clouds of midges hovered over the water upon which there were substantial numbers of craft: lighters carrying goods, tugboats, a rowing crew practising. Swans and ducks were very much in evidence too, unconcerned by the human invasion of their natural habitat.

People were out in force taking the air, May noticed, some sitting outside the riverside pubs on the towpath. She and Archie stopped at one and sat down on a bench, May with a glass of ginger beer while Archie had a pint of brown ale.

Inspired by his interest in her, she told him about her life in Tideway, her family and her current predicament, including the rift with her mother.

'I suppose I was stupid to believe him when he told me he loved me and was serious about me, but it was what I wanted to hear,' she confessed, feeling so much better for sharing it with someone. 'I've always been too reckless for my own good, according to my mother anyway. I listen to my heart rather than my head in life in general, and look where it's got me. In the club and my mother doesn't want anything more to do with me.'

'I'm rather inclined to be led by my feelings too,' Archie admitted, and went on to tell her that he was nineteen, that his mother had died when he was little and that he had been raised by his father. 'Dad's a rock-solid, down-to-earth sort of a bloke. I suppose he had to be with a kid to bring up on his own. He's got bags of common sense and uses it. Straight as a die, my dad.'

'I shall use my common sense in future,' May told him. 'I'll have to with a child relying on me. Once bitten . . .' She paused, looking at him. 'Not that I don't want the baby, because I do; more than anything.

But it would have been nice to have had it under different circumstances, rather than having it born into shame with its grandmother wanting nothing to do with it.'

'Mm, that is a pity,' Archie said, not patronising her by pretending that she didn't have a point.

'Mind you, I pity anyone who gives my kiddie a hard time,' she told him. 'They'll wish they hadn't when I've finished with them.'

'You're on the defensive already.'

'I am, aren't I?' she agreed lightly. 'It must be nature's way. The protective instinct is already in place.'

'The people around here are quite broad minded; well, more so than they would be in the country, I expect. But there will be some who will be a bit sniffy about it, I expect.'

'They'd better not be sniffy about my child when I'm around.'

'Hey, calm down,' he said, admiring her spirit. 'You'll do yourself an injury.'

'Goodness knows what I'll be like when it's actually born.'

'When's it due?'

'February.'

'You've a while to go yet, then.'

She nodded. 'Anyway, I'm sure you don't want to be talking about babies, a young chap like yourself,' she said. 'You'll want to have some fun on a Saturday night. You should be out with your mates looking for girls, not listening to my troubles.'

The only place he wanted to be was here with her. She was the loveliest creature he'd ever seen and he was eager to know everything about her. 'I'm quite happy; don't worry about me,' he assured her.

'I don't want to cramp your style,' she said.

'If I didn't want to be here, I wouldn't be,' he assured her. 'I can promise you that.'

She smiled at him. He really was the nicest person. 'Thanks for tonight,' she said. 'I love Auntie and Uncle to bits, but it's nice to have some young company.'

'I'm enjoying myself,' he said, and meant it. 'It isn't over yet, either. Would you like another drink?'

'Not for me, thank you, but you go ahead if you want one,' she told him.

'I will then,' he said. 'I won't be a minute.'

She was smiling as he strode towards the pub, his long legs making short work of the distance.

They stayed talking for a long time after he'd finished his beer, then he walked her home.

'Sunday tomorrow and a nice lie-in,' he said at her front door. 'I really look forward to that, having to get up so early all week to go to the fruit and vegetable market.'

'Will you lie in till dinner time?'

'No, nothing like that; eight or nine maybe.' He paused, looking at her in the gaslight glow. 'Fancy going out somewhere later?' he invited. 'There's usually a band playing in Ravenscourt Park on a Sunday afternoon.'

'Well . . .' she began.

'No strings,' he cut in. 'Just two people taking a break in the fresh air.'

'In that case, I'd love to,' she smiled.

Winnie and Albert came striding down the street, having been for a couple down the pub.

'Are you coming in for a bit of supper, Archie?' invited Winnie.

'Ta very much, Winnie. I don't mind if I do,' he replied.

It was all so easy-going and friendly, and the warmth wrapped itself around May and made her feel a part of things here in London. For the first time she felt really at home.

Her friendship with Archie quickly became an important part of May's life. His popularity rubbed off on her. He seemed to know everyone on the manor and any friend of his was a friend of hers. He took her into London to see the sights, to the picture palace, and Sunday afternoons were usually spent in Ravenscourt Park or walking by the river.

He was so much at home with Winnie and Albert, having known them all his life, it was almost like having a brother around. Though of course it wasn't quite like that, as May's latest letter from Bessie reminded her. She read the correspondence again while she was at the stall. Uncle had gone to the wholesaler's and Winnie was having a break at the café, so May was holding the fort.

Dear May,

Still missing you like mad but am glad you're settling down in London now. As that's where you're living you need to feel at home. This Archie you mention seems a real sweetheart. Is he really just a friend, though? From what you've said he seems smitten with you even though you insist there's nothing more than friendship between you. I'm really glad that you've got a friend.

Nothing much has happened here. Dad's home from the yachting season now and back to fishing. He must have been told why you're not here but I don't know the outcome because the subject is never mentioned, though they must talk about it in private. Mum is plodding along. You can never tell what she's feeling but I think she's sad; probably still grieving for Henry or missing you or a bit of both. You know Mum, she never says, just gets on with things. Sam seems to be shooting up all of a sudden and has gone into long trousers. He's left school and is working as an errand boy at the boatyard until he's old enough to go to sea with Dad. He needs to grow a bit more before then because of the physical strength needed for the job. He still doesn't want to be a fisherman, but feels duty-bound.

As for Jim and me, we are still going strong. He continues to be full of new ideas for the kids at school and because of this is more or less permanently at war with the headmaster, who is, as you know, very set in his ways. Jim's latest project is an essay competition with a prize paid for by himself, bless him, and a school play. The HM is dead set against both because of the extra work involved, even though it will all be done by Jim.

As for your question about an engagement, no sign of anything like that yet but I live in hope because I really want to marry Jim.

Sam sends his love.

I'll try to get up to London to visit some time soon.

Lots of love,

Bessie

She was about to read it again when Archie called out, 'Customer, May!'

The customer, a woman of about thirty, was looking longingly at the colourful shawls that were hanging up, a job lot that Uncle had got hold of cheap.

'Pretty colours, aren't they?' remarked May. 'A red one would suit you, against your lovely dark hair.'

'Yes, I do like it.' She looked about to walk away.

'Why not have a look in the mirror?' suggested May, darting from behind the stall, wrapping the red woollen shawl around the woman and holding a rather tarnished mirror in front of her.

The potential customer looked longingly at her reflection. 'I can't really afford it, with having the kiddies to clothe.'

'You've got to keep yourself warm as well with winter just around the corner. They're good-quality shawls; just the thing now the mornings are getting chilly,' said May. 'I can knock a bit off for you if you like.'

'I'm not sure.'

'Half-price. How will that do you?'

'I'll take it,' she replied at once.

'You won't regret it,' said May. 'Anything else today? How about a nice warm cardigan? Or gloves, perhaps?'

'No, nothing else.'

'Here you are then,' she said, putting the shawl into a bag and taking the woman's money. 'See you again soon, I hope. Ta-ta for now.'

'Well done,' praised Archie when the customer was out of earshot.

'I'm not sure I should have let her have it so cheap,' May said. 'I think I might be a bit of a soft touch.'

'You'll toughen up in time,' he said. 'You're a natural with the customers. Winnie and Albert are good teachers.'

'Not to mention a certain someone else not a million miles away,' she said jokingly.

Winnie and Albert's house was a small Victorian terrace in a back street. It was a humble abode, cosy and comfortable and spotlessly clean but unmistakably working class. It did, however, have two miracles of modern-day living that made it seem luxurious to May: an inside toilet that had been built on to the back of the house and a water tap in the kitchen. Practically every time May used either facility she waxed lyrical about them.

'Oh, how wonderful. How my mother would love to be able to wash the greens like this,' she said one Sunday morning as she rinsed the cabbage for dinner in the colander under the tap. 'It's a real treat, Auntie!'

'Are you still going on about the running water?' teased Winnie, who was beating the batter for the Yorkshire pudding with a fork. 'I should have thought you'd have got used to it by now.'

'I'm used to it but still not taking it for granted,' May informed her. 'Goodness knows when they'll get piped water in Tideway.'

'It is a bit off the beaten track, but they have got gas now so maybe it won't be too long,' remarked Winnie. 'There's talk of bathrooms being put in around here at some point in the near future. Imagine that, May. Water running directly into a bath. It'll put the rent up but it'll be well worth it.'

'I'll say.'

Albert came into the room with his hat and coat on. 'I'm off for a quick one,' he announced.

'Quick one, my eye,' said Winnie. 'A slow several would be nearer the mark.'

'Just an expression, dear.'

'Dinner will be on the table at two o'clock sharp,' Winnie informed him. 'So don't you hang about all afternoon talking to those cronies of yours.'

'As if I would.'

'Go on and leave us in peace.'

He went to her and planted a kiss on her cheek. 'See you later,' he said cheerily.

'Two o'clock or your dinner is in the bin.'

'Yeah, yeah,' he said as though he didn't believe a word of it, and left with a cheery ta-ta.

'Are you going out this afternoon?' Winnie asked May chattily.

'Yeah. Archie's coming to call for me. We're going to the park,' she replied.

'Good. I'm glad you're getting out a bit. You don't want to be stuck at home all the time with a couple of old codgers like Albert and me,' Winnie approved. 'Archie is a good lad.'

'I don't know if he'll want to be seen out with me when I really start to show,' mentioned May. 'I'm beginning to thicken round the middle already. My corsets are killing me.'

'They would be,' said Winnie sympathetically. 'You'll have to leave them off later down the line.'

'Not until I absolutely have to,' May told her. 'I don't want to set tongues wagging until it's absolutely unavoidable.'

'I'm sure Archie won't desert you when your condition becomes obvious,' opined Winnie. 'He doesn't seem the type to worry about gossip.'

'It will be very awkward for him, though.'

'No doubt about that,' agreed Winnie. 'But he's the sort to stay loyal to his friends.'

'I'll take it a day at a time and see what happens,' said May.

'That's all you can do, love,' agreed her aunt. 'But however things work out with Archie and the others round here, you'll have Uncle and me.'

May felt her eyes swim with tears at her aunt's kindness. How different she was to her sister Edie!

Ravenscourt Park was well attended as usual on a Sunday afternoon. But people were more inclined to be on the move because there was a nip in the air as autumn got under way. May and Archie listened to the band for a while then took a stroll, talking about this and that and enjoying the sunshine.

It was when they sat down on a bench by the lake and the roar of a train going over the railway arches receded that Archie dropped his bombshell.

'I've been thinking, May,' he began, sounding unusually apprehensive.

'Be careful. You'll give yourself a headache doing too much of that,' she joshed.

'I'm serious.'

'All right, what's on your mind?'

'I think that it might be a good idea for you and me to get married,' he announced.

'Married!'

'Yeah. What do you think?'

She laughed, assuming he must be joking.

'Don't laugh at me, May,' he said in a solemn tone.

'Oh, Archie, surely you're not being serious.'

'I wouldn't joke about a thing like that,' he told her. 'I kid around about most things, but not that.'

'But we're just friends,' she reminded him.

'And we still would be,' he told her.

'I don't see how—'

'Look,' he cut in eagerly. 'If we got married it would solve a lot of problems and be the best thing for you and the nipper. It would spare you both from a whole lot of pain in the future. As my wife you'd have respectability, and the child would have a father so wouldn't be looked down on.'

'But what about you in this grand plan?' she asked. 'What would you get out of it?'

'I'd get to be with you and your baby,' he told her plainly. 'You've probably guessed how I feel about you. I wouldn't have mentioned it this soon, but time is of the essence with the baby coming.'

She'd suspected his feelings went beyond friendship but had chosen to ignore the subject until now, since he had made no move in that direction. Now she knew she must make things clear. 'Archie,' she began hesitantly, 'I think the world of you as a friend but I could never love you in that way. I'm very sorry.'

His face muscles tightened slightly but he soon recovered. 'That's all right. I wouldn't force anything of that nature on you.'

'Oh, Archie . . .' She felt terrible.

'If you give it some serious thought you will see that there would be a lot of advantages,' he was keen to point out. 'You wouldn't have to go out to work because I would support you and the nipper.' He paused, looking at her. 'If that was what you wanted, o' course. So you wouldn't have to worry about getting the baby minded while you were out at work.'

'But it all seems to be about me and the baby, Archie.' She was concerned about him. 'That isn't fair to you.'

'I would get to be with you both so I would be happy,' he told her simply. 'All I would ask is to be the baby's dad and your husband . . . er, even though it wouldn't be in the full sense of the word, of course.'

She took his hand. 'Archie, you are one of the loveliest people I have ever had the good fortune to meet; a true friend. But I don't think I can do this. It would be far too one sided. It would ruin our friendship. We might even grow to hate each other.'

'Not necessarily.'

'There's a chance we will, and I don't want to risk it.'

'I admit it wouldn't be ideal, but it would solve a lot of problems.' He sounded very disappointed. 'Especially for the little one.' He looked at her entreatingly. 'But if you won't even consider it . . .'

'It wouldn't be right, Archie,' she said. 'Marriage should be a thing of love on both sides. It wouldn't be fair to you and you would eventually resent that. You might think now that you won't, but in time you will. It would be only natural.'

'Won't you even think about it? Please?'

'All right, I'll think about it,' she said to pacify him. 'Don't think I don't appreciate the offer, because I do. It's very good of you and I'm privileged to have you as a friend.'

'Yeah, I know,' he said cheerfully. 'I suppose I am pretty wonderful.'

'You must be stark raving mad to turn him down,' was Aunt Winnie's reaction when May confided in her that evening after Uncle had gone to see his pal next door. 'Completely bloomin' barking.'

'But I don't love him in that way, Auntie,' she explained. 'And I know I never will.'

'Someone in your situation can't afford to worry about something like that,' Winnie retorted. 'You've been open and honest with him about it and he's still happy to go ahead, so get on with it, girl. This is no time to be fussy.'

'It wouldn't be fair to him.'

'It would be if you made him a good wife,' opined Winnie, putting a different slant on it. 'If you do your very best for him and look after him well. You could always shut your eyes and think of the baby's father during you-know-what.'

'He says he won't press me as far as that's concerned.'

'He might very well say that now, but he's a man when all is said and done,' she said. 'Anyway, it would be your duty as his wife. He'd be doing his best for you and the nipper after all. So you'd have to put yourself out too. If I were you I would welcome the opportunity with open arms, for the baby's sake if not your own. There's only one way to protect that child when it's old enough to be hurt by people outside the family, and that's to provide it with a father and a ring on its mother's finger.'

'But we were going to manage before this came up,' May reminded her.

'Yes, and we still will if you can't make yourself marry Archie, but this opportunity has arisen and I think you should seriously consider it, because it will save you from a lot of pain. Not many girls in your situation would get a chance like this. So think long and hard about what a difference it will make to your child's life before you make your final decision. This is about the baby, May, as well as you.'

'I know, Auntie, and I will give it some serious thought.'

'Don't think about it for too long, though,' Winnie advised. 'We don't want you going into labour at the altar.'

'Oh, Auntie, you don't half exaggerate.' May laughed, but she knew her aunt was making a serious point.

'You must want your brains tested,' exploded Bill Mott when Archie confided in his father about his hopes of marriage to May. They'd always been close, and Archie was very open about things by nature. 'Taking on a woman who's carrying someone else's kid. Oh my Gawd! How did she manage to talk you into offering to do a silly thing like that?'

'She didn't talk me into anything,' he told him. 'I want to marry her, Dad.'

'You're too soft, boy, you always have been, as much as I've tried to toughen you up. You must get it from your mother, I suppose. It certainly doesn't come from me. You can't throw your life away bringing up another man's kid. I mean, she's a nice enough girl – and pretty too, I grant you – but pregnant . . . that's a real turn-up for the books. She keeps it well hidden, though not for much longer. You want to steer well clear, mate. I bet she kept quiet about being in the family way until she'd got you hooked.'

'She told me before we even went out together, as it happens,' Archie informed him, smarting on May's behalf at the insults.

'That's something in her favour, I suppose,' Bill admitted reluctantly. 'Like I said, she seems like a nice enough girl and I've got a lot of time for her uncle and aunt, but you are my main priority and I think you'd be wise to forget her and find someone else, someone without complications.'

'I don't want anyone else and I don't mind the complications, but you'll be pleased to know I probably won't be able to marry her anyway, because she isn't at all keen on the idea,' Archie told him. 'She doesn't think it's fair to me under the circumstances. It's very unlikely that she will accept.'

'That'll just be an act she's putting on to make her seem genuine and to get you even keener,' Bill told his son. 'It's working too, by the sound of it.'

'She isn't like that at all,' objected Archie, his voice rising. 'Honestly, Dad, you can be very hard at times. You barely know the girl; how can you judge her?'

'I'm realistic.' He'd had to be over the years. The death of his wife from pneumonia when Archie was a year old had all but destroyed Bill. She'd been so young and had meant everything to him. He'd wanted to die himself but had faced up to his responsibilities and forced himself to carry on, vowing to do his best for their boy, who was his pride and joy even though he wasn't the sort to show it with sentimental gestures. It wasn't easy raising a child on your own when you had a living to earn and no relatives to turn to. But Archie had grown into a fine man and Bill was proud of him, which was why he didn't want to see him hurt by some scheming young woman who'd dropped her drawers for the first bloke who asked and ended up in trouble. Archie was no Adonis, but he had a steady job and was a part of a thriving business that would one day be his, and he would be a catch for some nice, decent girl who was not carrying another man's child. 'Look, son, a girl in her position has got to look after herself and her kiddie, and that's what she's doing. I'm not blaming her for that; I just don't want you to be the mug that gets lumbered with her, that's all.'

Archie was furious now. 'I wouldn't be lumbered, don't you understand that, Dad? I would do it of my own free will because I want to be with her. I love her. I'm a grown man and I will do what I think is best, not what you think is right for me.'

'You do so at your peril, then.'

'I know that, but it will be my choice,' he said heatedly. 'I have to make my own decisions and live with my mistakes when I make them. You have to let go.'

'When have I ever interfered in your life before?' Bill came back at him.

'Well, you haven't since I've been grown up, I suppose,' Archie was forced to admit.

'Exactly! The need for it hasn't arisen before so I've left you alone. But now it's different and I shall give you my advice whether you want it or not, even though, as you have pointed out, you don't have to take it and probably won't. That girl is bad news,' he ranted, 'and you'd be wise to get rid of her.'

For the first time in his life, Archie wanted to hit his father, such was the strength of his feelings for May. He kept his hands clenched at his sides to keep control and felt ashamed of the impulse. He'd had a good few hidings from his dad as a nipper, like all young boys, but had never felt any violent urges towards him before. He was still his father, no matter how much they disagreed, and you didn't strike your own father, especially one like his, who had raised him on his own and made a good job of it. He took a deep breath to calm himself, the skin on his face and neck burning with rage.

'You're entitled to your opinion, Dad,' he said, keeping his manner reasonable. 'But if May agrees to marry me, I will jump at the chance and be the happiest man in London. If she'll have me I shall marry her with or without your blessing.'

Bill visibly flinched. 'Fair enough,' he said in his deep, gravelly voice. 'But don't expect me to come to the wedding.'

Archie was taken aback. He hadn't thought Bill would take his opposition that far. 'Don't worry, I won't do anything silly like that,' he ground out. Then he left the room and went out in the street to walk off his anger.

The next day on the market, when Archie had gone to get some small change and Bill Mott saw May go to the café, he asked the man on the hardware stall next to his to cover for him for a few minutes, handed him the money bag and followed her.

She was waiting to be served at the counter when he went in.

'You can sit down if you like,' he offered. 'I'll bring yours over. What are you having?'

'Thank you very much,' she said, smiling at him politely. 'A glass of milk and a slice of toast, please.'

When they were both seated at the table, May went to give him the money but he wouldn't take it.

'That's very kind of you, Mr Mott,' she said politely. 'Thank you so much.'

'I've been looking for the chance of a private word with you, as it happens,' he told her.

'Really?' She found Bill Mott rather intimidating in a one-to-one situation like this. There was something of the bruiser about him, being square jawed and broad shouldered with a wide nose and a mouth set in a determined line. 'Well now's your chance. What's on your mind?' she asked.

'I won't beat about the bush,' Bill began quickly. 'I understand that you have matrimonial designs on my son Archie, and frankly I don't like it, so I'm here to ask you to back off.'

Stunned, she stared at him. 'Me? Back off? If that wasn't so insulting it would be funny,' she told him.

'Oh really?'

'Yes, really,' she confirmed. 'Archie is the one who wants to get married. Not me. Oh no. There has never been anything like that between us. The whole thing is his idea. No one was more surprised than I was when he sprang it on me.'

'Look, I can understand that you need someone to make an honest woman of you, for the kiddie's sake,' Bill said as though she hadn't spoken. 'I can't say I blame you, but obviously my concern is for my son.'

'He told you about the baby, then?'

'That's right. But only because he's got this ridiculous idea about marrying you. Because it's so important to him he discussed it with me,' he informed her. 'He knows it won't go any further, so there's no need for you to have a go at him about breaking a confidence.'

'I have no intention of doing so,' she said tartly. 'I trust Archie to be discreet.'

'Anyway, I want you to think of him in all this. Go and find someone else to give your baby respectability and leave my Archie out of it.'

May was so angry she hardly knew how to contain herself. But somehow she managed not to set about him.

'As I have just said, you have got things the wrong way around, Mr Mott,' she said through tight lips, her eyes bright with rage. 'Archie is the one who wants to get married. I have told him I won't let him do it, but he doesn't seem willing to take no for an answer.'

'He's far too soft hearted and I've told him so.'

'In case you haven't noticed, Archie is a big boy now; old enough know his own mind.'

'You and I both know that reluctance to accept is just the line you are taking to make him all the keener. Archie is more gullible than I am. He believes every word you say,' Bill stated.

'And so he should, because I am not a liar . . .'

'Look,' he cut in. 'It's a hard world for women who find themselves in your position, I won't deny it, and I quite understand your motives. But I am asking you in a reasonable manner to look for someone else. I do not want some bastard kid in my family.'

For the second time in her life May found herself throwing liquid into a man's face. This time it was milk. As she got up to leave, Bill Mott was sitting at the table, too shocked to move, with white liquid running down his face and dripping off his chin.

A hush descended over the café and all eyes turned in their direction as May marched across the room and out of the door with her head held high. Until that moment she had been uncertain what to do about Archie's proposal. Now she knew for definite what her answer was going to be.

Chapter Seven

Bessie took May's unopened letter to work to read in her dinner break. All the fun had gone out of lunchtimes since her sister had left and she still missed their midday meetings where the highs and lows of the morning's work would be exchanged. She even looked back nostalgically on May's tirades against the horrid Mrs March. But today she had the letter to look forward to.

Settling down in the room behind the shop with her sandwiches, she opened the envelope excitedly.

Dear Bessie,

If you are not sitting down to read this, you had better do so before you continue because you are in for a huge shock. Ready, then here goes. Archie Mott and I got married yesterday. Yes, I can hardly believe it myself but it's true. I wanted you to be at the wedding more than anything but it was all done in a terrific rush by special licence for obvious reasons and I didn't have a chance to let you know in time. It was a register office marriage with boiled ham and mash at Auntie's afterwards for some of Auntie and Uncle's friends just to make it respectable. So you didn't miss the wedding of the year but I know you would have loved to be there anyway.

As you will have gathered from earlier correspondence, it isn't a marriage of love in the romantic sense. Archie, bless him, offered me the chance of respectability for myself and the baby and I decided to take it. I have been completely honest with him about my feelings for him and he still wanted to go ahead, so here I am a married woman. I intend to be the best wife ever to him and for the three of us to be a family when the baby comes. I am very fond of him, respect him enormously and consider myself privileged to be his wife. I hope I prove worthy because he really is the kindest, most generous man you could ever wish to meet.

We are living here with Auntie and Uncle until we can get a place of our own. They have both been truly wonderful and I love them to bits. Archie's father Bill is a different kettle of fish altogether, though, and doesn't approve of me at all. He didn't even come to the wedding, which hurt Archie no end, though he didn't say as much so as not to upset me. Bill Mott thinks his son could have done a whole lot better for himself with a nice unencumbered girl and I'm sure that's true, but it is me that Archie wants. Because his father won't accept me, things are very strained between the two of them, though Archie would never turn his back on him completely and I would hate that anyway. Bill has done a good job of bringing Archie up on his own, but he is a pig of a man from what I know of him. With men like him around it's no wonder women chain themselves to the railings in Downing Street and are willing to go to prison for women's rights. Of course I don't say any of this to Archie.

The two of them still work together on the stall but aren't good mates any more, which makes me sad, especially as I'm the cause. Whatever I think of him personally, he is Archie's father. Oddly enough, it was rather a dreadful incident between Bill Mott and me that finally made up my mind about Archie's proposal, but I'll tell you all about that when I see you. I do hope you can come soon. I miss you so much. Give my love to the others. I wonder what Mum will think of my new, respectable status when you tell her.

Love,

May

The letter made Bessie cry.

'Whatever is the matter, my dear?' asked her employer, coming into the room. 'Aren't you feeling well?'

'I'm quite well, thank you, Mr Parsons,' she said, hastily mopping her tears and trying to recover.

'There's something the matter, though?' he suggested kindly.

'I've had a letter from my sister and am feeling a bit emotional, that's all.'

'Oh dear! Are you sure you're in a fit state to be at work?' he asked with characteristic concern. 'Only you must go home if you are not up to it.'

'I'll be fine, really. I'm missing my sister, that's all, and feeling a bit sad after reading a letter from her.' She paused, then made a sudden decision. 'But may I ask you a favour?'

'Of course.'

'Could I leave work a bit early on Saturday, please?' she asked. 'Only I want to get the train to London.'

'I'm sure that can be arranged, my dear,' he said absently, and she was reminded again of his kind nature and how he deserved more respect from that awful daughter of his. 'Now what did I come in here for? Ah yes, a cup of tea.'

'I'll make you a fresh one,' Bessie said, cheered and excited at the prospect of seeing her sister again.

'Oh May, you didn't,' cried Bessie on Sunday morning. 'I can't believe you did that to your father-in-law.'

'He wasn't my father-in-law then, though, was he?' May reminded her.

'But how on earth did your chucking a glass of milk all over Bill make you decide to marry Archie?' Bessie was intrigued to know.

'It was what he said to make me throw the milk that made up my mind. He called my baby a bastard, and it brought the reality home to me that that was how my child would be regarded if I didn't do some-thing about it. So I decided that in the interests of the child, I couldn't let the chance to protect it pass me by. And, of course, I benefit from it too as I will be spared the misery of being an unmarried mother.'

'You did the right thing in my opinion,' put in Winnie.

'As long as Archie is happy about it, that's the important thing,' expressed Bessie.

'He's like a dog with two tails,' Winnie assured her.

'That's all right then,' approved Bessie. 'And there's always the chance that his father might change his mind about you later on, when he sees how happy you're making his son.'

'It doesn't seem very likely at the moment, but I shall keep trying to improve things, for Archie's sake.'

'Bill Mott isn't a bad bloke, and he's very well liked round here,' their aunt commented. 'He's a hard man, though; has been ever since we've known him. Very set in his ideas. It must have been a blow to him, losing his wife so young. He's never looked at another woman since. Archie has been his life, which probably explains his behaviour now.'

'And which is why I'm always telling Archie to visit him as often as he can, no matter how angry he is with him. It must be lonely for Bill living on his own and having bad feeling with his son after them being so close. I hate the idea of Archie falling out with him over me, though I know Archie is hurt by his attitude.' May sighed. 'Parents, eh! What with my mother disowning me and Archie's father wanting nothing to do with me, it's a good job I have you lot.'

The three women were in the kitchen preparing Sunday lunch. Archie had gone to see his father and Albert was in the other room reading the Sunday paper.

'I know your life is in London with Archie now,' began Bessie, 'but now that you're a respectable married woman, maybe you could come home to visit now and then.'

May had serious doubts about that. Her marriage had changed nothing as far as her relationship with her mother was concerned. Her new status didn't alter the fact that she had let Edie down, and vice versa. Yes, she had done wrong, but surely any mother worth her salt would stand by her offspring regardless of their mistakes and faults. Hers hadn't, and it still cut deep with May.

'If I did come it wouldn't be to see her; it would be to see you and Sam,' she told Bessie. 'She didn't want to know about me when I was in trouble, so I'm in no hurry to put myself out to see her now that I'm not.'

There was a tense silence, then Winnie said, 'Have you finished peeling those parsnips yet, Bessie?'

'Not quite.'

'Get a move on then, love,' she said in a jovial manner. 'I need to parboil them ready to roast.'

'Slave-driver,' her niece laughed, and the atmosphere became easy again.

Lunch was a jolly affair with plenty of jokes and laughter. Bessie thought May and Archie seemed very well suited, larking around together and enjoying each other's company. There might not be romantic love on May's side but there was plenty of affection. At times she seemed to be over-compensating a little.

'Have you got enough of everything, Archie?' she'd say, and 'Let me put a few more spuds on your plate.'

'Stop fussing and get on with your dinner,' he would tell her considerately. 'I'm big and ugly enough to look after myself. You concentrate on yourself.'

A heated discussion erupted during dessert when Albert commented on something he'd read in the paper: a crowd of angry students had struck a blow at the suffragettes by attacking one of their offices. They'd smashed the windows, carried some of the furniture into the street and made a bonfire of it.

'Serves 'em right,' declared Albert. 'They've no one to blame but themselves.'

'They're fighting for a just cause, Uncle,' May pointed out. 'They don't deserve that.'

'A just cause, as you call it, is an excuse for violence, is it?' he came back at her heatedly.

'The violence is probably exaggerated in the papers. Anyway, what else can they do to get themselves heard?' said May. She had bought the suffragettes' newspaper on occasions since she'd been in London so had more understanding of the subject now. 'It isn't right that women can vote in parliamentary elections in some parts of America, Australia, New Zealand and even the Isle of Man, but not in Britain.'

'Well if they had any sympathy from the public before, they've lost it now that they are using such violent methods, and that's been proved by the attack on their offices,' Albert went on, ignoring May's arguments. 'A lot of them are getting beaten up too. So you stay well clear of them, my girl.'

'Calm down, Albert,' advised Winnie. 'You'll give yourself indigestion.'

Bessie gave May a warning look and Archie said, 'I'm sure May isn't going to go all revolutionary on us, are you, love?'

I'm with the suffragettes in spirit, she thought, but she said evasively, 'I wouldn't do anything that would put any of you at risk, so you've no need to worry.'

'That's my girl,' said Archie.

'Are you looking forward to the baby, Archie?' asked Bessie to change the subject.

'Ooh, not half,' he told her with that enormous grin of his. 'I can't wait. No child will get a warmer welcome than this one will get from me.'

Archie's attitude towards May and the baby convinced Bessie that May had done the right thing in marrying him, and she had no doubt that he would be good and true to her. She wasn't sure if she could say the same thing about her sister, though. May would try her utmost, but carrying it through was another thing altogether. Marrying a man you didn't love would be difficult for any woman to cope with, and May had a particularly passionate and impulsive nature.

May walked with her sister to the tube station, from where Bessie would travel to Liverpool Street to get the train to Haverley. They walked through the Broadway, which although not as busy as usual, it being a Sunday, still bustled. There was a fair amount of traffic about: horse transport, motor buses driving willy-nilly and people crossing the road seemingly uncaring of any danger from traffic, everyone hurrying in the gathering dusk, the lamplighter turning on the streetlights.

'It's so different here,' Bessie remarked. 'I've never seen so many people out and about, especially on a Sunday night.'

'Next time you come I'll take you to the West End; you'll really see the crowds then.'

'You seem to have taken to life here,' observed Bessie.

'You get used to anything if you have to,' May responded. 'I was forced to come here, and it was traumatic at first, what with it being so different to the village and my being homesick. But now that I'm more settled, I think it suits me better than Tideway, if I'm honest. Village life is a bit too restricting for me, though I didn't realise it at the time, having known nothing else. I enjoy the bustle here and I definitely like having a degree of anonymity; the fact that I can actually go out and see people I don't know. I mean, everyone knows everyone else on the market and in the street where we live so there is a strong sense of community locally, but you don't feel under a microscope here the whole time, which is rather liberating. Tideway was like living in a goldfish bowl in comparison.'

'Sounds to me as though we've lost you for ever to town life,' suggested Bessie sadly.

'Tideway will always be home in my heart,' May made clear, 'and I miss you all to bits, but I suppose my future does lie here now with Archie.'

'Stop it, you'll make me cry,' Bessie said swallowing hard on a lump in her throat.

'I'll be in tears myself in a minute,' her sister said thickly. 'It was never my choice to go away, but you have to make the best of whatever direction life sends you in. If you can embrace it, as I have, so much the better. It could have gone the other way; I could have hated it. So I'm lucky.'

'It's been so good to see you anyway, May,' said Bessie as the station came into view.

'I can't tell you what seeing you has meant to me,' responded May warmly. 'Thanks ever so much for coming. It was the best wedding present I could have had. Shall I come to Liverpool Street with you and see you on to the train there?'

'Don't be daft,' Bessie said, adding jokingly, 'I'm quite capable of getting myself home. You Londoners aren't the only ones who know your way around.'

'A Londoner? Me? Well I suppose I am now, aren't I?'

'You certainly are, and you've taken to it like a duck to water.'

May went on to the platform with her and they had a heart-rending embrace before Bessie boarded the train. Then May turned and left the station and walked home, feeling dreadfully sad.

Bessie was feeling emotional too on the train journey home. Everything was so irreversibly different now. It was natural for siblings to grow up and go their separate ways, but she had never envisioned a time when she and May wouldn't live in close proximity. Some Tideway families went back for generations, and relatives lived close to each other. But May's life was in London now, and that infused Bessie with an aching sense of loneliness.

She wouldn't watch her sister's baby grow up. An occasional visit like this one was all there would be. May didn't seem keen to come home to visit; understandably so. Mum had said nothing about welcoming her back into the family now that her circumstances had changed, either.

Even apart from that, the environment in which someone lived must have an effect, and Bessie had already sensed a change in May as London life became her norm. There was a new confidence about her. She had never been shy and retiring, but now there was a touch of worldliness about her that hadn't been there before, and it made Bessie feel bereft. It seemed to come between them somehow, although nothing had been said.

Oh well, life moved on and you had to go along with it, she thought wistfully as the train drew into Haverley station. She'd be very glad to get home, especially to see Jim; she'd missed him over the weekend.

It was fully dark as she alighted from the train, and she drew her shawl around her more tightly against the autumn evening chill. Walking along the platform towards the exit, she was lost in thoughts of the weekend and looking forward to being home. She didn't relish the long walk along the stony path to the ferry after dark on her own, though.

'Hello, Bessie,' said someone as she was about to go out into the night.

'Jim!' she cried, smiling broadly. 'What are you doing here? We didn't arrange for you to meet me.'

'You didn't think I would let you walk to the ferry on your own in the dark, did you?'

'Knowing you, I should have guessed, you lovely man,' she said, flinging her arms around him impulsively with the sheer joy of seeing him, uncaring of the fact that there were other people about.

'Well, well, if this is the effect a weekend away has on you, you should go more often,' he laughed, tucking her arm into his as they headed for the ferry. 'No, I've changed my mind about that. I don't want you to go away too often.'

'I won't, don't worry,' she assured him. 'It was lovely to see May, even though it made me sad to accept the fact that she'll probably never come back to Tideway to live. I enjoyed seeing Auntie and Uncle but although they made me very welcome, I'm glad to be back here. A short visit to London is enough for me'

'Thank goodness for that,' Jim said, relieved. 'I thought you might be dazzled by it and want to follow her.'

'Not in a million years.' As they walked along the path, their footsteps crunching on the pebbles, the path dimly lit by an occasional gaslight, she chatted to him about the weekend, pointing out the highlights. 'I wish you'd been with me,' she said. 'It would have made all the difference.'

'I missed you more than I can say, Bessie,' he said, halting in his step suddenly and turning to her. 'I know it was only a day and a night, but the heart seemed to go out of everything without you.'

'Oh Jim, what a sweet thing to say.'

'I don't want to be without you again, Bessie,' he said. 'I love you so much.'

'I love you too, Jim.'

'Will you marry me?' he asked simply.

'Yes, I will,' she said without a moment's hesitation, the sadness of the day melting away.

'I don't have a ring because I didn't want to be too presumptuous,' he explained. 'Anyway, I thought you might like to go to Colchester with me to choose one.'

'I'd love that,' she said happily.

So life was changing direction for her as well as for her sister, and she welcomed it with open arms. You couldn't avoid change any more than you could halt the growing-up process. The way things used to be would always be important to her, but it was time to look to the future with Jim.

The ferryman was waiting when they got to the embarking point, arms entwined. Although the ferry officially finished at ten o'clock, he always waited for the passengers on the last train from London, whatever the time or the weather. Bessie and Jim were the last ones, so as soon as they were aboard the ferryman cast off, and the couple sat holding hands as the boat creaked and glided across the dark waters to the other side. It had been quite a day, thought Bessie, with the best possible ending.

★   ★   ★

'So, what do you think of that then, Edie?' George enquired when he and his wife closed their bedroom door behind them that same night. 'One daughter married and the other engaged.'

'At least Jim did the thing properly,' Edie said, turning her back to him while she slipped out of her clothes and into a long-sleeved, high-necked nightdress. 'He asked you if he could marry Bessie. That fly-by-night the other one has got herself hooked up with probably doesn't know the first thing about manners and decency.'

'May's husband sounds very decent to me, from what Bessie has said,' remarked George, changing into a flannelette nightshirt. 'Not many men would take on a woman who is pregnant with another man's child. He must think a lot of her to do that.'

'He must be soft in the head.'

'Bessie said he seems like a very nice young fella,' said George.

'He's a cockney barrow boy.' Edie snorted in a derogatory manner.

'What's wrong with that?'

'He'll be as common as muck.'

'Not necessarily,' disagreed George, 'He's a working man, the same as I am.'

'Hardly the same thing,' she said. 'Fishing is honourable and courageous.'

'Market traders are honourable people as far as I know,' he told her.

'They don't risk their lives every time they go to work,' she declared unreasonably.

'Not many people do, but all workers make a contribution. Anyway, I should think their sanity takes a bit of a bashing, dealing with women shoppers all day,' he said in a rare moment of humour.

'There's no need to be flippant.'

'Just teasing,' he said, climbing into the high bed. 'Anyway, under the circumstances, he couldn't come and ask me if he could marry May, as she's not even allowed in the house. I suppose we're lucky he didn't come here wanting payment for it.'

'George, what a terrible thing to say,' Edie said disapprovingly.

'Just being realistic,' he said. 'It isn't unknown in that situation for parents who can afford it to pay to save the family reputation. May has been lucky.'

'Why are you being so casual about it when it's such a serious matter?' Edie wanted to know. 'You don't seem the slightest bit bothered about what May has done.'

'I am very bothered about May's misdeeds and the consequences, though if I had had my way she would never have been forced to leave this house,

113

as you very well know, no matter what she'd done. But tonight I am thinking about Bessie and how happy I am for her,' he told her. 'It isn't every day a chap like Jim Minter asks for your daughter's hand in marriage. He is going to be joining our family and that pleases me no end. I think they are very well suited and I like him a lot.'

'Oh yes,' Edie agreed, sounding happier. 'Bessie couldn't do better than him. She always did have her head screwed on the right way, that one; unlike her wayward sister.'

'Give it a rest, Edie. I hate what she's done every bit as much as you do. But it's a reality and there is a baby on the way. It's time to let go; time to put things right. She's married now, so she won't bring shame on you.'

'You can't put broken china together again,' she said. 'I raised the girls to be pure and fine, to be decent upright human beings, and that is how she repays me. Being married doesn't alter anything as far as I'm concerned.'

By God she was hard, George thought. She'd never been a warm person; had always been very strait-laced and inhibited. But since Henry died there wasn't one iota of love in her. It was as though it had all been replaced by anger and resentment. She didn't seem to have loving feelings for anyone now, least of all him. He knew she would rather he had died than Henry. He could see it in her eyes and in the way she shrank back from him if he tried to touch her. He didn't really blame her. He thought it would have been fairer that way too. At least he'd had more years of life. But who were they to say who lived or died?

'People are all only human,' he pointed out. 'There's only so much a mother can do to make her children be what she wants them to be. In the end they are people in their own right, with failings like everyone else. Mistakes are part of life. We all make them.'

'Trust you to take her side,' she said accusingly. 'You're like Winnie; you've no standards, either of you. You always take Winnie's side against me.'

'That just isn't true,' George denied, his voice rising. 'I think Winnie is a nice person with a big heart and I sometimes stand up for her when you are doing her down, that's all.' He sighed into the darkness. 'You are a good woman, Edie, and a loyal and dutiful wife, but you are becoming increasingly hard to get on with. You'll drive everyone away in the end if you don't soften up a little.'

'If they go, they go,' she said tartly. 'Anyway, what do you know about being a mother?'

He could feel his temper rising so he said, 'I'm going to sleep now, Edie. I've got an early start.'

He turned on to his side with his back to her. He didn't attempt to kiss her good night, because the way she drew away from him hurt even though he was used to it. There were some things in life you just had to accept, and the fact that his wife couldn't stand the sight of him was one of them. Since he couldn't bring Henry back, he couldn't change anything, so he just had to live with it.

'You seem a bit down in the dumps,' observed Archie from the bed as May brushed her long hair at the dressing table. 'Has seeing your sister again made you homesick for your family?'

'It has a bit,' she admitted, because she knew she could be honest with Archie without upsetting him. In fact their relationship was built on honesty, about most things anyway. 'May and I were so close, you see. I miss Dad and Sam as well; even our dog Whistler.'

'You've left your mother out.'

'It's hard to miss someone who hates the sight of you.'

Having lost his own mother at such a young age mothers were very special to Archie. In fact, he had a somewhat rose-tinted view of them. As a species, they were beyond reproach for him.

'I'm sure she doesn't hate you; no mother could do that,' he told her. 'If there is any chance of putting things right with her, I should take it if I were you. You only have one mother and she won't be around for ever.'

'Yeah, yeah, I know,' she said, putting the hairbrush down on the dressing table and standing up. Unbeknown to her, she was an absolute vision of loveliness to Archie in her long nightgown, her hair flowing to her shoulders.

'Shall I go downstairs and get you a hot drink and a biscuit,' he offered. 'Would that cheer you up?'

Oh Archie, please stop being so nice to me, she said silently. Be horrid to me sometimes so that I don't have to be permanently filled with guilt for not loving you back. Don't love me so much, because I can't reciprocate. I wish I could, and I try every day, but it just won't happen.

'Getting into bed with you will cheer me up more,' she said, turning the gaslight off and feeling her way across to the bed. 'So here I am ready for a kiss and a cuddle. And you can stop worrying about the baby; it'll be fine.'

The darkness did have its good points, she thought, and this was one of those occasions when she was very grateful for it. She never, ever wanted Archie to know what an immense effort this side of things was for her, which he might do if he could see her face. He would be so hurt, and he didn't deserve that.

There were children on almost every street corner wanting a penny for the guy around Hammersmith way in the run-up to the Guy Fawkes celebrations.

'The little perishers,' remarked May over the evening meal with Archie and her uncle and aunt. 'I reckon some of them must have collected more than we earn in a week. Thank goodness the day has arrived at last so that we've seen the last of them for another year, and a good job too.'

'It's just a bit of fun,' remarked Winnie.

'Me and my mates used to go and stand outside the station with our guy,' said Archie. 'It was a great laugh and a decent little earner. We used to make enough money for fireworks as well as sweets for weeks afterwards. There were plenty of fights for the best pitches, though.'

'Your market skills were beginning to show themselves even then,' remarked Winnie.

'I don't know about that, but I used to thoroughly enjoy myself,' he told them. 'Still do, in fact. Are you all coming out to have a look at what's going on outside? There's a big fire on the green near the pub. I saw them building it.'

'Yeah, might as well,' said Albert.

'There'll be some fun about tonight for the kids and nice fireworks for us grown-ups to look at,' enthused Archie. He turned to May. 'We'll have a bonfire of our own when the nipper is big enough. That's something to look forward to, isn't it?'

'It's a year today since May's brother was drowned, Archie,' Winnie reminded him. 'So she's probably feeling a bit sad and not like going out enjoying herself.'

'No, it's all right, I'll come,' May said, not wishing to spoil things for the others.

'Sorry, love, I wasn't thinking,' said Archie. 'We don't have to go out. I'll stay here with you.'

'No you won't. We're going out,' she said, determined not to be a wet blanket. 'You don't have to stay indoors moping to show respect, and I've been thinking about Henry all day, bless him. He always enjoyed Guy Fawkes night and wouldn't want me to miss it on his account.'

'That's the way I look at it too,' said Winnie. 'He's been in my thoughts all day.'

So when they'd finished eating they all trooped out into the streets –

May a little slower than usual because of her extra weight – and watched the sky glow from fires in many back gardens, the whizz, bang and pop of fireworks and showers of golden rain exploding all around them. They joined the crowds at the communal bonfire and watched the kiddies enjoying themselves, then went into the pub and drank a toast to Henry.

Ostensibly May was her usual jolly self. But although she was here physically, her heart was in Tideway tonight. She knew that on special occasions such as this, it always would be.

In Tideway the celebrations were in progress the same as always. There were hot potatoes and soup and Edie's special parkin. But for the Bow family, November the fifth would always be synonymous with tragedy.

There was one new bright spark to make things go with a swing, though. As the local schoolmaster, Jim saw it as his duty to take an active part in all local events and did so with a great deal of enthusiasm. He was in his element tonight, making sure all the kiddies had a good time.

When it was all over, Bessie and the rest of the family went back to the cottage and drank a toast to Henry. Of course Jim had never known him, but he entered into the spirit. Bessie was proud of her mother, who had worked hard as usual to make the event a success, even though her heart must have been breaking.

Bessie added something to the toast: 'To our other absent loved one, May,' she said, and they all raised their glasses to her sister. Bessie doubted if her mother's heart was in that, but she found the small gesture rather comforting nonetheless.

Chapter Eight

'There's a lot of talk locally about a new market opening in the summer down at Shepherd's Bush, near the station,' Winnie mentioned casually to May as they walked through Hammersmith Broadway towards King Street one bitterly cold day in February of 1914. 'It's going to be a big one too, from the sound of it.'

'Archie said something about that,' responded May. 'Will it be competition for us?'

'I don't think so,' she replied. 'We're a small market mainly catering for the locals, who probably wouldn't fancy the extra walk, especially carrying a heavy bag of fruit and vegetables. Archie and his dad should be all right too.'

'That's good,' said May, feeling suddenly breathless from a sharp pain.

'Are you all right, love?' Winnie enquired, turning and noticing that her niece was having a struggle with the walk.

'Yeah, I think so,' she replied. 'Just feeling the effects of the extra weight and the cold weather. I have been getting a few twinges lately, too. I suppose that's normal at this stage in the pregnancy.'

'Maybe we shouldn't have come out shopping as you're so near to your time.' Winnie and Albert didn't open their stall for business on a Monday, so she and May were heading for the main shops in search of a few sundry items for the baby.

'I'm not all that near, Auntie. I've still a couple of weeks to go yet,' May reminded her. 'I don't want to be stuck indoors the whole time while I'm waiting. I'd be bored to tears and the time would drag even more than it is already.'

'Yeah, that's true. Don't mind me. I'm just an old fusspot,' admitted Winnie.

'The suffragettes haven't let the cold weather deter them, have they?' observed May, noticing a woman standing in the gutter selling the suffragettes' official newspaper. 'The poor thing looks frozen. She'd be better off standing in a shop doorway out of the wind.'

'She can't do that. If she steps on to the pavement while selling her wares, the police will charge her with obstruction and she'll be carted off to the nick,' Winnie explained. 'So she has to stand in the gutter.'

'That's terrible.' May was indignant on the paper-seller's behalf. 'Shall we buy a paper to show some support?'

'Yes, let's,' agreed Winnie. 'Better keep it out of Albert's sight at home, though. You know how he feels about the suffragettes. We don't want to set him off ranting.'

They were on their way over to the woman, who was holding up a copy of the newspaper with pride, when two rough-looking men approached her and a scuffle broke out.

'You're scum,' growled one of them, prodding her roughly. 'Filthy, 'orrible scum.'

'Lunatic,' added the other. 'You're a bloomin' disgrace to women everywhere. Get back indoors where you belong and concentrate on looking after your old man if you've got one. Though I doubt if anyone would want an ugly cow like you.'

A passing female joined in the affray, showing where her allegiance lay in an extremely vociferous manner. 'It's your sort who give decent women a bad name,' she yelled, wagging her finger at the suffragette while a crowd gathered around. 'You won't get anywhere with your daft campaign, you silly bitch.'

One of the men started aiming blows at the paper-seller, who fell to the ground and was kicked repeatedly.

That was enough for May. 'Oi,' she shouted, pushing her way through the crowds and confronting the men. 'Leave her alone, you spiteful pigs. What sort of man hits a woman?'

'What sort of a woman makes a show of herself on the street and deliberately causes trouble?' he retaliated, pushing May with such force that she was sent reeling and left struggling to keep her balance. 'Wanting to vote in elections when they know nothing about politics. A woman should know her place and stay indoors like she's meant to.'

Winnie was on the scene like a shot. 'Get your filthy hands off my niece,' she demanded. 'You ought to be thoroughly ashamed of yourself, you bully.'

'Mind your own business, you old bag,' returned one of the men, glaring at her.

'You leave her alone, can't you see she's pregnant?' roared Winnie, tackling the man.

'I'm not blind; of course I can see the state of her. She should be out of sight at home with her great big belly,' said the man, 'not out on the streets interfering in other people's business and making a show of herself with all this unwomanly behaviour. I know what I would do to keep her in order if I was her old man. I'd give her a right pasting. She'd know how to behave if she was married to me. Oh yeah! She'd know her place then all right. These mad activists are dangerous; they must be stopped, not encouraged.'

'You're the dangerous ones, bigots like you,' Winnie shrieked, hitting him with her shopping bag until he finally cowered back, but not before filling the air with some choice expletives.

May finally reached the paper-seller, who was sitting in the gutter, her hat lying in the road, her newspapers strewn far and wide. 'Here, let me help you up, though I can't bend down too far because of my bump,' she said, offering her hand and helping to pull the woman to her feet. 'Are you all right?'

'A bit shaky, but I'll live,' replied the woman. She looked to be in her mid-thirties, and was smartly dressed with a refined accent. 'I'm used to this sort of thing. We get far worse than that, I can tell you. Our organisation isn't for the faint hearted.'

The crowd dispersed, but a few female sympathisers lingered to help collect the scattered newspapers, offering the suffragette support while uttering some colourful adjectives about the men.

'You're looking a bit shaken up, dear,' commented Winnie. 'Will you let us take you home or back to your shop? I know there is a WSPU shop further down the street.'

'Oh no, that won't be necessary,' the woman said, brushing herself down and putting her hat back on. 'I've got papers to sell and I shan't go back until I've sold every last one.'

'That's the spirit,' praised May, though she was looking very pale herself because she suddenly wasn't feeling well.

'Yeah, well done,' added Winnie. 'We may not all be prepared to go to prison for the cause because personal circumstances don't allow it, but we appreciate that you're doing a good job.'

There was a sudden intake of breath from May. 'Oh no!' she cried in distress.

'Whatever is the matter, love?' asked Winnie, looking at her ashen-faced niece. She followed May's gaze downwards. There was a small puddle by her feet. 'Oh my good Gawd, your waters have broken.'

'I've been having twinges all day and thought it was just wind, because I'm not due yet,' said May, clutching her stomach and wincing. 'But now . . . oh, Auntie, I think the baby is starting.'

'You don't half choose your moments,' quipped Winnie, struggling to keep things light despite the anxiety of knowing that they were a good fifteen minutes' walk from home and the safe hands of the midwife. 'But don't worry. I'm here with you. I'll look after you.'

'Ooh, Auntie,' wailed May again. 'I've got a horrible pain.'

'What sort of pain is it?' she asked. 'Sharp, or more of an ache?'

'It's one that hurts,' May said, trying to calm herself with a joke. 'Ouch, not half it does.'

'It's sometimes a good while before things happen after the waters break,' said Winnie, taking May's arm. 'So we've plenty of time.'

'Things seem to be happening now,' May told her, trying not to panic. 'The pain is strong . . . Ooh Christ, here comes another one.'

'This is all my fault,' said the suffragette

'Oh yeah, and how do you work that out?' May tried to reassure her. 'It's just nature.'

'It was you helping me up that started things off,' she said.

'Don't be so daft,' said May. 'It would have happened anyway. I've been feeling a bit queer all day. It's my own fault. I shouldn't have come out.'

'We'll have to go to the shop for help,' suggested the suffragette. 'There are plenty of willing hands there.'

'We need to get her home and get the midwife in,' stated Winnie worriedly.

'I don't think we'll have time, Auntie,' May told her. 'I can feel the baby coming. I'm wanting to push.'

'Blimey,' said Winnie. 'But you'll be a long time yet. First babies take ages.'

'I don't think this one will,' May told her. 'I can feel it pushing down really strong.'

'The first thing we need to do is to get her to the shop,' said the suffragette again. 'We can organise some transport to take you home from there.' She put the papers in a bag and slung it over her shoulder. 'Here, if you hang on to the two of us, it might help.' As they started to walk across the road she said, 'My name is Constance, by the way.'

Winnie supplied her with both their names.

'I know this will seem like futile advice, May,' began Constance, 'but try not to panic. You're in good hands.'

'Don't panic?' May burst out. 'I'm about to give birth in the middle of the street. I think the odd flash of panic is permissible.'

'You're not going to give birth in the street, and if you do, you won't be the first,' said Constance.

'How do you know what's gonna happen?' May was belligerent from the effects of the pain.

'I've had four children of my own, so I suppose I can call myself experienced,' she said.

'Ooh,' groaned May, bending over. 'How much further is this bloomin' shop of yours? I don't know if I can make it.'

'If you can't, we'll carry you between us, won't we, Winnie?' said Constance calmly.

'We'll have a go,' agreed Winnie, liking the other woman enormously. 'But she's no lightweight at the moment.'

'I'd crawl there rather than make a show of myself in that way,' said May.

Naturally she'd known that labour wouldn't be a picnic. She had prepared herself for the pain and promised herself she would stay calm and not make a fuss. But she hadn't bargained on going into labour so publicly. Nor had she realised that it would hurt so much. No one had ever told her just what torture it was. There was this commonly held idea that because childbirth was natural, the pain was somehow bearable. Well it didn't feel very bearable to her at this moment, and there was worse to come, she was sure.

'We have an emergency, ladies, so all hands on deck,' Constance called into the shop when they finally arrived, May now doubled up and groaning. 'May here has gone into labour unexpectedly and we need transport to get her home before the baby comes.'

'Ooh, you poor dear,' sympathised a woman from behind the counter, where there were sashes and banners on sale in the Women's Social and Political Union official colours of purple, white and green. For those who couldn't afford the more elaborate insignia, there were penny badges and pamphlets. 'Come and sit down while we sort something out.'

'I can't sit down or stand up. I just want to die,' moaned May and let out a heart-rending scream. 'It's bearing down, it's coming. Oh my God! Help!'

With a pale and anxious Winnie assisting, Constance half carried May through to the next room, which was an office. There were women typing, others busy with bookwork, and in the centre there was a table around which several women were working, putting printed pieces of paper into envelopes.

'Move the table, everyone,' said Constance with authority. 'We've got an imminent birth and need somewhere to deliver the baby. The floor is the safest place.'

Within seconds the table was moved, someone had put some cushions from the typists' chairs on the floor underneath May and the room was empty except for May, Winnie and Constance, who had brought some clean towels, presumably from their washing facilities.

All the fear went out of May. She felt safe in the hands of these two capable women, even though they had no formal medical training. Although she yelled, sweated and swore through every contraction and vowed that no man would ever touch her again if this was the result, she did co-operate when they told her to push, until at last, after one last excruciating shove, the baby slipped out.

'It's a little girl,' said Constance, holding her up for her mother to see. 'A beautiful little daughter.'

Throughout the pregnancy, May had claimed that she didn't have a preference as regarded the sex of her baby, while secretly harbouring hopes of a daughter. So now that she was here, she couldn't have been more delighted.

'Congratulations, love,' said Winnie tearfully.

'A little girl, Auntie,' May gasped in wonder. 'Isn't that just the best gift I could have? I shall call her Constance, and she will be known as Connie.'

'Very appropriate.' Winnie turned to the suffragette. 'You've been an absolute marvel. Thank you.'

'I'm glad to have been of help.' Constance smiled. 'It's up to us girls to do what we can for each other.'

'Hear, hear,' said Winnie.

Half an hour or so later, May was ensconced in an armchair in the staff room with a cup of tea and a biscuit. She had her feet resting on a stool and a blanket over her. The baby, now washed and dressed in a gown of white winceyette with a white bonnet and matinee coat and wrapped in a shawl, all purchased hurriedly by Winnie from the drapery store across the street, was sleeping in her mother's arms. Winnie had gone to tell Archie, who would arrange transport to take mother and baby home.

One of the suffragettes came in, a young woman of about twenty. 'Are you all right in 'ere?' she asked. Her accent was much less refined than Constance's. 'Are mother and baby doin' well, as they say in posh circles?'

'We're doing fine, thanks to all of you,' replied May.

'It's given us all a bit of excitement anyway,' the woman said. 'It's certainly livened the place up a bit.'

'I should think you get enough excitement, doing what you do.'

'We don't all go out getting ourselves arrested, you know; a lot of it is just routine hard work.'

'Do you work here full time?' May wondered.

'No such luck,' she sighed. 'I'm in service in a toff's house full time. I come up here for a couple of hours on my afternoon off to help out.' She made a face. 'I'd lose my job if my employer found out; that's why I daren't go out selling the newspapers on the street in case I'm seen. Working here in the back office I'm not likely to get found out as long as I'm careful no one sees me coming in or out. The movement has got such a bad name, a lot of people are dead set against us. The family I work for certainly are.'

'My father and my uncle nearly have a fit every time they read anything about the campaign in the paper.'

'A lot of men are like that; quite a few women too, though don't ask me why, since it's for their benefit,' the young woman said.

'They're used to the way things are and can't see beyond the status quo, I suppose,' suggested May.

'Probably,' agreed the suffragette. 'Whereas people like me would love to get out there wearing a sash in public with pride, but because of all the opposition it just isn't possible.'

May nodded in an understanding manner. 'Do you get paid for working here?' she asked.

'Oh no, it's voluntary. I do it because I believe in the cause. Most of the routine work here is done by unpaid volunteers,' she explained. 'The women on the management who work for the movement full time get paid, though some of them don't need the money so they plough it back into campaign funds. We need all the dough we can get to keep the movement afloat. It's a costly business.'

'In the beginning it was made up of middle-class women, wasn't it?' commented May, who had read about the movement's origins.

'That's right. Nowadays women support it from all walks of life and from all over the country,' said the young suffragette proudly.

'Do you ever get to meet up with women from other places?' enquired May with interest.

'Yeah. At the big meetings in Hyde Park or Trafalgar Square you meet all sorts of people; from the north, west, everywhere,' she told her. 'The atmosphere is wonderful at those get-togethers: the warmth and feeling of unity, everyone joined together to support the cause. I just love it.'

'You're not afraid of going to those meetings for fear of being seen, then?'

'No. I feel safe because I'm not likely to be noticed among the crowds. Anyway, nobody from my employer's circle would be seen dead anywhere near a WSPU rally,' the woman explained. 'I'd hate to miss one of those. Some of the women bring their kids with them too. I suppose they want their little 'uns to grow up to have an independent spirit like their mothers. We've got housewives, cleaners, shop workers, skivvies as well as women from the gentry, and many of us have to support the campaign in secret because of opposition from family and employers.'

'It makes no difference what class you are or how rich; if you are a woman they won't let you have that fundamental right – the right to vote in a parliamentary election,' said May.

'Exactly,' she responded. 'For forty years women have been fighting this cause, and all to no avail. So Mrs Pankhurst and her daughters decided on a more vigorous approach since peaceful means didn't have any effect. It hasn't worked yet, but we'll keep on trying. It's terrible the way some of our members are treated. I don't get involved in any of the violence because I can't afford to go to prison and lose my job. My mum relies on the money I give her every week, you see. There are five kids younger than me at home.'

May nodded in an understanding manner. 'Constance seems very nice.'

'Yeah, she's one of the posh ones,' the young woman told her. 'Her ole man is worth a bob or two; he's one of the few men who doesn't object to the campaign, which is why she can go out selling the newspapers on the streets openly.'

'I see.'

The suffragette looked at May. 'Anyway, would you like another cuppa tea while you're waiting?'

'That would be lovely,' she said gratefully. 'Thanks very much.'

'I'll take the little one off you while you drink it if you like,' she offered.

'I can manage, thanks,' said May, feeling as though she didn't want to let her baby go, not even for a second. Motherhood was still so new, but her warm little bundle felt right in her arms.

Archie couldn't have been more thrilled with the new arrival if she'd been his own flesh and blood, and he made a terrific fuss of May after her post-natal sleep.

'She's a little cracker,' he said that night, peering at Connie, who was now ensconced in her cradle by the side of their bed. 'Still, with you as her mother she was bound to be.'

'Give over with your old flannel,' May joshed.

'Mind you, what a place to give birth, eh?' he said, smiling. 'I nearly died when Winnie told me. Still, they seemed like a nice bunch of people, those suffragettes.'

'They are just women fighting for a cause,' she said. 'Not the lunatics the papers make them out to be.'

'You know me; live and let live, I say,' he reminded her. 'They looked after you so they can do no wrong in my eyes.'

Through May's postnatal euphoria came a worm of unease at this further evidence of Archie's devotion to her. It sometimes felt like a burden, having someone love her like that, especially as he was such a good man. The responsibility of living up to it was enormous. He'd come to fetch them in a horse-drawn cab, every inch the proud father, as though he had convinced himself that Connie was actually his. Although May admired him for his support, and knew it was the only way forward for Connie, there was a slight niggle there too, because she'd never been quite able to forget Connie's biological father, and the sweetness and passion of their time together.

'She looks just like you,' Archie was saying now.

'She doesn't look like anyone except a baby yet,' May pointed out, feeling guilty for hoping that she might at some point see something of Connie's father in her.

'I disagree,' he said. 'She definitely has a look of you about her somehow.'

'All right, Archie,' she said, patiently affectionate. 'If you say so.'

He gave her a flash of his wide smile. 'Can I get you anything?' he asked. 'Winnie says beef tea will do you good.'

'I'd sooner have a cup of cocoa,' she said.

'Consider it done,' and he bounded from the room, eager to please as usual.

In the short time since giving birth to Connie, May had become certain of one thing: she was going to bring her daughter up to have the courage of her convictions and pursue her own beliefs, whatever they might be. She hoped the day would come when women who found themselves in her position weren't shunned by society and forced to marry any man who offered to rescue them from the purgatory of being an unmarried mother and their children from a life of misery. If they were lucky enough to find such a man.

Sadly, she knew that day was a long way off. Women didn't even have the right to vote yet, let alone anything as radical as acceptance of their failings as human beings. Still, while there were people with the spirit of the Pankhursts and their followers around, anything was possible.

*   *   *

It was a bright but bitter February Saturday in Haverley, and Bessie was cold to the bone as she organised the wedding party outside the church for the photographs. Digby had already taken several of the bride and groom on their own and now needed some group shots. Everybody was shivering, not least the bride, who still looked beautiful in a long-sleeved flowing white dress with a billowing veil.

'Ooh, it's cold enough to give you frostbite out here,' shuddered the mother of the bride, whose hat alone would take up a whole shot, thought Bessie. 'Can you get a move on with the photographs, please? I don't want my daughter catching cold.'

'We'll be as quick as we can,' said Bessie.

'The sooner the better,' the woman persisted. 'We're all freezing to death out here in just our wedding clothes.'

'To avoid any more delay than is necessary, could you all get into the groups as quickly as you can, please,' requested Bessie, shivering in the sub-zero temperature. 'Can we have the bridesmaids next, please? Bridesmaids, please, thank you . . . that's the way. If you could move in a little so that Mr Parsons can get you all in the shot. The two tiny ones at the front . . . that's the stuff . . . Just keep still for a minute if you would, please, girls. Smile for the camera. No, not giggle your heads off . . . just a nice pretty smile. Perfect.'

Usually Digby would take the photograph at this stage. But today this didn't happen, and Bessie went over to the camera, where he was in position under the black cloth. 'Are they all right for you, Mr Parsons, or should I rearrange them some more?'

To her amazement, the photographer crumpled and slumped to the ground, and lay there with his eyes closed.

'Oh, good grief,' Bessie said, while screams erupted all around her and the best man tried to calm the wedding party.

Bessie was quickly on her knees, looking at her horizontal employer. She felt for a pulse and found one, much to her relief. His eyes flickered open.

'What's happened?' he asked, looking dazed.

'You passed out,' she informed him. 'Don't worry. I'll get you to a doctor right away. He'll soon put you right.'

'I don't need a doctor,' he said, struggling to his feet. 'We need to get this job done.'

'I think it might be wise to see a doctor anyway, Mr Parsons. Just to reassure you,' she suggested kindly, confident that a man in his position could afford the fee. 'I'll take you right away in the trap.'

'Not before I've finished taking the pictures you won't,' he informed her. 'We can't let these people down.'

'But . . .'

'Don't argue, Bessie,' he ordered. 'Just go and get them reorganised into position, please.'

She noticed him swaying and held on to him. 'You're still a little unsteady,' she observed worriedly. 'Please let me take you to the doctor.'

The best man came striding over. 'How are you feeling, old chap?' he asked.

'A bit shaky but fine otherwise; must be the cold weather that sent me off,' Digby said in a brave attempt at vigour. 'Nothing to worry about at all.'

'Are you sure?' The young man looked embarrassed and rubbed the side of his nose with his forefinger in a nervous manner. 'I hate to seem heartless, but this has left me in a bit of a spot as regards the wedding photographs. It's my responsibility to see to it that all goes well, and naturally, the bride and groom don't want their big day to pass unrecorded.'

'And it won't, I assure you. My assistant will do the photographs,' declared Mr Parsons, sending Bessie reeling. 'I must admit, I'm not quite up to it myself at the moment.'

'Your assistant?' The man didn't look impressed as his gaze rested on Bessie.

'Yes. Your photographs will be quite safe in her hands, I promise you. She's been with me for several years,' stated Digby. 'She knows the job inside out.'

'But does she have any actual photographic experience?' asked the best man.

'It's your only option,' replied Digby, evading the issue. 'I'm not well enough to do them myself at this precise moment and you won't be able to get anyone else at such short notice. If you're not satisfied with the finished product, you don't pay me a penny and you get a full refund of your deposit. Will that suit you?'

'I suppose it will have to do,' he mumbled uncertainly. 'But if you don't get it done soon, the entire wedding party will be in hospital with pneumonia.'

'I'll wait in the nearest pub, Bessie,' Digby told her quietly. 'I need something to steady me and a sit-down in the warm.'

'I'll walk you over there.' Bessie was worried about him.

'You'll do no such thing,' he said in an uncharacteristic show of authority. 'You get on and do the photographs.'

She looked at him and knew she had no choice. 'Right you are, Mr Parsons,' she said.

Initially she was so nervous she could barely focus the camera lens, especially as the subjects were all so cold it was difficult to get a smile out of anyone. This was a big day for the newly-weds and couldn't be recaptured if she failed at the job. So she focused her mind on everything she had learned, issuing instructions from under the cover during the actual photography then coming out to arrange every new group. Gradually, as she became more engrossed, her confidence grew. How very glad she was that she had listened to Digby when he had taught her skills she had never thought she would use, especially about the importance of light.

She found her employer sitting by the fire in the pub looking better. 'All done,' she said. 'I've packed the equipment into the trap and I'm ready to drive you home as soon as you are.'

'Who said you'll be driving?' he asked.

'Mr Parsons.' It was her turn to be firm now. 'I do not want to end up in a ditch because you've come over queer. So please do as I ask and let me drive.'

Despite his protests she could see that he was relieved. That funny turn had given him a real fright, even though he was loath to admit it.

Joan Parsons showed not the slightest interest or concern about her father when Bessie got to his house and explained to his daughter what had happened.

'He'll be all right,' she said impatiently as Digby sank gratefully into his armchair. 'He's as strong as a horse.'

'I think he needs to see a doctor,' suggested Bessie. 'Just to be on the safe side.'

'If we want your opinion we'll ask for it,' snapped Joan. 'I'm going out and I have to get ready. I don't have the time to get a doctor and listen to what he has to say when there's nothing wrong with my father. All he wants is attention.'

'Joan is right, Bessie dear,' intervened Digby wearily as though he hadn't heard Joan's last comment. 'We don't want a big fuss over nothing. I'll see you on Monday. I know you mean well, dear, but Joan and I will take it from here.'

'I'll see you on Monday then,' Bessie said, with a sinking feeling that Joan was going to be unkind to him the minute she left.

* * *

130

That night in bed, Bessie's thoughts were concentrated on another matter altogether. There had been a letter for her when she'd got home from May, saying that she'd had a baby girl. It was such wonderful news Bessie couldn't sleep for the excitement of it. She had already written a letter to her sister and would get to London to see the baby as soon as she possibly could.

Thinking back on the events of the evening, it occurred to her that her mother's reaction to the news had been odd in the extreme. Bessie hadn't expected an outpouring of joy, given the dire situation between her mother and May, but Edie had been so offhand, it was almost as though the new baby wasn't her grandchild at all. It was sad, and Bessie was hurt on May's behalf.

Despite all of that, she was thrilled for May. It might not be too long before Bessie herself had a little one, because she and Jim had a summer wedding planned. She wanted her sister to be there, so May and her mother would have to meet then.

More immediate was the worry of whether the wedding photographs she'd taken today would be a success or a complete disaster. If it was the latter, the happy couple would have nothing at all to look back on and Mr Parsons would lose money; all because of her. Oh dear, what a day it had been! She would be glad when she knew one way or the other.

Digby was already at the shop when Bessie got to work on Monday morning. He greeted her with a smile, which she returned happily because she had been worried about him all day Sunday and was pleased to see him looking better. She had wondered if he would be well enough to come in to work after the incident on Saturday.

'The photographs are spot on,' he told her. 'I came in and developed them yesterday. I couldn't have done better myself. Come and have a look at the proofs.'

She followed him into the studio and they pored over the pictures together.

'They're not at all bad, are they?' she said, amazed and delighted at the standard. 'Phew I'm so relieved. You wouldn't have got paid if I'd messed them up.'

'You managed to get them smiling despite the fact that they were all freezing and fed up with the delay,' he said, looking at the pictures again. 'And you really have taken notice of what I've told you about the importance of light and how to use it. Well done, my dear. I'm very proud of you.'

'Thank you.' As he remained silent, Bessie turned to him. 'Oh my good-ness, Mr Parsons, you poor thing,' she said, seeing that he was whey faced and seemed about to pass out. 'You've come over poorly again. Let me help you into a chair.'

She managed to get him into an armchair they used for sittings and his head slumped forward on to his chest briefly but he didn't seem to lose consciousness completely. Inwardly trembling but ostensibly calm, she said, 'I'll get you a drink of water and help you on to a sofa in the waiting area where you'll be more comfortable.'

He ran the back of his hand across his brow, which was beaded with perspiration. 'I came over hot and dizzy again,' he said through dry lips. 'I feel so weak.'

'Yes, I can see that you're not well,' she said, handing him a glass of water. 'I'll make you a cup of of tea; that might help.'

'Thank you, dear.'

When she'd settled him on a sofa with a cup of sweet tea, she said, 'I really think I should go for the doctor now that you've come over faint again; just to get you checked out. I doubt if it's anything to worry about but he might be able to give you something to stop it happening again. You probably just need a tonic,' she told him gently. 'We don't have anyone booked for half an hour or so and it will only take me a few minutes to run down to the doctor's house. He might not be able to come right away but you can rest while we're waiting and I'll look after the shop.'

This time Digby didn't even begin to argue with her. 'Yes, I think some medical advice would be a good idea now,' he agreed.

After a thorough examination, Digby was told that he needed to go home and take it easy for a few weeks. The doctor wanted to keep an eye on him but thought the turns were due to his overdoing it and the fainting was a warning sign for him to slow down. He gave him a large bottle of tonic to correct any iron deficiency.

'It's all very well for him to tell me to go home, but how can I close the shop just like that?' he grumbled to Bessie after the doctor had gone. 'I can't let the business go to rack and ruin. I have responsibilities and bills to pay.'

'You won't have to let it go to rack and ruin. I will look after it for you,' she told him. 'I'm quite capable. I proved that to you on Saturday.'

'Saturday was one thing; running the whole place for several weeks single handed is a different matter altogether,' he pointed out. 'It will be too much for one person.'

'It will be a challenge, I admit, but I'm willing to do my best,' she told him. 'I feel sure I can hold things together just for a few weeks. It isn't as if it will be for ever.'

'There is also the fact that you are not an experienced photographer,' he reminded her. 'I've my reputation to think of. Some people only come here because of me.'

'There's always the thought that everything I have learned I have learned from you,' she reminded him. 'I can be sure to point that out to the customers.'

'Some of them might decide to go somewhere else if I'm not here,' he said.

'Indeed they might, so I'll just have to persuade them to wait until you come back if they won't let me take their photograph, won't I?' she said with a positive attitude. 'The bookings we already have in the immediate future for weddings and special occasions I will do myself. No one will argue about it, seeing as it will be too short notice to get anyone else.'

'I don't know . . .'

'I will make a good job of it, Mr Parsons; the reputation of your business is in safe hands, I promise you,' she said with a determined air. 'I proved that I can work with the camera on Saturday, and as for keeping up to date with everything else, I'll work later in the evenings to cope with that. Your health is the important thing, and you need to look after yourself while I take care of things here. No one is indispensable, remember; not even you.'

'You're a very kind girl, Bessie,' he said, beginning to warm to the idea, 'and I will do as you say. These fainting fits have really shaken me up, I must admit. But if you find it too much, you must let me know at once.'

She nodded, knowing that she would have to be on her knees before she would let on to him. He was a good man and deserved some time off and looking after, though she doubted if he would get much of that from his daughter.

'The first thing we must do is get you home,' she told him. 'I will have to close the shop while I take you. I got you home safely on Saturday so I'm sure you'll trust me to do it again today.'

'It's just as well you can handle the trap,' he said.

'You taught me, remember,' she said. 'You did it so that I could drive you to outside jobs if you didn't feel like it yourself. It's all part of my duties as your assistant.' She paused, looking at him, and held out his coat for him to put on. 'So, shall we be on our way, or are we going to stay here talking about it until we are both old enough to retire?'

'You can be quite bossy, can't you?'

'When the situation warrants it, yes, I most certainly can.'

He slipped his arms into his coat and she held out his hat for him.

'Right, Mr Parsons, let's get you home to take a well-earned rest,' she said, holding his arm supportively as they went outside into the bitter wind.

Over the next few weeks Bessie was on the earliest ferry in the morning and the last one back to Tideway at night. Her days consisted of working with the camera in and out of the studio, developing in the dark room, mounting and finishing the photographs and all her usual jobs as well: keeping the paperwork and the books up to date, cleaning, and working in the reception. She had to deal with irate customers who wanted Digby to take their photograph and needed a lot of persuasion before they would agree to let her do it; inevitably, some said they'd prefer to take their business elsewhere, but she managed to persuade the majority to give her a chance. It was a huge commitment she had taken on, and the responsibility was immense, as the reputation of Digby's business was on the line.

Sometimes she would have welcomed a helping hand with the day-to-day jobs such as cleaning and filing, because her great interest, she discovered during this period, was the actual photography, and the process, from camera to the finished product, was very time-consuming. She was meticulous at every stage.

If she had thought that Joan Parsons might help out a little, she was sadly mistaken.

'My father asked me to call in to see how you're getting on,' Joan announced one day, appearing in the shop.

'You can tell him that I'm doing just fine,' said Bessie, busy with some paperwork at the desk in the reception area. 'I've got someone coming to view some proofs in a minute and a family sitting right after that, so it's all go.'

'Aren't you the busy bee then?' Joan said mockingly.

'I am, as it happens,' Bessie confirmed in an even tone. 'You can give me a hand if you like. I could really do with someone to cover in reception while I'm working in the studio. It's very distracting having to come out in the middle of a sitting to see to someone who comes into the shop.'

'I'm not doing that,' Joan stated categorically. 'I don't work, as you very well know.'

'I thought you might make an exception on a temporary basis while your father is laid up,' suggested Bessie.

'You thought wrong then,' was her adamant reply.

'Oh well, it was just an idea,' said Bessie. 'How is your father now, anyway?'

'More irritating than usual, if that's possible,' Joan replied, sighing heavily. 'I shall be glad when he's gone back to work, which will be next week, I hope. I'm fed up with him hanging around the house getting on my nerves.'

Bessie felt a sharp stab of pity for her long-suffering employer, and anger towards this awful woman. 'It's his house, so he's entitled to be in it as often as he wishes, surely,' she pointed out.

Joan shrugged. 'That doesn't mean I have to enjoy his company, does it?' she retaliated. 'The silly old duffer.'

'Far from being a duffer, your father is a very clever man, and well respected by all who come into contact with him,' Bessie informed her sharply. 'He deserves your respect, especially as he keeps you in such comfort.'

'That is none of your business, Bessie Bow,' retorted Joan. 'As I've told you before, you are just the hired help around here, and don't you forget it.'

'I won't forget it, but neither will I grovel to you like your father does,' Bessie told her.

'One word from me and my father will give you your marching orders,' Joan threatened.

'I wouldn't be so sure about that if I were you. Who would run his business for him then?' retorted Bessie. 'You?'

'Don't be ridiculous,' Joan said with a pitying expression. 'There are plenty of people ready to step into your shoes.'

Sadly, Bessie knew that was true.

Fortunately the discussion came to an abrupt end when the shop door opened and the expected customers arrived to view the proofs of their recently taken photographs.

'Give my regards to your father and tell him that there are no problems here,' Bessie said to Joan in a valedictory tone. 'I'll call over to see him in a day or two.'

Joan flounced off and Bessie turned her mind to the business in hand. Fortunately the customers were delighted with the proofs and gave her a healthy order for mounted and framed copies. It gave Bessie a feeling of immense satisfaction. She enjoyed the job, and in some ways would be disappointed when Digby returned and was back in the studio, because then she would revert to the menial tasks and no longer have access to the camera, which had proved to be her forte. She was fascinated by the effect of light and the difference it made to a picture, and would love to explore the subject more fully.

One person who would be very glad when Digby was back at work was Jim, who hardly saw her these days. She had already left for work when he got up in the morning, and arrived home dog tired when the household was about to turn in for the night. She even had to go in to the shop on Sundays to clear the backlog of work, much to the utter disapproval of her pious mother. But the whole challenge was proving to be interesting and fulfilling. Experience was definitely the best teacher, and she had learned a lot in a short time, which would stand her in good stead on Digby's return.

Oh well, press on, she told herself as the family group arrived for their sitting and she welcomed them into the studio.

Chapter Nine

'Morning, Mrs Mott,' greeted Charlie from the junk stall respectfully as May pushed the baby in the pram down the market one fine morning in May. 'How's the little 'un today?'

'She's coming on a treat, thanks, Charlie.' May smiled. 'In fact, she seems to get more beautiful with every day that passes. But I would think that, wouldn't I?'

'It goes with the territory when you're a mum,' said Charlie's wife, coming over and peering into the pram. 'But in this case she really is a little sweetheart.'

'You won't get any argument from me about that,' said May, glowing with pride. She came to the market most days, primarily for shopping, but it always turned into a social occasion, because the stallholders were so friendly towards her. Everyone made a terrific fuss of the baby and May revelled in it.

'You've excelled yourself with this one, Archie,' the woman shouted across the road where Archie was working at the stall. 'I didn't know you had it in you.'

'I'm full of surprises,' he shouted back with his usual beaming smile.

'He's ready to get cracking on the next one, aren't you, lad?' Albert joined in with a hearty laugh.

'All in good time, Uncle,' May came back at him. 'This little one is quite enough for me for the moment.'

May did want another baby; not quite this soon, but she wasn't planning on leaving it long. Having fallen pregnant so young and unexpectedly, she'd had many secret moments of doubt as to her maternal capabilities. But motherhood suited her so well, she wanted more of it; a baby with Archie she knew would delight him. Her earlier concern about his head-in-the-sand attitude towards his non-biological paternity to Connie had faded, because he qualified in every way that mattered, being supportive to May and a loving father to Connie.

The baby had brought them closer together; almost as though she somehow made up for the missing element on May's side of the marriage. Connie was at the centre of their lives now, and never once since her birth had either of them mentioned the fact that Archie wasn't actually her father. He'd slipped into the role so well, it was easy to let the truth pale into insignificance. It obviously had for Auntie and Uncle too.

May had never been more in her element than she was now. She felt truly alive and vibrant. The world was a better place with Connie in it; every area of her life was more vivid and pleasurable because of her. When she remembered that her mother had tried to make her have an abortion, her blood ran cold. She still hated Edie for that. Thank God she'd not gone through with it; and three hearty cheers for Auntie Winnie for making it possible.

London life grew on May more strongly as time passed. Her days were spent in blissful motherhood, but at least one afternoon a week she went to the WSPU shop to help out for an hour or two, filling envelopes in the back office or working in the shop. Connie slept in her pram while her mother worked, and on the odd occasion that she woke and wanted attention, she got plenty of it from the other women as well as her mother. May had been honest with Archie about her voluntary work, and although he, like many other men, couldn't understand why having the vote meant so much to women, he didn't put up any opposition to her involvement. Albert thoroughly disapproved but accepted that there was nothing he could do about it, especially as his wife was now a supporter as well.

Now Connie began to whimper. May rocked the pram for a while, and when that failed to have the desired effect she took her out gently, cuddled her and began singing to her. But no lullaby for this baby! Oh no! Instead May broke into a hearty rendition of 'Alexander's Ragtime Band', jigging around, whereupon the baby smiled and chuckled while the stallholders looked on in amusement

'She's a girl and a half, that one,' Winnie remarked to Albert, who was unpacking some stock while they watched May's antics. 'It's a real treat to see her with that baby. She's a tonic.'

'She's a one-off and that's a fact,' agreed Albert, smiling affectionately.

'Having her and the little one around has enriched our lives, don't you think?'

'It certainly has. I don't know where she gets all these new songs from,' he mentioned.

'Ragtime, it's called,' his wife informed him, 'and May gets to know them from a friend of hers at the WSPU who is a maid in a big house.

She hears the new ragtime music at their parties and sings it in the office; the toffs dance their feet off, apparently. May's friend sometimes works extra hours to serve them at these do's, so she's well up in the latest things. Mind you, the postman is always whistling the songs too, and people buy the sheet music and play them on the piano. New songs soon get around.'

May was on her way over, wheeling the pram with one hand and holding the baby with the other.

'Hello, Auntie and Unc,' she greeted. 'Are you both behaving your-selves? I hope you're not causing any breaches of the peace or anything.'

They both laughed, enjoying her affectionate ribbing; glad she felt easy enough with them to do so.

'You're the one more likely to do that, with all this suffragette nonsense,' Albert said in a light-hearted manner.

'Now, now, Uncle,' May said in a tone of gentle admonition. 'You know we've agreed to disagree about that.'

'She's quite right, Albert,' added Winnie, who also now did an hour or so at the shop whenever she could find the time. 'We agreed that we wouldn't fall out over that.' She held her arms out for the baby. 'Can I have a hold of her to get me through the day?'

'Course you can,' replied May, handing her over gently. 'Then I'll take her over to see her dad. He'll want a cuddle as she's awake.'

As Winnie cooed and fussed over Connie, May remembered something.

'The postman came after you'd left and delivered something a bit special.'

Winnie narrowed her eyes questioningly. 'Oh yeah, and what would that be?'

'An invitation to Bessie's wedding next month,' May replied. 'She's invited all of us.'

'Blimey,' responded Winnie. 'I hope Edie has agreed to it, or we're in for the full blast of her icy treatment. Your mother is an expert at that if something doesn't please her.'

'I'm sure Bessie would have cleared it with her before sending the invitation,' said May. 'When she came to London to see the baby, she told me that she wanted us to be there and that it would spoil the day for her if we weren't, so she must have insisted. I don't want to upset Mum, but I wouldn't miss it for the world. I can't not be at my only sister's wedding.'

'Course you can't, love,' agreed her aunt. 'I wouldn't want to miss it either.' She paused, mulling it over. 'Edie has her faults, but I don't think she would do anything to wreck the day for Bessie. She'll be on her best behaviour.'

'I expect you're right. In the meantime, we've got Sunday to look forward to,' May reminded her, referring to the forthcoming suffragette demonstration outside Buckingham Palace.

'Another thing I wouldn't miss,' said Winnie.

'Have you told Uncle Albert that you're going?' May asked in a low tone while her uncle was busy unpacking some new stock out of earshot.

Winnie nodded. 'Oh yeah, I wouldn't keep it from him; that isn't our way,' she told her niece.

'What was his reaction?'

'He isn't pleased, naturally, but he wouldn't try and stop me,' Winnie replied.

'Same with Archie,' said May. 'He knows that sometimes I have to do what I know is right even if he isn't keen, and I would never do anything that would put him or Connie at risk. I want to go to add my support, but I shall keep well away from any trouble, especially as I shall have Connie with me because of the breast-feeding.'

'It's a pity it's come to the point where we even have to consider such things when the campaign is for something so fair and just,' said Winnie.

May nodded in agreement. 'Anyway, I'd better take madam over to see Archie then get on and do my shopping, or I'll never get home to do the chores.'

Watching her swing lightly across the road towards the fruit and vegetable stall, Winnie felt a surge of love so strong it brought tears to her eyes. Edie couldn't possible know the extent of the joy she had given to her sister when she'd thrown May out of the house. It was an ill wind indeed.

A frown furrowed her brow for a moment as she thought ahead to the wedding. For herself she could take anything Edie cared to dish out. She'd grown up with her sharp tongue so had a good deal of resistance to it. But she wouldn't stand back and see May hurt. Not under any circumstances. Hopefully Edie would behave herself for Bessie's sake. Winnie was deeply saddened by the family rift. Edie was a tartar, and she and Winnie had little in common and different views about practically everything. But they were sisters, after all, and Winnie was fond of her for all her faults.

There were banners galore outside Buckingham Palace on Sunday when May and Winnie joined the Votes for Women campaign groups from all over the country. North, south, east and west were represented here in large numbers. Mothers, daughters and granddaughters; there were even a good few grandmothers.

Many of the women wore official sashes. May and Winnie couldn't afford one of those so wore penny badges in common with most other working-class women, who simply didn't have the means to show their allegiance so grandly. Their less blatant commitment was also because they feared harm to their loved ones, as the anti-suffrage people had been very spiteful recently. The homes of some high-profile suffragette sympathisers had even been raided by the police, who had also stormed the campaign offices. The spirit of the movement was pride in one's commitment to the cause, but for people like May and Winnie, reality had to be faced.

There was a great feeling of comradeship among the gathering today. May and Winnie were with Constance and the others from their local branch, two of whom were holding a banner bearing the slogan DEEDS NOT WORDS. The atmosphere was noisy and jolly, with cheers of enthusiasm, the women united by the deeply felt ethos of their sisterhood, the spirit of their common cause drawing them together. There had been some inspiring speeches from the women on the platform, who were dressed entirely in the official colours.

There were stories of members' heroic prison experiences, and medals for valour were awarded to women who had been on hunger strike and suffered force-feeding in prison, a practice no longer used. Prison governors were now allowed to release starving women for one week before having them rearrested to finish their sentence. May and Winnie joined wholeheartedly in the cheers and the barrage of outrage from women around them at the use of this brutal practice.

'Downright cruel,' said Winnie.

'Wicked,' said someone near her in the crowd.

'Our members are being punished for being violent when we've been driven to it by the unfairness of the system, and all our militant acts have been planned so that no one gets hurt,' said a woman standing next to May with a little girl sitting on her shoulders. 'All we want is what we are entitled to: a say in who governs the country we live in. I've brought my daughter with me today because I want her to grow up believing that as a woman she has certain rights, and that you have to stand up for yourself and what you believe in or you'll be trampled on for ever.'

'We are being denied the basic right of citizenship,' added May, glad that she had come here today, and buoyed up with fervour for the occasion.

Opinions were exchanged and friendships made. There was laughter as well as anger. But eventually May felt the time had come to leave. So far Connie had slept through it all, but now she was beginning to be wakeful and she needed to be fed.

'I'm glad we came, but I think it's time we went, Auntie,' she suggested.

'Yeah, all right, love.'

But as they were about to move, a sudden hush descended on the crowd. Something was happening on the other side, too far away for them to see what it was through the masses. Word spread from onc to another that some women had tried to reach the Palace to present a petition to the King and had been arrested. The gathering drew back as mounted police went by, escorting policemen on foot who were holding on to the arrested women as they walked them past. The women had their heads held high and were supported by jeers for the police from the crowd.

Suddenly the atmosphere became hostile, the resentment palpable. Some of the indignant women tried to fight with the police, which got them arrested too. May and Winnie hurriedly weaved their way through the multitude and made their way home, stopping on the way for May to feed the baby, which she did furtively in an alleyway near the station, hidden from view by her aunt.

Although the meeting had turned ugly, May felt honoured to have been there; she knew she had seen history in the making. How much longer the fight for justice would have to go on, she didn't know. There was certainly no sign of the government relenting on the suffrage issue at the moment.

She and Winnie were quiet on the train on the way home, both immersed in their own thoughts on the matter. May knew that she would never forget the look on the suffragettes' faces as they were taken by the police: pale and angry, but indomitable spirit personified. Being in the company of such fortitude convinced May that the fight would eventually be won. It wouldn't be tomorrow or next week, but it would come. The issue wasn't going to go away, no matter how much the government wished it so. The characters of the women at the helm of the campaign were too strong.

There was an article in the paper the next day about the arrests, with a picture of the women being taken away by the police. It looked very dramatic.

'I hope you weren't involved in anything to do with that,' said Archie that evening over their meal.

'I support the campaign and was at the demonstration, so I was involved as far as that's concerned,' May pointed out. 'But no, I wasn't anywhere near any of the trouble.'

'But it could just as easily have been you they dragged away in hand-cuffs,' he said.

'No it couldn't; I stayed well away and didn't do anything to warrant arrest.'

'It could still be dangerous with that sort of thing going on around you.' He looked somewhat alarmed. 'You and the baby could have been hurt.'

'I would never allow that to happen,' May said adamantly. 'I've told you that and I mean it. If I didn't have Connie, I would be right there in the thick of it and in prison if necessary, but she needs me so I'll make sure I'm not carted off by the police.'

'That's right,' put in Winnie. 'We stay well away from trouble, which might seem cowardly to some of the more active members, but family comes first with us, no matter how strong our beliefs.'

'I should hope so too,' Albert put in.

'I didn't know all that much about the suffragettes until I came to London,' said May conversationally. 'Of course I knew the basics from what I read in the papers, but no one was involved in Tideway and there wasn't a local branch, so I didn't realise the strength of feeling you get when you are actually there at one of the meetings. If I'd grown up here I think I'd have got involved long ago.'

'You'd have been a right little militant,' Archie teased her, happy now that she had assured him of her responsible behaviour.

'I think I would too,' she agreed after some thought. 'So it's just as well for you that I know my first priority is looking after you and Connie.' She gave a wry grin. 'And while we're on the subject of your welfare, we need to get you a new suit for the wedding.'

'A new suit?' he said, as though she had suggested that he go out naked and roll in stinging nettles. 'There's nothing wrong with the one I've already got.'

'Nothing except that you've probably had it for donkey's years; you've worn it every Sunday since I've known you.'

'If it was good enough to wear to my own wedding, I'm sure it's good enough for your sister's.'

May mulled this over for a few moments. 'Yes, Archie, you're right,' she said, deciding to resist the urge to force a new suit on him just to make an impression on her mother, who would probably disapprove of him on principle anyway. 'You'll be fine in the one you've got if you'd rather not bother to get a new one.'

'That goes for you too, Albert,' Winnie told her husband, adding with a wry grin, 'Us ladies will have something new to wear, though, isn't that right, May?'

143

'Not half,' she grinned. 'And Connie will too; she's going to have the prettiest outfit I can find.'

'Uh-oh,' said Albert, grinning at Archie. 'This is gonna cost us, mate.'

'It certainly is,' confirmed Winnie. 'There's a wedding present to be paid for as well, remember.'

'Your sister will only get married once, May,' said Archie, 'so you just let me know what money you need. Get yourself and Connie something really nice to wear and don't worry about the cost.'

'Ooh, what a lovely man,' said Winnie lightly. 'You can tell they haven't been married long. It won't last.'

But May knew it would. Whatever she wanted for herself or Connie she could have with Archie's blessing as long as it was within his means. He would give them his last farthing even if it meant leaving himself destitute. She could weep at the generosity and kindness of the man. He deserved better than her, and that was a fact.

Today Bessie was on the other side of the camera. She was the one being asked to smile and to stand correctly. Not that she needed any bidding to smile; she couldn't stop on this her wedding day, which really was proving to be the happiest day of her life.

They had just come out of the village church after the service. It was a fine day in early July, the village resplendent in the sunshine, the river shining at the bottom of the hill. The new Mrs Jim Minter was wearing an elegant white dress with a modest neckline and a long skirt, her veil now swept back from her radiant face. Jim stood beside her in a new suit, proud and happy.

Bessie's day was made complete by her sister's presence here. She had been adamant with her mother about invitations being sent to the London branch of the family; she had made it clear that it would spoil her day if they weren't there. Edie had agreed without argument, whilst making it known, in that special way of hers, that she wasn't happy about it.

As far as Bessie could see, there didn't seem to have been any bad feeling so far, but she was deliberately blinding herself to anything that might be happening among the guests. This was her day, hers and Jim's, and she was determined not to let anything spoil it for either of them. They were having the wedding reception in the church hall and going on honeymoon to Clacton later on today, after which they would move into a cottage they were taking for rent in Tideway, in the next street to her family but closer to the waterfront.

144

Her parents had done her proud, she reflected. It was a well-known family fact that they had been putting money aside for years from Dad's summer earnings for both their daughters' weddings. Just mine, as it happened, Bessie thought sadly. May's hadn't cost them a penny; not even for a gift.

May's expulsion from the family was obviously painful for her, but she seemed to be coping, Bessie observed, seeing her sister smiling there in the crowd, dear Archie by her side holding the baby. She'd found an absolute diamond in him.

So had she herself, she thought, looking at Jim and meeting his smile with one of her own. This was the fairy-tale wedding she had always dreamed of, and every second of it was precious.

'Can we have one of the bride and groom looking at each other with . . . er, affection, please,' Digby was saying. 'Look as though you really mean it, please.'

'Certainly,' said Bessie, leaning up and kissing Jim on the lips as the camera snapped. 'Is that real enough for you?'

This caused a roar of laughter among the guests. Digby was smiling. He was now fully recovered to health, but Bessie knew he would be missing having her to assist him. As a married woman, especially the schoolmaster's wife, it wasn't done for her to work outside of the home, so sadly she'd had to give up the job she had so enjoyed, and Digby had a new assistant starting next week. It was a pity she'd been forced by convention to leave, because teachers weren't highly paid and her earnings would have been welcome. But that wasn't how things were done around here.

'Can we have close relatives of the bride and groom now, please?' requested Digby.

Jim's parents and other relatives came forward and were told to stand on one side of the happy couple, while Bessie's people were on the other.

'Smile, please, everyone,' instructed Digby. 'That's lovely. Just one more shot to make sure.'

The camera clicked on the happy faces. As May arranged her face into a smile, it occurred to her that no one looking at these pictures in the future could possibly guess the heartache that lay behind some of the smiles frozen in time by the lens of the camera.

All credit where it was due, thought May later on, Mum had put on a good show for Bessie. Trestle tables had been erected in the flower-decked church hall, all laid with pure white tablecloths, and the wedding guests were served with cold boiled ham and beef, new potatoes and salad, followed by trifle. After the speeches, the toasts and the cutting of the cake, the tables were cleared and a small band arrived to play for dancing.

Bessie and Jim took the floor for the first dance in keeping with tradition, but when the party was in full swing, Bessie went home to get changed into her going-away clothes. May took the opportunity to go with her while Winnie looked after Connie to give the sisters a much-needed few minutes alone together.

'It was a lovely wedding, Bessie,' said May, helping her sister off with her dress in the bedroom they had once shared. 'You looked absolutely beautiful. The best Tideway has ever seen.'

'I don't know about that,' Bessie said with a modest grin. 'But thanks anyway, sis. The dressmaker in the village made the dress and my going-away outfit.'

'She made a lovely job of it,' complimented May. 'Mum and Dad certainly did well by you too.'

'Yeah, they did, I must admit. The wedding was all I've ever wanted and I enjoyed every moment once I'd got over my nerves at the beginning.' She looked at May. 'Thanks for coming. It wouldn't have been the same without you.'

'I wouldn't have missed it for the world, even though my being here probably ruined it for Mum.'

'Don't be daft.'

'You're not going to try and tell me that she wanted me here,' challenged May.

'She would sooner die than admit it, but she's probably dead pleased to see you,' suggested Bessie. 'I don't expect she wanted a parting of the ways between the two of you any more than you did. No mother would want that. She's too proud to come down off her high horse, that's all it is.'

'I disagree. I think she was thoroughly glad to see the back of me and wants me out of her life for ever,' was May's honest opinion. 'There has always been something about me she didn't like.'

'Now you really are imagining things,' admonished Bessie. 'She treated us all the same.'

'Yeah, she did treat us all the same, but I think she had to force herself in my case.'

'Oh, May . . .'

'I'm not just being dramatic, Bessie. I've thought about it a lot since I've been away, and looking back, there was always something behind her

146

eyes; something I could never quite put my finger on but always knew was there. It was a feeling rather than anything I could actually see.'

'Probably because you were always so daring and independently minded,' suggested Bessie. 'That got you into more scrapes than the rest of us, so you were in trouble with Mum more often. It's as simple as that.'

'Very probably,' May said. This wasn't the time to pursue the matter. 'Anyway, it's all in the past now. I'm a married woman with a life of my own.'

'At least you and Mum have managed to be civil to each other today,' remarked Bessie. 'I thank you for that.'

'It's your wedding day; it would be a poor show if we couldn't manage to behave ourselves on such an important occasion, wouldn't it?'

'A wedding is the perfect opportunity to build bridges, I would have thought,' suggested May hopefully.

May shook her head. 'Sorry, sis. A spot of polite conversation is one thing; forgiving her for casting me out of the family and trying to make me murder my baby is quite another.'

'To be fair, she wouldn't have thought of Connie as a child at that time,' Bessie pointed out.

'No. She was just my disgrace and therefore potentially Mum's too,' said May. 'It's only since Connie has actually been here and I love her so much that I've realised the enormity of what I nearly did in the name of respectability.'

'It makes me shudder to think of it too,' confessed Bessie, standing there in her corsets as her sister hung her wedding dress up carefully on a hanger. 'But Mum was just doing what society made her. To her it was the only way.'

'That's why we can never truly put things right between us. She thinks I am wholly in the wrong and that she was unquestionably right. And while I accept that I broke all the laws of decency, I think that what she tried to make me do was a far worse sin than mine.' She paused. 'Anyway, enough of all that on your wedding day. Now let's get you into your going-away clothes so that you can stun them all over again at the reception.'

With her sister's help, Bessie slipped into a pale blue skirt in the new tapered line with a matching jacket that nipped in to her slender waist. Her blond hair – usually taken back off her face – was curled and worn loose to her shoulders under her cream hat.

'You look lovely,' complimented May with genuine admiration. 'You look just like Mary Pickford, only prettier.'

147

'It's nice of you to say so, but I don't think I'm quite in the film star league.' Bessie smiled. 'But I did sleep with my hair curled into rags to get it like this.'

'It was worth it; it looks gorgeous.'

'You look lovely too, May,' commented Bessie, running an approving eye over her sister, who was wearing a dress in a deep shade of pink, also in the new straighter line, with a large floppy cream hat with a pink feather.

'Thanks, kid.' May's eyes filled with tears. 'We'd better get you back to the party so that and your lovely new husband can slip away to the seaside for a romantic interlude.' She slipped her arms around her sister. 'I wish you all the luck in the world and I know you'll be very happy with Jim.'

'I miss you, May,' Bessie confessed thickly.

'Likewise,' responded May, feeling her sister's body shudder slightly against her. 'Now don't cry, because you'll make your eyes all puffy, and you don't want to go away on honeymoon looking anything less than your best, do you?'

Bessie drew away and they both laughed emotionally.

'Come on,' said May gently. 'Let's go back to the party so that you can knock 'em all dead with your outfit.'

After a fond farewell from May to Whistler, who was in his basket in the kitchen, the sisters left the cottage together and walked back to the church hall. May felt the closing of a door behind her, as though this truly was the end of an era.

The party continued after the newly-weds had departed in a shower of confetti. May and the others had to leave soon after, so May made a point of having a few quiet words with the people who mattered to her before it was time for them to go.

'How are things with you, Sam?' she asked. Her brother was now tall and gangling, not quite yet a man but out of school and earning his living.

'All right, thanks.'

'How are you enjoying working at the boatyard?'

'It's better than going to sea with Dad,' he said. 'I'm making the most of it because I'll have to join Dad on the boat soon.'

'You never know, you might get to like it.'

He made a face. 'There's no chance of that, but I'll have to do it because it's what is expected of me. Even when Dad retires I'll have to carry on the family tradition. It would break his heart if I told him I wasn't going to do it, and there's nothing I can do to change his mind. He knows it isn't what I want, but he won't relent on the subject. Still, he's crewing on the Marriots' yacht for most of the summer, so I can forget about it while he's away.'

Excitement shot though May at the mention of the Marriot name, but she forced herself not to ask any questions about the family as a way of finding out about William. She was disappointed in herself for feeling anything at all for him still. She'd tried her very best to expunge him completely from her memory.

'Fishing is an important job, Sam, bringing in food for people to eat,' she told him.

'I know, but I'm sure there are plenty of other people who would enjoy doing it more than I will.' He sighed. 'Take no notice of me, May. I must be a bit weird, I think. Fishing is the life blood of the village. Everybody else loves it. Trust me to break the mould by wanting to do something else.'

'You won't be the first to break the mould in our family,' she said 'I've beaten you to it.'

Having been told, when he was old enough to understand, what had happened to May, he flushed because it was a taboo subject and he was at an age to be easily embarrassed. 'I'll say you have,' he said bashfully.

'Maybe Dad will be less insistent later on,' she said. She had nothing more positive to offer on the subject, since family traditions here in Tideway were set in stone. 'Things usually do work out in the end.'

Sam smiled his shy smile. 'They did for you, anyway,' he said. 'Archie seems like a really nice bloke.'

'And what about my lovely daughter?' she asked, kissing the top of the baby's head.

'She's nice too.'

'Would you like to hold her? You are her uncle, you know,' May said, smiling.

Sam looked alarmed. 'I don't know anything about babies. I might drop her.'

May laughed. 'Don't panic. I won't force you. When she gets a bit bigger you'll be more confident. You can hold her then,' she said, but she felt an ache of sadness, because she didn't know when she would see any of them again.

'We really miss you around here, May,' he blurted out, as though reading her thoughts. 'It hasn't been the same since you left.'

'I know, and I miss you too, Sam.' She took hold of his hand with her free one and squeezed it. 'I might not get to see you often but I do think about you a lot, and if ever you want to come and visit, now that you're all grown up, you'll be very welcome.'

He said he might take her up on it one day, and she moved on to speak to some old friends. Then she and the others went as a group to bid farewell to their hosts, her parents. May had deliberately avoided being on her own with her mother for fear she might lose control and say what was in her heart.

'We're off now,' she said now, looking at her father, then her mother. 'It's time to get home to put the baby to bed.'

'Thanks for a lovely party, both of you,' added Archie. 'It was a really good do.'

'It did go off rather well, didn't it?' said George, who had had a good few beers and was in a jovial mood. 'All due to my wife here. She organised the whole thing in her usual efficient way; a lot of work it was, too.'

'A labour of love,' said Edie.

'The ladies are better than us men at organising this sort of thing, aren't they, George?' said Archie pleasantly. He had been warned by May to be on his best behaviour.

'No doubt about that. She's been in her element, haven't you, love?' said George, ever the supportive husband.

'I don't know so much about that. Things don't organise themselves, do they?' she said stiffly.

'They do not,' said Winnie, unable to refrain from comparing this well-organised wedding with May's rushed do and the fact that Edie and George hadn't even been there.

There was an awkward pause, then Albert said, 'Come on, folks, we'd better be going or we'll miss the train.' He shook George's hand. 'Nice to see you again, mate.' Then he looked at Edie. He'd always thought of her as a stuck-up, cold-hearted bitch, but he was under strict instructions from his wife to be nice to her today. 'And you, love. Thanks for a lovely day.' He looked away from her to the others. 'Now come on, you lot, or we'll be swimming across the river and walking back to London.'

They all moved through into the lobby and filed through the outside doors.

'I'll catch you up,' announced May impulsively, moving back to stand beside her mother.

Winnie looked worried by this, and Archie stayed by his wife's side protectively.

'Just give me a few minutes, will you, love?' May asked him. 'I won't be very long, I promise. I'll meet you down at the ferry. Don't let it go without me, will you?'

'As if I would,' said Archie, moving away.

Her father made a diplomatic exit too, leaving May alone with her mother outside the hall in the cool of the summer evening.

'I didn't think it would be right to leave without a few words, since we've both studiously avoided being alone together all day,' May told Edie.

'I've done no such thing,' Edie denied hotly. 'I've been busy making sure everything ran smoothly and looking after the guests. There are formalities to adhere to at a function like this.'

'So busy you didn't even have the chance to spend a few minutes with your first grandchild?' May said accusingly. 'Or are you still refusing to acknowledge her existence, even though I'm a respectable married woman now?'

'Don't make a scene, May,' Edie urged. 'I don't want the day ruined by your theatrics.'

'I've no intention of making a scene, Mum,' May assured her. 'I just want you to look at my daughter, your granddaughter.' She lowered her head to gaze at Connie, asleep in her arms. 'Look at her. See how beautiful she is.'

Edie did as she was asked, seeming awkward. 'Yes, she is a lovely child,' she admitted coldly. 'There. Are you happy now that I've said it? Are you?'

'At least you've looked at her, even though you did have to be forced into it.'

Edie shrugged.

'I am very glad I have her, Mum,' May said pointedly. 'She's the love of my life.'

'You got your own way then, didn't you?' rasped Edie through clenched teeth. 'Still, that's always been your mission in life: to get your own way.'

'I wasn't that bad, was I?' May could feel tears welling up and she forced them back.

Again Edie shrugged without speaking.

May looked at her mother's face, barren of all affection. 'Don't you feel any tinge of conscience about what you tried to make me do?' she asked her.

'Conscience?' Edie said flatly. 'You're the one with the guilty conscience, my girl, not me. You should be hanging your head in shame for what you did.'

'I will never do that,' May informed her firmly. 'I am proud of my daughter and you should be proud of her too. She's your own flesh and blood, for heaven's sake.'

Edie said nothing.

'What is it with you; are you afraid to feel anything?' May challenged her. 'You were never a warm-hearted woman, but did any feelings you did have die the day Henry drowned? Is that it, Mum? Or is it just that I was always the odd one out for some reason; the child you didn't much care for?'

When her mother lowered her eyes, May gasped. 'Oh my God, I am right. I always knew there was something.'

'Look, I brought you up and did my very best for you, and you repaid me by going against everything I ever taught you,' Edie said in a shrill tone. 'So don't come to me trying to put the blame on me, trying to make me feel bad, because it won't work.' She paused for breath. 'I taught all my children how to live like decent human beings. I instilled in them the difference between right and wrong.'

'I'll say you did.'

'I even gave you a chance when you were in trouble, and you threw it back in my face.' She went on as though May hadn't spoken. 'So don't try and imply that I turned my back on you without good cause, because I didn't. Yes, you have a beautiful daughter, and you have been lucky enough to find a good man, so you have come up smelling of roses. But that doesn't alter the fact that you let me down in the worst way possible.'

May stared without speaking at her mother's hard face, her own eyes hot with tears now.

'Anyway, you have your people waiting for you at the ferry, so go home and leave me to enjoy the rest of the party in peace,' Edie said in a subdued, rather weary manner.

Without another word, May turned away and headed for the ferry, the baby propped against her shoulder. Just before she got there she stopped to wipe her eyes and compose herself. Even now her mother had the power to hurt and humiliate her. She would never, ever forget the expression on her face when she had asked her if she had been the child in the family she hadn't taken to. Edie hadn't needed to say anything. All May needed to know had been there in her eyes.

'There you are at last,' exclaimed Archie. 'I thought I was gonna have to come and drag you away from there. Here, let me take the nipper to give you a break.'

'Sorry I held you up,' she said as he took the baby from her. 'I just needed a few words with my mother.'

'As long as you're here now, that's all that matters,' he said with his usual good humour. 'We should be in good time for the train.' He looked at her. 'Are you all right?'

'I'm fine,' she fibbed.

In the boat they sat close together, the baby sleeping in his arms.

'Thank you, Archie,' she said.

'What for?'

'For being you,' she said tenderly.

Edie didn't go straight back to the party; she walked in the opposite direction to May along the main street that ran parallel with the waterside. Although she had been careful to keep her feelings hidden in front of May, her nerves were in shreds and she was trembling all over and feeling sick. Did May have no sense of decency at all; no respect for the status quo and the people who had brought her up? How was it that she could make Edie feel as though she was somehow in the wrong? It really was most unfair.

She had a sudden image of the baby sleeping in her mother's arms, her small face in sweet repose inside the pink frilly bonnet. A nasty little worm of compunction tried to insinuate itself into her psyche, as May's words echoed over and over in her mind: 'what you tried to make me do'.

But Edie had only been trying to protect her family from disgrace. She didn't make the rules that gave girls in trouble such terrible lives. She couldn't have known then that May would come out of it smiling, though she should have had the sense to guess, knowing the way that one was, with her daring ways and wilful spirit. She'd heard a whisper down the family grapevine recently that May had even got involved with those dreadful suffragettes. Trust her to support something so outrageous. It was typical.

Edie decided that she wasn't going to spend one more moment worrying about what might have happened because of what she had tried to make May do in her best interests. The child had survived, so there was nothing to feel bad about. But she kept seeing the baby in her mind's eye and thinking how close she had come to never making it into the world, all because of Edie's own slavish dedication to propriety. It was the way she was; the way she had been brought up. You couldn't change the habits of a lifetime.

She took a deep breath to calm herself, then went back inside to the party, where the band was playing the new ragtime music and the younger guests were doing a peculiar dance she was informed was called the Turkey Trot. Naturally Edie didn't join in. That sort of thing was far too undignified for her.

May sat on the train next to Archie, glad that he and Albert were engaged in conversation so that she could be quiet with her thoughts. Auntie Winnie was dozing. Try as she might, May couldn't put her mother out of her mind or dismiss the pain the meeting with her had left her with.

She looked down at her child sleeping in her arms and thanked God for her. The two of them had a new life with Archie and her uncle and aunt in London. The past must be eradicated as far as possible. She owed it to Archie and her daughter to devote herself to them.

A man sitting opposite in the carriage opened his newspaper, revealing front-page headlines and a picture of the Austrian archduke who had been assassinated along with his wife while on a visit to some place called Sarajevo. The murder had been all over the papers for the last few days. Although May could see that it was a shocking tragedy for two people to be shot in cold blood on the street while going about their business, and she was deeply sympathetic, she wasn't quite clear as to why it was such headline news here in England.

She asked Archie. 'I mean, it's so far away,' she said. 'It's very sad, but why is it such big news for us here?'

'We're an important nation and these things can escalate,' he explained. 'There's been trouble in that part of the world for a long time. This has stirred things up good and proper. It's world news, love, and will be in the papers all over Europe and beyond.'

'I'm still not sure exactly why, though,' she persisted, having a thirst for knowledge.

'It's world politics, love,' he explained. 'If powerful nations such as Germany and Russia get involved, then the sparks will really fly and who knows what will happen?'

'War, you mean?'

'No, not necessarily. I don't suppose it will come to that,' he said so as not to worry her. 'And if it does, it won't be anything much.'

'Will it affect us?'

'Dunno, but I shouldn't think so,' he replied. 'I should forget all about it if I were you. It's oceans away from us.'

'A terrible business about the archduke and his wife,' Albert joined in.

'Killed in broad daylight just like that. They got the bloke who did it, but the damage is already done. I reckon there will be more trouble out there for sure.'

The men carried on talking about it, but May concentrated on her baby, who had become wakeful. Rocking her gently, she thought little more of the assassination in some far-off country.

Chapter Ten

'What I can't understand is why *we* have to go to war if Belgium is invaded by the Germans,' said May, during a discussion with the traders at the market one morning in early August when she paid her usual visit with Connie in the pram.

'Because of an ancient treaty,' explained Archie, supported by others in the group, everybody full of the news dominating the headlines at the moment, customers and passers-by lingering to add their comments. 'In 1839 Britain promised to help defend Belgian against any attacker, so we are obligated to honour that commitment if the worst happens.'

'Even now, after all this time?'

'Of course. A promise is a promise, no matter how old it is,' he opined. 'The Germans don't think Britain will honour such an old treaty and fight for Belgium. Some of our politicians are doubtful about it too, according to the papers. But I bet we will.'

'And all of this because the archduke and his wife were murdered in Bosnia?' May queried.

'That brought things to a head, but they reckon it was just the excuse the big nations were waiting for and that's why it's escalated into a major crisis,' explained Archie, who was not an educated man but who was a staunch patriot and an avid reader of newspapers and had been following the current situation closely. 'There's been trouble brewing for ages in Europe. Now that Germany has declared war on Russia and France, things are really serious. The Germans want to invade Belgium in order to defeat France, so we'll have to go to war with Germany if they disregard our warning.'

'It seems very drastic to me,' said May, who hated the idea of war and, rather naively, was unable to see why it couldn't be avoided. 'Our country going to war over something that has nothing to do with us because of some ancient promise. It doesn't seem fair.'

Archie and the others in the group looked at her with a mixture of disapproval and astonishment.

'Oh May, what a thing to say,' said Archie in a tone of heated admonition. 'Of course we must honour our promise. We couldn't possibly renege on our pledge and allow the Belgian people to be invaded by the Germans. Belgium is a neutral country and should be respected as such. We can't stand back and let the Germans ride roughshod over them. It wouldn't be right.'

Whereas May viewed the prospect of war with horror, the others seemed to relish the idea; were even rather excited by it.

'Anyone would think you wanted a war,' she said to Archie disapprovingly.

'I don't want it, of course I don't. Nobody does; but if that's what it takes to right a wrong, then that's what it will have to be.'

'He's right, May.' Even Winnie opposed her on this one. 'But it will all be a long way from here. It'll be over in no time.'

'It would be better if it didn't happen at all,' insisted May.

'It isn't that simple, love,' said Albert.

'Where's your patriotic spirit, May?' urged Archie, giving her a rare frown. 'We all have to stand together at a time like this and be proud of our country and its honourable nature.'

'No one could be more proud of their country than I am,' she stated categorically. 'I just don't happen to be very keen on the idea of war, that's all. There must be other ways of putting things right.'

'Sometimes there just isn't any other way when there are bullying nations to contend with. Anyway, there have always been wars,' Archie pointed out. 'But they don't affect us ordinary people. We have a professional army to fight for us.'

'You just don't get it, do you?' May said, her voice rising. 'I'm not worried for myself; just about the fact that people – whoever and wherever they are – are going to be fighting and lives will be lost, no matter how short the war is. I can't understand why they can't find another way round it.'

'You'll just have to accept that there isn't any other way and stop going on about it,' he told her.

'I think it might be a good idea for you to take your wife out tonight, Archie,' intervened Winnie, moving swiftly on to defuse the tension. 'It might take her mind off all the talk of war, though it'll be hard to escape it wherever you go just at the moment. I'll look after Connie for you. It'll give me a chance to have her to myself. As you don't get to go out together very often, why not make a night of it and go to the West End to see a show? You might get in at the Palladium.'

'Do you both the world of good,' added Albert.

'Would you like that, love?' Archie asked May.

'Yeah, I think I would,' replied May, who still enjoyed the bright lights, though she didn't get out of an evening much since she'd had Connie. A break from the house would make a nice change; it would give her the chance to wear the outfit she'd bought for Bessie's wedding. 'In fact, I think I'd like that very much indeed.'

'That's settled then,' said Winnie happily. 'Tonight, Albert, we are baby-sitting.'

'Fair enough,' he agreed happily. 'But if young Connie screams the place down, I'm going down the pub.'

'Typical male reaction,' she grinned.

The Palladium and the Tivoli were both fully booked, so they found a picture palace showing a film starring May's favourite female film star, Mary Pickford. The auditorium was crowded, the screen misted slightly by the pall of cigarette smoke that hung over everything. The audience shouted at the actors at the slightest provocation and were almost beside themselves in the exciting scenes, the drama emphasised by the pianist at the front turning up the speed and volume accordingly.

Archie smoked numerous cigarettes, and he and May shared a bag of toffees. She grabbed his hand during the scary parts when the heroine looked certain to meet her maker but was saved in the nick of time by the hero.

'Well, did you enjoy it, May?' Archie asked when the lights went up and they joined the crowds heading slowly for the exit. 'It's taken your mind off all this war talk, I hope.'

'Yeah, it was lovely,' she said. 'Mary Pickford reminds me of Bessie on her wedding day with all those lovely curls.'

'Bessie does look a bit similar to her, now that you come to mention it,' he remarked casually, running his eye over his wife's slim figure so prettily enhanced by her pink outfit. 'You look like a film star tonight in your posh clothes.'

'You don't look so bad yourself,' she told him.

Outside in the streets there were people everywhere: some moneyed types in evening dress pouring out of theatres and high-class restaurants; some ordinary folk just here because the West End always drew a crowd. There was usually a buzz in the air here, but tonight there was something else too; a kind of frantic excitement, May thought. The reason for this soon became evident. A rumour spread through the crowds that an important announcement was imminent. People were heading towards Buckingham Palace and Trafalgar Square, singing the national anthem. No one seemed in the least eager to go home.

No one, that is, except May.

'We have a baby to get home to,' she reminded Archie, who was completely caught up in the atmosphere and suggested while they were having supper in a back-street café just off Leicester Square that they join the crowds heading for the Palace, because the King and Queen were expected to come out on the balcony. 'I don't want to take liberties with Auntie. It wouldn't be fair to her.'

'Winnie won't mind holding the fort for a bit longer,' he assured her. 'You know how she loves to look after Connie. She can't get enough of it.'

'I'd rather go home, if that's all right with you.'

'But it's a historic occasion, May.' He was full of it. 'We'll feel more a part of it here in the crowds.'

'Archie, love, the last thing I want to do is spoil your fun, but I simply cannot get excited about the outbreak of war, so I'd rather go home if you don't mind,' she told him. 'But there's no need for you to come with me. You stay and enjoy yourself along with the rest of the bloodthirsty masses.'

'Don't be daft,' he said. 'I wouldn't leave you to go home alone in these crowds.'

'I'll be absolutely fine, honestly. I'm an adult and as such am quite capable of getting around on my own,' she was keen to point out. 'You stay if you want to, but for the life of me I can see nothing even remotely thrilling about being told that this country is at war.'

'It's patriotism that's rousing the people,' he informed her. 'Finish your food and we'll go. I am not going to let you go home on your own at this time of night.'

They dropped the subject and chatted about other things while they finished their pie and mash. When they left and were heading for the station, there was a sudden sound of cheering, which grew and spread to every corner of the crowds on the street. Everyone stood still for a moment, the men waving their hats as they gave voice to their feelings. The news had finally broken. Britain was at war.

'There you are, Archie,' May said tartly. 'You were in the thick of it when history was made after all. You'll be able to tell Connie that when she's grown up.'

'Yeah,' he said, too full of patriotic fervour to notice her acid tone. 'Let's go home now, if we can get anywhere near the station.'

'This lot will be here all night, I reckon,' she said as they picked their way through the multitude.

All around them was the roar of merrymaking.

'They all seemed very pleased,' May observed, 'and I'm blowed if I can understand why.'

'Because our country is not shying away from its responsibilities, that's why,' Archie told her with an air of buoyancy. 'But as I told you before, it's nothing for you to worry your head about. We won't be affected here at home.'

He couldn't have been more wrong.

As well as the fact that the war was the sole topic of conversation among the population of London, the newspapers were full of dreadful stories about German crimes against humanity, which caused a wave of anti-German feeling.

When May went to the WSPU offices to do her voluntary work, she found the shop closed. Constance and some of the others were there clearing out, and she told May that the campaign had ended and orders had come from the top for all members to concentrate their energies wholeheartedly on the war effort on the home front. Within a week of the outbreak of war, the Liberal government released all suffragette prisoners on the understanding that their campaign would cease.

Despite her horror at the thought of war, May couldn't help but be infected by the general mood of patriotism, though the harsh reality of the situation really hit home when recruitment posters appeared every-where, with a formidable and compelling picture of the famous army general Lord Kitchener pointing his finger above a caption that read: YOUR COUNTRY NEEDS YOU. Apparently the experienced, well-trained regular army wasn't large enough to cope with the magnitude of the task ahead of them, and volunteers were urgently needed.

Men responded to the call in their thousands. You couldn't walk past the recruiting office in Hammersmith for the crowds of men queuing to take the King's shilling. The newspapers were filled with stories about recruiting offices all over the country being swamped and men turned away because the staff couldn't cope. All young men, it seemed, wanted to join up.

'They're good lads,' said Archie one evening over their meal. 'They know where their duty lies.'

'I hope you haven't got any daft ideas about joining them,' said May. She cared deeply for Archie and didn't want him to get hurt.

'It's every young and fit man's duty,' he said, obviously keen to join the queues at the recruiting office,

'You're a married man,' she reminded him. Concern for his own life wouldn't deter him, but care for her and Connie most certainly would.

'They won't be away for long,' he said evasively. 'Everyone knows it will be all over by Christmas.'

'Your duty is here with us,' she pointed out. 'It's different for the single men without responsibilities.'

'Don't let anyone outside of these four walls hear you say that, love, especially the wives of the boys who have joined up,' said Winnie gravely. 'Everybody has gone war mad. The general feeling is that it's our duty as women to encourage our men to join up.'

'So now I have to feel guilty because I don't want my husband to go away to war,' said May.

'Nobody *wants* their husbands and sons to go—' Winnie began.

'Uncle is too old, so you'll be all right,' May cut in crossly.

'May,' rebuked Archie. 'Don't take it out on your auntie just because you're angry with me.'

'It's all right,' said Winnie, putting her hand on May's arm. 'I can see that you're upset.'

'Sorry, Auntie,' she apologised. 'I shouldn't have said that. It wasn't fair.' She turned to Archie. 'I'm not angry with you in the least; just a bit afraid for you.'

'There's no need to be,' he assured her. 'I am not going to join up, so you can rest easy. There are so many volunteers anyway, they are turning people away.'

'Thank the Lord for that,' said May. 'Now perhaps can we talk about something else apart from the bloomin' war.'

Christmas came and went and there was no sign of any soldiers coming home victorious; just wounded men returning and tales of some who never would. German warships had reportedly shelled some coastal towns in the north of England, killing and injuring civilians, and there was a lot of talk of possible civilian bombings by German Zeppelins. All of this added fuel to the war fever and did wonders for the recruitment campaign.

May did what she could for the war effort, given that she had a baby to look after. She knitted furiously for the troops, and helped out at various fund-raising events organised by Constance and her colleagues. Winnie and Albert were considering the idea of giving up the stall if the war continued and going to work in one of the munitions factories nearby.

Lord Kitchener's unforgiving expression on the poster continued to reach the conscience of every fit young man, and the queues at the recruitment offices grew ever longer. It wasn't only the finger of Lord Kitchener that pointed at those who hadn't answered the call. Members of the public were doing it too. The accusation of cowardice was being aimed in their direction, quite viciously in some cases.

May and Archie didn't mention the subject of his joining up. But their silence on the subject was beginning to come between them, May sensed, and it worried her through the bitterly cold January days.

Winnie was a great believer in the value of a night out to lift the spirits, and thought that there were few ills a night at the music hall couldn't alleviate, if only for a couple of hours. So, having perceived her niece to be strained and not her usual cheerful self, she suggested that she and May go together one evening in January.

'I'm sure Archie will look after Connie, won't you, love?' she said cheerily. 'You know how good you are with her.'

'I don't mind in the least,' he said in his usual amiable manner. Unlike most men, who steered well clear of an infant until it was an interesting, house-trained child, Archie took an active part in Connie's welfare. He didn't venture too deeply into women's territory by bathing or changing her, but he was very confident with her and played with her, cuddled her and rocked her to sleep. 'You go off and enjoy yourselves. It'll be a nice break for you.'

So it was that May and Winnie, with Archie's blessing, set off for the music hall in their best coats and hats one evening in January.

The house was silent. Connie was asleep upstairs in her cot and Albert had gone down the pub for a quick one. Archie sat in the armchair reading the newspaper and mulling over the painfully conflicting situation he found himself in. On the one hand, he had responsibilities here at home with May and Connie; on the other, he had a duty to his country and felt guiltier about his failure to fulfil it with every day that passed. Things were being said on the market, too; some customers had taken their business elsewhere. He had a broad back; he could take any amount of criticism from other people. It was the grinding self-castigation that got to him, almost like a physical pain.

The newspapers were playing the war news down, but it was obvious that men were getting killed over there in France, and here he was sitting in a comfortable armchair baby-sitting while soldiers in their thousands

163

sat in the trenches in the bitter cold, hoping they managed to dodge enemy bullets and live to see another day. Most of his mates had enlisted now, even some of the married ones, and that exacerbated Archie's feelings of guilt. He was a young man and he was needed over there.

But he was needed here too. Apart from the physical and emotional support May needed from him, what about income? It was a costly business bringing up a baby. Still, the situation was the same for every other working man. For the unemployed it was a gift, as the army paid a wage that could go directly to the wife. So May wouldn't starve, but neither would she get as much as Archie could give her working on the stall. Then there was his father to consider; he was getting on a bit in years now and couldn't be expected to run the stall on his own, what with being up early to go to the wholesale market to buy stock. Archie doubted if Bill would take anyone on, because it had always been a family business and he was traditional about such things.

The relationship hadn't been the same between them since he'd married May but Archie still cared a great deal about his dad. Bill had made it abundantly clear that he thought every fit young man should join up, and told Archie not worry about the stall, so that wasn't the main problem. May was. It was a dilemma indeed. He would do anything in the world for May, but this issue was tearing him apart to the point where he was beginning to hate himself every bit as much as did the woman who had pinned a white feather on him the other day in Hammersmith Broadway.

The sound of the baby crying upstairs recalled him to the present with a start, and he hurried up to the bedroom, where she was standing up peering through the bars of the cot. At nearly a year old, Connie was almost walking on her own. She was a proper little sweetheart and he thought the world of her.

'Come on then, you crafty little minx,' he said, lifting her out of the cot gently. 'What is it, eh, missy? Do you want a bit of attention, fancy a cuddle?'

She continued to grizzle.

'Shush, shush, darlin',' he said softly. 'Everything's all right. Daddy is here.' He lifted her so that her head was resting on his shoulder and walked up and down with her, singing a nursery rhyme. When she still didn't seem ready to settle, he took her downstairs and sat in an armchair with her in his arms, singing to her softly.

There was a cheerful roar of approval in the auditorium as the interval ended and the curtains opened for the second half of the show. Enveloped by the warmth of the audience and the noisy appeal of the entertainers in this smoky theatre, it was easy to relax and let your problems slip to the back of your mind for a while. It wasn't possible to forget the war, though, because the songs were ardently patriotic and the entertainers persuasive in their appeal to the young men in the audience to enlist at a desk behind the stage at the end of the show.

The comedians were particularly powerful in that their serious plea came in the midst of humour. The laughter was hearty, the songs emotive. Everybody rose to their feet when one of the female singers – normally associated with comic songs – gave a serious and emotional rendition of 'Rule Britannia'. Being in the presence of such an outpouring of emotion, it was impossible not to be affected. With tears in her eyes, May was imbued with a sense of unity with the people joined together by adversity; she was at one with them.

She hadn't really been in the mood for a night out but had come along because her aunt had seemed so keen and she hadn't wanted to disappoint her. Now she was very glad to be here.

'Well, did you enjoy it, love?' asked Winnie, linking arms with her niece as they set off on the walk home.

'Very much, Auntie,' she replied. 'Thank you for suggesting it. It was a lovely idea.'

'That's all right, love,' Winnie said, glad that the evening had been a success. 'There's nothing like a good show to blow away the cobwebs, I always think.'

It had certainly done that for May. She hadn't felt so clear headed since the outbreak of war.

When they got home, they found Archie dozing in the armchair with Connie asleep in his arms.

Touched by this evidence of fatherly devotion, May gently woke him and together they went upstairs and put Connie back in her cot.

'Thanks for holding the fort tonight,' she said a bit later when they were drinking cocoa in bed.

'That's all right, love,' he said. 'You enjoyed yourself, that's the main thing. Everybody needs a break.'

'It certainly cleared my head,' she told him, 'and although it breaks my heart to say this, if you want to join up, you have my blessing. I'll be behind you all the way.'

His body softened with relief against her, and she knew in that moment just how worried he had been about not answering the call to fight for his country. 'What about you and Connie, though?' he asked, concerned for them as usual.

'We'll be all right, the same as all the other wives and girlfriends and mothers whose boys have gone away. So don't you worry about anything here. I'll take care of everything and keep the home fires burning. You must follow your heart in this decision, Archie. I'm sorry it's taken so long for me to come to my senses. It was wrong of me to influence you. Do what you think is right, and whatever your decision, you have my full support. We all have to pull together to fight this war. It's my job to let you go if that's what you want.'

He turned to her, and his smile was so wide, anyone would think she'd just told him he'd come into money. 'Thanks, May,' he said. 'You're a diamond.'

'Let's finish our cocoa and settle down,' she said, leaving him in no doubt as to what she had in mind. 'We need to make the most of the time we have left together.'

Never had a beverage been consumed with such speed as his was that night.

'Could I have a word, please, Mr Mott?' asked May.

Archie's father replied with a question of his own: 'What could you possibly have to say that I would want to hear?'

'If you give me a chance I'll tell you.'

It was a few days later and they were in the market café. May had been shopping with Connie in the pram when she'd noticed Archie's father going into the café, leaving Archie holding the fort at the stall. Needing to speak to Bill Mott privately, she had followed, taken Connie out of the pram and gone inside.

He raised his eyes and tutted irritably. 'Can't a man have a cuppa tea in peace?' he grumbled.

'Look, I know you don't like me and I can't say that I'm keen on you, but we have one thing in common: we both think the world of Archie. He's joined the army and will be going away as soon as he gets his papers, so I think it's time you and I had a chat.'

Sighing heavily, Bill waved a hand towards an empty chair at the table. 'As this is a public place I don't suppose I can stop you sitting down. So do so, for Gawd's sake, before you drop that child.'

May seated herself with a struggling Connie on her lap. Bill Mott gave the little girl a spoon to bang on the table.

'She wants to go down on to the floor, that's what she's after,' explained

May. 'She can get around a bit if she holds on to something and she can't get enough of it. But here isn't the place.'

Bill Mott was a man of definite views, a bigot in many ways, but he wasn't totally without manners. 'I would offer you a cuppa tea and something for the little 'un, but I don't fancy the idea of getting soaked to the skin again,' he said drily.

May gave a wry grin. 'There'll be nothing like that,' she told him. 'I promise you.'

'There had better not be,' he said grimly. 'I can't answer for my actions if there is.'

He went to the counter and brought back a cup of tea and a bun for May and a biscuit and milk for Connie.

'Thank you, that's very kind of you,' May said politely.

'Just get on with what you have to say, then leave me in peace to have my break,' he said roughly.

May held the glass to Connie's mouth. She spilled more than she drank because she was used to drinking from a bottle, but May wiped her down and got on and said her piece.

'I'm not asking you to like me or approve of me as Archie's wife,' she began, 'but I do think it would be a good idea for us to forget our differences and join forces while Archie is away so that he can go off to war with an easy mind, knowing that things are being looked after here in his absence.'

Bill looked aghast at the suggestion. 'Join forces . . . in what way?' he asked, eyeing May suspiciously.

'You let me help you out on the stall,' she replied. 'Obviously I'm tied because of Connie, but at least I can cover for you while you have a break now and then. I'll bring her with me and make sure she doesn't suffer by it. Everyone at the market loves her.' She made a face. 'Present company excepted, of course.'

'Absolutely not,' he stated categorically. 'There'll be no need for you to do anything of the sort. I shall manage my business perfectly well on my own. I've been at this game a long time, you know.'

'Exactly, and you're not as young now as you were when you started out.'

'Cheeky cow.'

'I didn't mean to be rude, but it's true, and if you think about it you will see that there is sense in what I say,' she told him determinedly. 'I was thinking that it will be a very long day for you without Archie to help. You'll have to be up early to go to the wholesale market, and without a break all day, it will be too much. I know Archie is worried about you; he says that you will never employ anyone from outside of the family.'

'He's right about that.'

'There you are, then. I know you don't consider me to be family, but technically I am,' she reminded him.

Bill drank his tea slowly, looking at her warily over the rim of his cup. 'What are you after?' he asked. 'Why would you offer to help me? Is it money you're after? Yeah, that must be it. Your sort are all the same; out for what you can get.'

It was hard for May not to act on impulse, but in the interests of improved relations she held her tongue and kept her hands well away from her tea cup.

'I won't rise to the bait and be upset by that remark,' she told him. 'The reason I am offering is probably beyond the comprehension of someone like you. But believe it or not, my motives are not self-seeking. I want to help because you are Archie's father and I want him to go away to war knowing that the two people he loves most in the world will look out for each other in his absence. I'm not asking for a job. I'm not offering to be a full-time assistant or even a part-time one. I couldn't anyway because I have a baby to look after and she is my first priority. I am merely offering you the chance of cover for times like this when you need a break, or any odd errands you might need running, or help at busy times like Saturdays when you have a queue waiting. Yes, I know that you stallholders cover for each other now and then, but there will be times when you need more than the odd ten minutes. The question of money hasn't even entered my head.' She gave him a hard look. 'Soldiers' wives don't find it easy to manage, so I've heard, and if I need to, I will do something to earn a few extra shillings, even if means skivvying for a couple of hours a day, but I wouldn't take money from you, even if I was on my uppers.'

He looked at her through a cloud of smoke from his cigarette. 'And I wouldn't take help from you if I was on my knees.'

'Then you should be damned well ashamed of yourself for your lack of patriotic spirit,' she came back at him. 'Look, Mr Mott, it took me a while to get into the spirit of the war and to know that I have to do my part by letting Archie go with a good grace. Men are showing great courage out there in France; the least you can do is to get along with your son's wife while he is away.'

'I don't see why I should. After all, he won't be any the wiser, will he?' Bill pointed out.

'That's very true,' she said. 'But it's hardly the point. We are supposed to be pulling together.'

'Why can't you get it into your head that I don't want you or your sprog anywhere near me?' he said.

Her hand edged towards the tea cup and she forced it back and said in a dignified manner, 'All right, if you really don't want Connie and me in your life, then there's nothing more to be said. So I'll finish this and we'll be on our way. It's a pity to waste it.' She looked at her daughter, who was nibbling her biscuit and staring thoughtfully at Bill in that unwavering way that infants had. Her milk was only half finished. 'Are you going to drink your milk, darlin'?'

As May reached her hand forward to pick up the glass of milk, her daughter had the same idea and her chubby little fingers got there first, knocking the glass on to its side and sending the contents all over Bill's front.

'Oh Christ, not again,' he burst out, standing up and spreading his hands in a helpless gesture. 'You're a bloody savage.'

'I'll get a cloth,' said May, put at a disadvantage by the mishap. She picked up a now screaming Connie and went to the counter, coming back with a cloth. 'Here, hang on to the baby for me while I clean you up.' She handed the child to him. 'I am very sorry. This time it really was an accident.' She looked at him, ignoring his furious expression. 'If you could hold her higher up by your chest so I can mop it off your trousers . . . That's it, thanks.'

He looked most uneasy holding the baby, as though she might have the habits of a viper, while May got the worst of the spillage off his clothes, mopped the table and took the cloth back to the counter.

'Come on, sweetheart,' she said to her daughter, who had stopped crying and was now being held more comfortably against Bill's upper chest. 'Let's go and see Daddy, then we'll get our shopping done and go home.'

But Connie seemed to like it where she was and snuggled into Bill's shoulder, smearing soggy biscuit crumbs all over his coat. When May took hold of her firmly and dragged her away, she opened her mouth and emitted an ear-piercing scream, reaching out her arms to Bill, face red and wet with tears.

'We're going now, and you're going in your pram with dolly, all warm and cosy; won't that be lovely?' May said persuasively, rocking her in her arms. 'There, there, shush, shush.'

As Connie calmed down and the crying abated, May said to Bill Mott, 'For some reason she wants to stay with you. She's too little to know that you're a nasty, vindictive man with a closed mind and an evil tongue. I really don't know how you came to have such a fine son as Archie. He must have inherited his lovely nature from his mother; he certainly didn't get it from you. I came to see you today in the spirit of friendship, and you've thrown it back in my face, so you can work yourself to death while Archie is away as far as I'm concerned.'

With that she marched out, put her daughter back in the pram and set forth to do her shopping. She was so angry she could hardly contain herself. How did sweet-natured Archie come to have such a horrible man as a father?

Archie was whistling and singing around the house in his usual way, as though he didn't have a care in the world, the evening before his departure to an army camp in the country. No one would guess that he was going away in the morning to be trained for battle.

Such was the public's confidence in victory, you sometimes heard of men going off to war singing cheerful songs like 'Pack Up Your Troubles', but May knew her husband wasn't as blasé as he seemed. It was in his nature to be jolly, and he was always singing and whistling, but it was just a little too boisterous this evening. The strain in the atmosphere was palpable. They were both being overly nice to each other.

Knowing Archie as she did, she guessed that the battlefield wouldn't be his main worry – he was too fired up with a sense of duty and pride in his country for that; he wanted to be there in action with all the others – it was leaving her and Connie that would bother him most at this stage. Though of course, any sane man going away to war must surely be apprehensive, even though they considered it the height of cowardice to admit it.

He was in their bedroom, sitting beside Connie's cot watching her sleep, when Winnie called up the stairs to him.

'Someone to see you, Archie,' she said.

They both went down. Much to May's amazement, it was Bill Mott.

'Just popped round to say a final ta-ta and wish you luck,' he said to Archie. Winnie and Albert made themselves scarce in the kitchen. 'I know I said goodbye to you after work but I want you to know that I'm proud of you, son.'

May could see by the look in his eyes and the slight tremble of his mouth that Archie was very touched, but he just shrugged and said, 'Thanks, Dad. But I'll hardly be gone any time. It'll probably be all over by the time I get there. You concentrate on looking after yourself. I hope you

170

manage on the stall without me. I reckon you'll have to take someone on, though. I know you say you can cope but I can't see how one pair of hands will be enough.'

'I'll see how it goes,' responded Bill with a casual air. 'But don't you worry about anything here at home. Your missus and I will look out for each other, so you can go away with an easy mind and concentrate on the job.'

Puzzled, Archie looked at him and then at May, who was as astonished as Archie was by these words. He transferred his gaze back to his father. 'You and May?' he said. 'Looking out for each other?'

'Yeah, that's right,' Bill confirmed.

'But you don't get on,' Archie reminded him.

'You're talking in the past tense,' Bill said, astounding May further. 'That's all behind us.'

'Really?' asked Archie.

'It's at times like this that families need to stick together, so that's what we are going to do,' explained Bill.

'I couldn't agree more, Mr Mott,' said May uncertainly, but delighted by his sudden change of heart and the fact that Archie was obviously pleased.

'You've taken a load of my mind, I can tell you,' Archie told him. 'I've been worrying myself silly about the pair of you while I'm away. But if you're going to support each other until I get back, that isn't nearly so bad. I'm really chuffed. You know how much I've always wanted you to be friends.'

'Well now we are, so you can stop worrying,' said Bill Mott, beaming at his son.

'Why don't the two of you go down the pub for a pint together as you won't be seeing each other for a while?' May suggested on impulse. 'Father and son together; it will do you both good.'

Archie looked at her and then at his father. 'See what a lovely wife I've got, Dad,' he said, smiling proudly. 'She encourages me to go out drinking, whereas some wives would give a bloke a whole load of earache over it.'

'I said a pint, not a pub crawl,' she grinned, though in actual fact she wouldn't have minded if he'd come home blind drunk on this occasion. Any man about to risk his life for his country was entitled to let his hair down on his last night of freedom.

'Get your coat then,' said Bill, heading for the door as though in a hurry to leave. 'Come on now, boy, don't hang about. I'll wait for you outside.'

'Ta-ta love,' Archie said, kissing May briefly on the cheek. 'Shan't be very long.'

'You stay as long as you like and enjoy yourself,' she said warmly.

'I'll do my best.'

As soon as she heard the front door slam behind them, her expression changed, her brow furrowing at the thought of what he would soon have to face. Encouraging your man to do his duty was one thing; wanting him to do it was quite another!

Having said all his goodbyes the night before, Archie slipped from the house before it was light the next morning with one last private embrace with May at the door. She didn't make a big thing of it because she knew he didn't want that.

Later that morning, when she went to the market for her shopping as usual, she headed straight to the Mott stall to speak to Bill. He was serving a customer so she waited until he'd finished, smiling and expecting a warm welcome.

'What do *you* want?' he asked in a surprisingly hostile manner, his eyes cold and hard.

'I just wanted to say how pleased I am that you've had a change of heart.'

'Oh yeah, and what change of heart might that be?' he asked in a supercilious manner.

'About Connie and me, of course,' she replied, puzzled by his attitude. 'What else would I be talking about?'

'I've had no change of heart,' he told her.

'But when you came round last night you said—'

'I didn't mean a word of it,' he cut in. 'It was all just for Archie's benefit. I thought you would realise that. You must be even dimmer than I thought.'

'You devious old sod.'

'Look, you wanted Archie to go away with an easy mind, and so did I, so I took a few liberties with the truth. What's wrong with that?' he wanted to know.

'It's downright deceitful.'

'But he went off smiling this morning, and that's all that matters to me,' he said. 'So you and I can carry on as before and no harm done. What's so terrible in that?'

'To your corrupt little mind, nothing, I suppose.'

'Good, that's settled then,' he said, ignoring her barb. 'We can continue as usual and completely ignore each other while he's away. We'll have to

172

put on some pretence when he comes home on leave, I suppose. Still, we'll worry about that when the time comes.'

She looked at him long and hard. 'Is that really what you want, Mr Mott? For us to stay strangers?' she asked, her eyes never leaving his face. 'Really and truly what you want?'

'I wouldn't have said it if it wasn't, would I?' he replied, irritated. 'Cor blimey; talk about thick skinned. What more can I say to get it into your dull little head that I want you to stay away from me?'

'Nothing more, you pigheaded old bigot,' she burst out. 'I won't come near you again and that's a promise.'

'Thank God for that,' he said.

'My feelings exactly,' was her parting shot. 'You are the rudest man I have ever come across and I never want to speak to you again.'

Turning away, May pushed the pram over to her aunt and uncle's stall, fuming. It said something about the strength of feeling some people had about girls who got themselves into trouble that they would rather be lonely and overworked than accept a helping hand from anyone who had made that mistake, even though that someone was now proving herself to be a good wife and mother.

If she hadn't treated his son right Bill would be entitled to think ill of her. Also, she could understand that he would want a grandchild of his own, not have to pretend to be grandfather to a child with no blood tie. But surely that was no reason to treat May with such venom. He and her mother were two of a kind. They were completely rigid in their opinions and determined not to budge. It made May feel sad as well as angry, though she couldn't understand why it mattered to her so much in the case of Bill Mott.

'Ooh, you don't look any too happy,' observed Winnie. 'Are you missing Archie already?'

May couldn't count the number of times she had thanked God for her aunt, and she did so again now, wholeheartedly. She wanted to bare her soul to her about Bill Mott but held back because she knew that Auntie would go straight over there and give him a tongue-lashing in her defence. Nobody upset Winnie's niece and got away with it. May didn't want her auntie and uncle to fall out with Bill on her account. It would cause an awkward atmosphere on the market, especially as they had been friends with him for years.

So she just said, 'Yeah, course I am.'

'I shall miss him about the place too,' confessed Winnie. 'He's such a larger-than-life character. Always happy, is Archie. Still, I don't suppose he'll be away for long.'

173

'Let's hope not.'

'Come and have a cuppa with me in the café, love. That'll cheer you up,' Winnie suggested.

'Thanks, Auntie, but I won't if you don't mind,' May said, having an overwhelming need to be alone with her thoughts. 'I'll just do my shopping and go home to get on with the chores.'

'See you later then,' said Winnie.

There was only one person May wanted to be with at this moment, and that was her sister Bessie. She was the one person she could unburden herself to about anything at all, and she needed her so much right now. Oh well, chin up, she told herself as she did her shopping and walked home. She was lucky she had dear Aunt Winnie, whose loyalty and support never faltered.

Anyway, Bessie had problems of her own; in her last letter she'd said that Jim had joined the army too. May hoped she was bearing up under the strain. She did miss her so.

Chapter Eleven

June 1915

Dear May,

I hope you are well, and managing to keep your spirits up without Archie's cheery presence to keep you going. It's very hard to have our men go away to war but we have to put a brave face on it because it's much worse for them. I miss dear Jim during every waking moment and I expect it's the same for you.

The good news from me is that I am expecting a baby at the end of the year, and I couldn't be more delighted. As luck would have it, they gave Jim some home leave recently so I was able to tell him then and he was thrilled to bits. He thinks he'll be going to France some time soon so he'll have that lovely news to keep him going; something special to look forward to when he comes home.

There's bad news too, I'm afraid. My ex-employer Digby Parsons has died since I last wrote. It was very sudden; a heart attack, apparently. It was a terrible shock and I'm very sad about it as he was a sweet man and I was fond of him, as you know. I was very touched because he left me his camera and photographic equipment in his will. His instructions are for me to have it and use it because, in his opinion, I have potential as a photographer and he wants the things so precious to him to be used by someone with an interest and flair for photography. Isn't that lovely?

When Jim was home on leave I was able to take a picture of him in uniform, and very grand he looked too. I have the photograph framed and sitting on the mantelpiece so I can look at it whenever I feel like it. It makes him feel closer somehow. I've done a few of local lads who are going away to war, for their wives and mothers, and they have all been very pleased with the finished product.

Portraits of servicemen in uniform are very popular at the moment, which is understandable. I only charge a small amount on top of the cost of the film and developing, but I do ask anyone outside of the family to pay a token fee as it isn't easy to manage on a soldier's pay, as I'm sure you are finding out for yourself by now. With a baby on the way I can't afford to be casual about money. The photographic conditions are very makeshift, though. I use my front room as a studio because the light is good in there, and I do the developing in Dad's garden shed.

Mum says I should move back in with them now that Jim is away to save the rent on this place, but I want to keep a home of our own for Jim when he comes back, if I possibly can. You need the privacy when you're married as I'm sure you know. I love our little cottage, mine and Jim's, so I'll just have to see how it goes and hope that he isn't away for too long.

Mum and Dad are much the same and Sam can't wait to join up when he's old enough, more than ever now that he's out with Dad on the boat full time. Of course he's much too fond of terra firma to join the navy so it will be the army for him if the war isn't over by then.

How is everything in London? Have you had many air raids? We've heard that there have been some but they say that the newspapers aren't allowed to report any details so we don't know where they are. Please write soon and let me know the latest. I still miss you and wish we could see each other more often. I must come and see you soon; maybe before I get too huge, though I'm fattening up nicely already.

Much love to Auntie and Uncle and a big hug and kiss to Connie from me.

Love,
Bessie

Sitting on the sofa with her writing pad on her lap, Bessie addressed the envelope and stuck on the stamp. Glancing around the room where she and Jim used to sit together when the work of the day was done, the morning sun now filtering through the net curtains, she was pierced with longing for Jim's return. It was a dear little cottage at a different angle to her parents' home, so that the front of the house had a good view of the waterside.

Now she set off for the postbox along the sun-washed street, the tiny front gardens in full bloom with such favourites as hollyhocks, roses

176

and marigolds. The tide was out and the ferryman was punting the boat across from the other bank because the strip of water was so narrow he didn't need the oars. Although there were plenty of people about on the main thoroughfare that ran parallel to the river – all with a few friendly words for her as they passed by – the ambience here was one of quiet timelessness.

Along the waterside, things were not as busy as in pre-war times. Fishermen still worked along the quays, but there were fewer of them. Most of the young men had joined up: some had become soldiers; many, already being seamen, had gone into the navy; others were working on merchant ships.

There were restrictions in force now for the remaining fishermen. Each smack needed a permit and was only allowed to fish in certain waters off the coast. The population locally had been enlarged temporarily by the servicemen billeted here and in Haverley as well as at Colchester barracks, because the government had feared that the Germans might invade by coming in to land on the Essex coast.

Bessie and most other villagers had found this rather a daunting prospect in the early months of the war, but as time passed and no such invasion happened, confidence grew. The village threw itself into the war effort: there were knitting groups to make socks, scarves and sweaters for the troops, and fêtes, jumble sales and concerts in the church hall to raise money.

Now she dropped the letter into the postbox and headed home. As she approached the ferry landing point, the boat arrived and her heart sank as she saw Joan Parsons step out.

The drawback of her legacy from Digby had been carefully omitted in Bessie's letter to May. There was no point in having her sister fret about the trouble Bessie was having with Joan Parsons over it. Digby apparently hadn't been as wealthy as his daughter had imagined – which wasn't surprising considering the lavish way she used to spend his money – and although she had inherited his house and all his worldly goods apart from those he left to May, she no longer had the income from his business to maintain her lifestyle. Having staunchly refused to learn her father's craft, and being of an idle disposition anyway, she couldn't step into his shoes and keep the business going to pay the overheads and create a personal income for herself.

The shop and studio had only been rented by Digby and were already let out to someone else. Because of these factors, Joan begrudged Bessie her small inheritance and thought most ardently that she should return

177

the photographic equipment to its rightful owner. Bessie was not a greedy woman, and had Joan been left in poor circumstances, she would have considered complying with her wishes. But Joan was well placed financially.

By the look on her face now, Bessie was in for another ear-bashing.

'I was just coming to see you,' Joan announced.

'This will save you the walk to my house then, won't it?' Bessie replied tensely.

'Have you reconsidered your decision?' she demanded.

Bessie heaved an eloquent sigh. 'Your father made the decision when he made his will.'

'I should have been the sole beneficiary,' Joan declared. 'I could take this to court.'

'But you won't because you know you don't have a case,' suggested Bessie.

'The silly old fool didn't know what he was doing,' Joan said spitefully. 'I could claim that he was of unsound mind.'

'You wouldn't stand a chance with that, given that he was still working until the day before he died.'

'Why don't you just do the decent thing and let me have the stuff that belongs to me?'

'Because I was very honoured that your father wanted me to have it,' she replied. 'It's a personal thing.'

'It's greed, pure and simple,' argued Joan.

'What would you do with it if you had it anyway?' Bessie enquired.

'Sell it, of course, since my dear father has left me with a house to maintain but nothing to do it with, and very little to live on from week to week.'

'The money you would get from the photographic equipment wouldn't last you any time at all,' Bessie pointed out. 'It's old and hardly worth anything in financial terms.'

'It would be something to tide me over.'

'Not for long, I can assure you.'

'What am I supposed to do, then?'

'You could get a job,' suggested Bessie. 'There's plenty of work about for women nowadays because of the war.'

The look Joan gave Bessie could surely have withered Lord Kitchener himself. 'Don't be ridiculous,' she rasped. 'People like me don't go out to work.'

'Maybe they didn't before the war,' Bessie informed her, 'but everything is different now. Women of a higher social class than you are rolling up their sleeves and getting jobs in factories, on the post and the railway, filling vacancies left by the men who have gone away to war. There are all sorts of opportunities these days.'

'I am not going out to work.'

'Why not sell your big house and get a smaller one?' Bessie recommended, trying to be helpful. 'You could live on the difference.'

'I am not selling my house.'

'Take some lodgers, then.'

Another contemptuous look headed Bessie's way. 'Me a landlady?' she exploded. 'Are you completely mad?'

'In that case, your only hope is to find a husband to support you.'

'Fat chance of that, since all the eligible men are away at the war,' Joan snorted.

Bessie cast a studious eye over the other woman. She was dressed in a fashionable silk dress in pink with a matching parasol and pretty shoes, her hair styled into kiss curls beneath her up-to-the-minute toque-shaped hat. It would be difficult for any woman not to look beautiful in that outfit, but somehow Joan didn't. She looked elegant and grand but not beautiful. In fact she was rather plain.

But Bessie had a sudden moment of insight and saw beyond the public persona to a young woman feeling desperate about her situation. She had been pampered and spoiled to such an extent that now that her support had gone, she was helpless. Digby had created a monster who couldn't cope without him.

'Do you have any relatives who could advise you as to what to do?' Bessie enquired in a kindlier tone. 'Aunts or uncles perhaps who might help you to invest the money wisely if you were to sell your house and get a smaller one?'

'I've plenty of aunts and uncles but none of them want to be bothered with me for some reason,' Joan replied.

It seemed incredible to Bessie that Joan really had no idea how her rude and selfish behaviour might offend other people. Her father had pandered to her so completely, she obviously thought it was acceptable.

'I don't know much about house sales, as I've always lived in rented accommodation, but I believe there are professional people who deal with that sort of thing.'

'Why should I sell my house?' Joan burst out furiously, her eyes filling with angry tears. 'What right do you have to tell me what to do? You're nothing.'

179

'I have no right at all,' said Bessie, rattled but managing to stay outwardly calm. 'I was just trying to help.'

'Give me what is rightfully mine then, if you want to help,' she demanded.

'I have nothing that is yours,' Bessie came back at her, determined not to be bullied into doing as she asked. 'Your father left it to me because he wanted me to make good use of it, which I am doing. It was given to me because he judged me to have a flair for photography. It means a lot to me that he made that gesture. He wouldn't want it to be sold.'

'In what way are you using the equipment, exactly?' asked Joan, narrowing her eyes suspiciously.

'Taking photographs, of course,' Bessie replied. 'I wouldn't be cooking the dinner with it, would I?'

Joan gave her a questioning look. 'Are you making money from it?' she demanded.

'I don't know if you could call it making money, but I do charge a small fee to non-family members to cover the cost of materials and a token amount for my time,' she replied.

'Oh, that is downright disgusting,' Joan lashed out. 'You are capitalising on my father's death, making money with his things, things that don't belong to you.'

'How many more times must I tell you: your father wanted me to use the equipment, which is why he left it to me.' Bessie could feel her temper rising and her heart palpitating, which couldn't be good for a woman in her condition. 'My husband is away at the war and I have a baby on the way. I need every penny I can get, so I can't afford to give the photographs away, no matter how much I might want to.'

This previously unknown news of Bessie's circumstances enraged Joan even more, for some reason. 'Oh, so you're pregnant, are you? I thought you'd put on weight lately,' she said, becoming angrier with every syllable. 'You think you've got it all, don't you? A husband, a baby on the way and equipment that belongs to me. You money-grabbing bitch. The only reason you were kind to my father was so that he would leave you something when he died.'

Almost of its own volition Bessie's hand flew through the air and landed on Joan's cheek with a whack, and while she stood there holding her face in a state of disbelief that anyone would have the audacity to stand up to her in such a way, Bessie delivered a few home truths.

'You have more in material terms than I shall ever have,' she began. 'You would still have a lot of money to play with if you were to sell your big house and move into a smaller one, whereas I shall probably live from hand to mouth in rented property for the rest of my life. That is what people of my class do. But we have values, integrity and love for each other, something you will probably never experience. So don't come here demanding something that belongs to me. That equipment is mine and I am *not* going to give it to you.' She paused for breath. 'So what are you going to do? Break into my house and steal it one night while I am sleeping? Try it and you'll have the police at your door.'

The other woman was standing aghast, still holding her face. Suddenly she lunged at Bessie and laid into her, punching her around the head and shoulders then giving her an almighty shove in the chest that sent her staggering over the bank. She landed with an almighty thump on the mud of the river bed, shock waves reverberating throughout her body.

Joan herself seemed astonished by her own actions. She just stood staring at Bessie as she struggled to her feet, slipping and sliding, her clothes covered in dark brown slime.

'If my pregnancy is affected because of this,' Bessie warned her breathlessly as she eventually got to her feet, bedraggled and mud covered, 'I will make sure you suffer, believe me. So you had better pray to God that all is well.'

Pale with fright, Joan turned and ran towards the ferry without another word, leaving a shaken Bessie to walk home alone. She had taken quite a tumble and was feeling upset and worried for her baby, her legs trembling.

One thing she was sure of. She wouldn't see Joan Parsons around here again for a while. Attacking a pregnant woman was low, even by her standards. Surely Joan, as self-obsessed as she was, must be feeling ashamed of herself.

Once Bessie had washed and changed her clothes she felt a lot better, but she took things easy just to be on the safe side. At least she was past the three-month stage, which was said to be the most fragile time in a pregnancy. As the day wore on and there didn't seem to be any ill effects from the fall, she went round to see her mother. Most days she called in at Berry Cottage for a chat and to take the dog for a walk, something she still enjoyed and that reminded her of Jim.

She wasn't planning on telling her mother about the events of the morning because she didn't want to worry her. But as it happened, Edie had some news of her own and was far too full of that to notice that her daughter looked pale and strained.

'I'm thinking of getting a job,' she announced over a cup of tea in the kitchen.

'A job? You?' Bessie was so surprised she spilt her tea.

'There's no need to look so shocked,' admonished her mother. 'I'm not a complete dimwit, you know.'

'Of course not,' Bessie assured her in a definite tone, mopping up the spilled tea with a cloth. 'I just can't imagine you going out to work. You've always been such a great believer in the idea that a woman's place is exclusively in the home.'

'I still am, but there's a war on and we all have to do our bit to help,' she said. 'Besides, the money would come in handy. The new fishing restrictions are making it even harder for your father to make a decent living. Mrs Todd next door has just started work at the factory making army uniforms. She said they need people urgently and they give you training.'

'I think it's a very good idea, Mum,' responded Bessie, though she had doubts as to how her mother would interact with her workmates, given that she was so prim and proper and not the most social of souls. 'Are you thinking in terms of part time?'

'Oh yes. I wouldn't want the family to suffer by it. I'll make sure your father and brother always have a clean house and a meal on the table when they get in.' She paused as though choosing her words carefully. 'And I'm sure there will be times when you might need my help when the baby comes. Though the war will probably be over by then so that we can all revert to normal.'

'I'm banking on the war being over by then,' Bessie told her. 'I'll be very disappointed if Jim is still away when the baby is born.'

'Everybody thought it would be over by Christmas last year, and here we are in the summer and still no sign of an end to it,' said Edie. 'Still, we live in hope. I don't see how it can drag on for much longer.'

'Me neither,' agreed Bessie.

To Gentle Jim Minter, as his army mates called him on account of his mild-mannered nature, victory seemed nothing more than a distant dream as he marched with his platoon in the driving autumn rain through the muddy fields and orchards of France. He was drenched to the skin, dirty, exhausted and demoralised. The reality of war was very different from the picture they had painted at the recruitment centre.

He had known it would be a challenge, of course, but he hadn't expected to see troops mown down in rows by enemy machine-gunners, or soldiers so heavily laden down by the packs they were forced to carry when they went into battle that they staggered rather than walked and were easy targets for the enemy.

Jim would never forget seeing his comrades dropping in their hundreds in a recent battle; the shortage of shells on the British side meant that they hadn't even been able to put up a proper fight against the German machine-gunners, so there had been no breakthrough.

Somehow, and he would never know how, Jim had survived while others died around him; a profoundly traumatic experience and something that he knew would haunt him for the rest of his life, however short that might be. There was no skill or trick to staying alive as far as he could see. It had nothing to do with being faster, cleverer or braver than the next man. It seemed to him to be a lottery. You did your best and lived in hope.

A few couldn't take it. Some of them, not much more than boys, had tried to run away and had been taken away and executed. The slightest sign of cowardice was rewarded by death, and the names of those who died in this way were read out to the rest as a warning. To Jim it was utterly barbaric.

Still, at least he was having a break from the trenches, living under shell- and gunfire, the conditions unimaginable: the itching from the lice, the rats biting while you slept and the stench of rotting dead soldiers. It was surprising how such horror became commonplace when you lived with it day after day.

It seemed unpatriotic to even have thoughts of discontent. This was a war so what had he expected when he'd rushed to the recruiting office so eager to do his duty? Action, yes; pride in his country also, but not the complete disregard for human life he experienced on a daily business.

He thought of his sweet and lovely Bessie and ached with missing her. He hoped she was all right and that all was well with the pregnancy. It was thoughts of her and home that kept him going during the long days of boredom and exhaustion interspersed with periods of terror and despair. Fear was a permanent state, and any man who claimed not to be frightened must be lying. Steering his thoughts back to his wife, he knew he was lucky to have Bessie. He had hardly been able to believe it when such a beautiful young woman had taken a fancy to a skinny schoolteacher like him.

At one time he had hoped they would be blessed with a son, but not now. Boys grew into men and could be called upon to fight for their country. He never wanted any child of his to have to go through this. So a daughter was what he wished for now; a little girl with her mother's looks and beautiful nature.

An explosion rent the air, followed by gunfire.

'Here we go again,' said the soldier next to him as they fell to the ground with rifles at the ready.

'Yep,' said Jim. 'Let's get the buggers this time.'

'That's right. The sooner we get the job done, the sooner we can go home.'

The men focused all their energies on the job in hand. Kill or be killed, that was the premise here. Oh to be in England, thought Jim, reciting the first line of the poem in his head to calm him. Oh to be in England with Bessie on a summer's day, or any day at all . . .

Bullets whizzed past his head and shells exploded nearby. The man next to him was hit by a bullet and after a brief cry lay still. Jim continued firing. Somehow he had to survive this carnage for Bessie and the baby.

'Well I'll be blowed,' said May, reading the latest letter from her sister one morning over breakfast in the late autumn. 'Good grief. You won't believe it, Auntie.'

'Tell me what it is then, girl, for goodness' sake, before I die of curiosity,' Winnie urged her.

May gave Connie – who would be two in a few months – a helping hand with her porridge. 'Mum's got a job,' she announced.

'No! She never has!'

'She has. She's working in a factory making army uniforms, and even more surprising, she likes it.'

'Get away. I can't imagine Edie going out to work, let alone in a factory.'

'Neither can I. But Bessie says she seems to be getting along fine with the other women.' May glanced through the letter again. 'She runs her day like a military exercise so that the household isn't disrupted, apparently. She gets up at the crack of down to do the household chores and always has a meal ready for Dad and Sam when they come in from work. She prepares all the meals ahead and does the ironing at night.'

'That's typical of Edie,' remarked Winnie. 'She always has been a most diligent housewife and wouldn't have her household routine upset for anything. Not even a war.'

'Always puts the family first, eh, Auntie,' said May with a bitter edge to her tone. 'Always the devoted mother.'

Winnie lowered her eyes, picked up her tea cup and drank slowly. 'We are what we are, love,' she reminded her niece. 'I'm sure she did her best for you when you were growing up. You can't discount that because of what happened later.'

'Are you defending her?'

'Yes, I suppose I am,' she replied thoughtfully. 'She is my sister, after all, and she does have her good points. Personally I'd like to see the two of you patch things up. It isn't right the way things are at the moment. I know you feel that way too.'

'You must be very perceptive then, Auntie,' May said. 'Because I'm not sure how I feel about it myself, except that I'm still hurt that Mum chucked me out.'

'In your heart you'd like to have it put right. It isn't in you to bear a grudge.'

May looked at her, puzzled. 'How come you know so much about me?'

'You and I have become pretty close this last couple of years,' Winnie replied. 'With everything that's happened, and living in the same house.'

'Yeah, that's true.' May grinned, teasing her. 'You're a wily old bird, though.'

'Oi, you. Not so much of the old.'

'Seriously, Auntie I think the time for reconciliation with Mum has passed,' she said.

'It isn't too late.'

'Talking of being late, won't you be late for work?' said May, in a swift change of subject.

Winnie looked at the clock on the wall. 'I'm all right for a minute or two.' She helped Connie guide the spoon of porridge directly into her mouth rather than via her ears and hair. 'I've got time for another cup of tea. Do you want one?'

May nodded and Winnie refilled their cups. 'It must seem odd having to worry about a time clock instead of Uncle Albert,' suggested May. Her aunt and uncle had given up the stall until after the war and both worked in war factories now. Uncle Albert was on an early shift and had already gone to work.

'Not half,' she said. 'I miss the market something awful and can't wait to get back to it after the war. Still, we all have to do our bit, and the money is good in the factory.'

'I'd do it myself if it wasn't for Connie, but I don't want to get her minded.'

'Your place is with her, love,' opined Winnie. 'You don't want to miss a single moment of her while she's little. She'll grow up soon enough.'

'Yeah, I know,' May agreed, taking into account the fact that since her aunt hadn't any children of her own, she viewed these things with a certain wistfulness. 'And I do what I can in the way of voluntary work for the war effort. As long as I can take Connie with me, I'll do anything.'

'Never underestimate your role as a mother, dear.'

'I don't, Auntie. I love being a mum,' she told her. 'She's growing up too fast. It's time I had another baby.' She looked at her aunt. 'It would be nice to have one with Archie.'

'He'd be all for that.'

'I'll just have to hope that he comes home soon so that we can get started on it,' she laughed.

'You'll get no argument from him about that side of it,' chuckled Winnie.

'I don't even know where he is, let alone when he's coming home,' May said. 'They're not allowed to say much when they write. The letters are censored anyway. He's in a foreign field somewhere, and that's all I know.'

'Let's hope it won't be too long before the war is won and he is home for good,' said Winnie, finishing her tea and rising. 'In the meantime, I have to go to work.'

'I'll do the clearing up and get your shopping for you down the market,' said May.

'Thanks, love. That will be a great help.'

'The least I can do is to lend a hand with the domestics while you're out doing war work.'

Winnie gave her a hug, seeming oddly emotional suddenly. 'You're a good girl,' she said, wiping her eyes with the back of her hand and turning to Connie. 'You've got a mummy in a million, Connie; a real diamond.'

'All this flattery,' smiled May, laughing it off. 'I shall think you're after something if you keep on.' She gave her aunt a look. 'Only teasing. I would never think that of you.'

'I should hope not.'

For some reason that May didn't understand, the air was suddenly fraught with emotion and May felt wet eyed herself. How very peculiar, she thought, as her aunt scuttled off and she herself finished feeding Connie.

Most of the food stalls in the market were still operating – mainly manned by men beyond the age for military service or women – but some of those that traded in less essential items had closed down for the duration of the war while their owners had either gone into the services or on to war work.

Because of the bad feeling that existed between Bill Mott and herself, May never bought her greengrocery from his stall now that Archie wasn't working on it. But as she wheeled Connie through the market in the pushchair to get her shopping that morning, she noticed that his stall was empty, with no sign of life. She was immediately concerned, because Bill never normally missed opening for business. She asked the man on the pie stall if he knew where he was.

'He'll be at home nursing his injuries, I expect.'

'Injuries?' A knot drew tight in May's stomach. 'What's happened to him?'

'He got into a fight with a bloke in the pub last night,' he explained.

'No . . .'

'Oh yes. They had a right old ding-dong,' he told her. 'The pub landlord threw them out and they carried on fighting in the street.'

'What on earth was a man of his age doing fighting?'

The man shrugged. 'The bloke said something that offended him and there was no stopping him. He was like a mad thing. I've never seen anything like it.'

'Was he badly hurt?'

The man gave her a direct look. 'The other bloke was a lot younger and fitter than him, put it that way,' he explained. 'So I'm not at all surprised that Bill isn't up to work today.'

'Oh, that stupid man,' she exclaimed, saying goodbye to the trader and turning and hurrying off towards Bill's house, wheeling Connie in the pushchair.

Bill lived in a small terraced house in a Hammersmith back street. May had to knock at the front door for a long time before it was finally opened.

'Oh, it's you,' said Bill gruffly when he opened the door clad in a red woollen dressing gown. He peered at her painfully, one of his eyes black and badly swollen. The other eye was puffy, and there was a bruise on his cheek and several angry-looking grazes on his face. 'What do you want?'

'You are your usual charming self then,' she said with irony. 'Have I got you out of bed?'

'No. I was up. I just hadn't got round to getting dressed yet,' he told her. 'Why are you here?'

'I should have thought that was perfectly obvious,' she answered. 'I heard what happened last night and I've come to see if you're all right.'

'So now that you've seen that I am, you can go, can't you?' was his gruff reply.

'Come off it. I've got eyes in my head. I can see that you are far from all right.'

'What business is it of yours anyway?'

She replied with a question of her own: 'What is a man of your age doing fighting in the street like a common lout? You ought to be thoroughly ashamed of yourself.'

'Clear off and leave me alone,' he demanded.

'I certainly will not. I'm coming in.'

'No you are not.'

'Oh don't be so damned ridiculous, man,' she admonished sternly. 'You need someone to do something about those cuts and bruises. Let me come and do it. And don't raise your voice or you'll upset my daughter.'

Connie was already squirming to get out of the pushchair so May unstrapped her, whereupon she ran up to Bill smiling with her arms up.

'Grandad can't pick you up at the moment, darlin',' said May, taking her daughter's hand and walking past Bill into the hall. 'He's hurt himself.'

'I'm not her—' began Bill, following her inside and closing the door.

May held up her hands in a restraining gesture. 'I know all about the technicalities, but don't go on about it now; not in front of Connie, please.'

He sighed heavily. 'Oh well, as I'm obviously not going to get rid of you until it suits you, you might as well come on through.'

They went through to his kitchen, a narrow slit of a room surprisingly well kept for a man living alone. His first-aid kit consisted of an old tin of ointment and some bandage. May did her best with those, washing the wounds with some clean rag while he sat obediently on a kitchen chair, wincing every so often.

'What was the fight about anyway?' she asked.

'That's my business.'

'I'm only taking a polite interest.'

'Well don't,' he snapped. 'You know it isn't welcome.'

Connie, who was standing by her mother's side clutching a rag doll that she took everywhere with her, started crying.

'Now see what you've done with your nasty manner,' May reproached. 'Children are very sensitive to atmosphere. She thinks you're angry.'

'I am.'

'There, there, sweetheart,' said May, washing her hands and picking her daughter up. 'It's all right. Grandad was only joking. He isn't really cross.'

When the child was pacified, May asked Bill if he'd had any breakfast.

'Not yet,' he said.

'Would you like me to cook you something before I go?' she enquired.

'No thanks. I've been living on my own for a long time and am quite capable of cooking for myself.'

'I know that. I'm only offering because you're poorly, not because you deserve it with your nasty rude manner, or because I approve of a man of your age fighting,' she told him. 'I'll make you a cup of tea anyway. You go and sit down.'

'Biccy,' said Connie hopefully, having heard tea mentioned and drawing her own conclusions.

'In the larder,' said Bill and hobbled off into the other room with Connie trailing after him.

When May went in with the tea and biscuits, Connie had climbed up on the sofa next to him. May gave her a biscuit, which she nibbled happily.

'I must say you keep the place very nice,' mentioned May in a complimentary manner, handing Bill a cup of tea.

'There's no need to sound so surprised,' he said. 'You women aren't the only ones who can keep home, you know.'

'So I see.'

'I've been at it for a very long time,' he reminded her. 'I ought to know how to do it by now.'

She felt a pang. It must be lonely for him, not having anyone with whom to share his life. But to suggest such a thing would be an invitation for a scathing rebuke, so she said, 'You'll be having some time off from the stall, won't you?'

'A day or maybe two, no more,' he told her. 'A soon as this eye has gone down a bit I'll be back. I can't afford to be without an income for long.'

'It's probably pointless for me to say this, but I'll help out if you like, though I know you wouldn't trust me to go and buy your stock for you.'

'You're right. I wouldn't.'

'I can give a hand on the stall until you're properly back on your feet,' she offered.

'There'll be no need. I can manage perfectly well on my own, thank you.' He was adamant. 'We've been through all this before. I thought you'd accepted it and would stop giving me earache.'

'This is different,' she persisted, refusing to give up. She was convinced he needed some help. 'You've taken a beating and you might not feel on top form for quite a while, but as you're such a stubborn old git I'll keep shtum about it and let you get on with it on your own.'

'Good.'

'You are your own worst enemy.'

'That suits me.'

She left soon after that, after a screaming match with Connie, who didn't want to go. It was peculiar the way she seemed to have taken to Bill, because he didn't do anything to court her favour. He barely took any notice of her as far as May could see. But something about him obviously met with the child's approval. Heaven only knew what it could be, as he was the most hateful of men.

'How is he?' asked the pieman when May went back to the market to finish her shopping.

'He says he's fine, but he looked very battered and bruised to me.'

'I'm not surprised, the way he was going at it,' he said. 'It's a wonder he didn't kill the other bloke.'

'Why didn't someone stop him?' May wanted to know. 'A man of his age shouldn't be brawling, especially with a younger, fitter man who should have known better; surely someone could have dragged them apart.'

'We tried, believe me, but Bill Mott is a very proud man and he was seething with fury,' he told her. 'If someone offends him there's no holding him back. And if someone says something he doesn't like about his family . . . well, he's like a man possessed.'

'What was it all about anyway?' she said. 'Did someone insult Archie in some way?'

'Not Archie.'

'Who then?' she enquired. 'He hasn't got many other relatives around here.'

'It was you, of course.'

'Me?' Fear shot through her. Surely no one could have found out about Connie not being Archie's child and said something defamatory, could they? 'Why would anyone say bad things about me behind my back? I don't know any of his drinking mates.'

'They've seen you around, though, and they like what they see,' he told her.

'Why insult me then?' she asked naively.

'They didn't mean any harm; it was just a bit of fun. You know what young fellas are like when they've had a few to drink; and they weren't even talking to Bill. You could even call it flattering, but Bill didn't see it that way.'

'What on earth was it?' she asked. 'You've told me this much; you'll have to finish it now.'

'All right, it was like this. We were all at the bar, and Bill overheard this young bloke talking about you to his mate. He was saying how gorgeous you are and how much he'd like to . . . well, how much he, er . . . fancied you, but in more graphic terms, if you know what I mean. Well, Bill went raving mad. He said he wasn't having his daughter-in-law insulted in such a vulgar way and dragged the bloke away from the bar and landed him one. The young chap tried to hold him off with respect to his age, but Bill went for him and the man had to defend himself, and then I think he lost his temper. You couldn't really blame him, the way Bill was going at him. Anyway, the landlord threw them both out of the pub and we thought it would end there. But no, Bill wouldn't give up and went for him outside on the street. The other man stopped and walked away in the end. We all held on to Bill so he couldn't go after him.'

May shook her head. 'Oh that stupid man,' she sighed. 'I could throttle him.'

'Bill's a good bloke,' said the pieman. 'He hasn't had it easy, losing his wife so young. He's made a fine job of bringing Archie up on his own and family is everything to him. I don't think he keeps in touch with other relatives, so you and Archie and young Connie are all he's got.'

'Yeah, I suppose we are,' she said, not wishing to enlighten the man about the true state of affairs between herself and her father-in-law.

'Give him my best when you see him,' said the man.

'I will,' she said.

Well, well, thought May as she finished her shopping. So Bill Mott wasn't quite so unfeeling as he seemed and had accepted her into his family even though he was loath to admit it; otherwise why would he have overreacted in such a way to what he saw as an insult towards her? Ostensibly Bill was the sort of man to steer well clear of; he was an ill-mannered bigot, best avoided. But he was her husband's father and he mattered to her. Now that she knew he had a heart beneath his horrid rude persona, she had something to work on. One thing was for sure, she wasn't going to give up.

Two days later Bill was back on the stall, still looking much the worse for wear, but at least the swelling on his eye had gone down. As soon as she arrived at the market, May got him a mug of tea and a cheese roll from the café.

'What's all this?' he wanted to know when she handed them to him.

'To help you through the morning,' she explained. 'I know you won't leave the stall to go and have a proper break until dinnertime, so I've brought something to you.'

'But I didn't ask—'

'Oh stop arguing, for goodness' sake, man, and enjoy,' she said, and walked on wheeling the pushchair. Connie smiled and waved to him.

'What a kind thought,' remarked the customer he was serving. She wasn't

191

a regular so didn't know his personal details. 'You're lucky to have such a caring daughter. Such a lovely young woman, and what a dear little granddaughter.'

'She isn't my daughter,' he explained.

'Oh, sorry, I just assumed . . .'

'She's my daughter-in-law,' he heard himself say, as though he was proud of it.

'Even luckier, then,' said the customer. 'Not all in-laws are so helpful. My son's wife can be a right little cow with me if the mood takes her, and I know plenty of other people with the same sort of problem. I should make the most of yours if I were you. She looks like a real sweetie to me.'

When the flurry of customers had passed, Bill sat down on a stool he kept behind the stall to drink his tea and eat his roll, realising how very much he needed them and enjoying them immensely. He did miss being able to take a break when he felt like it now that Archie wasn't around. It was a long day on his own. 'What a kind thought,' the customer had said. It *had* been very kind and he hadn't even thanked her. Being brutally honest with himself, he knew he would have thrown the gesture back in her face if she hadn't left before he'd had the chance.

He cast his mind back to the other day when she'd come round to the house to see if he was all right and he'd given her short shrift. She was very determined; he'd say that much for her. He could see her now over at the cooked meats stall. Syd who ran the stall came out and was talking to the little girl. He could hear the childish laughter from here. May was laughing too.

Archie's missus was very popular around here and everybody made a fuss of the nipper. Of course they didn't know the truth; they thought she was an ordinary decent girl and the child was Archie's. To look at May you would never guess. She always had a cheerful word for everyone and the baby was very well looked after. Archie had never been happier than since she'd been in his life.

Why would she bother with a man like Bill who made a point of being hateful to her? As the customer had said, in-laws didn't always get on. It must be because of Archie she was taking such trouble. And Bill had never seen her so much as look at another man, contrary to what you'd expect of a girl with her history.

He began to feel uneasy as he recalled the effort she had made with him and the way he had treated her. It was easy to forget the truth about her when she behaved like any other young mother. And then

192

it occurred to him that that was exactly what she was: a young mother doing her best while her husband was away at war, and looking out for her husband's dad.

The awful things he'd said to her in the past came flooding back, shaming him so that his skin burned. Yet she hadn't given up on him. She had wanted to make things work between them. Suddenly Connie's origins didn't seem to matter; just the fact that she was here, with her dimply smile and her trusting eyes.

Bill wouldn't blame May if she turned her back on him altogether after the way he had treated her, but he had to try to put things right. He looked over; she was loading her shopping into her bag and putting her purse away as she shared a joke with old Syd before walking away.

Committing the ultimate sin as a market trader, Bill ran after her without even stopping to arrange cover.

'Oh 'ello,' she said when he caught up with her. She was smiling and he could see a spark of determination in her eyes, as though she was refusing to allow herself to be upset by him. 'I hope you haven't come chasing after me to tell me to keep away from you again, because you'll be wasting your time and energy. I'm very thick skinned as far as that's concerned.'

He smiled, and much to his shame felt tears rushing into his eyes.

'Blimey, Mr Mott, you'd better be careful you don't crack your face with that grin,' said May, pretending not to notice his watery eyes. 'The muscles aren't used to it.'

'I've come to . . . well, er, that is, I was wondering if you and the little 'un might like to come to the café with me for a cuppa. We need to talk. I've been a pig.'

'I won't argue with that.'

'Will you come?' he asked. 'It's a peace offering; a chance for me to say sorry properly.'

'What about the stall?'

'I'll ask Syd to keep an eye on it for ten minutes,' he told her.

'In that case, we'd love to, wouldn't we, Connie?' she said looking down at her.

The little girl smiled her irresistible smile, and the three of them headed for the café.

Chapter Twelve

Bessie emerged from the chemist's shop in Haverley with a bottle of the apothecary's special concoction for her mother, and walked slowly down the cobbled street towards the stony path that led to the ferry. It was a bitterly cold afternoon at the end of November, and an aching rawness seemed to penetrate through her clothes to her bones. The light was already fading and her instinct was to hurry, but at eight and a half months pregnant the most she could manage was a kind of slow waddle.

When she'd called on her mother earlier she'd found her struggling with a raging temperature and a hacking cough, apparently having barely managed to finish her shift at the factory. In the absence of a chemist's in Tideway, a trip across the river had been necessary, and Bessie was always willing to oblige despite her current vastness. There were a few more shops to look at here, though the big stores were all in Colchester, which was out of the question for her until after the baby was born.

There was an exciting rumour in the village about the new motor buses coming to Tideway and running a service to Colchester at some point in the near future, which would change all their lives. But no one knew if it was true or when it was likely to happen. It certainly wouldn't be until after the war. New projects of any significance were held up until then, so it would continue to be Shanks's pony for the present.

Bessie's pregnancy had been a healthy one, but she'd had enough of dragging herself around at this late stage and was eager for the birth. She had a hankering for a son; a little boy who would grow up to be a man of principle like his father. Her hopes that Jim would be home for their child's birth had been abandoned, as there seemed to be no sign of an end to the war. There was talk of the press being heavily censored, so Bessie guessed that civilians weren't being told how things were really progressing at the front line. According to some, the newspapers had been instructed by the government to overstate the successful battles and play down the failures.

But the growing number of wounded servicemen around couldn't be hidden. Even small places like Tideway and Haverley had their casualties. No matter how much the press maintained optimistic reporting, people were beginning to see for themselves the terrible cost of the war.

To help maintain a positive attitude, Bessie focused her mind on the arrival of her baby and keeping a clean and comfortable home ready for when Jim returned. In his last letter he'd mentioned being in trenches somewhere but hadn't named the location. He didn't say much at all except that he was well and looking forward to coming home. At least she'd heard from him and knew that he was alive; that was the important thing.

Now she found herself touched by nostalgia when she passed the shop that used to be Digby's studio and was currently a rather scruffy iron-monger's store. In Digby's day the shop had been so special, with its shiny front and gallery of photographs in the window, a black-and-white striped awning adding a touch of class overhead. Now there was a dismal display of hammers, nails and enamel washing-up bowls. Poor Digby. He'd been such a sweet character and a gifted man. If his daughter hadn't been too idle to learn his trade, she could have carried the business on in her father's tradition. Thankfully, Bessie hadn't seen or heard anything of Joan since that last violent altercation.

In the interests of her pregnancy, Bessie had been forced to take a break from her photographic work at home because it was too physically demanding while she was carrying so much excess weight. She wondered how Jim would feel about her continuing when he came home expecting to be the sole bread-winner. Only time would tell.

Reaching the outskirts of the village, she was almost paralysed by a feeling of exhaustion, a dull pain nagging in the small of her back. Needing to take the weight off her feet, she eased herself down on to a low garden wall to rest before she started on the long walk along the pebbly path to the ferry.

'Are you all right?' asked a male voice, and looking up she saw a sailor.

'Yes thanks. I'm fine; just a bit weary and in need of a breather,' she replied. 'It doesn't seem any distance from the village to the ferry normally, but when you're eight and a half months pregant it seems to go on for ever.'

'I can imagine.' He looked at her with a grin. 'Shouldn't you be taking it easy at home rather than stepping out, especially as it's getting dark?' he asked in a tone of friendly concern.

'I probably should. But my mother needs medicine and she isn't well enough to go for it herself,' she explained.

'Wouldn't the neighbours have helped out if you had asked them?' he enquired.

'Normally they would, but there didn't seem to be anyone around today,' she told him, realising as she spoke how changed by the war everyday life was in the village. 'A lot of the women are out at work because of the war nowadays.'

'Mm, there is that.'

'Anyway, it's boring sitting around at home just waiting, so I was glad of an outing.'

'I wouldn't mind some sitting around at home,' he told her chattily. 'I'm going back off leave the day after tomorrow. Still, I mustn't complain, I was lucky to get some shore leave. I only got it because the ship I was on went down.'

'Ooh, that must have been frightening.'

He shrugged. 'It was a bit. But I lived through it, so I'm not complaining.'

'Most of the men in our village joined the navy; that's the natural thing as they are nearly all seamen.'

'Your husband?'

'No, thank goodness. He's a dry-land man; a schoolteacher, actually. He joined the army instead. I'm from a fishing family, and having lost my brother to a storm at sea and seen my mother live in permanent fear for my father all my life, I steered well clear of anyone of a seagoing nature.'

'The army boys aren't having a picnic out there in the trenches, from what I've heard,' he said, frowning, 'though you won't see much about it in the papers.' Realising his tactlessness, he added quickly, 'You know how these thing get exaggerated in the telling. I'm sure your husband will be doing fine.'

'I certainly hope so.' She paused. 'The war will end eventually and along with it all the worry. If you're married to a seaman, being in fear for their lives is a permanent state.'

'I suppose it would be.'

Tall and broad shouldered, he looked to be in his mid-twenties and had dark smiling eyes and a ruddy complexion typical of a seagoing man. He had taken his cap off on meeting her to reveal short dark hair. 'I haven't seen you around here before,' she remarked.

'No, I'm not a local. I live a few miles down the coast towards Brightlingsea,' he informed her. 'I'm going to visit someone in the next village to Tideway. I don't know when I'll get home again, so I'm doing the rounds of friends and relatives.'

'What do you do during peacetime?' she asked, taking a friendly interest.

'I'm a seaman,' he replied with a wry grin. 'Definitely to be avoided for someone with your views on the matter.'

She laughed. 'All right, point taken,' she said lightly. 'The world is full of seamen's wives who have managed to stay sane. I am in a minority.'

'I don't have a wife so am not guilty of sending any poor woman mad,' he told her.

With some difficulty Bessie got to her feet. 'Well, I'd better make a move. My poor mother will be waiting for the medicine and it's cold sitting about. I feel heaps better for the break, though.'

'Here, hang on to my arm if it will help,' he suggested.

It wasn't proper to take the arm of a male stranger, but she did so anyway because she really was finding the walk one heck of a drag. 'That's better,' she said as they walked on slowly. 'I hope I'm not holding you up.'

'Not at all. I'm in no particular hurry,' he assured her. 'But don't get any ideas about having your baby until you get home. I'm a practical sort of a bloke and will turn my hand to most things. But delivering a baby . . .' He drew in his breath in mock concern. 'I'm not sure if I'd be up to that.'

'I'll try and hang on then,' she laughed, spirits raised by his easy-going company. The walk to the ferry didn't seem nearly so tiring with someone to talk to. They chatted all the way, about the usual things: the war, the weather, stories that had been in the newspapers. They touched on the subject that had been on everyone's lips for the past few months: the sinking by German torpedoes of the transatlantic passenger liner *Lusitania* on the ship's journey from New York to Liverpool last May. Over a thousand civilians were drowned, many of them women and children.

'Germany has promised to stop attacking passenger ships,' the man mentioned. 'Probably because they're afraid that America will come into the war on our side, as there were some Americans among the death toll.'

'I wish the Americans *would* come into it,' Bessie said. 'We need all the help we can get to bring this horrible war to a conclusion. There doesn't seem to be an end in sight.'

They got back on to less depressing subjects and he told her that he thought Tideway was one of the prettiest villages in Essex. She said she hadn't seen many of the others but she wouldn't want to live anywhere else.

When they alighted from the ferry on the other side, with him helping her on to dry land, she said, 'I only live across the street. I can manage now.'

'I'll leave you to it then, if you're sure,' he said pleasantly.

'I'm quite sure. Thank you for making the journey home so enjoyable.'

'It was a pleasure to meet you.' He smiled.

'Likewise,' she responded. 'Good luck with the war when you go back off leave.'

'I hope all goes well with the baby,' he said. 'You take care of yourself now.'

'I will.'

Smiling, she watched him in the gaslight as he strode off along the main street in the opposite direction to where she was going. What a lovely fellow, she thought; he had transformed an arduous walk into a pleasure. It was then she realised that she didn't even know his name. He was just a passing stranger who had raised her spirits and made her day. Because of him she felt like a human being instead of an oversized baby carriage. She walked along the street to deliver her mother's medicine with a smile on her lips.

Two weeks later, after a long and difficult labour, Bessie gave birth to a son, a fine healthy boy to whom she was enslaved at first sight and who she immediately decided to name after his father,

'He'll be known as Jimmy, though,' she told her mother after the midwife had gone and the baby was washed and dressed in a white winceyette gown. Edie had taken time off work to look after Bessie during her lying-in and was in her element having a baby to care for again. 'To avoid confusion.'

'That's a very good choice, dear,' Edie approved. 'I'm sure Jim will be delighted.'

The whole gamut of emotions – doubt and fear; agony and ecstasy – Bessie had felt during the childbirth experience suddenly welled up inside her and she burst into tears.

'It's natural to feel a bit weepy after giving birth,' muttered Edie awkwardly. She wasn't good in this sort of situation, not being a tactile person even with her own family. Inhibition had always prevented her from offering much consolation when anyone was in distress; even when the children were little she'd found it difficult to fully let go and comfort them. Demonstrativeness just wasn't in her nature, so to give someone – especially an adult – a cuddle would be alien to her. 'Having a baby takes a whole lot out of a woman. So a darned good cry will do you good.'

'I suppose so, Mum.' Bessie wept copious tears. 'It's such a momentous occasion. I wish Jim was here to share it with me and see his little son in his first hours.'

'Yes, I can see that must be very hard for you,' said Edie, rather stiffly.

'Let me take the baby from you for a while and you can have a good sleep. Every woman needs that after giving birth. It works wonders.'

'I miss him so much,' sobbed Bessie, keeping her son close to her. 'It hurts not to see him for so long. It's a continuous pain. I so want him to be here.'

'There's nothing you can do about it, so you'll just have to be patient for a while longer.' Edie bit her lip, trying to think of something helpful to say as well as struggling to stifle her tendency towards irritation. 'As soon as you feel up to it you can write to him; that will make you feel better. Just think how the news that he has a son will cheer him up out there in France.'

At that moment Bessie wanted someone to wrap their arms around her and make her feel loved. But she knew that her mother didn't indulge in such things, so she dried her tears and said, 'Yeah. I'll write to him as soon as I can.'

'You get some rest now. I'll look after young Jimmy for a while and bring you a cup of tea later on.'

'I'd rather keep him with me, Mum,' she said. 'I'll put him in his cradle next to me in a minute while I sleep.'

'As you wish,' said Edie. 'I'll bring you a cup of tea before you settle down.'

'Thanks, Mum. That would be lovely.'

Alone in the room with her sleeping baby, the silence soothing and embracing her, Bessie looked down at the tiny scrap of humanity in her arms. She had never experienced feelings at this level of potency before. The sadness of moments earlier was swept away by the power of this great love for her son. She knew in that moment that she would give her life for him if it was ever necessary.

'We'll keep each other going until Daddy comes home, little Jimmy,' she whispered, kissing his tiny brow. 'He's going to be so proud of you.'

In the kitchen, putting the kettle to boil on the hook over the hot coals of the range, Edie was struggling with her own feelings of guilt for not giving her daughter the physical comfort she had needed just now. This sense of inadequacy wasn't new to her. She had experienced it many times while she had been raising her children. Although she had done her best for all of them in her own way, there was always a sense of compunction lurking because of her restrained nature.

Sometimes she wished she could be more like her sister Winnie, who would put her arms around a complete stranger if she thought it would help. Though on second thoughts she wouldn't want to be like her. Winnie's warm and outgoing nature had been a curse at times, causing trouble for herself and other people.

Thinking of Winnie led to thoughts of May, and she was pierced by conscience over the way she had treated her. Once again she tried to convince herself that she had done the right thing. Anyway, things had turned out better than could have been hoped because May had found a husband up there in London, and according to Bessie she enjoyed her life there. An outgoing girl like May would be more suited to the metropolis, with all its modern facilities and entertainments, than a quiet little place like Tideway. Her life as an unmarried mother would have been a misery here. So Edie had nothing to reproach herself about as far as that was concerned. In fact she would even go so far as to say that she had done May a favour.

'That was the best Christmas dinner I've had in many a long year,' said Bill Mott as he finished a portion of Christmas pudding and put his spoon down on the plate. 'Thank you, and my heartiest compliments to the chef.'

'The chefs,' corrected Winnie. 'It was a joint effort between May and me, so she deserves her share of the credit.'

'Thanks, love,' he said, smiling at his daughter-in-law.

'A pleasure,' responded May. 'I'm so glad you decided to join us today, Bill. I couldn't bear to think of you being on your own at Christmas.'

'I'm glad I came too,' he said.

'Piggyback, Grandad,' chirped Connie, who was getting to be a real chatterbox, even though they sometimes couldn't make head or tail of what she was saying.

'Not now, darlin',' said May. 'A bit later, perhaps, when Grandad has had time to digest his meal.'

'We'll play this afternoon,' he told her.

'Promise?' she chirped.

'I promise.'

'I'm surprised that food is still reasonably plentiful,' remarked Albert conversationally, 'given what the German U-boats are doing to our merchant ships. Apart from that period at the beginning of the war when people were panic-buying and creating shortages, things have been much the same as usual.'

'Our reserves must be lasting out well,' Bill mentioned. 'Things are bound to change eventually, though, if the war goes on for much longer.'

'Let's just be grateful for today, shall we, and enjoy all the good things we have,' said May. 'I suggest that we drink a toast to absent friends.'

'Good idea,' said Winnie.

Albert got a bottle of port from the sideboard and they all raised their glasses to loved ones past and those who couldn't be here. As well as Archie, May also remembered Henry, Bessie and the family in Tideway.

May had been to see her sister and the baby as soon as she'd got news of the birth, by which time Bessie was up and about again. Connie had been thrilled to go on the train to see her new cousin. Bessie had been radiant, though sad that Jim wasn't around to share in her joy. May had paid a dutiful visit to the family home and received the usual restrained welcome from her mother. She'd had a good chat with Sam, though, who told her that he was planning on joining the army as soon as he was old enough. His father's eagerness for him to do his duty to his country meant he put up no opposition, though help on the boat wasn't easy to find these days, as all the young men were away in the services.

Recalled to the present by the jolly babble of conversation here at the table, May noticed how contented Bill looked as he made a great fuss of Connie. She was imbued with pleasure that a friendship had emerged from the initial acrimony, for his sake as well as hers. He was a different man to the surly, bigoted one who had refused to accept her into his family. Now she really believed there was nothing he wouldn't do for her and Connie, and he enriched their lives. She wouldn't take money from him for herself but she didn't refuse when he wanted to help with Connie's welfare, because she knew it gave him pleasure.

She stood in for him on the stall every day while he went for a break, and helped on a regular basis on Saturday mornings when Winnie was able to look after Connie. For this she did accept the wage he insisted she have, which helped her to manage.

Now that she and Bill were friends, her aunt and uncle welcomed him into their family circle too. He came for Sunday dinner every week and in return he supplied them with fruit and vegetables free of charge; enough to last them for a few days. Of course Archie had been led to believe erroneously that she and Bill had buried the hatchet before he went away. Now there would be no need for pretence when he came home. Dear Archie; it wasn't much of a way to spend Christmas, being away at war. She did hope he was safe and managing to keep his chin up.

*   *   *

'Come on, Archie, let's have one of your stories,' urged one of the men from his dugout in the trenches where Archie and his mates lived. They had all been in the front line and were now in the support trenches, resting out of the direct line of fire but still vulnerable from enemy snipers and shelling. 'We've got to try and stay cheerful somehow on Christmas Day, and you're our only hope. No one tells a joke like you do.'

'I'm not sure I've got any new tales left,' responded Archie. 'I've been entertaining you lot with 'em for months. I haven't got a never-ending supply, you know.'

'One of the old ones'll do, mate; as smutty as you like,' said another of the men. 'It's the way you tell 'em that has us in fits. It don't matter that we've heard it before. You ought to be on the music hall; you're as good as any of the comic turns on the stage. Come on, make us laugh.'

Laugh? Archie felt more like crying, sitting here in this unsanitary hellhole, cold to the bone and with his feet in their usual sodden state. Their orders were for all men to change their socks every day and rub their feet with whale oil to protect them from trench foot, but it was a waste of time, because it was impossible to keep their feet dry. The floor of the trench filled with water as soon as it rained, which it seemed to do all the time lately. And the water always rose above the duckboards.

They each had a dugout, which was a hole carved in the side of the trench in which there were boards for them to sleep on. They could hang a ground sheet or a blanket over the front from a hook in the trench if they wanted privacy when they slept, but not many men bothered, having been robbed of all normality for so long.

'Let me finish this fag and I'll try and think of one,' Archie said now.

'Good old Archie,' said someone.

'Things are pretty quiet today; perhaps they're going to have a truce like they did in some parts of the trenches last Christmas,' suggested one of the men.

'I wouldn't bank on it,' said another. 'We're all more fed up than we were a year ago and keen to get the war over. The Hun probably feels the same.'

Morale was low among the ranks. They had been promised an early victory; had been assured that their army was far superior to that of the enemy. In actual fact they had been let down by bad planning, which had cost many men's lives, as well as a lack of ammunition, which had meant that the front-line troops didn't always have the proper back-up.

Archie was smoking his cigarette, deep in thought, but he wasn't trying to come up with a joke to tell the lads; his thoughts were all of May and Connie and all the rest of them at home, but mostly of May. He didn't know what the time was but it was afternoon, so they would probably have had their Christmas dinner and would be sitting by the fire eating sweets and playing with Connie. Just imagining the scene made him hurt with yearning for warmth and comfort and the feel of May beside him.

'We're still waiting, Archie,' said one of his mates, recalling him to the present.

'Right,' he began, scouring his mind for inspiration. 'This bloke goes into a pub with a parrot on his head . . .'

Watching him, the men were smiling in anticipation as he spoke, slowly spinning out the tale. He was a natural entertainer and they relied on him to keep them sane. 'The barman asks him why he has a parrot on his head, and he says—'

The sentence remained unfinished. The ground shook with the thud of an explosion as shells exploded nearby and splinters whizzed overhead. The sound of gunfire rang in Archie's ears, echoing over and over again.

'Happy Christmas, boys,' he said as a stray bullet hit one of his pals. The man was still for a moment before falling to the ground. 'Happy bloody Christmas.'

Underneath the house where May and Connie lived with Winnie and Albert there was a coal cellar that expanded out under the street. The coalman delivered the coal into it by opening a lid in the pavement.

Winnie and the others used it as a shelter when the Zeppelins came over. Armed with candles and blankets, they went down some stone steps behind a door near the front of the house and sat there among the coal and the spiders until the danger had passed. It wasn't easy when they had had a fresh delivery of coal because of lack of space, but they managed. Uncle Albert didn't come down, as he liked to watch what was going on in the skies. Many people stood in the street watching, and cheered when Allied guns hit an enemy plane and it retreated emitting smoke.

Because of Connie, May always took cover during the raids. The noise was terrifying: the sound of explosions and the roar of anti-aircraft gunfire from Wormwood Scrubs. Surprisingly, Aunt Winnie was always very frightened at these times. Being the woman she was, she tried hard to hide it, but her pallor and her trembling hands gave her away. May did her best to cheer her as she sang songs to comfort Connie, who was too young to realise the danger and thought the whole thing was a bit of lark.

One day in the spring of 1916, Bill gave them something that changed things for the better in the shelter and brought a whole lot of fun into their lives. Being a man of the market and in the know with shadowy characters who had goods for sale about which no questions were asked, he could sometimes obtain luxury items at a cheaper price than in the shops. Often they were artefacts that no one else they knew had because they hadn't yet become available in ordinary retail outlets.

This was how he came by the wind-up gramophone and some records, which they took down to the cellar to drown out the noise of the bombs and guns. As the weather turned milder and there was less coal in the cellar, they could make themselves more comfortable. Even Winnie was less afraid with ragtime music to listen to instead of the frightening sounds outside.

They had fun with the new music machine in the house too, especially May, who loved dancing and was always singing along with the tunes. Winnie joined in, and with Connie they jigged around the room. May found a book about how to do the new dances and picked them up quickly. Connie loved to dance, so the house was always filled with music and laughter. Winnie adored having May and Connie there and dreaded the day when they and Archie would move into a place of their own.

Albert sometimes complained about the place being full of women making a racket all over the house, but Winnie knew that he enjoyed it as much as she did.

One day in June, when little Jimmy was six months old, Bessie took him to London for a visit, and the two sisters and their offspring had a day out in the West End, visiting the glamorous Selfridges store, which had been opened in 1909.

'I've never actually bought anything here,' confessed May, as they walked through the luxuriously scented departments selling make-up and perfumes, and the beautiful clothes and furnishings and homeware the sisters could only dream of ever owning; everything displayed so attractively.

The public were urged on posters by the proprietor Gordon Selfridge to 'Spend the Day Here'. May and Bessie didn't exactly do that but they did stay a while without making a purchase, though they did splash out on a cup of tea and cake in one of the cafeterias.

'It's like another world,' said Bessie dreamily. 'I have never seen anything like it before.'

'It does us good now and again to see how the other half lives,' said May.

'As long as it isn't often enough to make us discontented with our lot,' said Bessie.

'As long as Archie comes home from the war in one piece, I'll be content,' said May in more serious mood.

Bessie nodded. 'Same here with Jim,' she said. 'Nothing else really matters.'

'Have you heard from him lately?'

'Yeah, I do hear from him now and again. He sounds quite cheerful,' she replied. 'I think perhaps they are told to say that to keep our spirits up at home.'

'Archie's just the same,' May said. 'Still, as long as we hear from them, we know they are alive.'

'Exactly.'

May decided to change the subject quickly before they both got maudlin. 'Have you started the photography again since having Jimmy?'

'Yes, I have, as a matter of fact,' Bessie replied. 'I had so many people asking me, I went back into it sooner than I intended. Everyone wants a photograph of their loved one in uniform just in case the worst happens, and men going away want a photo of their wife or girlfriend to keep with them.'

'I suppose they would do.'

'I can't do jobs far outside of the village – weddings or home portraits – because I don't have any transport, but I do what I can,' she said.

'Do you take Jimmy with you?'

'Mum sometimes has him, but if she's working I take him with me,' she said. 'He's still quite portable. It won't be so easy when he's running around. Still, Jim might be home by then and he may not want me to continue.'

'There is that.'

'Sam is making himself useful,' Bessie went on. 'He starts work on Dad's boat early so he's free in the afternoons, and he goes with me on outside jobs sometimes; he helps to organise the groups, gives a hand with the developing and so on. He makes a good assistant, as it happens. He's interested in the photographic process, which helps.'

'You're making a little business of it, then?'

'Only in a very small way. But I must admit that a bit of extra cash helps.' She kissed the top of her son's head. 'Clothes for him keep me poor.'

'We know all about that, don't we, Connie?' May said to her daughter, who was sitting next to her aunt eating a bun and watching Jimmy's every move. She thought he was wonderful and wanted a brother of her own to play with.

'It's so good to see you, May,' said Bessie, becoming emotional. 'I still miss you around the village. It's the traditions we used to share. I always thought our kids would grow up together and be as close as we are.'

'I wanted that too.'

'You'll have to persuade Archie to come to live in Tideway when he comes home,' suggested Bessie, joking.

'Do you know, I believe he would do that if it was what I really wanted; there isn't much he wouldn't do for me, bless him,' May told her. 'But he'd be like a fish out of water away from London, so I would never ask it of him.' She looked at her sister. 'I think I would be too now, to be perfectly honest.'

Bessie looked disappointed. 'Oh well, we'll just have to make sure we visit each other as often as we can so that the children don't grow up as strangers.'

'Unless you move to London, which I know you never would,' said May. 'But for now I think we'd better be making our way home or we'll hit the rush hour.'

They made their way to Marble Arch and took the tube to Notting Hill Gate, where they had to change trains. As they headed for the platform to get the Hammersmith train, May clutching Connie's hand tightly, and Bessie with Jimmy in the pushchair, May vaguely noticed a soldier walking in their direction; he looked like an officer of some sort, with a flat peaked cap.

'May,' he said, startling her, and her eyes widened as she found herself looking into the face of the father of her child. He was smiling at her as though she was a sight for sore eyes.

'You!' she gasped, feeling the blood drain from her face and her heart beating fit to bust. 'William.'

'Yes, that's right,' he said, looking delighted to see her. 'Quite a coincidence; us meeting in the metropolis when there are so many people about, especially as I'm away most of the time. I just happen to have a spot of leave.'

She nodded dumbly, trying to gather her wits. He was a soldier so deserved her respect, whatever he'd done to her personally. 'Have you seen any action?' she asked eventually.

'I've seen my share,' he told her. 'I'm going back to France tomorrow.'

Again she nodded.

'I didn't expect to see you in London,' he said.

'Didn't you?' she asked, instinctively refraining from giving him any more information about herself.

'No. I associate you entirely with Tideway.'

'Us country girls get around, you know,' she said lightly.

'So I see.' He looked down at Connie and smiled. 'Hello, and what's your name?' he asked.

'Connie,' she replied sweetly.

Instinctively May held her daughter's hand even tighter, as though William might take her away. She knew this was a gross overreaction, as he wouldn't be interested in a child from an affair that had meant nothing to him. A man of his type was likely to have any amount of liaisons with women. Anyway, he'd known nothing of the pregnancy so wouldn't even make the connection.

'Mummy, you're hurting me,' objected Connie, now a beautiful little girl coming up to two and a half in a summer frock, her dark curls bouncing on her shoulders.

'Sorry, darlin',' she said, loosening her grip.

'Come on, May,' shouted Bessie, who had gone on ahead. 'The train is coming in. Hurry up or we'll miss it and have to wait for the next one.'

'We have to go now,' May said quickly to William. 'Come along, Connie.'

'May I . . . er . . . please don't go just yet. Surely another minute won't hurt. At least tell me where you—'

But she had gone, hurrying towards her sister.

'Who was that soldier you were talking to?' enquired Bessie with casual interest.

'Just a stranger asking me the way to another platform,' May fibbed, so shocked by her reaction to seeing the father of her child again she wanted to push it to the back of her mind. To her shame, all the old feelings were still there: the heady excitement; the pulses racing; the wanting to be with him.

They hurried on to the platform with the crowd and boarded the train. When the doors closed behind them, May experienced a mixture of relief and disappointment. For a second back there, she had thought he might follow her; had even hoped that might happen. Now she was safe from temptation, but it left a horrible feeling of emptiness.

Oh Archie, she said silently. You're such a good man and you deserve better than me; a woman who still harbours unrealistic romantic feelings for a man who let her down. Thank God it was just a passing moment.

So much had changed since she had last seen William. The world had gone to war; she had pulled herself out of despair and got married and had a child and was now more at home in London than the village of her birth. But some things never changed, and her feelings for William Marriot certainly hadn't. But they were only feelings and as such could be controlled and forgotten, which was exactly what she was planning to do.

The preliminary bombardment that preceded any battle started towards the end of June and went on for days. The attack had been planned in great secrecy, the men were assured. They were also told that the Germans and their trenches would have been blasted by the bombardment and the barbed wire destroyed by the time they went over, so they would have no trouble getting through. All they had to do was climb over the trench parapet and advance at walking pace towards the enemy in waves of about one thousand, as they had been trained to do.

Jim Minter was among those who would go over first. They had come up to the line during the night, laden with their packs but marching at a smart pace and singing cheerful music-hall songs to keep their spirits up. Now, on this beautiful sunny July morning, Jim was in the trench waiting for the order. His insides were griping with terror, as always at this point before a battle, but having been told that everything was in place for an easy victory, he wasn't as paralysed with fear as he had been in the past. At the same time he wanted to go in and get the job done and then get as far away from it as possible. Something happened in a situation like this, when you went over wondering if you would live to see the next minute; it was beyond fear, a kind of ghastly acceptance of whatever lay in store.

All the men's rifles were checked by the officer, and they had their final briefing, then the order came and the troops clambered up and over the parapet into no-man's-land.

Archie was in the same battle that day, in another British division. The moment he went over the top at the Battle of the Somme was the moment he lost all trust in the military hierarchy as he witnessed carnage on a gigantic scale.

Contrary to officers' promises, the wire that should have been destroyed wasn't even damaged and the deep enemy bunkers remained intact, so the Germans were able to effect mass slaughter of the British troops from them. It was so horrific as to be barely believable. There were dead men underfoot and dropping all around him, good pals some of them; bullets whizzing past him, shellfire blasting in his ears so that he couldn't think straight; smoke almost blinding him and making him retch and want to vomit.

Although he had been in combat before, the shock of this catastrophic violence bewildered and disorientated him for a few moments and he stood where he was, trying to get his bearings. Then he did the only thing that was open to him: he moved on towards the guns, heading for almost certain death.

Chapter Thirteen

One Sunday morning in September, Tideway was buzzing with excitement as news spread about a German Zeppelin that had crashed in flames in the middle of the night in a field just outside a nearby village, only narrowly missing some cottages there. According to rumour, the enemy aircraft had released its bombs over London, where it had been hit and damaged, and had then headed for the Essex coast and the North Sea, hoping to make it home. But it hadn't even got as far as the Channel.

Everybody in Tideway was talking about it, an assortment of stories circulating from those villagers who had been to have a look at the wreck the instant they heard about it. They were besieged with questions on their return.

'What about the people in the cottages?' asked someone. 'Were they hurt?'

'I don't think so, but I do know that they were terrified and hid in the cupboards.'

'The poor things; what a terrible ordeal.'

'Did the Germans try to kill them?' another wanted to know.

'No, nothing like that. Apparently they just got out of the burnt-out Zeppelin and walked down the lanes and gave themselves up to a village policeman.'

'They must have known they wouldn't stand a chance if they went on the run.'

'I bet the people in the cottages were glad to see them go. I know I would have been.'

'Not half,' agreed one of the villagers.

Even as they spoke, people were flocking out of Tideway to grab a glimpse of a piece of history with their own eyes; mostly on foot, some on bicycles or horseback or by pony and trap.

'How about coming with me to take a look, Bessie?' suggested Sam when she went over to Berry Cottage with Jimmy to discuss the development, having heard about it from her neighbours. 'It isn't often anything happens around here. We don't want to miss the little bit of action that does come our way.'

'It's a bit morbid going to look at someone else's misfortune, don't you think?' she said.

'No one was killed,' he reminded her. 'Anyway, it's war and they are the enemy.'

'I'll look after his nibs if you want to go, Bessie, to save you wheeling the pram along those bumpy lanes,' offered her mother. 'I'll go over to your place with him for part of the time anyway, as his toys are all over there.'

'Why don't we all go?' suggested Bessie. 'It's Sunday so Dad isn't working.'

'I wouldn't walk across the road to see a German bomber, let alone a few miles,' snorted George.

'I don't fancy it either,' added Edie. 'It seems a bit bloodthirsty to me.'

So Bessie and her brother set out along the lanes together, the trees at the sides tinged with glorious autumn colours, fallen leaves underfoot.

At least the outing took Bessie's mind off the grinding worry that grew more all-consuming with every day that passed without word from her husband. Every morning she looked out for the postman, but no letter arrived. Today being a Sunday she was spared the agony because it was the postman's day off.

When they got closer to their destination, the crowds going the same way got denser, pouring in from all directions from villages all over this region of Essex. Bessie and her brother took a short cut across a field only to find that hundreds of others had had the same idea and the lane at the other side was congested. Bessie had never seen so many people in one place at the same time. Everyone was very congenial, though. There was almost a party atmosphere.

'You'd think we'd come to see some sort of royal event rather than an unfortunate enemy aircraft, wouldn't you?' Bessie commented. 'The crowds are just as excited.'

'Which just goes to show what narrow lives we lead,' remarked Sam jokingly. He was a young man hungry for excitement, and although there was plenty of drama in the North Sea in stormy weather, he was keen for the sort that came from the wider world. He'd get plenty when he was of an age to go in the forces, if the war was still in progress. Now that conscription had been introduced, he didn't have to feel so guilty about leaving his father to find someone else to work for him on the boat. 'I mean, we get all thrilled if there's something other than cold meat for dinner on a Monday.'

'Oh, come on, Sam,' objected Bessie. 'Our lives aren't that dull. Mine isn't, anyway.'

'Just joking.'

But today their lives weren't going to be enriched by any added adventure, as it seemed that they had had a wasted trip. Sightseers were walking back disappointed, with the news that the Zeppelin was now so well guarded by the men of the Lancashire Fusiliers that no one could get near enough to see anything.

However, Bessie and her brother weren't easily deterred and continued to pursue their course, eventually reaching their goal only to find that they weren't allowed within viewing distance, though with a bit of ducking and diving Sam did manage a glimpse of a piece of the wreckage, so it wasn't a completely pointless journey. Serendipity was in the air too, because on the way home he got talking to a girl of about his own age and seemed quite smitten. The couple arranged to see each other again.

'Something good came out of it, then,' Bessie said to her brother when they left the girl at the ferry.

'Yeah,' he said dreamily.

'She seems like a nice girl. Very pretty.'

'I didn't notice,' he said, his blushes belying his show of youthful nonchalance.

When they got back to Berry Cottage, Bessie knew immediately that something was wrong.

'What's happened?' she asked nervously, seeing the worried expression in her mother's eyes. 'Where's Jimmy. Has he been hurt? Is he poorly?'

'Jimmy is fine,' Edie assured her through tight lips, her face paper white. 'He's asleep in his pram in the back garden.'

'What is it then, Mum? Has something happened to Dad?' Bessie needed to know, though she was dreading the answer because it was obviously something serious. 'You look as though you've just seen a ghost.'

Edie bit her lip anxiously and took something from her apron pocket. 'This came for you while I was over at your house,' she managed to utter finally in a shaky voice, handing Bessie a telegram.

Bessie burned from top to toe then turned to ice, her heart beating erratically. Trembling, she opened the envelope, her eyes hardly able to focus on the words. All that leapt out at her was 'painful duty to inform

213

you' and 'killed in action July 1st 1916'. She handed the piece of paper to her mother, who passed it to her husband as he came into the room.

Vaguely Bessie was aware of words of kindness and comfort. She went through the motions of acknowledgment but her hearing seemed to be impaired suddenly. She felt distant, vague and oddly numb.

'I have to get Jimmy,' she heard herself say in a high, thin voice. 'I have to go home.'

'I'll come with you.'

'No, Mum, not now.'

'But you can't be on your own at a time like this.' Her mother was aghast at the suggestion. 'You need your family around you at the moment.'

'Later,' she said. 'I need to be by myself for a while now. I'll be back.'

On jelly legs she went out into the garden to collect her sleeping son.

'Why not leave him here with us?' suggested her mother. 'Just while you get over the initial shock.'

Bessie didn't reply. She couldn't explain to anyone why she needed to be alone with her baby so badly at this moment. He couldn't give her words of comfort or share her pain. But it was essential to her to feel his warmth, to smell his baby scent and listen to him breathe. She needed his life force close to her.

'I'll be back later on,' she told them and wheeled her son to their own little cottage, to the home she had been looking forward to sharing with Jim again one day soon.

'It's just you and me now, Jimmy,' she whispered as she lifted the baby out of the pram and sat down on the sofa with him in the small living room with its view of the waterfront that she and Jim had so enjoyed together.

Jimmy whimpered, having been woken from his nap, then started to grizzle. She spoke to him softly and stroked his brow until he quietened then struggled to go on the floor. She sat him down with his toys and watched him play with his wooden bricks through a blur of tears.

Of course, as a soldier's wife, she had known the risk Jim was under but had forced herself to stay positive. She had doggedly refused to contemplate her single parenthood as permanent and had been steadfast in her belief that they would eventually be reunited to raise their son together. But harsh reality now had to be faced and she must be strong for Jimmy. Falling apart simply wasn't an option. Her boy needed her and she would always be there for him. He was her life now.

She wanted to cry until there wasn't a tear left in her with the sheer pain of her loss, and with fury at the slaughter of a young man with his life ahead of him. But she daren't give in and weep, for fear she would never stop.

Quite how it had happened Archie had no idea, but it was now early November and he was still alive, despite the fact that the Battle of the Somme had raged for months and was still going. All the lads knew the battle was lost, though. Occasionally the German lines were pushed back a little, but there was no breakthrough; just a staggering loss of life. Day after day the fighting continued and somehow he had survived.

'Somebody up there must like us, I reckon,' remarked one of his mates when they were away from the front line during a rest period. The men were sitting around talking and smoking in the support trench.

'Sometimes I think that's debatable,' responded Archie, drawing hard on his cigarette. 'I mean, what are we saved for except a living death? Because that is what this is. We're not human beings any more; just stinking, lice-ridden fighting machines.'

'Blimey, it isn't like you to be so down in the mouth, Archie,' commented the soldier. 'We rely on you to keep us cheerful. If you get low we're all done for.'

Although it was in Archie's nature to stay cheerful whatever the circumstances, it was becoming increasingly difficult for him in the foul-smelling, rat-infested trenches. He'd seen too many men die, lost too many pals. He was the only one left of his original group. Most of the men with him now had been sent in to replace the casualties, so he hadn't known them long, but his ability to entertain had soon been noticed and he tried to keep them happy. The poor sods. How long would they last when they went back to the front line? he wondered. His own luck would run out eventually, too. On the law of averages, it was bound to.

'Me down in the mouth; never let it be said,' he responded now, managing to feign good spirits. 'It's time for a joke or two, I reckon. Right, lads, what do you call a deer with no eyes?'

'Dunno,' said someone. 'What do you call a deer with no eyes?'

'No idea,' chuckled Archie. 'No eye deer; get it?'

This raised barely more than a smile.

'You can do better than that, Archie,' said someone. 'We want a proper adult joke. Something for men only; a bit on the blue side.'

'Right. There's this bloke of ninety-two who's married to a girl of eighteen, and he goes to the doctor . . .'

The men listened as he dragged out the story in an amusing manner, their horrific circumstances put temporarily to the back of their minds.

'You're popular today, May,' remarked Winnie at breakfast one November morning as she handed her niece three letters.

May glanced at the envelopes, recognising the handwriting. She felt a surge of relief when she saw that there was one from Archie. There was also one from Bessie and the third was from Constance, the suffragette, with whom May had corresponded on an occasional basis since they'd stopped working together at the WSPU office.

She opened Archie's first.

'He's all right, thank goodness,' she told her aunt. 'He says a bit more than usual, which means he can't be in the front line; they're not allowed to say anything then. Nothing about the war, though, as usual. He says he's with a good bunch of blokes, and he's having enough food and is in good health. I think perhaps they have to say that so we won't worry. Anyway, he hopes we are all well and is looking forward to coming home after the war.'

'At least he's safe.'

May nodded. 'Phew, what a relief; every time I get a letter I thank God for it,' she said.

Finishing her porridge, she opened the letter from her sister, promptly burst into tears and wept without restraint.

'Whatever's the matter, love?' asked her aunt, getting up and putting her arms around her shaking shoulders. 'What's upset you so much?'

May handed her Bessie's letter.

'Oh, Auntie, it's so awful. Poor Jim; poor Bessie,' she sobbed. 'Oh dear, whatever will she do? She adored Jim and will be heartbroken.'

Being of a similar temperament to May, Winnie burst into floods of tears too.

'Cor blimey. It's like being at a ruddy funeral in here with you two,' remarked Albert, coming into the room. 'What's got into the pair of you?'

'It's Bessie's husband Jim,' Winnie informed him thickly, her handkerchief held to her face. 'The poor lad has been killed in action.'

'Oh no . . . oh, I see,' he said, tutting and biting his lip. 'That's a real shame.'

'It's a calamity. There's too many men getting killed; soon there will be more people in mourning than out of it,' declared Winnie hotly. 'There are black hats everywhere around here on a Sunday. Hardly a splash of colour anywhere. It's downright heartbreaking. Something should be done to bring this war to a conclusion. All these young men being wiped out.'

'Bessie says she doesn't want me to rush down to Essex straight away with the cost of fares being as they are,' May mentioned, looking at the letter again. 'She says she's doing all right. She's determined to be strong for little Jimmy. She's got Mum and Dad and Sam behind her.'

'The baby will keep her going,' said Winnie. 'And they won't be able to have a funeral, so it isn't as though you'll need to go to that to help her through.'

'I want to see her as soon as I can, though, Auntie. She needs me, so I shan't leave it too long,' she declared. 'Meanwhile, I shall get a letter in the post to her today.'

Winnie picked something up off the floor. 'You dropped your other letter in all the upset,' she said, handing May an envelope. 'You probably don't feel like reading it just now, but it might be important so you'd better take a look.'

'I hope it isn't more bad news,' muttered May, made to feel vulnerable by the contents of Bessie's letter.

It wasn't bad news. In fact it was rather an interesting proposition from Constance. She was apparently running a day nursery for the children of women on war work and needed an assistant.

May read some of the letter out loud.

'I've had one of my helpers leave to go to work in a factory and am looking for someone to take her place. I wondered if you might be interested. You are experienced with children having one of your own so you would be ideal, especially as you and I work well together. I can't tell you what a tremendous help it would be to me if you could come on board. I want someone I can trust to look after the children properly and you are just the person. You could bring Connie with you so she'll have plenty of playmates and you wouldn't have to worry about getting her looked after. The pay isn't a fortune because I only have a small wages budget on account of the fact that I don't charge too much. It wouldn't be worth the mothers' while going out to work if I did, as they are all from poor backgrounds. But your money would be paid to you regularly every week.

'There is a snag, however: the nursery is quite a distance from you, between Notting Hill and Paddington. It would be a long walk with a little one and the bus fare would add up over the course of a week and make a hole in your wages.

'I do have a bicycle you could borrow if this would help. It would save you a great deal of time and money if you do decide to take the job.

Perhaps your uncle or father-in-law could fix a little seat on the back for Connie to sit on. I'm sure she'd find the ride great fun. I hope you are interested in working with me and look forward to hearing from you at your earliest convenience.'

'Well, that sounds like just the job for you,' Winnie enthused. 'Are you going to do it?'

'I would love to do it, Auntie,' replied May, still shaken by the news from Bessie but brightened by this opportunity. 'But there are a couple of snags.'

'Which are?'

'Firstly, I don't know if I would be any good with children in large numbers,' she confessed.

'I don't see why not. You're wonderful with Connie,' Winnie pointed out with enthusiasm. 'I think this would be ideal for you, especially as you can take Connie with you. It will be good for her too, to have company of her own age.'

'I love my own child to bits, but other people's kids are a different matter altogether,' May admitted.

'There is that, but I'm sure it won't be a problem.' Winnie thought that a job outside the home would be good for May, in that it would take her mind off the war and Archie's part in it. Especially now they'd had this terrible news about Jim.

'I might end up throttling the little perishers if they play up,' May said.

'I'm sure you wouldn't, dear,' her aunt reassured. 'You'd find the patience if you needed to. Anyway, you could give it a try, and if you find that you aren't suited to it, you can always leave. You can't work with kiddies if you're impatient.'

'Exactly.'

'What was the other snag?'

'I can't ride a bicycle.'

'That's easily solved,' stated Winnie in a positive manner. 'Get the bike over here and teach yourself. We'll help you. Not that either of us can ride a bike, but we can hold it for you until you get your balance. That's what people do, I think.'

'I might just do that, Auntie,' May agreed, her mind returning to her sister. 'With a bit of extra money coming in, I'll be able to afford to go and see Bessie without breaking the bank.'

'Good girl.'

'Meanwhile I will write a letter to dear Bessie and get it into the post on my way to the market.'

'I shall write one too,' said Winnie, becoming sad again. 'I'll do it as soon as I get home from work.'

They all fell silent as though simultaneously paying their respects to Jim.

As the U-boat campaign against British imports continued and food reserves began to get low, queues appeared in shops and markets in the London area. The shortage of grain led to the introduction of a new type of bread made from flour mixed with powdered potatoes or beans, and margarine became a substitute for butter. Food prices rose and coal was in short supply. The fervent patriotic support for the war at the outbreak was wearing decidedly thin among the public, especially as the death toll from abroad continued to rise. Nobody had expected any of this when they'd waved their men goodbye.

Some light relief might have been found by onlookers on the streets of Hammersmith as May learned to ride a bicycle. She was dressed in trousers, which until the war had rarely been seen on a woman. They were still considered somewhat outrageous by some older people but were the only sure way of keeping a girl's modesty intact while in the saddle.

Up and down the street she went, with Winnie, Albert or Bill Mott running beside her, holding the bike steady and shouting instructions until she got her balance, which, she was told, once gained would remain for ever. There were occasional wobbles, even a tumble or two, and hoots of laughter, but it wasn't long before she was off on her own, riding around the streets, practising to make sure she was thoroughly competent before she put Connie on the back. When she finally did, the little girl thought the whole thing was a delight and couldn't get enough of it.

So it was that one morning early in the new year of 1917, mother and daughter set off together wrapped up in warm coats and bright red matching scarves, hats and gloves that May had knitted from wool she had got in a sale, riding through the London streets towards Paddington alongside horse-drawn vehicles, motor cars and omnibuses. May was surprised at how quickly they reached their destination and arrived feeling pleased with herself, invigorated and ready for her next challenge.

It wasn't more than a few minutes, however, before May seriously questioned her judgement in agreeing to take the job. To say the place was chaos was an understatement. It was more like complete anarchy: ragged children running riot, shouting and screaming and completely out of control; one or two quiet little souls standing on the sidelines looking tearful; a few sitting forlornly at the tables to one side of the room.

Constance and a female assistant looked harassed and, as far as May could see, completely ineffective. Connie, who was not normally a shy child, took one look at the scene and clung to her mother, close to tears.

'It's a bit hectic at the moment as you can see; they'll settle down for the day soon. We haven't got into our stride yet,' explained Constance.

May nodded.

'Am I glad you're here, May,' Constance went on. 'Another pair of hands will make all the difference. When you and Connie have taken your coats off, I'll show you round.'

The nursery was on the ground floor of a large house. Constance was apparently renting the whole of the downstairs for the nursery. The babies and toddlers were in one room, being looked after by an experienced nanny. There were rows of cots and high chairs and a small play area where those who were old enough were sitting on the floor with an assortment of baby toys.

'You will be helping my other assistant, Mary, with the two to five year olds,' Constance announced as they went back into the main area, where Mary was trying, rather unsuccessfully, to keep order. Constance then showed May a room leading off, which had been made into a dining room with child-size tables and chairs.

The older woman adopted a confidential manner. 'The children who come to us are from poor or disadvantaged families, and their manners aren't exactly top drawer,' she informed May. 'We discourage bad language here but it's second nature to some of them at home so it's a bit of an uphill struggle. At least the war has given their mothers the chance to improve their situation by earning some money, which is the reason I set up a nursery with reasonable fees. I don't take anyone whose parents can afford to pay more. The children here don't have luxuries but they are properly looked after and well fed.'

Again May nodded.

'You'll need to be strict with them or they'll run rings around you,' Constance told her. 'They're little villains, some of them. Discipline is the key to good order here.'

'Mm.'

'So let's work begin then, shall we?' she decided as they walked into the bedlam that was the two to five year olds. 'Now then, children,' she shouted in a foghorn voice. 'Quieten down now, all of you . . . at once, please.'

After the command had been repeated several times with increased volume every time, order finally prevailed, but only just. May was reminded of her own childhood. Edie had been strict, particularly with May, and there had never been much money around, so she and Bessie had had to help around the house from quite a young age. But not this young; their pre-school years had been spent in the security of knowing that their mother was close at hand at a time when they were as yet untroubled by discipline outside of the home.

These children were little more than babies, not yet ready to fight their own battles. May's heart broke to see the shy ones standing at the side looking petrified while the others ran roughshod over them. This was a nursery, not a prison camp. The children needed more than just discipline and something to occupy them through the long day; they needed fun and to feel loved.

'Can I have some leeway when dealing with the children?' May enquired of Constance. 'You know, use my own judgement.'

'Of course, as long as it fits in with our daily programme,' she replied.

'Which is?'

'Milk now, dinner at twelve, tea at four o'clock and collection at six at the latest.'

'And in between?'

'They play with the toys, what few there are of them, do crayoning, that sort of thing,' Constance informed her. 'We keep them amused as best we can to help the time pass.'

'Read to them?'

'Story time is in the afternoon,' Constance told her. 'But for now could you get the crayoning things out of the cupboard and get them sitting down at the tables?'

'Certainly. But first I'd like to introduce myself to them.' She looked down at her daughter. 'Shall we go and say hello to all the children, Connie, and tell them our names?'

Connie nodded sheepishly, and together they walked into the pandemonium.

'Hello,' said May to a little girl who was standing tearfully at the side of the room. 'My name is May and this is Connie. I'm going to be helping to look after you. What is your name?'

'I want me mum,' she said, ignoring the question. 'I don't like it 'ere. I want to go 'ome.'

'Ah, that's a shame,' said May gently. 'Connie and I don't know if we'll like it yet either, as we are new. Do you think you could help us get to know the others? Would you like to come with us to tell us who they all are?'

The child looked uncertain.

May took her hand and led her gently towards the others. 'What did you say your name is?' said May craftily.

'Lily,' she replied.

'All right then, Lily, let's have some names. That little boy in the grey jumper will do for a start. What's his name?'

''Enry,' she said.

'Thank you.'

May introduced herself to each child individually. Some swore at her; others regarded her with indifference. One little girl told her tearfully that she had wet her knickers. May assured her that she would be back to see to the problem when she'd met everyone else. There were clean children, and ones who didn't look as though they'd seen a bar of soap in weeks; cheeky ones, sweet ones and those in between. All of them had one thing in common. They each needed individual attention at some point in the day.

May got the crayoning things out of the cupboard and set the children up with paper. Some had no interest whatsoever and just wanted to run wild around the room. Those who persevered were helped by May. She made a point of remembering every child's name and gave personal attention to all of those who wanted it, including Connie, who enjoyed having so much company whilst still having her mother close at hand. Constance suggested that May might like to read the afternoon story, and there wasn't a sound to be heard in the room while she did so.

By the time May had finished her shift, her apron was covered in paint and crayon in various colours, as well as gravy stains from helping the children at lunchtime. She had heard the language of navvies issued from the mouths of babes who knew no better; dealt with the adorable, the not so good and the downright wicked; and enjoyed every moment.

As she cycled home with Connie, her mind was racing with ideas to make the nursery a more enjoyable experience for the children. One idea in particular came into her mind and she couldn't wait to suggest it to Constance.

'Are you sure this isn't too much for you now that you're a working woman?' said Bill Mott when she turned up for her stint at the stall on Saturday morning.

'Of course it isn't,' she said, putting out some more carrots and tidying the display in general. 'I'm young and fit. A session on the stall isn't going to hurt me.'

'I know that,' he said. 'But I thought you might want some time to yourself as you're working all week. It's very good of you to help me out.'

'Nonsense. I thoroughly enjoy it,' she told him. 'Anyway, I wouldn't want to rob Aunt Winnie of her chance to have Connie to herself on a Saturday morning. That's the highlight of her week.'

'I bet young Connie enjoys it too.' He smiled. 'I'm guessing that Winnie spoils her rotten.'

'She probably does but I let it go; she's in charge so her rules apply for the morning. She's the nearest thing Connie has to a grandmother, so I like them both to enjoy themselves.'

Bill looked sad.

'Sorry,' she said, putting her hand on his arm. 'I didn't mean to open up old wounds for you.'

'You haven't, love,' he assured her. 'They've never really healed, even after all this time. I'm glad to be a grandad to her, especially as your own folks live a good distance away.'

'Mine probably wouldn't be grandparents to her even if they lived next door,' she said, 'especially my mother.'

'You haven't managed to patch things up, then?'

'No. She's never forgiven me for getting pregnant the wrong side of the blanket and she's refused to accept Connie. That's the bit that hurts.'

'It's a real shame,' he said.

'Yeah, it is a disappointment to me, but that's life. You step out of line and you have to pay the price for it. Still, things have worked out well for me. I'm closer to my auntie than I ever have been to my mother. Aunt Winnie is an absolute rock. I was always very fond of her before – she always visited us regular when we were growing up – but since I've been in London and have got to know her better, I think she's the tops. So that makes up for the fact that things aren't good with my mother.'

'Thank Gawd I came to my senses before any more time was wasted,' he said. 'I would hate not to have you and Connie in my life now.'

'Likewise,' she said.

The more Bill got to know May, the more he liked her. In fact, she was a proper little diamond. 'You're the best thing that ever happened to my Archie,' he told her. 'I know I wasn't happy about it when you got married, but I was wrong to doubt you. You obviously think the world of him and you're the best wife any man could have: trustworthy, loyal and devoted. I know you would never let him down in any way at all.'

May wished she shared Bill's faith in her. But when she thought back to the brief meeting with William Marriot, and her feelings for him, she wasn't quite so sure. Archie had become very dear to her and she truly believed she would do anything for him. It was what else she might do that bothered her, because there was a wild and passionate side to her nature that he didn't satisfy, and that, if put to the test, she wasn't sure she could control.

A rush of customers arrived and a queue formed. As she and Bill worked together, serving and passing the time of day with the punters, she pushed such doubts from her mind. It wasn't right even to think of another man in that way while her husband was away at the war. If Archie was spared — and the news from abroad was not good, with the death toll rising daily — she would make sure she stayed faithful to him.

Recalled to the present, she realised that there was a discussion in progress about the rising price of food and the coal shortage, which was really biting hard in this cold January weather. Coal was rationed according to the number of rooms a family had in their house, and the allowance per room wasn't much.

'At least there's more space to shelter from the air raids in the coal cellar with no bleedin' coal in there,' said one cheery middle-aged woman as May emptied some potatoes direct from the scales into her shopping bag. 'It's an ill wind, as they say.'

'I bet you're not so cheerful when there's no fire in the grate of an evening,' said another woman in the queue.

'I bleedin' well ain't,' said the other, cackling. 'You should hear me swear when I'm sat there in me armchair with three pairs of long drawers on as well as me coat, hat and gloves. I'd go to bed to keep warm but me ole man would take that as an invitation. Nothing cools his ardour, not even me long woollen drawers. I'd sooner run round the block a few times to keep warm than put up with that sort of carry-on in this cold weather.'

People waiting to be served laughed. This was the real world, thought May: ordinary people making the best of hard times and managing to smile despite everything. Archie away fighting in God only knew what conditions was reality. Romantic notions about some good-looking chap who couldn't give tuppence for her anyway were just immature fantasy and should not be treated with any degree of significance. This down-to-earth turn of mind comforted her and boosted her confidence in herself.

'Mind how you go now, and try to keep warm,' said May to the woman as she went on her way. 'Next, please, ladies. A pound of carrots and a couple of onions? Coming up right away,' she said, putting the required items on the scales and entering into the friendly chit-chat that the customers enjoyed and expected from their regular market trader when they did their shopping.

What an asset she was to the business and to his life, thought Bill, watching her.

The afternoon story had been toppled from its position as favourite item of the nursery day by a new feature that May had introduced and that they called Song Time. With the help of Bill Mott and his cart, she had brought the gramophone to the nursery together with some nursery-rhyme records and her own ragtime music, and the kids had a whale of a time.

For the first part of the session they danced to the music, the word 'dance' being interpreted in the loosest possible way. They moved in or out of time to the music in whatever way they pleased, most of them merely jumping up and down with great gusto, some of the girls showing a little more grace and twisting around or skipping round the room. The whole idea of it was for them to have free movement. This they did with huge enthusiasm.

This rather manic episode was followed by singing along with the records. The kids adored this. Even though May played the same few discs every day, they couldn't get enough of it. They loved the familiarity of the songs as they got to know them. It even brought some of the more reserved ones out of their shells. May led the singing and enjoyed every moment.

The job had become more than just paid employment to May. It was more of a purpose. Her aim was to make the nursery a warm-spirited place, not just somewhere the children were dumped every day merely to be supervised, an experience dreaded by some of the less outgoing ones. She wanted it to be a place where the mothers could leave their little ones in the sure knowledge that they would be content, not just left to sit on the floor all day playing with or fighting over the few toys available.

Constance's forte was the running of the nursery, making sure the food was ready and the children's basic needs were catered for, as well as the business side of things. May helped anywhere she was needed but mainly looked after the entertainments, and she spared no effort to keep the children amused, along with Mary, who only came in part time.

The women worked well together. It was the most rewarding of occupations and May was surprised by her affinity for it. There were bad moments, of course: children fighting, being sick or having accidents with their ablutions. But most days she cycled home feeling as though she had done something worthwhile. She had never thought of herself as a patient person, but she needed patience in barrowloads in this job, and much to her surprise and gratitude, it had come to her.

Chapter Fourteen

The seasons changed, another year passed but the war continued to drag on, despite America having come into it, bringing fresh troops and heart to the exhausted Allied armies and new hope to civilians everywhere. French place names, previously unknown to most ordinary English people, became sorrowful household names as horrific battlefields where their husbands, sons and sweethearts were dying. Such places as the Somme, Ypres, Passchendaele . . .

As though finding it necessary to test the human race to the nth degree, nature intervened in the autumn of 1918 by sending a virulent and deadly flu epidemic that swept across the globe affecting fighting troops and civilians alike. Known as Spanish flu, it spread through communities whose people were already weakened by wartime hardships.

In late September it arrived in Britain, and soon gained momentum. News of its ghastly progress spread by word of mouth as well as through the newspapers, who reported the extent of the fatalities. When people began to get sick in Tideway, Bessie found herself in a state of permanent fear for her little boy. Already made vulnerable by the death of her husband over two years ago, she could feel panic rise if Jimmy had so much as a sniffle.

'The newspapers are putting the wind up us all,' remarked her mother one day in October. 'But we mustn't take too much notice of what we read. They concentrate on the dramatic side of it, but not everybody dies from the disease; lots of folks get better too, and no one in the village has perished from it yet. Keep an eye on the boy but try not to get yourself in a state about it. Jimmy is nearly three; he's old enough to pick up on fear. You don't want him turned into a nervous wreck. If illness comes, we'll deal with it. Unless that happens, you must try not to worry.'

With great difficulty Bessie took heed of what her mother said. Fortunately she was very busy, which helped her get things into perspective. Finding it almost impossible to manage on her war widow's pension, she had taken on more photographic work. As her reputation spread, along with word of the reasonable prices she was able to offer because she worked from home, she soon had enough work to make ends meet, given that Jimmy was her first priority, which meant that her time was limited.

She took on a small amount of outside work – weddings and community events – but could only operate locally because she still didn't have transport. An extra pair of hands would have been useful, but her one-time helper Sam was away in the army now that he had turned eighteen. With hard work and expediency she managed, but it became increasingly obvious to her that she was going to need proper paid help and shop premises if she was to make a real success of her business. Meanwhile she needed to get some money behind her, and wait until after the war, when things settled down and people were released from war work, before she took someone on.

It hardly seemed possible that more than two years had passed since Jim's death. It seemed like only yesterday she had received the black-edged telegram. Yet at the same time it felt like forever since she had seen him. Sometimes she fancied that he was with her in spirit, giving her strength and support. Other times there was nothing; it was as though he was gone from her completely, and she hated that feeling. She was still a young woman but she knew there would never be another man in her life.

Now she had to go to the shops for the day's provisions and post the letter she had written to May last night.

'Come on then, my little soldier,' she said to her son, who had a lot of his father in him; the same gentle nature and compelling brown eyes. 'Let's get your hat and coat on.'

'Are we going to see Grandma?' he asked.

'Grandma is at work, but we'll call in to see Grandad if you like,' she informed him.

'Yippee,' he cried, as Bessie's father was a favourite of his. Bessie was glad they were pals, because it gave Jimmy a much-needed male influence in his life.

Holding hands as they walked along the waterfront to the village butcher's, grocer's and post office, they paused a while for Jimmy to watch a family of swans glide by. He loved the river and its wildlife and enjoyed spending time with his grandfather when he was working on his boat on the hard.

It was a beautiful autumn morning with a hazy blue sky, chilly but still, the air tinged with the ambrosial scent of the season. Lots of people were out and about: fishermen working on their boats or chatting in groups;

women with their shopping baskets; young mothers wheeling prams. The silver sprats the fishermen hadn't been able to sell at market gleamed in the sunshine as people helped themselves.

Every few yards someone greeted Bessie and her son, the boatmen making a fuss of Jimmy because they all knew and liked his grandfather. When they finally got to Berry Cottage, she was surprised to find that her mother wasn't out at work as she'd expected. She was upstairs in bed, an unprecedented event for Edie during the daytime.

'I've never known your mother take to her bed before, no matter how poorly she's feeling,' her father confided worriedly. 'She was a bit off colour yesterday but nothing to speak of. Then she woke up in the night feeling terrible and just didn't feel well enough to go to work this morning. She must be bad to do that. I hope she hasn't got Spanish flu.'

'I'm sure it won't be anything as drastic as that,' said Bessie, hoping to reassure. 'I'll go up and see her.'

'She said to tell you that you're not to go anywhere near her in case it is that. She doesn't want you catching it and passing it on to the little one.'

He did have a valid point but she couldn't ignore her sick mother. Noticing that her father was shivering, she said, 'There's no fire in the hearth, Dad.'

'No. Your mother was too ill to light it,' he told her, illustrating just how much the household relied on Edie. 'I haven't got around to it. I'll do it in a minute.'

'The place is freezing. Just because the sun is out doesn't make it warm indoors, not in October,' she pointed out, drawing her shawl tight. 'You keep Jimmy amused while I get the fire going.' She looked at him. 'You don't look too good yourself. Are you feeling all right?'

'I don't feel very well, to tell you the truth,' he replied. 'It'll just be a cold coming, I expect.'

'You sit down while I get the fire going, then I'll make you a hot drink and see if Mum wants anything. If I catch the wretched flu thing it's just too bad. People need looking after when they are sick and the pair of you need me here right now.'

'I think we do too,' he was forced to admit.

By the evening of that same day, both her parents were tucked up in bed and Bessie had moved into Berry Cottage temporarily to look after them.

'It's very good of you, dear,' said Edie gratefully when Bessie took them up some beef tea. 'I'll never forgive myself if you catch it, though.'

'If I do, I do. There's no point in worrying about it, and I'll keep Jimmy well away from you,' she said. 'So relax and enjoy a bit of pampering.'

'I wish I could,' muttered her mother, looking pale and shivery, her lips dry and chapped. 'But I feel too ill to enjoy anything.'

'Should I go and ask the doctor to come over?' enquired Bessie. She looked at the clock. 'It isn't too late to get across the river. The ferry will still be running.'

'Lord, no,' protested Edie. 'We don't have money to burn and we certainly don't want to pay out for the doctor for just a touch of flu. He'll be run off his feet anyway with so many people going down with it. They say you should go to bed and keep warm if you've got the symptoms, and that's what we're doing. We'll be all right, won't we, George?'

'Mm,' he mumbled from under the bedclothes.

'All right, we'll see how you are in the morning,' Bessie agreed. 'In the meantime, let's have those hot-water bottles and I'll refill them for you. I've already got the kettle on.'

Clutching the stone hot-water bottles, she hurried downstairs, checking on her sleeping son on the way.

Two days later George Bow was on the mend. He was still weak but he was up and about, though not quite well enough yet to take the boat out. Edie showed no sign of improvement but still refused to let them get the doctor.

'Your father isn't working so there'll be no money coming in,' she reminded her daughter, who was keen to get medical advice. 'We don't want to dip into what he made in the summer from the yachting just for a doctor when the thing will heal itself in nature's own time. That money is to help us through the winter.'

'I'll pay the doctor from the money I earn from my photographic work,' Bessie offered.

'You most certainly will not. You need to hang on to that.' After a lifetime of frugality, it was second nature to Edie to be tight with money. 'You don't have a husband to support you and you have a child to bring up. I shall be really upset if you get the doctor.'

'We'll see how you are in the morning then,' Bessie finally agreed, 'and if you're still no better I *am* getting the doctor whether you like it or not.'

George came to his daughter's bed in the early hours of the next morning, fully dressed in his outdoor clothes.

'I'm going for the doctor for your mother,' he told her in a whisper after he'd woken her. 'She's worse. She's burning up and her chest hurts. The poor woman can hardly breathe.'

Fear shot through Bessie but she tried not to show it, careful not to alarm him. 'The ferry won't be running at this hour,' she pointed out.

'I'll take my own boat across.'

'But you're still not properly better yourself,' she reminded him. 'You shouldn't be out in the cold in the middle of the night. It will make you ill again.'

'I'm not bothered about that,' he told her. 'Your mother needs medical help and she's going to get it. Don't worry about me. I'll be all right.'

Bessie didn't even suggest that she go for the doctor herself, because she had never been allowed to learn how to use the boat. The place for Tideway females was considered, most definitely, to be on dry land.

'Whatever you think best, Dad.'

'Keep your eye on her while I'm gone.'

'Of course.'

Leaving her son sleeping peacefully, Bessie pulled on her dressing gown and went to her parents' bedroom, while her father went out into the night.

'Come on now, Connie, stop playing with your porridge and eat it properly,' said May forcibly. 'We have to get ready to go to the nursery.'

'Can I help you put the music on today when we are there?' the little girl asked.

'Maybe. If you're a good girl and finish your porridge now,' her mother replied.

'Why do I have to eat it?' the child wanted to know.

'Because it'll make you strong and healthy,' Winnie told her, 'and also because Mummy said so.'

'I sometimes wonder who's in charge, her or me,' May laughed. 'She can be a little madam when the mood takes her; a proper little bossy-boots.'

Connie thought that was hilarious and roared with laughter, her whole body exuding delight.

'Whoops. You've done it now,' said Winnie, looking at the child affection-ately. 'Once she gets the giggles there's no stopping her. She can't eat her breakfast for laughing now.'

'We're going to be late if you don't get on and finish your breakfast,' admonished May, though she couldn't help but smile at her daughter's exuberance. 'And you'll miss the chance to get a turn on the scooter, because someone else will have bagged it.'

This crafty reminder did the trick and Connie began to make short work of the food.

'You won't be able to be late next year when you go to school,' Winnie mentioned casually.

'That's a point,' added May. 'We'll have to be out sharp in the mornings then.'

'Will I like it at school?' the child asked.

'Ooh yes,' replied May, though she secretly dreaded the day she had to send Connie out on her own, away from the safety of her mother's protection. 'You'll be a big girl then.'

Could she really be coming up to five years old? It hardly seemed possible. The speed with which time passed frightened May, because Connie's childhood was so very precious to her. As the little girl got older, May could see a lot of her father in her: the way she smiled and held her mouth; the fleeting indefinable look in her eyes that made May's heart leap because it reminded her so vividly of William Marriot. Just when she thought she had successfully relegated him to the past, biology raised its head and reminded her that she still wasn't quite over him.

But Connie was her *raison d'être*; thoughts of her father mere incidental irritations. Everything was worthwhile because her daughter was in the world. May was beginning to want another baby rather desperately now, to satisfy her own maternal urges and also because she didn't want Connie to be an only child. It would too lonely for her later on. Of course it was already too late for any further children to grow up close in age to Connie, and because of the wretched war, there was nothing May could do about it. She just had to wait until Archie came home and pray to God that he did. She already knew how he would feel about having a child – their first together. He would be all in favour.

A knock at the door recalled her to the present. Winnie went to answer it while May got firm with Connie, who had begun to dawdle again. 'Come on now, love, get on and finish your breakfast; there's a little dear.'

'May . . .' Winnie had re-entered the room.

'Who was it, Auntie?' she asked, perceiving the pale, anxious face. 'What's the matter?'

Shakily Winnie handed her a telegram. 'It's addressed to you. Sorry, love,' she said in barely more than a whisper.

'Oh.' May froze completely. 'It must be about Archie,' she uttered through dry lips, her hands trembling so much she could hardly open the envelope.

Winnie didn't say anything; she just watched and waited, ready to offer solace.

Staring at the words, May read, 'Mum very ill. Please come at once. Bessie.'

'It isn't Archie, it's Mum,' she told her aunt. 'She's very sick. I've to go at once.'

'Oh my Gawd,' cried Winnie, clutching her head. 'I'm coming with you. I'll have to leave a note for Albert.'

'Bessie wouldn't have sent a telegram if it wasn't really urgent,' remarked May. 'We'll have to leave right away. I don't want to let Constance down, but today I have no choice. There's no time to let her know.'

Within ten minutes they had left the house en route for Liverpool Street station.

'She's been asking for you, May,' said Bessie when Winnie and May arrived. 'And you, Aunt Winnie. In fact she seems quite desperate to see you both.'

'Oh.' May thought her mother must be delirious to be asking for her, given the situation between them. 'What's actually the matter with her?'

'Pneumonia,' replied Bessie.

There was a gasp from May and Winnie; they both knew what that meant.

'She had Spanish flu at first, then complications set in and we had to get the doctor.' Bessie was looking whey faced and drained. 'He said we have to prepare ourselves for the worst. Dad is with her. He won't leave her side. The doctor has been wonderful. He's been in and out in between his other calls every day since she took really bad. He's told us not to worry about the cost. He'll just charge us for the one visit.'

'That's good of him,' responded May numbly.

Bessie nodded. 'You two go up to see her,' she suggested. 'I'll stay down here and look after the children.'

She looked at her niece and managed a smile. 'Well, Connie, aren't you all grown up now, and so pretty with your lovely frock and hair ribbons.' She took the little girl's hand and led her away gently, choking back tears. 'Come and see your cousin Jimmy.'

Edie was barely conscious when May and Winnie went into the bedroom, which smelled of cough medicine and poultice, the air infused with the sour odour of illness.

'Here's May and Winnie come to see you, Edie,' said George, looking pale and exhausted. 'You've been fretting about seeing them. Well, they are here now.'

May sat down by the bed, shocked to see her mother so ill; she was pale and emaciated, a mere shadow of her former self. 'We got here as soon as we could, Mum,' she told her. 'Sorry to hear that you're not feeling well.'

With a sense of urgency bordering on desperation, Edie reached out for May's hand and clutched it tightly. 'I'm so sorry, May, sorry for everything,' she said, her voice barely audible. 'Can you find it in your heart to forgive me?'

'Of course I can,' she replied without hesitation, all the rancour of the past eradicated by the words she'd never thought she would hear her mother utter. 'I did all right in the end anyway; found a good husband to look out for me and Connie. It's all in the past; gone and forgotten.'

Edie was frail and rambling. 'I thought it would be for the best,' she said weakly. As she continued to speak, it was as though she was referring to someone other than May, her mind obviously confused. 'She was so young, she had always been headstrong, so I thought it was the right thing; the only thing really under the circumstances.' Beads of perspiration suffused her face. May dabbed it with a cold flannel and dried it gently with a towel.

'Don't worry about it, Mum,' May tried to reassure. 'We're friends again now. That's the important thing.'

'I tried to treat you all the same, but sometimes . . .'

'It's all right, honestly,' May told her, holding Edie's hot bony hand in hers, surprised by her admission. 'I knew I wasn't the favourite child, but it doesn't matter.'

'Sorry.'

For the first time she could remember, May could feel real deep-felt emotion – maybe even love – exuding from her mother, and she was overwhelmed by it, tears streaming down her face. All she wanted now was to give wholehearted reassurance to a sick and feeble woman. 'I'm sorry too, for giving you such a lot of headaches. I know I was a handful.'

Edie seemed to drift in and out of consciousness, the rattle of her chest filling the room. Then she came to again. 'Winnie . . . is my sister Winnie here?'

'I'm here, Edie,' said Winnie, taking May's place at the bedside and holding her sister's hand.

'I'm sorry if I got it wrong and made you suffer,' Edie said almost in a whisper. 'I just didn't know what else to do.'

'I know dear, I know,' Winnie assured her. 'You always acted with the

234

very best of intentions.' She looked at her sister with affection. 'You were always the practical one.'

'One of us had to be,' said Edie.

'You're right there.'

Edie became very distressed as she struggled for breath. Half an hour later she slipped away with her family around her. Her husband kissed her and closed her eyes. For the first time ever, their daughters were shown evidence of their parents' love for each other.

'Dad's in pieces,' mentioned May when the three tearful women went back downstairs, leaving their father sitting by his dead wife. 'It seems strange to see him like that. He's always been such a strong man.'

'He'll be lost without her and that's a fact,' stated Winnie, wiping her eyes.

'I just can't believe it,' wept Bessie.

'Nor me,' added May tearfully.

'This time last week there wasn't a thing wrong with her,' Bessie went on. 'I should have got the doctor to her earlier. But she was so dead set against it.'

'I doubt if it would have made any difference, love,' opined Winnie. 'There isn't any medicine to cure this new flu epidemic, which is why people are dying in thousands.'

'You did everything you could,' May assured her sister. 'You've nothing to reproach yourself for. It was her time. That's why she's gone. Not through any lack of care on your part.'

The back door opened and Connie burst in from the garden, her entrance followed by screams from outside.

'Jimmy's fallen over and grazed his knee,' she informed them with an air of seniority about her, adding dramatically, 'it's bleeding.'

As Bessie went to see to her injured son, Winnie said, 'You certainly don't get a chance to wallow in your own misery when there are kids about, which I suppose is a blessing.'

'I'm glad Mum made her peace with me before she went,' confessed May emotionally. 'I was surprised to hear her admit that she'd felt differently towards me than the others. She said she'd tried not to treat me differently, sort of admitting that she had done. That's what I took it to mean anyway. Perhaps she hadn't wanted another child so soon after Bessie and that's the reason. I always thought I must have imagined that. I suppose every mother has her favourite, and I wasn't hers.'

'She seemed to be good to you, from what I could see,' Winnie told her.

'Oh yeah, she was a good mother. She couldn't be faulted in that way. It was just a feeling I had that there was something about me she didn't like; that she was irritated by me. It was never anything you could put your finger on, though, and it's only in retrospect as an adult that I've thought about it.'

'I think you might have been imagining most of it,' suggested Winnie.

'Very probably. The fact that she made her peace with me before she died means the world to me,' May confessed. 'She seemed keen to put things right with you too. I suppose that was about the rift caused between the two of you when I fell pregnant and you took my side . . .' She paused. 'Only she seemed to be going back into the past, didn't she?'

'She was just rambling,' said Winnie quickly. 'She was in some other place when all that came out.'

'I'd like to think she knew what she was saying when she spoke to me, though some of it didn't make a lot of sense, I must admit,' confessed May. 'It was as though she was talking about someone else and not me. She said *she*; not *you*.'

'I think she was a little confused at times, but I'm sure she knew what she was saying when she made her peace with you,' said Winnie, moist eyed.

'For the first time in my life I felt real love coming from her,' May said, starting to cry. 'And now she's gone.'

Bessie came in carrying Jimmy, followed by Connie and Whistler.

'I'll just put a bandage on his knee,' she said. 'Can someone put the kettle on and make some tea?'

May and Winnie agreed in unison and they all moved into the kitchen. The dog sat at the bottom of the stairs as though sensing something was wrong.

'Poor thing,' said May, fondling his head. 'Dogs know these things. He's as sad as we are.'

'Can we have a dog, Mum?' asked Connie, who adored Whistler. She stroked him and put her face against his fur affectionately.

'One day, maybe, when we get a place of our own,' replied May, wondering how everything could be going on as normal when their mother was dead upstairs and their father grief-stricken. She supposed it must be because life had to go on, no matter how bad people were feeling.

As well as her grief to endure, Bessie was forced to accept the fact that she would have to give up her little cottage and move in with her father, who needed her close at hand. Someone had to look after him, and May was too far away and had commitments in London.

Bessie did regret having to return to the nest, to a home with her mother's stamp all over it, leaving all her carefully chosen furnishings behind in the cottage where she had planned to raise her own family with Jim. She was spared the bother of having to sell the furniture because the landlord wanted to rent the cottage out furnished, so he bought it all from her as it stood; rugs and curtains as well.

One thing she was determined not to give up, though she suspected she might have a fight on her hands to keep it, was her photographic work. There were two main obstacles: firstly, when her brother came home there would be two men and a child to cook and clean for, which would eat into her time; secondly, there was the question of space.

Where could she actually have her studio at Berry Cottage? Living alone with her son she had worked around it. Sharing a home with other people would be very different. Somehow she would have to find a way, because she needed to work. The main reason was financial: the war widow's pension she got from the government wasn't enough to support her and Jimmy decently. But she wanted to work for personal reasons too. She had learned a lot about photography and knew she was good at the job. Digby had known that too, which was why he had left her the equipment. She was determined not to let it all go to waste just because she happened to be a woman.

Because they were in the early stages of mourning, May and Winnie didn't think it was appropriate for them to join in the revelry and rejoicing too wholeheartedly when the Armistice finally came at eleven o'clock on the morning of 11 November 1918. But it was too much of a momentous event not to take any part at all, and May wanted Connie to recognise the fact that the longed-for peace had arrived at last. Mothers came to collect their children as workplaces closed for the day and people took to the streets to celebrate, so the members of the nursery staff were free to go.

May cycled home ringing her bell along with the church bells pealing out, boy scouts sounding bugles, police whistles shrilling, dustbin lids clanging and people cheering and singing. When she got home, her uncle and aunt were back from work and out on the street, where people were hugging each other and cheering to mark the end of the war.

Collecting Bill Mott on the way, they all hopped on a bus and joined the crowds in the West End, where they caught a glimpse of the King and Queen as they made an informal drive through the centre of London to Hyde Park. Connie sat on Bill's shoulders waving her flag and cheering.

After four long years of war, it was finally over. Obviously Edie's death overshadowed everything, and May was dreadfully sad, but she couldn't help but rejoice that the war was finally ended and the men could come home.

The festivities were still in full swing in the West End when May and the others got home. Albert and Bill wanted to carry on for a while longer so went to join the celebrations at the local pub. Winnie stayed home to keep May company, and after Connie was in bed they sat together in the parlour with a bottle of port they had got in for Christmas, having decided that the Armistice warranted a glass or two each.

'It's been such a peculiar few weeks,' said May, a little mellow after a couple of drinks. 'With Mum dying and the Armistice coming more or less at once.'

'Yeah, it's been an emotional time for all of us.'

'It's a pity Mum didn't live to see the end of the war, isn't it?'

Winnie nodded, looking sad. 'The cost of the war will really come home to people when the celebrations are over and the men return in much smaller numbers than they went out in.'

'There is that,' agreed May. 'I pray to God every day that Archie will come marching home. I had a letter a week ago so I know he's survived. And as far as we know Sam is all right too.'

'They'll be back, don't worry, and what a celebration that will be,' declared Winnie.

She poured them another glass; they were both feeling increasingly relaxed with every sip.

'I keep thinking about Mum,' sighed May.

'Me too,' mentioned Winnie. 'Edie and I didn't always see eye to eye, but she was my sister when all is said and done, and I was fond of her.'

'All that stuff she said just before she died,' May began. 'I can't get it out of my mind. I keep going over and over it, as if I'm trying to make sense of it.' She paused. 'It was as almost as though she was trying to tell me something.' She sipped her drink, losing her inhibitions and suddenly able to talk about this very personal subject.

Winnie stayed silent.

'I don't know why it matters so much to me, Auntie,' she went on, leaning further back in her chair. 'I mean, it was never a big issue, just an occasional feeling of things not being quite right when I was growing up.

She ended the rift between us, that's the main thing.' She thought for a moment. 'But she wasn't apologising to me about that, I'm sure of it. There was something . . . something else she wanted me to know, but time ran out on her.' May looked at her aunt. 'I suppose I'm imagining things again, am I?'

Putting her glass down carefully on the table beside her, Winnie looked at her niece with a grave expression. 'No, you're not, as it happens,' she told her. 'I think there was something she wanted you to know too.'

'Oh?' May was surprised. 'I thought you said I was reading too much into it when I mentioned it the other day.'

'Yes, well that was then to stop you upsetting yourself in the immediate aftermath of losing your mum,' Winnie told her. 'Now I have had time to think about it, and you are obviously going to torment yourself over it, so I am going to tell you something that will make it all very clear to you. But it will come as quite a shock. So brace yourself.'

May sat forward. 'Auntie,' she began in a questioning manner, observing Winnie's serious expression, 'what is it? You're scaring me.'

Winnie hesitated, then picked up her glass again, took a large swallow of the comforting liquid and blurted out, 'My sister Edie, your mother as you have always known her . . . er, she wasn't actually your mother.'

'Of course she was my mother,' stated May. 'What on earth are you talking about?'

'Edie brought you up as her own, and I think she made a very good job of it, but she didn't actually give birth to you.'

'I don't understand.' May was bewildered. 'Why are you saying these things?'

'Because I think you have a right to know. I haven't been able to tell you before because I promised Edie I wouldn't. She thought it would have made it difficult for her to raise you as her own. Now you are grown up and Edie can't be hurt, so it's time you knew the truth.'

'What truth?' May clutched her head. 'Auntie, I don't know what you are going on about and I don't like all this stuff. Did my real mother die? Who was she?'

'No, she didn't die,' replied Winnie, managing to keep her voice steady. 'She's sitting here with you.'

The silence was so intense, even the ticking of the clock seemed deafening. Then May burst out, 'You? You are my mother?'

'Yes, and very proud of it I am too.' Winnie sounded confident, but she was actually distraught and dreading the explosion she knew would come, fearing that she would lose May's love and respect completely.

May blinked. 'So why have I been led to believe otherwise? Why didn't you bring me up?' she asked.

'I was fifteen when I fell pregnant with you . . . I was in no position to.'

'What about my father?'

'That doesn't matter.'

'It does to me.'

'He was a member of the household where I worked as a housemaid.' She saw the question in May's eyes. 'No, he wouldn't have stood by me, and that is definite.'

'You didn't even tell him, did you?'

'I would have been dismissed immediately if I had, and I couldn't afford that. I had to send money home even though I was living in as a house-maid,' she explained. 'So I tightened my corsets and plodded on. I worked for as long as I could, which was up until the last few weeks before you were born. When I got near to my time, Edie – who I had taken into my confidence early on – told my employer that I was ill with bronchitis and would be staying with her until I was better. So I stayed with Edie and George but kept out of sight of the neighbours in case they twigged. Edie kept very much to herself in those days – she didn't take part in village affairs – so when she appeared with a new baby, no one had reason to suspect that it wasn't hers. I was back at work within a few days. I couldn't afford to be off work so didn't bother with the traditional lying-in.'

'The man . . . er, my father might have married you if he had been given the chance.'

Winnie shook her head.

'You don't mean . . .'

'Yes, he was already married. But it wouldn't have made any difference if he hadn't been. I was nothing to him.'

'Oh, Auntie.'

'Young housemaids have been seduced by their lords and masters since time began,' she told her. 'But I was too young and naive to realise that at the time.'

'But a married man . . .' May said disapprovingly.

'They can be very powerful, these upper-class types. I was flattered by his attention and fell for him.'

'Was my father a rapist?' asked May.

'No.'

'So you . . .'

'Yes, that's right.'

'Oh, I see.'

Her aunt raised her eyes.

'Yeah, all right, like mother like daughter,' conceded May, getting her aunt's drift. 'But at least in my case the man wasn't married and I kept my baby. I didn't just give her away. I faced up to my responsibilities.'

'And so did I,' Winnie said defensively. 'Before you judge me, just listen to the facts.'

'But . . .'

'Listen.'

May sat back in the chair in despair. She had been beginning to feel a bit tipsy from the port. Now she was stone-cold sober.

'As you know, Edie was a lot older than me and she was in a stable marriage.'

'What about George? How did he feel about it?' asked May.

'He was all for it. You know how kind and easy going he is. They already had Henry and Bessie, so you fitted in very well. Edie took you from me immediately after you were born, and made me promise never to say a word to anyone for your sake.'

'Oh, so it was all your sister's fault, was it?' May said cynically. 'Nothing to do with you.'

'No, that isn't what I am saying at all,' Winnie came back at her. 'Edie has always been very practical. When a problem needed solving, she got on and solved it.'

'It's a wonder she didn't try and make you do what she tried to make me do.'

Winnie looked at her.

'Oh . . . so I nearly didn't get born at all.'

'There was never any chance of that happening,' Winnie assured her. 'I absolutely refused.'

'Thank God for small mercies.'

'I know you're very hurt, darlin', and you probably won't believe this, but giving you up was the hardest thing I have ever had to do,' Winnie told her. 'But Edie had everything that I didn't. She had a home, and a husband who was willing to bring you up as his own in an established family. I was just a kid with nothing except a job as a housemaid, which I would have lost if I'd kept you.'

'What about your parents?'

'My mother would have thrown me out if she had known, but as I was living away from home, she never got to know,' she explained. 'Our parents were very strict about anything of that sort, which is where Edie

241

gets her strong views from. But it isn't only Edie; you know what people are like about that sort of thing,'

'You could still have kept me,' opined May miserably. 'I kept Connie.'

'Yes, you did, and you were able to do so because you had an aunt who took you in and gave you support,' Winnie reminded her. 'If you hadn't had your uncle and me, you and Connie would have been in the workhouse. If I hadn't gone along with Edie, that's where you would have been born, and God knows what sort of a life you would have had then. Children were separated from their mothers so you wouldn't have been with me. As it was, you had a stable environment and a place in a good home with three meals a day and clean clothes to wear.'

'And I'm supposed to be grateful to you for that, am I?'

'That's up to you,' she said. 'I'm just pointing out the reality of the situation.'

'I suppose telling me was the least you could do for me after a lifetime of disregard,' said May, the shock and disappointment making her spiteful.

'I never disregarded you.' All through the years Winnie had sent money to Edie whenever she could to help with the cost of clothing and feeding May until she was old enough to go out to work. But to mention it would be a cheap bid to win her over and might make May feel even worse. 'You had a damn sight more than I could have given you.'

'And a mother who didn't want me around because I wasn't her own child and she resented having to bring me up.'

'That just isn't true,' argued Winnie. 'Edie didn't resent it. She might have been a bit of a tartar but she was basically a good woman and gave you an excellent upbringing. All right, so she didn't stand by you when you were in trouble, but she would have behaved in the same way had it been Bessie in that sort of bother. It had nothing to do with you not being her daughter in the biological sense. It was her obsession with respectability that caused that; the way society is and the way we have both been raised.'

'If you say so.' May's harsh words were tumbling out almost of their own volition. The pain of knowing that the woman she had always admired for her strong, independent spirit, endless capacity for humour and warm heart had abandoned her at birth was so strong it made her want to hit out; she needed Winnie to feel some of what she herself was feeling now.

'Edie did her very best for you,' Winnie continued. 'All right, sometimes you felt different. Edie wasn't a saint; she was just an ordinary woman doing her best, and I suppose sometimes she might have got frustrated with bringing up a family, like anyone else. You were always a bit of a wild child, like me, whereas Bessie was placid, so whatever the circumstances you would have been in trouble more often than her by your very nature. Don't tell me you didn't have a happy childhood, because I won't believe you. I've been there, remember. I've seen how you were. I used to visit on a regular basis when you were children, if you recall. I kept a close eye on you, and if I'd thought Edie was being unfair I would have told her, on the quiet. But as far as I was concerned you were healthy and happy with a life that I could never have given you.'

May shrugged.

'How do you think that felt, May? Just imagine how you would feel if it was you and Connie in a similar position,' challenged Winnie. 'It used to break my heart because I couldn't have you with me like I wanted. Sometimes you have to live with your own broken heart for the good of another.'

'Does Uncle Albert know?'

'Of course he does. I wouldn't have kept something as important as that from him. I told him before we got married. I didn't want any secrets between us.'

'Why didn't you take me back after you got married?' she asked. 'You could have had me then without causing a scandal.'

'You were eight years old by then, and what sort of damage would it have done to you, eh?' Winnie replied. 'To take you away from your brothers and sister and the life you were used to would have been cruel. Anyway, I promised Edie I wouldn't tell you until you were old enough to cope with it.'

'I'll never be old enough to cope with it, if I live to be a hundred,' announced May, completely in thrall to her emotions. 'How can anyone cope with the fact that they were given away at birth? That is the ultimate rejection. I've been living a lie. Both you and your sister have been lying to me through your teeth all my life.'

'I'm sorry, love, I really am.' Winnie was full of remorse. 'All I can say in my defence is that I really did think I was doing right by you, and that throughout it all I never stopped loving you or ceased to be sad that I'd lost you. I wasn't able to have any more children, so you could say that justice has been done.'

May said nothing.

'The sadness of losing you never went away – it just got worse as you grew up,' Winnie explained. 'Until fate took a hand in it and I got you back, in a manner of speaking, when you came to live here.

This past few years has been the happiest time of my life. I've loved having you here.'

The younger woman looked at Winnie in a way that made her wince.

'Sad? You?' she said thickly. The qualities she had so admired in her aunt now seemed only to make her appear callous. 'You wouldn't know how. Everything is just a laugh and a joke to you.'

'Things aren't always what they seem, as you very well know,' Winnie retaliated. 'You are exactly the same as I am in that respect. When you are sad or worried no one would ever know, because you laugh on the outside. That's what I've been doing all my life. It's my way of coping, the same as it is for you. You get that part of your personality from me.'

May stood up. 'Sorry . . . Auntie, but I can't deal with any more of this right now. I need to be on my own.'

'All right, love,' said Winnie. 'Sleep well.'

The good-night kiss she always received from May was noticeably absent, and Winnie was in despair. This was one occasion when she couldn't stay cheerful, because she had a terrible suspicion that she was about to lose the person who meant everything to her.

Chapter Fifteen

Whatever the complexities of the situation, and however justified Winnie might have been, the fact of the matter, from May's point of view, was that the woman she had always known as a favourite aunt was actually her mother who had seen fit to give her away at birth. It took some getting used to. As much as May might wish to brush it aside and behave as though nothing had changed between herself and Winnie, that simply wasn't possible, because everything had.

No amount of sensible reasoning or in-depth thought on the subject could alter that. With her intellect May could understand why Winnie had felt it necessary to behave as she had, but her emotional self was in turmoil. It wasn't a matter of self-pity – that wasn't in her nature anyway, and she accepted the fact that she had benefited from Winnie's decision – it was a feeling of worthlessness that came from personal rejection. Her sensible side told her she was being unreasonable; her heart told her that she was an unwanted child and that Winnie had taken the easy way out. Her anguish went far deeper than her mind; it was more a wounding of the soul.

Because she suspected that she would take her trauma out on Winnie by saying hateful things to her if she continued to live in the same house – in which case the entire situation would be impossible – she made a decision.

'I'm moving out, Auntie,' she informed her the next morning after breakfast, when the two women were washing the dishes in the kitchen. Connie was in the other room with Albert. Everyone had the day off because of the Armistice. 'I'm sure Bill Mott will put Connie and me up for the time being. Until something more permanent can be arranged.'

May saw Winnie wince at her decision but she got no satisfaction from it, only more pain. It was not her intention to hurt the other woman. It was simply that the state of affairs was an emotional minefield, and so she knew she had to leave.

'Oh May, don't do this,' Winnie begged. 'Please don't. We'll get through it between us, I promise you, if we give it some time. I know you've had a shock, but we get along so well, all of us living here; don't spoil it. You and I are both the same people we always were before the revelation. Nothing has changed.'

'Everything has changed for me, Auntie.' She looked at the older woman gravely. 'I shall continue to call you that. I will never call you Mother.'

'Of course not,' Winnie agreed. 'I wouldn't expect or want that. But there's no need to move out; none at all. You're happy here. Connie is content. It works very well.'

'Not any more it won't,' May insisted. 'We'd have to move out anyway at some point when Archie comes home; into a place of our own.'

'Of course, but don't go prematurely and with bad feeling,' she urged.

'I have to do it. I'm so sorry.' May was driven to be adamant by the power of her instincts.

'But Connie will miss me and Albert . . .'

'Don't worry, I won't stop Connie from seeing you,' she assured her. 'I wouldn't make a child suffer because of the way adults carry on.' She gave Winnie a direct look. 'Anyway, you are her grandmother, aren't you? You are entitled to see her. I shall bring her to visit on a regular basis, but that is where the contact between you and me will end.'

Winnie's face was bloodless. 'There's no need for any of this,' she said, her spirit beginning to return. 'All right, so I did wrong in your eyes, though others might see it differently. I'm a human being, and as such I don't always get things right. Do I have to pay for it for the rest of my life?'

'I'm not trying to punish you,' May insisted, hating herself for what she was doing but feeling compelled to continue. 'Honestly I'm not.'

'Aren't you?' said Winnie in an accusing tone, eyes narrowed, lips tight, her skin suffused with red anxiety blotches. 'Are you absolutely sure about that, May?'

'Yes, I am. I am merely being realistic,' she told her. 'Us living here won't work any more and neither will the relationship between you and me.'

'I see. I rejected you – to your way of thinking – so now you are rejecting me.'

'No, it isn't like that at all.'

'It's exactly like that, despite the fact that you won't or can't admit it, even to yourself,' retorted Winnie, who although terribly hurt, had far too much gumption to sit back and take everything May was throwing at her without at least stating her case. 'You want to hurt me as I have hurt you. Never mind the reasons or the facts of the matter. You want to go away and lick your wounds and make sure I suffer in the process.' Tears began to roll down her cheeks, and she wiped them away with the back of her hand in a gesture of defiance. 'All right, if that's the way you want it, you go. I'm done with begging and pleading. You are old enough to make your own decisions; far be it from me, the wicked mother, to try and influence you.'

She turned away from May towards the sink and plunged her hands into the washing-up bowl.

May stood for a moment watching her shoulders shaking from her stifled sobs, then, resisting her natural instinct to comfort her, she left the room, choking back the tears.

'Blimey, that's some family secret,' gasped Bessie. It was a week or two after the Armistice, and May had told her the truth about her origins. They were sitting on a bench by the Tideway waterfront, the children playing on the grass nearby. 'I can't believe it.'

'It took a while for it to sink in with me too, and I'm still not used to it,' confessed May. 'I didn't want to tell you such a personal thing by letter, and I wanted to see how you and Dad are bearing up anyway, so I decided to hop on to a train and turn up on the doorstep.'

'I'm very glad that you did,' Bessie assured her. 'It's lovely to see you.'

'Even though I'm not your sister?'

'Don't be ridiculous, May,' admonished Bessie. 'There's more to being sisters than the blood tie. Anyway, we're cousins, which is the next best thing.'

'It's a heck of a shock to take straight after Mum's death,' May told her. 'I shall always think of her as my mother, even though she was actually my aunt.'

'Of course you must think of her in that way. She's the one who brought you up.'

'Exactly!

'So how are things between you and Aunt Winnie?'

'Finished altogether. I've moved out of her place and am staying with Archie's dad for the time being. Bless him, he didn't ask any questions; just welcomed Connie and me into his home without hesitation. I suppose he thinks that Auntie and I have just had an ordinary falling-out.'

'That was a bit drastic, wasn't it?' questioned Bessie with a furrowed brow. 'Uprooting yourself and Connie like that and dealing Aunt Winnie such a blow.'

247

'What else could I have done?'

'Stayed there and worked it out, of course,' she replied without hesitation.

'What is there to work out?' May was keen to know. 'The woman is a fraud. After what she did to me, you don't think I'm going to carry on thinking of her as my favourite aunt?'

'I think you're being very hard on her, and that isn't like you, May,' Bessie said disapprovingly.

'Of course I'm hard,' defended May. 'Anyone would be in the circumstances.'

'Not necessarily. You didn't suffer by it, did you?' Bessie pointed out. 'You grew up with the boys and me and we had a good family life. Personally, I'm glad that Auntie handed you over. I wouldn't have grown up with you as my sister if she hadn't.'

'There is that,' May conceded with reluctance. 'But I was always the one in trouble with Mum, you must admit.'

'Only because you were the naughtiest,' Bessie said bluntly. 'I don't think it had anything to do with what we now know as the true circumstances. Come on, May, you were always into some sort of mischief, you must admit that. You were a right little daredevil; far worse than the boys ever knew how to be. Mum couldn't let you get away with it, could she? She had to exercise some discipline. Surely you must accept that, especially now that you're a mother yourself.'

'All right, so I wasn't always an angel, but it was more than that,' May persisted. 'I always knew there was something different about me.'

'Well I never suspected anything untoward, and I certainly didn't notice any difference in the way Mum treated us. You always seemed happy enough to me. We all were as children, most of the time anyway.'

'I'm not denying it,' May conceded. 'And I have a new respect for Mum and Dad now. It couldn't have been easy having another kid to bring up, another mouth to feed. A child that wasn't their own foisted on them. That's the bit that hurts, Bessie: that my real mother gave me away. She let someone else take the responsibility and the worry. Can't you understand how awful I feel for having given people who weren't my parents such a burden, especially as I was a bit of a handful?'

'Now you're just piling the agony on yourself unnecessarily,' reproved Bessie. 'They obviously thought of you as their own.'

'I don't know how anyone could just hand a child over; absolve themselves entirely of all responsibility.'

'You know the reason why she did it, though, so why be so hard on

Auntie . . . and yourself?' asked Bessie. 'You've always loved Aunt Winnie. She made a great fuss of you when we were kids and she's the same person she always was. She hasn't changed because you now know something about her that you didn't know before. I'm sure she would have kept you if that had been possible. Remember, she was very good to you when you got pregnant and Mum turned her back on you. Why cast her out of your life, especially after we've just lost Mum?'

'How can you trust someone who has lied to you all your life?' May asked.

'It depends why they lied.' Bessie looked at her. 'Obviously I can't know what it actually feels like to have to cope with what you are dealing with, which is why I can't understand why you can't find it in your heart to forgive Aunt Winnie. I can only try to imagine how hard it must be. But I'm sure it isn't impossible.'

'It isn't really a question of forgiveness; it's more a feeling of worthlessness within myself knowing that I was given to a couple who already had two children and were forced to take on another one.'

'You don't know that they were forced into it. It was more likely that Mum didn't leave Auntie much choice in the matter,' Bessie suggested. 'You know what she was like about any sort of scandal, and she could be very forceful, as you know from when you were in trouble.'

May made a face. 'It hurts to know that I was just a scandal that had to be dealt with.'

'It's all a very long time ago and you can't change anything, so live with it and don't bear a grudge,' Bessie suggested. 'Personally, I've always been comforted by the fact that you had Aunt Winnie and Uncle Albert to look out for you in London.' She stared at her hands. 'It seems such a shame to throw that lovely relationship away.'

'I don't need anyone to look out for me. I can stand on my own two feet,' said May sharply. 'Anyway, I've got Bill. And Archie will be home eventually.'

'Have you got any idea when that will be?' asked Bessie to defuse the rising tension.

'No. None at all. Demobilisation is going to be a very slow process, according to the papers, because there are so many men for the government to bring home. I'll expect him when I see him; next year sometime, probably. I suppose it will be the same with Sam.'

'Yeah, we know he's alive, but when he'll be home is anybody's guess.'

'The poor things,' said May with feeling. 'As if they haven't been through enough for their country. Now they've got to wait for ages to come home.'

'Many fewer will be coming home than went out there,' remarked Bessie.

'That's for sure. At least I know that my husband will be back at some point. There are plenty of women who don't know whether to expect their boys or not; those who have had notification that their men are missing, and those who haven't heard at all.' May paused, looking sad. 'Then of course there are people like you who know their loved ones won't be back. It must be very hard for you at the moment.'

'I must say, all the victory celebrations had a hollow ring to them for me,' admitted Bessie. 'Still, it's wonderful that peace has come at last and the killing is over.'

'How is it working out for you, living back at home?' May enquired.

'It isn't the same as having my own place, and I was disappointed to leave my cottage, of course, but Dad and I get along well enough, so it's fine.'

'What about your photography work?'

'Non-existent at the moment,' she replied. 'I had to cancel all my bookings when Mum fell ill, and now that I've moved back home I have nowhere to work. But Dad has said that I can clear out the attic and use it as a studio. When Sam comes home, he will be back in the room he used to share with Henry, so the box room in the attic is empty apart from junk. The garden shed will be my dark room as before. Actually, the camera should work quite well, because the light in the attic is excellent. The fan light provides plenty of natural light. Of course, the set-up won't be ideal; it'll be small and makeshift, but it isn't as though I'll charge top prices or have people queuing on the stairs at this early stage. I really need a shop to work from if I'm to make a proper living, but it will do for now. And there is the advantage of having Dad around to keep an eye on Jimmy while I'm working. I managed before and I'll do so again if Dad isn't at home, but it makes it easier on occasions. Dad and Jimmy are such good pals. In fact, I think his grandson is helping Dad to cope with his grief for Mum.'

'I'm glad about that.'

'What about your job?' asked Bessie.

'I don't have a job now that the war is over,' May informed her. 'Constance is closing the nursery down. There will be no call for it now that war work has finished. All our mothers worked in war factories.'

'That's a shame. You enjoyed that sort of work, didn't you?' she said.

May nodded. 'I really did. It was handy, too, because I could take Connie with me and she enjoyed it.'

'Perhaps there will be other jobs available working with children?' suggested Bessie.

'Not now that the war is over and the men will be coming home to claim their jobs back,' said May. 'Women will be back in the home again so will have no need for a nursery of that kind.' She paused thoughtfully. 'To tell you the truth, Bessie, what I really want is another baby of my own.'

'Seriously?'

'Oh yeah. I love being a mum and I've been feeling broody for ages,' she said, smiling. 'Connie is growing up much too quickly for my liking.'

'I should let Archie get properly in the door before you get cracking on it,' said Bessie with a wry grin.

'No chance. I'll have him up those stairs before you can say welcome home,' she joked. 'And having been away for so long, you won't see him hanging back.'

Bessie gave her a warm smile. 'It's nice to hear you laughing again, May,' she said. 'Don't waste time on bad feeling with Aunt Winnie. Life really is too short, and Auntie is such a dear.'

'We'll see,' May said to pacify her sister, though at the moment she couldn't envisage any sort of reconciliation with Winnie, even though she missed her dreadfully.

'We'd better make tracks,' suggested Bessie. 'It's time to go home for tea.'

They called the children and walked back along the quay in the direction of home.

'Your cottage is still empty, then?' May remarked as they passed it along the way.

'Yeah, I don't want it to stay that way for too long so that it gets that sad, derelict look, but at the same time I'm dreading someone moving in,' Bessie confessed. 'It's selfish of me, but I shall feel as if they are trespassing on my property; using the furniture that was meant for Jim and me.'

May nodded. 'It's a damned shame you had to lose that,' she said.

'There are worse things,' Bessie pointed out. 'You can see them every day in the street: men who have lost limbs; people pale with grief because they've lost a loved one, even more than one in some cases. We're only a small village, but we've got our share of dead and wounded. A house is nothing compared to the suffering there is around.'

'You're right. I'm sorry it's fallen to you to stay with Dad, though,' May told her. 'I would have done it willingly if circumstances allowed me to move back here. I've never had a place of my own, so I wouldn't have noticed the difference.'

'I don't mind,' Bessie assured her. 'My cottage was never going to be the same without Jim, and your first priority is Archie.'

'I'm established in London now,' May explained. 'I've got Connie's name down for a local school, and yes, I do have to put Archie first. He could never live outside London.'

'I've lost Jim; Dad's lost Mum. It makes sense for us to share a house,' Bessie said.

'You're company for each other, then?'

'Exactly. And when Sam comes home, it will be some male company for Dad.'

Not for the first time, May observed with admiration her sister's graciousness. She seemed to take everything in her stride without complaint; she always had. There was no doubt in May's mind that Bessie was the better natured of the two of them.

They arrived at Berry Cottage and went inside, where the dog jumped up to greet them. May felt the familiar ambience and scent of childhood wash over her: floor polish, carbolic soap, fresh bread and the lingering smell of yesterday's dinner. She was so glad she had decided to stay overnight. It wasn't as though she had anything to rush home for. The country air was good for Connie, too.

That same night, after everyone had gone to bed, May was feeling restless, and it seemed that she wasn't alone in this. Hearing someone moving around downstairs, she guessed it was her father, as Bessie had mentioned that he didn't sleep well these days. May, who was sleeping with Connie in Sam's unoccupied room, got out of bed, careful not to wake her daughter. She pulled on a dressing gown, crept from the room and went down the stairs.

Her father was sitting by the dying embers of the fire in the chilly room, the gaslight turned down low. He looked up as she came in.

'What's up, May? Can't you get to sleep?' he asked.

'I'm not finding it easy,' she replied. 'I heard you down here so thought I'd come and keep you company for a little while. Bessie said that you haven't been sleeping so well lately.'

'No, I haven't. There's something about the night when you're missing someone,' he said. 'It always seems much worse than in the daytime, I don't know why.'

'Aah, I'm sorry that you're having such a hard time, Dad,' she said sympathetically. 'We're all sad but, it must be awful for you, after being married to Mum for so long.'

'It isn't good,' he told her. 'But I'll get by. They say it gets easier with time.'

'Would you like a hot drink?'

'Are you having one?'

'I'll have one with you if you like.'

'In that case, a cup of cocoa would be nice.'

She made the drinks and settled in the armchair opposite him by the fire.

'I've been wanting to have a chat with you, Dad,' she remarked.

'Oh yeah,' he said, looking at her. 'Is it about anything in particular?'

'It is, as it happens,' she replied. 'I just wanted to thank you for all you've done for me throughout my life.'

'Oh? What's brought this on all of a sudden?' he asked, cradling his mug in his hands and looking at her in a questioning manner over the rim.

'I know the truth,' she explained.

'The truth about what?'

'About me, of course.'

'What about you?'

Because this matter was such a huge issue to May, it seemed odd to her that he didn't seem to know what she was referring to. But he seemed genuinely puzzled.

'About me . . . not being your actual daughter, of course,' she told him.

He stared into space as though peering through the mists of time and trying to remember.

'Oh, that,' he said at last, as though it was of very little consequence. 'I suppose you had to find out sooner or later, and you're old enough to deal with it now.'

'I was thinking of you, not me,' she explained. 'It must have been hard taking on someone else's child.'

'No, not at all; of course not; not for Edie and me,' he said in a definite tone. 'You were family and needed a good home, and it was our job to provide it since Winnie couldn't do so and we could. Neither of us ever saw it any other way or hesitated for a moment. You were ours almost from the minute you were born, and I can't remember ever thinking of you in any other way than as my own child. I've always been a family man, as you know. I enjoyed having kids around the place, the more the merrier. But of course your mother did all the hard work of raising the family, and you were a part of that.'

'You were always there in the background supporting her, though, and I thank you with all my heart for everything you've done for me through the years,' she said.

'It's a parent's job,' he told her. 'And I'll never feel as though I'm not your dad, so thanks aren't necessary.'

'Perhaps I can find a way to do something for you in return,' she said.

'There is no debt for you to pay back, May; none at all,' he assured her in a firm tone. 'But there is something you can do for me that would make me happy.'

'Anything, you only have to name it.'

'I would like it if you could come and see us a bit more often and bring that lovely little girl with you,' he said. 'She's a real charmer; full of life and mischief. Just like you were at her age. You both get it from Winnie. She's always been a livewire.'

'I haven't been coming to Tideway because of the rift between myself and Mum. It made things awkward because I thought she didn't want me around,' she said. 'But I promise I'll come on a regular basis in future.'

'Thanks, dear.'

They sat together into the small hours, talking sometimes, comfortably silent at others. May realised that it was the first time she had ever had a conversation with George on her own like this. It was a cathartic experience.

'I think I might be able to get off to sleep now,' he said eventually. 'So I'll go up.'

'You go to bed and I'll wash the cups and go up when I've done that.'

'Night then, dear,' he said.

She went over and planted a kiss on his cheek. 'Night, Dad.'

The next morning May left Connie at Berry Cottage with the others and went alone to the cemetery. She tidied her mother's grave and stood there offering thanks to a woman whose generosity she had never recognised. How easy it was to take people for granted, she thought remorsefully. She stayed there for a long time in silent conversation with the woman who had raised her like a mother. Then she walked slowly back to the cottage.

Bessie went to the ferry with her that same afternoon.

'Come back soon,' she said, hugging her sister and her niece before they clambered into the boat.

'We will,' promised May.

As the ferry left the bank, Bessie and Jimmy waving like mad, May had tears in her eyes. She felt so dreadfully sad at leaving them; at leaving the place. The latter surprised her, because she couldn't usually wait to get away.

Time passed and life moved on as people adjusted to peacetime. Women over the age of thirty were able to vote for the first time in the general election at the end of December. Officially it was their huge contribution during the war that had earned them the vote, rather than the suffragettes' pre-war methods. But many women, including May, believed that they would never have won the battle without the work of the suffragettes. She was proud to have been associated with them.

Very gradually men started to trickle back from the war to be reunited with their families, the sacrifices made by so many becoming obvious as lists of the fallen began to appear on war memorials. The number of disabled men on the streets of London increased as men with broken bodies and missing limbs were discharged from hospital.

May was deeply distressed to see so much disablement. The papers were full of advertisements for bath chairs and invalid tricycles. There was even something called a spinal carriage on sale; an oblong basket on wheels for those who couldn't even sit up. It upset her to see so much tragedy. Could anything ever be worth this?

Connie started school after Easter 1919 and took to it at once. With time on her hands, May helped Bill on the stall as often as he needed her.

The situation between May and Winnie remained the same. May took Connie to see her and Albert regularly and the two women were civil to each other, but the spontaneous warmth that had always existed between them had gone. Winnie had dropped her apologetic manner and matched May's forced indifference, though she was the same old warm and cheery person with everyone else, especially Connie.

The long wait for Archie's return came to an end one August evening when there was a loud rat-a-tat at Bill's front door. May went to answer it.

'Well that's a fine thing,' Archie said as though he'd never been away. 'I go away and come home to find you've moved house. Good job I'm not the sort to take offence. I might have thought you were trying to avoid me.'

'Oh Archie, you fool,' said May, beaming at him. 'I wrote to tell you.'

'That's the forces mail for you,' he said jokingly. 'You can always rely on it . . . to let you down.'

'Come here,' she said, wrapping her arms around him. 'Oh Archie, it is good to see you.' She shouted into the living room: 'Bill, there's someone to see you.'

Bill appeared, his face breaking into an enormous grin when he saw who it was. 'And about bleedin' time too.' He shook Archie's hand and slapped his back in an affectionate male way. 'It's good to see you, son.'

Her husband wasn't quite as emaciated as May had feared; maybe because the fighting had been over for some time and the men had been given more to eat. He was a lot thinner than before, though, and was she imagining it, or was he being just a little bit too jovial?

'So what was it like?' she asked when they were settled down in the parlour drinking tea. 'Tell us all about it.'

'I'd sooner talk about what's been happening here,' he told her. 'How is Connie?'

'Sound asleep at the moment, but fit and thriving,' she replied. 'You'll see a big change in her, though; she's growing up fast and goes to school now.'

'I can't wait to see her.' He took a long swallow of his tea, looking at May. 'How come you're living here? I couldn't believe it when Winnie said you'd moved out.'

'I thought I'd come and try your dad's patience,' she said jokingly, intending to tell him all about it in private some other time.

'I'm very pleased she did,' said Bill.

'But we don't want to talk about us; we want to know all about you,' May urged. 'You're the family hero. How did you get on out there?'

There was a brief silence during which May realised that she shouldn't have asked.

'I did all right,' Archie replied finally. 'I must have done because I'm home.'

'And now that you are home at last we can arrange a party for you,' suggested Bill, smiling enthusiastically. 'We must have a good old knees-up to welcome you back.'

'No, don't do that, Dad,' said Archie quickly, and May perceived how exhausted he was. 'I don't want anything like that if you don't mind.'

'All right, son,' he agreed. 'I'll make do with buying you a pint whenever you feel up to it.'

'Now you're talking,' Archie approved. 'That's more my sort of thing.'

'I don't mind if you want to go out for a drink later on tonight,' said May.

'On my first night home?' responded Archie. 'I think I must be married to an angel.'

'Far from it,' she grinned, 'and if you come home late rolling drunk, you'll see how true that is.'

He didn't come back late or drunk, just pleasantly squiffy. But May's plans to welcome him home in the traditional marital way were not to be. He fell asleep without even kissing her good night. Poor thing, she thought, he must be absolutely worn out for that to happen, because Archie was a man with a healthy sexual appetite.

Unbeknown to May, Archie wasn't asleep, only pretending to be, because it was easier. He'd longed to be home; had yearned to be here in this bed beside May. He hadn't expected to feel disorientated and distanced from her by the things he'd seen in the trenches, things he still saw in his mind's eye: endless horrific images, and the pain of losing mates. Since he'd been back, he'd been infused with a frightening feeling of displacement and a sense of being in a different world to his wife, his father and everyone else here at home.

This was something he could never have predicted, and it was a bitter blow after being away for so long and wanting to be home with every fibre of his being. His comrades at the front had seen the same things and shared the same experiences, which bonded them like nothing else could. Here he felt alone and isolated. And worst of all he felt out of his depth – shy, even – to be sleeping with a woman after so long.

It was easy enough to play the clown downstairs and in the pub, but here in the intimacy of the bedroom it was more difficult. As for making love to his wife, that was out of the question. He couldn't even kiss her good night for fear of collapsing in tears like some gutless weakling. He wanted to cry in her arms and have her comfort him like a child. But he would never allow her to see him like that. He was a man, not a mouse. She wanted a lover, not a hopeless apology for one.

Surely these awful feelings would only be temporary. This terrible aliena-tion must be due to the shock of a new environment after so long in primitive conditions, and would disappear when he had settled back in. At present all he wanted to do was sleep and not dream, though that wasn't so easy nowadays.

He could feel May awake beside him; he could hear her breathing, and knew by the way she was moving around carefully so as not wake him that she wasn't asleep.

'Sorry, May,' he said suddenly.

'That's all right, love,' she said, leaning over and kissing the back of his head. 'We've all the time in the world. You just get the rest you deserve.'

Her kindness and understanding caused tears to meander down his cheek on to the pillow, and he stifled the urge to weep for fear she would hear him. She must never know how deeply the war had affected him. It was his duty as a soldier and a man to protect her from it. The war was over. It wouldn't be right to inflict the reality of the front line on civilians when they were happy and enjoying life again. Especially his wife, who he loved with all his heart, even though he didn't feel physically able to show her that in the way a husband should.

There was great excitement in Tideway when motor buses came to the village. The service ran from Tideway to Colchester and made life a whole lot easier for the villagers, though not everyone could afford to use it often, as the fare was threepence single and fivepence return, which was quite a lot out of the average wage packet. So some people still walked or went by bicycle.

However, the bus worked out cheaper and more convenient than taking the ferry and the train to Colchester, and provided it wasn't used too often, it was an affordable luxury for most people.

Bessie found it immensely useful because it meant she could collect some of her photographic materials personally instead of paying for delivery; do some shopping for any clothes she and Jimmy needed; and keep up to date with current styles of photographic presentation by looking in the windows of the town studios. Three-year-old Jimmy enjoyed the bus ride and the visit to a café they had as a treat.

Bessie and Jimmy were walking home from the bus one day in August when she noticed signs of life in the cottage that had once been hers and Jim's. The front door was open but she couldn't see anyone around, and the net curtains she had so proudly put up at the windows prevented her from seeing inside.

A pang went through her, but she was pleased that there was someone in there again, breathing life into the place. She couldn't wait to tell her father.

'Someone has moved into my old cottage,' she burst out as soon as she went in through the back kitchen door. 'I wonder who it is; I hope it's a young couple with a family. It's such a lovely spot to raise kids.'

'Sorry to disappoint you,' said a male voice. She went into the parlour, where a youngish dark-haired man, big and burly with a weatherbeaten look about him, was sitting on the couch opposite her father and next to Sam, now back in civvy street. 'I'm a widower without any kids. So it's just me and my dog, I'm afraid.'

His voice faded out as recognition dawned for them both.

'Hello again,' Bessie said, smiling at the friendly stranger she had talked to on her way home from Haverley just before she'd had Jimmy.

He stood up and shook her hand.

'Nice to see you again,' he said, casting an eye over her and grinning. 'You've lost a lot of weight since we last met.' He looked down at Jimmy, who was at her side. 'All went well, then? He's a fine-looking boy.'

'Thank you,' she said. 'You won't get any argument from me about that.'

'As you know each other, there's no need to introduce you,' said her father, hoping for an explanation.

'We met in passing once a few years ago and had a good chat but we didn't get around to exchanging names,' the man said, his large square hands seeming enormous against the tea cup he was holding. 'I'm Bob Lacey, and you'll be Bessie. Your dad and Sam have been telling me all about you.'

'We met down at the quays,' explained her father. 'I invited him up for a cuppa to welcome him to the village.'

'I should hope so too. Welcome to Tideway,' Bessie said warmly. 'I'm sure you'll be happy at the cottage.'

'How could I not be when it's all so beautifully done inside? By you, I understand.'

She nodded. 'What brings you here?' she asked.

'I've always loved this village, and there's nothing to keep me in Brightlingsea now that my wife isn't around,' he explained. 'The poor dear was killed in an air raid while I was away at sea. I didn't want to stay there after I got demobbed; too many memories to make me feel sad. I heard through the grapevine that there was a cottage here for rent, so here I am.'

'Sorry to hear about your wife,' Bessie sympathised.

'Thank you. It's a few years ago now.' He paused thoughtfully. 'Must have been before you and I met last time, but I couldn't talk about it then. I'm getting better at that now.'

'Are you a fisherman?' asked Jimmy.

'I am indeed,' Bob replied.

'I'm going to be a fisherman when I grow up.'

'Not if I have anything to do with it,' said Bessie. 'I've had enough of that sort of worry. When Dad retires from the sea, I don't want anyone else from this family giving me a headache in that way.'

'I shall still be out there, I suppose,' said Sam, now settled back into civilian life but still hankering for something other than sea fishing for a living.

'Someone has got to go and get the fish for your plate,' Bob pointed out pleasantly.

'I know that, but I would willingly give up eating it if it meant that men didn't have to risk their lives to get it for us,' Bessie said in a light-hearted manner.

'You can't keep a seaman from the sea,' her father put in. 'If he didn't fish he'd do something else on the ocean. It's in our blood, isn't that right, Bob?'

'Spot on,' agreed their visitor. 'We'll keep going out there until we're too old to cope with it physically. Only then will we do something on dry land. So there will always be worried wives and mothers of seafarers.'

'It's getting too much for Dad now because it is so physically demanding,' stated Bessie. 'And don't deny it, Dad. All those early mornings and coping with keeping the boat afloat in bad weather; it's taking its toll.'

'It's what I'm used to,' George reminded her. 'And it's helped me cope with losing your mother. But yes, you're right, I probably will have to find something a bit easier before too long. It isn't a job you can easily do into old age, even though some men do.'

'Anyway, I must be off,' stated Bob, rising purposefully. 'I've plenty still to do to get myself settled in, and I'm sure you've things to do.'

'Do you fancy meeting up for a pint down the Quayside Arms tonight?' asked George. 'It'll give you a chance to get to know a few of the locals. I'll only be staying an hour or so because I have an early start in the morning, but it will make a break.'

'Yeah, I'll enjoy that.' Bob turned to Bessie. 'It was nice meeting you again.'

'Likewise,' she responded, seeing him to the door. 'Good luck with your new life in Tideway.'

'Thank you. I'm sure I'll be happy here.'

Watching him stride away, a handsome figure in a rough, windswept sort of a way, she thought for the second time what a nice man he was.

Her father and brother echoed her thoughts when she went back inside.

'He won't have any trouble fitting in around here,' opined George. 'He a genuine sort, and that's what we like in Tideway.'

'He's got a cracking boat too,' added Sam. 'A fair-sized one as well. He can't be short of a bob or two, but there's nothing boastful about him.'

'He'll be looking for hands, so that will bring a few more jobs to the village.' George gave a wry grin. 'Whether you like it or not, Bessie, fishing is how the majority of men in this village earn their daily bread.'

'That doesn't mean I have to like being attached to any of them,' she came back at him.

'Will you take me down the quay, please, Uncle Sam?' asked Jimmy, who was in his element by the water. He adored his Uncle Sam, who was very good with him, spending hours patiently playing with him.

'Yeah, if you like,' replied Sam. Turning to Bessie he added, 'Is that all right with you?'

'As long as you keep an eye on him down by the water, that will be fine.' She looked at the clock on the mantelpiece. 'I'll need him back in half an hour for his tea.'

'Will do,' agreed Sam. 'Come on then, nipper. Let's go and see what's doing down at the waterfront.'

Bessie stood by the gate watching them walk down the hill; uncle and nephew comfortable and happy together. It gave her a warm feeling inside, but she couldn't help wishing that she was watching father and son instead.

Chapter Sixteen

Being a sunny-natured sort of a person, able to maintain a positive persona whatever her true feelings, it was unusual for May to be outwardly depressed. But a month or so after Archie's return she found herself struggling to stay bright when she was feeling so hellish inside. Her husband might as well still be in France as far as the distance between them was concerned.

Ostensibly Archie was his old self when in company and around the house if Bill and Connie were there, except perhaps a little less exuberant, and he behaved normally towards May for the benefit of others. But when they were alone together the atmosphere was unbearable, their conversation guarded and never personal to themselves. She told him about her rift with Winnie and the reason for it; he duly sympathised. They talked about Connie and Bill, and about the rising cost of living, but they never mentioned the fact that the intimate side of their marriage had not resumed since he'd been back.

Usually such an uxorious and home-loving man, Archie had taken to going out drinking of an evening and coming home late and often the worse for wear. Was it her fault? wondered May. Had he fallen out of love with her? Perhaps he'd met a French girl while he'd been away. Surely not; not Archie! But there was no denying the fact that his attitude towards her was entirely different to that of the man who had bade her an emotional farewell nearly four years ago.

It was as though he couldn't bear to touch her and hated even being near her. It was extremely demoralising for May. To exacerbate the situation, she seemed powerless to do anything about it. If she tried to broach the subject or ask him what the problem was, his mood blackened and he refused to discuss it. Not being the type normally to hold back, she was on the point of exploding but managed to control herself. She didn't want to give him a hard time. He had, after all, been away at war, so generous allowances had to be made and she must be patient.

But the whole thing was dragging her down and reaching a point where she didn't know how much longer she could stand it. To lower her state of mind even further was the situation between herself and Winnie. She ached for the loss of their closeness. Seeing Winnie on a regular basis because of Connie and feeling the distance between them was a constant source of pain.

Things finally came to a head between herself and Archie one night in late September when he didn't come home until two o'clock in the morning. Now he was pushing his luck to an insulting degree, and she told him so when he finally came to bed.

'I don't mind you going out and having fun. God knows you've earned some enjoyment,' she said, trying to keep her voice low so as not to disturb the rest of the household. 'But I don't deserve to be treated like this; as though I'm some sort of repellent intruder in your life.'

'I don't treat you like that.'

'You do.'

'You're imagining things.'

'I certainly am not. You're behaving as though I'm not a part of your life, let alone your wife,' she insisted. 'Where have you been until this hour anyway, or am I not allowed to ask? You couldn't have been at the pub, because they've been closed for hours.'

'I've been at a club listening to jazz music, if you must know,' he told her. 'It's in the basement of a pub and they have a licence to stay open late. I went with a few of the blokes after closing time at the local.'

'Jazz? You?' She was astounded. 'I thought your idea of music was a sing-song round the piano.'

'That just shows how wrong you are, doesn't it?' he came back at her. 'Anyway, it isn't the music so much as the atmosphere that I enjoy.'

'Anything rather than come home to your wife,' she said, her anger turning to sadness. 'Talk to me, Archie. Please talk to me. This sort of behaviour isn't like you.'

'It must be,' he claimed. 'I wouldn't be doing it otherwise, would I?'

'Is there someone else?' she felt compelled to ask. 'Have you met someone else?'

'No.' He sounded sober suddenly, his manner grave; there was no exaggerated outburst of protest befitting a guilty man. 'There is no one else. You must never, ever think that.'

He was sitting on the edge of the bed with his back to her.

'I believe you.'

'I should bloody well hope so.'

'All right. There's no need to swear and bite my head off.'

'Sorry, May . . . I'm sorry about everything.'

The genuine contrition in his voice warmed and encouraged her.

'Then let's talk about it and try and put things right,' she suggested. 'We are both unhappy with the way things are at the moment. Let's try and get things back to normal.'

'Don't go on at me, May,' he said, his mood becoming irritable again. 'I'm tired.'

'You're drunk more like, and I'm fed up with it, Archie; absolutely sick to death,' and she turned on her side and curled up into a ball.

She heard him moving about until he turned out the gaslight and got into bed. He lay with his back to her as usual, which she saw every night as a fresh statement of rejection. How to improve the situation between them eluded her, because whatever it was that had come between them was something from outside. How could she fight back when she didn't know who or what the enemy was?

'He's nursing a hangover again, I suppose,' surmised Bill Mott disapprovingly during a brief quiet spell at the stall. May had gone there to give her father-in-law some support after she'd taken Connie to school, guessing that Archie wouldn't turn up for work until late and miss the morning rush.

'He's just tired, I think,' she fibbed in her husband's defence, polishing some apples with a clean cloth and arranging them into a display.

'I didn't hear him come home last night, but I suppose it was late again.'

'It was rather,' she was forced to admit. 'He was at some club listening to jazz music.'

'Jazz music? Archie! Good God alive. Whatever next? I thought that was just for the toffs.'

'Apparently not.'

'Archie is the sort of man to enjoy a game of darts down the pub with the piano going,' announced Bill. 'Not hanging around some den of iniquity listening to wild, degenerate music that attracts the lowest of the low.'

'That's going a bit far, Bill,' she said in a tone of mild admonition. 'I like jazz music myself, what I've heard of it anyway. I'd like to go with him sometime to hear some more.'

'The way he's carrying on at the moment, you're not likely to get invited.'

'Sadly, that's true.'

'It's downright disgusting the way he's behaving, and I shall tell him so in no uncertain terms,' ranted Bill. 'He's a married man and as such he should be at home of an evening with his wife, not out gallivanting. I daren't think of the money he must be spending. There'll be none of his demob money left at this rate.'

'Don't be too hard on him,' May urged. 'He has given a large slice of his life for his country, remember.'

'Some poor devils gave all of their lives for their country,' Bill pointed out. 'He's dancing on their graves; that's what he's doing. And what about those who have come back without legs or arms or sight?'

'In all fairness, Bill, Archie can't be blamed for having survived or for coming back with all his faculties,' she pointed out.

'No, but he's showing disrespect for his less lucky comrades as well as for you by behaving as he is. He is a war hero and he should behave like one,' he stated. 'I don't know why you're making excuses for him.'

She wasn't entirely sure either. Perhaps it was because Archie had been so good to her until now. He'd married her knowing that she'd been pregnant with another man's child and had been an exemplary husband for much longer than he'd been a bad one.

'I married him for better or worse,' she reminded Bill. 'He never put a foot wrong before he went away to war. We have to make allowances.'

Once again Bill was troubled by his conscience for ever doubting the sincerity of this young woman. To think that he had thought she wasn't good enough for Archie. At the moment it was the other way around.

'I agree up to a point, but he's taking liberties,' he stated. 'I mean, where is he now when he should be at work? At home pampering himself after too much beer last night, and his wife has to come and stand in for him.'

'It's no hardship,' she assured him. 'I enjoy working here, so don't worry about me.'

'That isn't the point, May,' he told her, his anger rising toward his errant son. 'His behaviour isn't on; it really isn't.'

'All right, Bill. Don't upset yourself about it,' she urged him in a kindly manner. 'It's just a phase he's going through. He'll get over it. Let me deal with it. It isn't your problem.'

'No, I suppose it isn't.' He paused in thought. 'Look, May, it isn't my place to interfere between the two of you, and I wouldn't do that. But I need to tell him to liven his ideas up as regards his work here on the stall.'

266

'That's between you and Archie.'

The conversation was brought to a sudden halt by a flurry of customers.

'Hello, Mrs Green, and how are you this morning?' greeted May, smiling at a regular customer as though she hadn't a care in the world.

Arguments between Bill and Archie, awkward silences between May and Archie and a miserable atmosphere filling the house: that was the pattern of life in the Mott household as the glorious sunshine of autumn faded into the iron-grey onset of winter. Connie was the saving grace because they all made an effort when she was around. But children were often more perceptive than they were given credit for.

'Don't Daddy and Grandad like each other?' she asked one evening when May was putting her to bed.

'Of course they do,' May replied, taken by surprise by the child's insight.

'It doesn't seem like it to me . . . they are always cross with each other,' declared Connie. Her memory didn't stretch to before Archie had gone away to war, so he had been a stranger to her when he'd arrived home.

'Everybody gets angry at times,' May told her. 'But it will be all right in time. Things will calm down eventually.'

'Perhaps Grandad didn't want Daddy to come back,' she suggested.

'Of course he did,' May assured her emphatically. 'He wanted it very much indeed.'

'Well, I wish he hadn't come back. It used to be nice before he came home,' she blurted out with childish candour. 'He's always grumpy and making Grandad sad. I don't like him. I wish he would go away again.'

'That's a horrid thing to say, Connie,' admonished May, shocked at the child's words, which brought home to her just how serious the situation was. 'Your daddy is a very brave and good man.'

'Why does he have to be so nasty, then?'

'I don't know, love,' she said, kissing Connie good night. 'But he will be better, I promise you.'

May confronted Archie, who was in the armchair reading the paper when she went downstairs.

'This has to stop, Archie, right now,' she burst out, so angry she disregarded the fact that Bill was in the room. 'Connie is feeling the bad atmosphere you are creating and it's upsetting her, so let's have an end to it. Whatever you feel about me, don't take it out on her. She's five years old, for heaven's sake. It isn't fair.'

267

Archie looked shocked. 'I don't take anything out on her,' he denied, genuinely surprised at the accusation. 'I wouldn't do that. I think the world of Connie.'

'Well show it a bit more, then,' May demanded while Bill made a diplomatic exit. 'She doesn't remember you from before you went away so you need to build a new relationship with her, and that isn't going to happen without some sort of effort on your part. Children notice these things. She says you're grumpy, and she's right. So give us all a break and start behaving like a grown-up. I'll put up with anything for myself, but when our daughter is upset, I won't have it, Archie, do you understand? Do us all a favour and pull yourself together.'

With that she stormed off into the kitchen. At that moment she would have given anything to leave the house and go round to see Auntie Winnie, to be nourished by her warm and caring personality. But that wasn't possible, so she heated some water in the kettle for the washing-up, put some soda in the bowl and attacked the dishes with angry vigour.

Life had taken a turn for the better for Bessie, mostly because she was seeing a lot of Bob Lacey, who had fitted into Tideway as though born to it. He'd become pals with her father and brother and the affinity she had felt for him at that first meeting had grown into a close friendship. She did not want another man in her life, but Bob's warm personality was a cheering influence, especially as memories of her dear Jim still made her sad.

Bob brought fun into her life again with his easy-going charm, and – being a seaman with a large boat – he won instant approval from Jimmy. Bob fished on a larger scale than George, employed several hands and also had a share in a boat-hire business further down the coast, so he wasn't badly off. He hadn't been in Tideway long when he became one of the few car-owners in the village, buying a second-hand saloon car and taking Bessie and Jimmy out and about in it. He and Bessie also had occasional evenings at the cinema in Colchester together, while George or Sam stayed home with Jimmy.

The car wasn't the most reliable of machines and tended to break down on regular occasions, but somehow Bob managed to get it going again and off they would go. A spin in the car was a real treat for Jimmy too, and they went out into the countryside most Sunday afternoons.

It was years since Bessie had felt this light hearted. She wasn't sure if she should be enjoying herself this much, as strictly speaking she was still in mourning for her mother. But having lost her husband, her brother and her mother already, and still only twenty-five, she was acutely aware that life was to be lived while you had it.

Bob's cottage had a more lived-in look to it than when she had been in residence, to say the least. He tended to leave things lying about. Books and magazines about boats, newspapers, and the odd jacket or jumper slung over a chair. Bessie constantly reminded herself that it was his home now, not hers, and how he lived was none of her business. It was a struggle, though, not to tidy up after him.

It was odd seeing Jimmy sitting on the furniture she had chosen and pulling back the net curtains she had made to look out of the window, which he did a lot because the cottage looked directly over the water-front, and he adored that.

'I don't know how you're going to keep him away from the sea when he's grown up,' Bob mentioned one day when she and Jimmy had called over and her son was peering out of the window into the wintry November day. 'It's in his blood.'

'It must have slipped a generation, then,' she told him. 'Because it isn't in my blood and it certainly wasn't in his father's.'

'It's there, though,' he told her. 'I recognise it because I had it too from an early age. My father wasn't a fisherman. He had a boat-hire firm, which is now partly mine, and that was what he wanted me to go into. But I wanted to be out on the ocean, not hiring boats out for other people to go.'

'Of course, I realise that living in a place where everything revolves around the tide and the wind and boats and sails and nets is bound to have an effect,' she remarked.

'You wouldn't move away to dissuade him in his formative years, would you?' he asked, frowning.

'No, of course not,' she replied. 'When he grows up it will be up to him how he earns his living, I just hope he chooses not to earn it by going to sea.'

'I'm glad you're not going to move away,' he told her. 'I'd miss you if you weren't around.'

'Moving away?' put in Jimmy worriedly, having heard only part of the conversation and misunderstanding. 'I don't want to live anywhere else.'

'We're not going anywhere, sweetheart,' Bessie assured him. 'So don't you worry your head about it.'

A glance passed between Bessie and Bob. It was a look that warmed Bessie's heart. There had been so much sorrow in her life, it was good to have some happiness. At that moment she felt as though everything she wanted was here in this room. Somehow she knew that Jim wouldn't mind. He would hate her to be lonely and miserable.

There were two things May had kept up since the war: one was her friendship with Constance; the other was the use of her bicycle, which Constance had said she could keep. The two things complemented each other nicely, because Constance lived in Kensington, which was quite a long walk for a short visit, so May cycled there.

It wasn't a close, soul-baring sort of a relationship. It was more an occasional afternoon with a cup of tea and a chat about things in general, mostly outside of the home. Constance was in a different class to May, her husband being professional and well heeled, but the gap could be bridged when they were together because they shared the same sort of views on important issues and had bonded during their time with the suffragettes, and later at the nursery.

Visiting Constance gave May a much-needed break from the abysmal situation at home, with things still impossible between herself and Archie. To his credit he had been making a noticeable effort to make friends with Connie these past few weeks since May had flared up at him about it, but their own relationship hadn't improved at all. There were occasion glimpses of how things used to be, which heartened her, but then he would withdraw into his shell again and they were back to square one.

Cycling home from Constance's along a leafy avenue one afternoon in November, May was thinking over the enjoyable conversation she had just had with her friend. They had talked a lot about something that was headline news at the moment: Viscountess Nancy Astor had become the first woman MP. Both May and Cosntance were delighted about it and hoped it paved the way for other women to follow. Nancy Astor herself had been quoted in the papers as saying that she hoped that even the humblest of women would follow the precedent she had set.

It was a nice idea but somewhat far-fetched in May's opinion. She couldn't realistically envisage lower-class women following in Nancy Astor's footsteps. They didn't have the confidence and were all too busy bringing up their kids and making ends meet anyway. Immersed in thought about the subject, May didn't notice a car overtaking her, but when it came so close that it made her wobble and almost fall off her bicycle, she rang her bell furiously and shook her fist at the driver.

'Maniac,' she fumed loudly. 'You ought to be banned from the roads with your noisy, smelly machines.'

The car pulled into the kerb ahead of her and the driver got out and marched towards her aggressively. She got off her bike and braced herself for an altercation.

'I hope you've come to apologise,' she shouted at him before he even got near to her.

'I most certainly have not,' he roared back fiercely. 'You're a menace on the road, a danger to other people, weaving all over the place and not keeping your mind on what you're doing. You should throw that heap of old iron on the scrap heap and walk. We'll all be a lot safer.'

'You could have killed me.' She was almost beside herself with rage at his insulting manner. 'Hogging the road like that. Who the hell do you think you . . . ?' Her voice tailed off, her breath catching in her throat.

'May,' he uttered.

'William,' she responded, then, gathering her wits, added, 'I might have known it would be you or someone like you, thinking you own the road.'

'You haven't changed, then,' he said, smiling at her, all anger melting away in the pleasure of seeing her. 'You're still ready to take on the world.'

'Not the world,' she corrected. 'Just selfish people with no thought for others.'

'You really were all over the road on that bike, May,' he claimed. 'But let's not argue about it.'

'I'll argue with you any day of the week,' she returned spiritedly. 'There are bullies like you everywhere these days in their wretched motor cars with their poisonous fumes.'

'It's progress, May,' he pointed out. 'You should embrace it, not complain about it.'

'Spoken in the true condescending spirit of a car owner to someone who isn't and is never likely to be,' she said.

'Never mind all that backchat. It is so good to see you,' he blurted out, sounding genuine. 'Don't let's waste time quarrelling. How have you been?'

'I've been absolutely fine,' she said, managing not to add 'no thanks to you'. 'How about you?'

'Yes, I'm all right,' he replied. 'I managed to survive the war with all limbs intact. So I suppose you could say that I did very well.'

'You were lucky,' she said coolly.

'I know.' He ran an approving eye over her. 'I love the outfit,' he said. She was wearing trousers with a bright red jacket and beret she had managed to get on a second-hand stall in the market. 'You look really good. Even more beautiful than I remember.'

'The clothes are practical for cycling,' she said quickly, trying not to be affected by his flattery. It wasn't easy, because it was a long time since anyone had told her she was beautiful and it was heady stuff. 'I've been visiting a friend and it's a long walk from where I live, so a bicycle is the answer.'

'Where *do* you live?'

'Never you mind.'

'You've got posh friends if they live around here,' he said.

'You're not the only person of means with whom I am acquainted,' she informed him haughtily.

He shrugged, seeming thoughtful. 'Why wouldn't you speak to me when our paths crossed in the station that time?' he asked eventually.

'Isn't it obvious?'

'No. Not to me.'

'I didn't think we had anything to say to each other then and I don't now,' was her icy reply. 'Frankly, I don't know how you've got the brass neck to expect me to.'

In an instant, his mood changed from light to serious.

'Can we talk, May?' he asked earnestly. 'I've so much I want to say to you. I've thought of you so often over the years.'

'There's nothing you can say that I would want to hear,' she told him firmly. 'I have to get home anyway. I don't have the time to hang about the streets.'

'Just ten minutes,' he said. 'We can talk in my car.'

'No.'

'Please . . .'

'I'm on my way home and I must go because I have to collect my daughter from school. You shouldn't be suggesting such things; you are a married man.'

'I only want to talk.'

'Ten minutes then,' she heard herself say, angry that she had allowed herself to be persuaded.

The car had soft seats and smelled of leather and lingering cigar smoke.

'Right, get to the point then,' she said, staring above the shiny dashboard through the window at her bike parked in the kerb. 'You haven't got long.'

'I'm sorry about what happened,' he said.

'So was I about the way you lied to me. But I was never sorry that I got pregnant,' she informed him. 'Never, ever!'

'Pregnant?' he said, aghast.

272

'That's right.'

'You never said anything about that.'

'As you were about to marry someone else, it was hardly fitting, was it?' she said. 'I have the most beautiful daughter, so you're the loser in all this.'

'I know I am,' he admitted. 'I knew it the minute I let you go.'

'I didn't see you running after me.'

'You said you never wanted to see me again.'

'Of course I did,' she said. 'I'd just found out that you were a liar and a cheat.'

'Would it have made any difference if I *had* come after you?' he asked.

'Not really. You were committed to someone else and I wouldn't have broken that up,' she told him. 'But at least it would have been a gesture. Maybe I wouldn't have felt quite so cheap if you'd made an effort.'

'You were never cheap,' he stated categorically. 'Anyway, I did try to see you but you disappeared. Your father was tight lipped about it when I asked about you. He said you'd got a job away somewhere and had left home. I couldn't get anything out of him at all. I made a few discreet enquiries in the village but people just said you'd left to work away.'

'My mother threw me out because I wouldn't abort the baby, so I went to live with my aunt in London,' she explained. 'Mum was terrified of scandal and wouldn't have so much as a whiff of it in her house.'

'I'm so sorry, May,' he said again. 'Sorry that you were forced to leave your home village because of me.'

'As it happens, it worked out well for me. I'm much more suited to town life,' she said. 'My husband is a Londoner and wouldn't want to live anywhere else.'

'Husband!'

She looked at him, her eyes bright with anger. 'So you thought I was ruined and scarred for life because you let me down, did you?' she said in a brittle tone.

'Not at all. It's just that . . . I didn't know what had happened to you after we split up,' he said. 'I'm surprised to hear that your mother didn't stand by you.'

'She didn't, but my aunt did,' she informed him. 'She was with me every step of the way and I owe everything to her. Then I met a nice chap who wanted to marry me, knowing the situation that I was in. That's what I call love.'

'The little girl who was with you at the station . . .'

'Yes, that's Connie.'

'My daughter?'

There was a brief hiatus. 'A mere technicality,' she said briskly. 'My husband is her father in every way that matters. He is the one who is bringing her up and providing for her.'

'Yes.' At least he had the grace to look sheepish. 'I suppose I asked for that.'

'Did you have any other children . . . within your marriage?' she enquired.

'No. The marriage didn't last long,' he replied. 'It was more a business arrangement than a marriage and it didn't work out. What a big scandal that was in our circles at the time. Oh yes, the folks didn't like that one little bit. I was away at the war for most of the time. But I moved out of the house and got a flat just down the road from here as soon as the war ended.'

'You might find it hard to believe, but I'm sorry it didn't work out for you.'

'It's my own fault for marrying the wrong woman.' He tried to laugh it off by adding, 'At least I'm away from the arguments, which is better for her as well, and the flat is much more convenient for the office.'

'I suppose it would be.' The clash of their different worlds made her feel uncomfortable. How could anyone equate the end of a marriage with convenience? 'Well, I had better be getting on my way,' she said hurriedly. 'I need to get back to collect Connie from school.'

But he stopped her by saying, 'Of course, the real reason my marriage didn't work was because I was still in love with you.'

'Oh please, don't insult my intelligence by coming out with rubbish like that,' she said.

'It isn't rubbish,' he claimed. 'I mean every word.'

'Look, William, I've grown up a bit since I was seeing you and these days I don't fall for the first flattering remark that comes my way.'

'I could give you and Connie a good life if you would let me, May,' he said, seeming genuinely keen. 'Neither of you would want for anything.'

'We don't want for anything now,' she was quick to point out. 'Nothing that matters anyway. Besides, you are a stranger to Connie.'

'I would soon get to know her, if you gave the word,' he persisted. 'I want to make it up to you both for doing you wrong all those years ago. I want us to have a life together. The three of us.'

'Doesn't the fact that I'm a married woman mean anything to you?' she asked.

'Of course it does. I'm not a complete monster. But having been through the war and managed to survive when so many others didn't, I am aware that life really is too short to waste a moment. If things are wrong for you and they can be put right, get on and do it, that's my motto.'

'Marriage is for ever as far as I'm concerned,' she made clear.

'In a perfect world it would be, but our world is very flawed and so are we as human beings. This man you married gave our child a name and saved you from disgrace, and for that I am deeply grateful to him,' he said. 'But now you should be with the man you really love.'

'You think I . . . ?'

'I know you do,' he stated with the confidence of his class. 'I saw it in your eyes when you recognised me.'

'You arrogant—'

'You can call me what you like,' he cut in, 'and I know I deserve it. But I recognised it in you because it is in me too.'

She reached for the door handle. 'I'm getting out of here before you come out with any more silly assumptions.'

He leaned over and touched her arm firmly in a restraining gesture.

'It doesn't matter how far you run or how much you deny it, it will always be there, May. Look at me and tell me that you don't have feelings for me and I'll leave you alone,' he said.

'I do have feelings for you . . . pure hate,' she said without looking at him.

'They say that is akin to love.'

'That's just a myth created by people like you for their own ends,' she told him.

'Does your husband make you feel how you felt when you were with me?' he asked.

'Better,' she lied. 'So let me get out of here and go home to the people who really do love me.'

'All right, I'll respect your wishes.' He put his hand in his coat pocket and took out a small card, which he handed to her. 'My address is on there and it's only a stone's throw from here. If you change your mind . . .'

'I won't.'

'If you need anything at all, just write to me or call in to see me. You'll always be welcome, any time,' he continued, ignoring her interruption. 'I know you don't trust me, and with good cause, but I really do want to do right by you and Connie now. So if you need money or support of any kind, you know where I am. I can help you in a big way and it would give me a great deal of pleasure.'

'Don't patronise me.'

He shrugged. 'If you want to take that attitude I can't stop you, but it is a genuine offer.'

'How do you know I didn't marry a man as rich as you are?' she asked.

He ran his eye over her clothes, which were made from cheap cloth, and her bicycle, which was not exactly in pristine condition. 'Just a hunch,' he said.

She fled from the car, mounted her bicycle and pedalled away with speed. The meeting had really unnerved her and she was bewildered by her response to him. One thing she did know for sure: her feelings for William Marriot were still as strong as ever. She pulled over into the kerb by a drain, dismounted and held the card over the grille. Standing there for a long time, she found herself unable to drop it through the bars so that it would be lost to her for ever. She simply could not close the door that had been so unexpectedly reopened. She would never use the details on the card, but neither could she bring herself to dispose of them.

Putting the card back into her pocket, she got back on her bicycle and cycled towards home.

Winnie was a worried woman. May's cheerfulness was just a little too forced, and Winnie could tell from seeing her that she was unhappy. That gave her a dragging sensation inside. The feeling was so intense, she truly believed that she would throw herself under a train if she thought it would make May's sadness go away. Such was the strength of the maternal bond, which she had had ever since May was born. No one had ever known how she had winced and smarted over the years on receiving news of any illness or misfortune of her daughter.

Archie wasn't looking any too happy either, and rumour had it that he was out late most nights, drinking a lot and getting up to goodness knows what. Of course she couldn't say anything, as she and May were barely on speaking terms. But she did find an opportunity to speak to Archie one day in the café.

'Mind if I join you?' she asked.

'Help yourself.'

'So what's going on between you and May?' she enquired bluntly, sitting down at his table with a cup of tea.

'Nothing that I know of,' was his guarded reply.

'Why are the two of you so miserable, then?'

'Who said we are?'

'Me. I'm saying it,' she told him. 'That girl is breaking her heart and you are as miserable as sin too, even though you're doing your best to hide it. You've been a different man since you got back from the war.'

'Have I?' he said abruptly. 'You know more than I know myself, then.'

'Don't get clever with me, boy,' she admonished.

'What do you expect when you come here questioning me about something that is personal between May and me?' he came back at her crossly. 'You shouldn't be asking about someone else's private affairs. It isn't right.'

His point hit home with a jolt and she smarted from it. 'Yeah. You're quite right, Archie. I shouldn't,' she agreed. 'It's just that the two of you mean a lot to me and I hate to see you both so unhappy. You should be rejoicing being together again after so long apart.' She sipped her tea. 'I'm sorry, Archie. Take no notice of me. I'm just a nosy old woman who should know better than to ask.'

'It's all right, Winnie,' he said, his tone softening. 'I understand. I know how much May means to you. I know about . . .'

She looked at him. 'She told you?'

He nodded.

'So I suppose you hate me too now.'

'No, of course not,' he assured her. 'I wouldn't dream of judging you about something so personal. I hurt for May, though, because she seemed so upset about it when she poured the story out to me; really cut up. If you want to know the truth, Winnie, I think it's a shame she fell out with you over it, because the two of you were so close. She needs you more than ever now.'

Winnie immediately picked up on that. 'There is something wrong, then,' she said.

He gave her a wry gin. 'You're crafty when you want to know something, Winnie Trent.' He paused. 'Look, it hasn't been as we thought it would be when I got back, that's all,' he confessed. 'My fault, not hers.' He opened his mouth to say something else, then changed his mind. 'But we'll work it out between us eventually, don't worry.'

'Sooner rather than later, I hope.'

'I hope so too,' he said. 'But we'll just have to wait and see what happens.'

'You know where I am if you need me,' she told him. 'Meanwhile I must finish my tea and go back to work.'

Watching her go, he felt a salty lump in his throat at the depth of her concern for May. He'd said that he and May would work things out, but he had no idea exactly how, since they grew more distant with every day that passed. It was his fault entirely. He wanted to put things right, so much. He'd tried to on a few occasions. But somehow he couldn't do it; he couldn't shake himself out of the awful isolation that parted them, and he was so ashamed.

Chapter Seventeen

The consequences of her father's death and the war had forced Joan Parsons to open her eyes to the practicalities of life, albeit it with some reluctance. The problem of the reduced circumstances her bereavement had left her in had been solved by the need for women to help with the war effort, which made going to out to work fashionable rather than something to be looked down on. Even middle- and upper-class women without her financial problems had joined the ranks, and eventually Joan had accepted, somewhat miserably, that there was no other way.

She had sold the big family house and now lived in a small cottage nearby. After all her father's debts had been paid there was very little money left, but her job at the munitions factory meant she could afford to live. She had hated the work with a passion and loathed her workmates even more, but the wages had been essential, and at least she hadn't had to be ashamed of going out to work.

It had certainly toughened her up, too. She was no longer the helpless female she now realised she had been before. She'd bobbed her hair and wore trousers as a matter of course. The problem was, it was now December 1919, the war had been over for more than a year and only the most menial jobs were available for women now that the men had come back and rejoined the workforce.

So Joan was left with a serious dilemma. Unless she worked, she had no means of financial support. She had no husband to look after her, unlike the married women who had gone back to being housewives in their droves after the war. She had had the occasional love affair but was still single at twenty-five. So she had to find a husband to keep her, or spend the rest of her life working behind the counter in the ghastly grocery shop in Colchester where she was currently employed. A man had to be found and wooed pronto. She didn't think she could stand another day behind this wretched counter, weighing out tea and slicing bacon.

Of course she would have to lower her sights as to the social standing

279

of the man, since she no longer moved in the circles she once had. She lived as working class but considered herself to be middle class, with the attitude and social graces she had been brought up with up. But she had no intention of settling for someone entirely without means just because she was desperate; she needed a man who could keep her to a reasonable standard. A small businessman perhaps; someone with a successful store might be all right. It wasn't ideal, but as the wife of a shop-owner at least she would have financial security and some sort of standing in the community.

Her ability to attract a suitable candidate shouldn't be too much of a problem if she really put her mind to it. She was not exactly a beauty, but she knew how to make the best of herself and had a very good figure. She'd had her moments with men but had never been able to sustain a relationship for any length of time. The reason eluded her. The men always seemed to get bored with her before things had a chance to get serious. Well, she was going to have to make one last in the long term now, because she had no intention of being a shop girl for the rest of her life.

Damn and blast her father for leaving her in this mess, she cursed. Thoughts of her father led to reflection on his one-time assistant, the awful Bessie Bow. Annoyingly, Joan's conscience occasionally troubled her as she remembered the last time the two had met, when she had lost her temper and pushed Bessie over on to the river bed. Although remorse wasn't normally an emotion that featured in Joan's life, she had been haunted by the incident from time to time over the years in the worry that her old adversary might have lost her baby as a result. To cause a miscarriage was low even by Joan's standards. She'd given Tideway a wide berth since then, to avoid seeing her.

Now she pushed all thoughts of Bessie Bow from her mind and concentrated on the immediate problem of finding a husband at the earliest opportunity. She no longer attended social occasions at which she might meet someone suitable and be formally introduced, so she would just have to keep her eyes open during the normal course of her everyday life and seize any opportunity that came her way.

As it happened, Joan didn't have to wait long before spotting a likely candidate. Just a few days later, when she was out for a walk in Colchester during her dinner break, the pale winter sun spreading its heatless light on the streets of the ancient town, she saw him. Of course, he might already be married, but she would find out once she got him into conversation and draw back immediately if he was. She wanted a meal ticket for

280

life, not just a brief liaison to spice things up for some chap whose wife didn't understand him. He looked to be a few years older than her and was a dark-haired, well-built man with a healthy complexion.

He was outside a church peering into the engine of a motor car. There was an air of ownership about him, and it was this that alerted her to his potential. He must have some substance to own a car. All right, so it wasn't exactly top of the range, and the man wasn't the last word in refinement by the look of his clothes. But she had to be realistic in her search, since a fellow with a brand-new car and all the fashionable gear to go with it wouldn't be short of female interest and might not give her a second glance.

The man put the bonnet down and turned the starting handle, whereupon the engine sprang into life. He looked very pleased with himself. It wasn't normally done for a woman to strike up a conversation with a strange man on the street, but she was too much in need to concern herself about the usual formalities.

'Well done,' she said, judging this to be a good opening gambit; she knew that no man could resist flattery. 'You look as though you are a man who knows exactly what he's doing when it comes to motor cars.'

'I have my moments,' he responded, smiling. She moved forward, and as she drew closer she could see that he wasn't bad looking, if a little on the rugged side. He was dressed in a tweed coat and his hair was blown askew by the wind. But he was reasonably presentable in an outdoors sort of way. Anyway, she couldn't afford to be too choosy, not with the dratted birthdays coming round ever quicker these days. 'But I'm not an expert, I must admit. It was more by luck than good judgement.'

Modest, too; Joan liked that, because she didn't want someone who was going to lord it over her. 'I was impressed anyway,' she said with feigned admiration.

'Nice to know that somebody is,' he said jovially, and she was encouraged by his obvious pleasure in her remark. It was vital she keep him talking for long enough to arouse his interest in her. 'I enjoy messing around with engines.'

He might not be sophisticated, but he was very well set up physically, she observed on closer inspection. The next thing was to find out if he was married.

'Are you one of those men I've heard about who drive your wife mad by neglecting her while you tinker with your car engine?' she asked craftily.

'I'm a widower, actually,' he informed her in an even tone. 'So that isn't a problem.'

Perfect, she thought, trying not to show her glee. 'I'm sorry to hear that,' she said in her best sympathetic voice. 'It's no age to lose your wife.'

'That's what war does, isn't it?' he said 'It takes people before their time.'

She nodded in an understanding manner, delighted with her progress so far. He would be hers for the taking if she made the very best use of her assets. 'It does indeed,' she said, giving a caring little sigh.

Desperate to keep the conversation going, she decided that a return to the topic of the car would be her best bet, so engaged in questions that she knew little or nothing about, such as the horsepower and the machine's fuel capacity, listening as though riveted to what he had to say, smiling and using her eyes in all the right places. All was going brilliantly until there was a shout from inside the church grounds, where a wedding party was posing for photographs.

'Bob,' called a female voice from the other side of the gate. 'Could you be a dear and keep Jimmy amused for a few minutes, please? He's bored stiff and under my feet and I need to concentrate.'

'Yeah, coming, love,' he agreed at once, smiling towards the owner of the voice. 'You should have done as I suggested and left him with me in the first place.' He glanced briefly at Joan but she could tell that he barely saw her; he only had eyes for the woman who had summoned him. 'Duty calls. Nice to have met you.'

And before Joan could say another word, he had left the car ticking over and was striding towards that damned Bessie Bow, who was taking wedding pictures with the equipment that was rightfully Joan's. As for Joan's concern about Bessie losing the baby, she needn't have worried. The kid was there as large as life. When she remembered all the time she'd wasted thinking she might have been responsible for damaging her pregnancy, her blood boiled. Another thing too: this man Joan had had her eye on for herself wasn't the man Bessie Bow had married. Her husband had been a skinny weed of a man. She remembered seeing them once together. What had happened to him she had no idea, but she did know it was grossly unfair.

How did she do it? Joan couldn't even get one man, and Bessie Bow had managed to get two. They were obviously on close terms; you could see it in the way he was talking to her and then taking the child's hand as though he was his father. Having dispensed with her son, Bessie turned back to the wedding crowd.

Incandescent with rage and completely out of control, Joan marched through the church gate and across to this happy little gathering. She grabbed Bessie roughly by the arm, causing her to swing round.

'What's going on . . . ? Oh, it's you,' exclaimed Bessie, pulling away from Joan. 'What on earth are you doing here?'

'Watching you,' Joan replied, scowling at her. 'Watching you in your illegal practices.'

'I haven't seen you for years,' said Bessie, taken aback by this interruption and embarrassed by it, coming as it had in the middle of a job. 'I thought you must have moved away from the area.'

'No, I'm still around, living in Haverley and determined to get justice for what you did to me.' She turned to the wedding guests and stepped forward. 'This woman is a fraud,' she announced in a loud voice. 'She is taking photographs with equipment that belongs to me. She has no right to be doing this, no right at all.'

A hushed murmur ran through the crowd. The bride looked as though she might burst into tears.

'If you have a grievance, I suggest you take it up with the photographer after our pictures have been taken,' said the best man, stepping forward and confronting Joan. 'We booked her in good faith and we want the photographs finished; in fact we demand it. Your personal problems have nothing to do with us, so please allow the photographer to continue.'

Bessie was mortified. 'I'm so sorry about this, everyone. Your photographs will be taken as arranged, don't worry,' she assured the man. 'Just give me two minutes to sort this out.'

She drew Joan to one side. 'What are you trying to do?' she demanded in a low voice. 'Put me out of business?'

'That wouldn't be a bad idea, since you shouldn't be in business anyway, using equipment that belongs to me,' Joan told her.

'Oh no, not that again.' Bessie was irritated. 'I thought you would have grown up and got over that silly nonsense by now. Go away, Joan. Clear off.'

'It's no good your trying to brush it aside, you scheming bitch,' rasped Joan, moving forward and grabbing Bessie, at which point Jimmy started to cry and Bob stepped in, removing Joan from Bessie and marching her towards the church gate.

'I don't know what all this is about, but you're not wanted here,' he said, ushering her through the gate and closing it behind her. 'So keep away.'

'She's got you in her clutches, has she?' Joan protested. 'I wonder how her husband feels about that.'

'Her husband is dead,' he informed her.

'Oh.'

'I've no idea what you've got against Bessie, but I'm warning you to stay away from her.'

'She's using my father's equipment and trading on his name,' Joan came back at him.

'I'm sure that Bessie is completely ethical in the way she conducts her business,' Bob defended.

'She's got you fooled good and proper.'

'It isn't my way to be rude to a woman,' he told her angrily. 'But you're an exceptional case. So go away before I really lose my temper, and let the people continue with their wedding photographs in peace.'

'I'll go, but you can tell Bessie that she hasn't heard the last of me,' she said, then turned and walked away.

Back outside the church Bessie was getting on with her work underneath the black cloth over the camera.

When she emerged, Bob said he would take Jimmy for a ride in the car while she finished the job. The little boy was looking quite tearful after seeing his mother attacked. Bessie was grateful and relieved. The altercation with Joan had unnerved her, especially as it had been played out in front of clients.

Bob really was a dear. Thanks to him she was able to take on outside work a little further afield now, provided that he was around with the car to drive her there. As weddings were usually at a weekend, when he wasn't at sea, it worked out well. Bob had suggested that he teach her to drive so that she could use the car herself, because she was now receiving requests to take official photographs at civic events and schools. She was planning to take him up on his offer. It would shock the people of the village, who had only just got used to cars being driven locally by men. A woman at the wheel would really set tongues wagging.

Meanwhile she had to try to repair the damage to her reputation caused by Joan Parsons by finishing this job in a professional manner. Then she was going to do whatever it took to bring this feud with Joan to a conclusion. She couldn't risk having the embittered woman turn up again while she was working. It had to be brought to an end once and for all.

Bob didn't want her to go.

'Leave it to me,' he said when she explained the history behind the altercation with Joan and told him about her plans. 'I'll go and see Joan Parsons and make sure she never bothers you again.'

'Thanks for the offer, Bob, but I have to go and see her myself. It's a personal issue between her and me.' She was adamant. 'Otherwise I'll always be under threat from her. This thing needs to be resolved once and for all. You can help me by staying with Jimmy while I'm out.'

'Do you know where she lives?'

'Not at this precise moment. But I'll soon find out. I shall ask around in Haverley,' she told him. 'Someone will know. It's that sort of a place.'

'I still think you should let me deal with it.'

'Absolutely not, Bob! I appreciate your concern, but this is one of those problems I have to deal with myself,' she insisted. 'I'm old enough to fight my own battles. I've got used to doing that since I lost Jim.'

'That doesn't mean you can't accept a helping hand from a friend now and then, surely?'

'No it doesn't, and I will,' she told him. 'But not as far as this is concerned. This one is for me personally.'

'Oh well, if you feel that strongly about it, I'd better let you get on with it,' he'd finally conceded.

Now, having asked in one of the local pubs as to Joan's whereabouts, Bessie was walking up the path of a cottage in a row on the outskirts of Haverley, far more modest than the previous Parsons address. With a great deal of trepidation she knocked at the door.

'You,' greeted Joan in a hostile manner, her cold eyes even icier than usual. 'What do you want?'

'To get things sorted out between us once and for all,' Bessie informed her briskly. 'I do not want a repeat performance of today ever again. Can I come in, please?'

'No you can't. Clear off.'

As Joan went to shut the door, Bessie pushed her weight against it with enough force to get herself over the threshold. Joan put up a struggle to keep her out but Bessie managed to stay on the inside of the door, which led straight into a living room with wooden beams and country-style furnishings.

'Right,' began Bessie when Joan finally admitted defeat, 'I want to know exactly what it will take to satisfy you and stop all this acrimony. It's gone on for long enough.'

'You know the answer to that, so why ask?'

'So . . . if I was to give you everything your father left to me, you would shut up, would you? Is that what you're saying?'

'Of course.'

'And what would you do to annoy me after that?' demanded Bessie. 'When you'd sold the stuff and spent the few pounds it would raise? I don't believe this grudge you've got against me would go away because

285

it doesn't actually have anything to do with the photographic equipment. It's much more personal than that.'

'Oh yeah, so you think you can read my mind, do you?' Joan said cynically.

'It isn't all that difficult,' replied Bessie. 'You're not the most subtle of people.'

'A proper little know-it-all, aren't you?'

'I could give you everything you think is yours,' said Bessie, ignoring her jibe. 'It wouldn't be right, because your father wanted me to have the things, but I would do it to get you off my back. I'm not so sure it would achieve anything, though, because you hate me for myself, and all this talk about my stealing your inheritance is just another stick to beat me with. If I gave it to you, you would find something else to torment me with. What I want to know is what I have ever done to deserve your spite.'

'Why should you have everything?' asked Joan.

'Everything? Me?' Bessie was astonished by this statement. 'I don't know how you've come to that conclusion. I'm a widow bringing a child up on my own with very little money, which is why I try to earn some extra by doing photography work.'

'You won't be on your own for much longer, though, will you? You've already got someone in tow.'

'I have no plans to remarry,' Bessie made clear. 'Anyway, that has nothing to do with this issue. I want this vendetta you've got against me to come to an end. I am sick and tired of it.'

'You were always artful,' accused Joan, as though Bessie hadn't spoken. 'Always trying to worm your way into my father's affections, pretending to like him and agreeing with everything the silly old fool said.'

'I didn't *pretend* to like him,' Bessie said angrily. 'I *did* like him, and if I agreed with him it was because he was right. He knew far more about photography than I did. As well as liking him, I also respected him.'

'Heaven only knows why. The man was an idiot.' Joan waved her hand around the room. 'Look at the way I have to live now because of him; in some hovel and having to work for a living.'

'A hovel,' cried Bessie. 'If you call this a hovel you have led a very sheltered life. It's a very pretty cottage that many people would give a lot to live in, and as for working for a living, that won't hurt you.'

'He should have left me well provided for.'

'He might have been able to if you'd not spent his money faster than he could earn it.'

'How dare you speak to me like that?'

'And how dare you accost me while I'm working; making a laughing stock of yourself and upsetting a bride on her big day?' Bessie's temper rose. 'You can have the stuff your father left me and I'll find the money to replace it somehow. I want nothing more to do with it or you. I'm warning you, Joan, if you come near me ever again after I have handed the things over, you'll live to regret it. I'll involve the police if I have to.'

'Don't you threaten me,' ordered Joan, lunging towards Bessie, grabbing hold of her and shaking her hard. 'You're nothing: just hired help, the lowest of the low.'

'Once I was the hired help, it's true,' returned Bessie, managing to push her away. 'But not now. Oh no! Now I am my own boss. So get your hands off me, you ridiculous apology for a woman.'

'Why, you . . .'

Bessie cried out in agony as Joan grabbed her hair and pulled it hard, then drew her long fingernails across Bessie's face. 'You're a savage; you want locking up,' she gasped.

'Get out of my house before I kill you,' shouted Joan, and Bessie didn't doubt that she would do it, because her temper was wild and she was capable of anything.

'I'm going, don't worry. I don't want to spend another second with a lunatic like you.' Bessie was shaken and breathless at the violence of the woman. 'Arrange to have the equipment collected as soon as possible. I want it and you out of my life.'

With a handkerchief held to the wound on her face, she opened the door and hurried out into the cold night air, her legs weak in the aftermath of the attack. The air was piercingly cold and the trees and bushes white with frost as she walked to the ferry, wondering if she would have enough in the fund she had been building up to open her own shop with which to replace the equipment she was going to give up to Joan. Somehow she would find the cash, because without the equipment she couldn't work at what she did best. She needed to provide for Jimmy into the future, and her means of doing this was about to be taken away. Damn Joan Parsons, she thought; damn her to hell!

The ferry had just arrived, and the few passengers on board alighted hurriedly, shivering against the weather. Bessie stepped on to the boat, gave the ferryman a ha'penny for her fare and sat down on the wooden seat.

'Not many customers about tonight,' remarked the ferryman. 'People are at home by the fire on a night like this unless they have to go out.'

'You still come out whatever the weather, though, don't you, Mr Tyler?'

'Aye, it's me job,' he replied. 'There might not be many people about but you have to be here for those that are, don't you? It's what I'm paid for.'

Seeing her pull her shawl tighter around her, he said, 'There isn't a train due in so I won't wait for any other fares. I'll get you across straight away, m'dear. Don't want you catching pneumonia on my account.'

'Thank you.'

He was about to set off when there was the crunch of footsteps on the path.

'Aye aye, another customer,' he said. 'You're just in time. Come aboard, m'dear.'

Bessie's heart sank. In the glow of the ferry lantern, Joan Parsons stepped into the boat.

'You've followed me,' accused Bessie.

'That's right,' Joan confirmed. 'I'm coming to get what's mine before you change your mind.'

'You won't be able to carry it all,' Bessie pointed out. 'Not the developing equipment.'

'I'll take what I can manage and get the rest collected another time,' she told her.

'As you wish,' conceded Bessie. 'I wasn't planning on moving away with it, though, so it will be quite safe.'

'I'll be happier when some of it, at least, is in my possession,' Joan announced.

Shrugging, Bessie fell silent, looking at the lights on the opposite bank and longing to be there. She was cold and miserable and would be thoroughly glad to get home.

About halfway across the river the boat started to bump and sway. It juddered so violently Bessie thought for a moment that it was going to turn over. Then it started to head up the river instead of across, obviously out of Mr Tyler's control.

'We've hit a pack of ice floes,' explained the struggling ferryman. 'The tide is running in fast and altering our course. I need to get the head of the boat round.'

'Can I help?' offered Bessie.

'No. You stay where you are,' said Mr Tyler in a definite tone as the boat rocked and rolled frighteningly. 'I need to keep the weight even. If you stand up we'll all end up in the water.'

Joan started to scream hysterically. 'Oh my God, it's going to turn over. We'll all drown,' she shrieked. 'Help, help! Somebody, anybody, help!'

'Calm down, for goodness' sake,' admonished Bessie firmly. 'Mr Tyler knows what he's doing.'

'There's no need for alarm,' the ferryman assured them, puffing heavily as he fought to get the head round. 'I'll get you home safe. But please stay as still as you can.'

His plea fell on deaf ears as far as Joan was concerned. She was far too obsessed with self-preservation to bother about the rest of them, and leapt to her feet yelling, 'The boat is going to turn over and I can't swim. I'll drown, I'll drown. Help! Help! For God's sake, somebody help us.'

'Sit down, please,' ordered the ferryman, still struggling against the forces of nature. 'You'll have us all in the water if you carry on like this, so calm down for all of our sakes.'

But Joan was out of control, laughing and crying simultaneously. Something had to be done quickly, and Bessie stood up and slapped her face to bring her out of it.

It stopped the hysterics instantly. But Joan wouldn't sit down; she stood where she was as though paralysed.

'Come on, Joan,' said Bessie in a kinder tone and with admirable patience. The other woman was obviously distressed, and this was no time for a shouting match. 'Sit down next to me. We'll be all right.'

At that moment, the ferry rocked so violently, Joan was thrown off balance. As a surge of water flooded the boat, she slipped over the side into the black waters. Bessie didn't hesitate. She threw off her shawl and boots and went in after her.

Bessie's breath was taken from her by the bitter temperature of the water. It was numbingly cold and she was completely winded but trying not to exacerbate the situation by panicking. What a blessing it was that she had been taught to swim by her brother, she thought, as she got her breath and her bearings and swam around looking for Joan in the dark.

She could hear her splashing and choking and swam towards the sounds until she located her, but she was unsuccessful in trying to help her because Joan was struggling and fighting for her life.

'Try not to panic,' Bessie said, getting behind her and gripping her underneath her shoulders, keeping her head above water. 'I can get you over to the bank but I need you to cooperate. Stay calm and let me do all the work.'

But Joan was far too frightened to take any notice and fought against her, swallowing water and retching. Bessie could feel her slipping from her grasp.

'Please, Joan, I can't help you if you fight against me,' she urged, her lungs almost bursting as she struggled for breath. 'Try to relax and leave it all to me. I won't let you down so long as you stay calm.'

At last Joan stopped struggling, and Bessie somehow – and afterwards she never knew how – got her to the bank. They came ashore much further downstream than the ferry landing point, as she had been helpless against the tide so had had to go with it.

The ferryman had got the boat in and was running towards them carrying Bessie's boots and shawl, followed by a crowd of villagers, who always seemed to know when any sort of drama had occurred.

'We're all right,' Bessie assured them as they fussed around the two women, offering help in the lamplight. 'We just need to get inside in the warm and get these wet clothes off. Come on, Joan, it'll only take a few minutes to walk to my place.'

Bessie was shivering so much her teeth were chattering as the two of them walked along the waterfront together.

'Why did you save me?' Joan asked Bessie later when Bob had gone home. Jimmy was asleep in bed, and the two women had bathed in a tin bath in the kitchen and were sitting by the fire in the parlour drinking cocoa. Having offered Joan a bed for the night as it was too late for the ferry, Bessie was wearing a red woollen dressing gown; Joan had on an old navy blue one her host had managed to find for her.

'What a question,' replied Bessie. 'Instinct, I suppose. It's natural to help when someone is in trouble.'

'But we can't stand the sight of each other.'

'That's quite true,' Bessie agreed. 'I wouldn't see you drown, though, not when I have the means to save you.'

'All I ever do is cause trouble for you.'

'I'll say you do,' admitted Bessie, not wishing to deny it. 'But you can't not help someone because you don't like them, can you? You'd have done the same for me, even though you hate my guts.'

'I wouldn't have because I can't swim.'

'If I was in trouble in a way that you could help with, you would,' said Bessie. 'It's a natural instinct.'

'Not for everyone,' Joan replied. 'I'm not sure if I have that kind of thing in me.'

'I shall have to make sure I'm never in trouble when you're the only other person around, then, won't I?' said Bessie, making a joke of it.

'Anyway, thanks for what you did,' Joan said, sounding unusually subdued and sincere. 'I owe my life to you.'

'Ooh, don't get too nice, Joan.' Bessie smiled. 'It might be too much of a shock to my system. I shall begin to think that you are sickening for something.'

'Well, I can't afford to upset you as you're giving me a bed for the night, can I?' Joan came back at her, entering into the joke much to Bessie's surprise.

'That wouldn't stop you if you were riled about something,' said Bessie. 'You'd walk all the way home via Colchester rather than keep it to yourself.'

'Am I really that difficult?'

Bessie nodded. 'I'm afraid so,' she informed her. 'You're an absolute nightmare.'

'Oh.' A silence. 'Look, I won't take your equipment,' declared Joan, out of the blue. 'I wouldn't dream of it now.'

'Oh yes you will,' Bessie came back at her in a definite tone. 'I want it safely in your hands and you out of my hair. I'll find a way of replacing it somehow.'

'I don't want it,' Joan confessed. 'I never did. Not really. I just didn't want you to have it.'

'Why?'

'I was jealous, I suppose. Always have been; ever since you first went to work for my father.'

'That seems crazy to me. You always had more of everything than I did, in a material sense.'

'You were always happy,' Joan explained. 'And you had my father's respect.'

'That's one thing you never seemed to want,' remarked Bessie. 'In fact, you actively discouraged it.'

'You're right. I did. But neither did I want you to have it,' Joan tried to explain. 'It's the way I am. I have a very jealous nature. I hate other people to have anything that pleases them. I don't know why.'

'You could have had your father's respect so easily if you'd taken the trouble to get to know him and been a bit kinder to him,' Bessie told her. 'He would have been thrilled to bits if you'd taken an interest in what he did for a living. I'm sure he would have wanted nothing more than to leave his entire business to you for you to carry on the tradition.'

'As it was, there was nothing to pass on except the equipment he left to you,' she said.

'He did his best,' said Bessie.

Joan nodded in agreement. 'I know.' She sighed. 'Anyway, you keep the camera and all the rest of the stuff, and good luck to you. There'll be no more trouble from me.'

Bessie looked at her suspiciously.

'You have my word,' Joan assured her. 'It's over, Bessie. I promise you.'

This time Bessie really did believe she meant it. 'I must admit it would be a huge relief,' she told her. 'I can't really afford to replace it, but I would do so somehow if I had to.'

'If you marry that chap you're seeing you won't need to work,' Joan suggested.

'We have no plans to marry at the moment, but if we were to at some time in the future, I wouldn't give up photography because I have a real interest in it, thanks to the way your father taught me,' Bessie informed her.

'Married women aren't supposed to work now that the war is over,' Joan pointed out. 'It isn't considered proper.'

'That's just too bad,' said Bessie. 'It isn't as though I would be taking a job from a man who needs it. I've made my own job, and I will create one for someone else if I can afford an assistant later on. I'm not going to waste a talent that was nurtured in me by your father.'

'I'd sooner be a kept woman myself,' said Joan. 'Blow working if you don't have to.'

'Each to their own,' was Bessie's response. 'But photography is a hobby as well as a job for me. I really enjoy it. There's so much more to it than just taking a picture of someone in their finery. It's all about getting the best image and capturing the moment.'

'It's very nice for you to have that but quite beyond me, I'm afraid,' admitted Joan with an air of resignation. 'So it's the wrong side of the counter for me until I find myself a husband.'

Bessie couldn't pretend not to be relieved to see the end of the feud and to be able to keep the equipment. What an extraordinary night it had been!

Chapter Eighteen

With all due credit to Archie, he spared no effort to make Christmas a happy time in the Mott household, especially with regard to Connie. His recent efforts to improve his relationship with the little girl had taken effect, May observed. During the run–up to the big day he threw himself into the festive spirit, bringing home holly, mistletoe and a huge Christmas tree, which he dutifully helped to decorate. He sat patiently at the table making paper chains with Connie out of coloured paper, and teased her gently about what might be in Santa's sack for her.

Having spent so much time riding on the back of her mother's bicycle, Connie desperately wanted a small one of her own, and she was all smiles on Christmas morning when a shiny new one had been delivered overnight along with a wooden pencil box, a baby doll, a whip and top, a skipping rope and various other delights, along with a stocking filled with little gifts and an orange in the toe.

May and Archie had worked together to make it all possible for her, and the day passed pleasantly enough, both of them devoting their time and energy to the child and making sure that Bill enjoyed himself. Together they took Connie out on her new bike in the morning and in the after-noon they visited Winnie and Albert. Ostensibly everything was fine.

But in reality May's heart was breaking and she sensed that Archie's was too. She could tell that he was deeply depressed despite his cheery front and for some reason he didn't seem willing to make an effort to put things right between them.

To add to May's emotional havoc was the remorse that plagued her because she hadn't been able to get William Marriot out of her mind since seeing him again. He excited her in a way that Archie never could, and he claimed to want her and Connie to be with him.

Being only human, she was tempted. As well as her passion for him, she couldn't help considering the practical side of things too, much to her shame. With William her daughter would have the best of everything money could buy, and good connections as she grew up, while May herself would enjoy financial security and luxury as a matter of course. Whereas the best Archie could offer was food on the table, some sort of basic accommodation of their own at some point in the future, cheap living and a market background.

Even apart from her own feelings, was she right to deprive her daughter of her birthright? she asked herself in bed on Christmas night. Should she give Connie the chance of a better life in the material sense, a higher standard of living for them both, especially as Archie no longer seemed able or willing to offer May love? He'd even taken to coming to bed after she was asleep, so he couldn't make his feelings much more obvious. Even now, on Christmas night, she was in bed alone. But she had married him for better or worse and she took that commitment seriously. It was a dilemma indeed.

Archie sat in the armchair downstairs, smoking and mulling things over. He was losing his wife and he didn't seem able to do a damned thing about it. It wasn't that he didn't care – May and Connie were everything to him – it was more that he felt empty of passion, was the only way he could describe it. He still felt irreversibly distanced from May, from his father; from everyone. He'd managed to make some sort of a connection with Connie recently after May had given him earache about not making any effort, but none of it felt real. He was going through the motions because he knew it was the right thing to do, but he felt as though he was acting.

He could pretend with Connie but not with May. It had to be real for her and he just couldn't make it happen. He was dead inside. She deserved better than an apology of a man. A woman like her could have anyone and he should set her free. But he wasn't even brave enough to do that.

Perhaps he could give her a break; suggest that she have a night out sometime soon while he stayed home and looked after Connie. It wasn't a permanent solution but it might give her a lift. It would be a rest from his presence anyway. He would speak to her about it in the next few days.

Winnie put on her best hat in front of the mirror in the hall and pushed a stray lock of hair under it. A Saturday night out with her husband at the Palace Theatre was just what she needed. January was always a swine of a month, with the cold weather and everything seeming so dead and dismal after Christmas. In the warmth and colour of the music hall she could forget the bitter wind and her chilblains. It might even take the edge off the pain of her rift with May for a while, as well as the worry of knowing that all was not well between May and her husband.

Every day Winnie saw Archie at the market, and sometimes May was there helping on the stall. Normally such a cheery pair, all the fun seemed to have gone out of both of them. It had never been a marriage made in heaven but they had made the best of things and seemed very happy together. May had even appeared to love him after a while.

Now Winnie would do anything to take the sadness out of her eyes, but what could she do, since she wasn't even permitted to offer a shoulder to cry on or a listening ear, the way things were between them? Oh well, no good would come of fretting about it. She'd made a mistake in her life and now she must take her punishment. She must live with sympathy for May whilst being powerless to help. That was the painful part. Chin up, girl, she told herself. Put a smile on your face for your husband's sake.

'I'm ready, Albert,' she called, putting on her scarf and gloves and giving herself a final once-over in the mirror. 'We'd better get going or we won't have time for a drink before the show starts.'

He appeared in a dark overcoat, showing a stiff white collar and tie underneath. 'Come on then, love, let's go,' he said, taking his best cap off the hall stand and putting it on.

Winnie took his arm and they walked down the street in the direction of the Broadway.

That same evening on the bus going along Hammersmith Broadway, May was looking out of the window, observing how vibrant and busy it was: a typical Saturday night, with crowds surging towards the theatres and cinemas, the pavements thronged with people visible in the gaslight, the pubs packed to the doors, some men even braving the elements and standing drinking outside on the street. Hammersmith was well known as a centre of entertainment; some said it was second only to the West End of London.

The bus moved intermittently. There was always a tangle of traffic here and tonight was no exception. Motor cars and petrol buses vied for position with horse transport, cyclists, dogs treating the road as their own and pedestrians crossing anywhere they fancied, regardless of the traffic hazards. Had she not wanted to feel as though she was going out for the evening, so was wearing a skirt and her best coat, she would have been out there in the chaos on her bicycle.

It was a while since May had been out of an evening, and she could sense the buzz of excitement as people headed for the palaces of pleasure.

She felt a pang, remembering how she and Winnie had sometimes enjoyed a visit to the cinema or the music hall together. There was something about a busy town after dark, especially on a Saturday night, that gave her a special feeling of exhilaration, perhaps because she was a country girl so it was all relatively new to her. She remembered how thrilling she'd found it when she'd first come to live with Auntie in London.

Tonight, however, she wasn't a part of the hedonistic masses. She was on her way to the more refined location of Kensington to visit Constance. It had been the only thing she could think of to do on her own when Archie had suggested that she might like to go out for the evening while he looked after Connie. Had things been different between herself and Aunt Winnie she would have been in the crowds out there heading for a show or a film. But they weren't, so she was going visiting instead. At least it would be a break from the strain of pretending that everything was fine between herself and Archie. He'd probably be glad of her absence too, she thought sadly, though she did actually believe that he had made the suggestion entirely for her benefit.

Constance had told her to feel free to call at any time, so May was taking her at her word and coming unannounced. If it wasn't convenient she would simply turn around and go home. Hammersmith on a Saturday night was great fun with company but no place for a young woman on her own, especially later on, when there would be a fair amount of inebriates out on the streets.

But right now the bus was still crawling through the chaotic Broadway, pulling up sharply every so often to avoid running down some merrymaking pedestrian. Eventually they progressed slowly onwards and May alighted at her stop and walked towards the elegant Regency abode in a salubrious tree-lined square where Constance lived with her well-off husband.

When she got there, however, she found herself hesitating. She stood outside in contemplation for quite a long time; then, without any prior intention and a great deal of compunction, she turned around and walked in the other direction before turning off into a side street, her heart racing.

'Everyone is out and about tonight by the look of it,' observed Albert as he and Winnie reached the Broadway and were enveloped by the crowds, most people dressed in their best.

'Good luck to 'em, I say,' Winnie responded. 'There's nothing like a Saturday night out to set you up for the week. We all deserve a bit of fun now and then.'

'Wotcha, you two,' said someone, slapping a hand on Albert's shoulder.

Turning, they saw Percy, who had a fish stall on the market. He looked as though he had already had a good few to drink. 'Are you out boozing?'

'No. We're going to the music hall,' replied Winnie. 'But I expect we'll have a quick one before the show.'

'Why don't you come with me on a pub crawl?' he invited. 'That will be much more fun.'

'You look as though you've had more than enough already, Percy,' commented Winnie. 'Your missus won't half give you what for when you get home.'

'I haven't had much,' he denied blearily. 'I came out early for a couple of snifters.'

'More like half a dozen large ones by the look of you,' said Winnie light-heartedly.

'Yeah, well, maybe I 'ave 'ad a few; you know how it is,' he said, his words slurred. 'One leads to another, and—'

'Before you know what's happening you can hardly stand up,' cut in Winnie. 'I should go home to your wife while you can still walk if I were you, Percy.'

'Well we're off anyway,' said Albert, eager to get away because they had plans of their own.

'My wife is a very understanding woman,' drawled Percy, numbed by alcohol to other people's concerns. 'She knows I don't mean any 'arm.'

'Anyway, we'll see you at the market on Monday,' said Winnie, also anxious to be on their way. 'Ta-ta.'

'Ta-ta,' he returned, swaying precariously as he went to cross the road.

'Hey, watch where you're going, Percy,' warned Winnie as he stepped into the path of an oncoming bus.

As he paid no heed, Winnie ran forward and pushed him to safety, but as she did so, she lost her footing and staggered. The bus juddered to a halt, but not before Winnie was knocked to the ground by it.

Pandemonium broke out all around him, but Albert was paralysed with fear as he stared at his wife lying motionless in the road close to the front wheels of the bus. A crowd formed almost instantly.

'She just walked out in front of me,' the bus driver was saying to the crowd emotionally. 'I didn't stand a chance of missing her. I slammed on the brakes as hard as they would go but I couldn't stop the bus quickly enough. Oh God help me; I've killed someone.'

'Move back, please, folks,' said a police constable who had arrived on the scene and was blowing his whistle for assistance. 'I'll send someone for an ambulance.'

The white mist cleared and Albert stepped forward and kneeled down beside his wife, explaining to the constable who he was as he tried to hold him back.

'Winnie,' he said, on his knees beside her, his voice gruff and barely audible. 'Winnie love. You'll be all right. I'm here with you. An ambulance will be coming soon. Just open your eyes . . . Please talk to me . . . Don't you dare go and die on me. You can't do that. Please, please stay with me. You can't leave me, Winnie. Come on, love. You know I'm lost without you.'

But Winnie lay just where she had landed, on her back with her eyes closed. Albert clasped her hand, praying and willing her to stay alive.

May walked up a flight of steps to the front door of an imposing building in an elegant terrace in Kensington, an address that was etched so indelibly in her memory she needed nothing to refer to. She pressed one of several buttons, with names at the side, on a brass plate at the side of the front door. It was answered promptly.

'Hello, May,' he said, smiling at her. 'I knew you'd come sooner or later.'

'Hello, William.'

'Come on in then,' he invited, standing back and opening the door wider in a welcoming manner.

She didn't respond; just stared at him in the light of the hallway. Even at home, faced with an unexpected visitor, he was as immaculate as ever.

'Well don't stand out there in the cold,' he urged her, his voice deep, vowels perfect. 'Come on in.'

Hesitating for only a few seconds more, she stepped into the luxuriously appointed hallway of the flats. As soon as the outside door was closed he opened her arms to her. Against all her better judgement she went into them.

Archie was snoozing in the armchair when there was a loud banging at the front door.

'All right, all right, there's no need to knock the door down,' muttered Bill as he went to answer it.

'It's Winnie,' announced a distraught Albert as he came charging into the living room, puffing from exertion and causing Archie to leap to his feet. 'She's been knocked down by a bus and is in hospital. She's in a really bad way.' He clutched his head. 'Oh, Bill, she's barely alive.'

'Oh good God,' said Bill, clutching his throat. 'Can we go and see her, or are they only allowing relatives to visit?'

'There are no restrictions; she's that ill. I've only left her because in the odd moments when she's conscious she's asking for May and seems to be upsetting herself because she isn't there,' he explained. 'I need her to come at once. Although Winnie is barely conscious, the fretting isn't helping her. The two of them haven't been on good terms lately and I think Winnie wants to put it right while there's still time.'

'May isn't at home, mate,' said Archie worriedly. 'She's gone out for the evening.'

'Ooh my Gawd.' Albert clutched his head, looking desperate. 'She needs to be there.' His voice was distorted with emotion as he choked out, 'Winnie might not have long.'

'I'll get her there. You leave it to me,' Archie assured him. 'She's only gone to see her friend Constance. I'm sure the address will be around somewhere. I'll find her, don't worry.'

'I'd be very grateful to you,' said Albert.

'You go back to Winnie, mate. I'll soon sort this out.' He turned to his father. 'You'll stay with Connie while I go and get May, won't you, Dad?'

'Of course I will.' Bill put his hand on Albert's shoulder. 'All the best, mate. Give my love to Winnie. I'll come and see her as soon as I can.'

'That goes for me too,' said Archie, already on his way upstairs to the bedroom in search of an address for Constance. The most likely place was May's dressing-table drawer where she kept her personal sundries; a private place where he would only ever venture in the case of an emergency such as this.

Bill had gone to his room and Archie was pacing up and down in the parlour, his mind in turmoil, the peculiar numbness he'd experienced since the war now replaced by feelings so strong they were almost unbearable: anger, disappointment and sheer terror at the thought of losing May. He knew she wasn't with Constance this evening because he'd run to the Broadway and got a cab to the address he had found for her, but Constance had neither seen her nor been expecting her.

His first thought had been for May's safety, imagining she might have met with an accident on the way here or been harmed in some other way. But then he remembered seeing a personal calling card in her drawer when he'd been looking for an address for Constance. At the time he'd been so preoccupied with worry about Winnie, it hadn't fully registered. It wasn't until May hadn't been where she'd said she'd be that the awful significance dawned. She was with *him*, and Archie was devastated.

He'd rushed back home to get the address. He was going to have to go there and confront her and Marriot, because May was needed at the hospital. This would bring the whole thing into the open and a decision would have to be made. If she chose the father of her child over Archie, then he wouldn't stand in her way no matter how deep the pain. He'd always known that Marriot was the love of her life. May had been honest with him from the start about that. He just hadn't realised that she was seeing him again. It wasn't like her to be underhand, and he felt dreadfully let down by her.

Still, what did he himself have to offer her in comparison to Marriot? Bugger all was the answer to that. He hadn't even given her any decent company since the end of the war. It was no wonder she had turned to someone else.

Anyway, now was no time for worrying about their marital problems. He was on his way to the front door to go and find May when he heard her key in the lock. He felt physically ill with tension, his muscles so tight they ached.

'Archie,' she said, looking sheepish. 'I'm glad you're still up, because I've got something to tell you.'

So this was it; she was going to tell him that she was leaving him for William Marriot. She was going to take Connie and go. She didn't need to continue; he could see it in her eyes.

'Not now, May,' he said quickly. 'There's something very important I have to tell you.'

'Oh.' She looked at him, observing the worried expression, the pallor. 'What . . . what's happened. Is there something wrong with Connie?'

'No. Connie is fine.'

'Thank God. But what . . . ?'

'It's Winnie,' he informed her. 'She's been run over by a bus and is in hospital.'

Watching her face flush then become bloodless, her skin suffused with perspiration as she looked about to pass out, he eased her gently into a chair.

'How bad is she?' she asked tremulously.

'They're not sure she'll make it,' he replied.

'Oh no.' Her voice broke and she put her hands to her head. 'Please God, not that.'

'She's asking for you, May,' he explained. 'I know the two of you haven't been getting on lately, but she wants to see you now. It's urgent. There might not be much time.'

'I'll go right away,' she said, already on her feet, her body trembling.

'I'll come with you,' he asserted. 'If we hurry we might catch a bus; if not, we'll have to take Shanks's pony.'

'What about Connie?'

'Dad will listen for her. He's gone to his room but he won't sleep for worrying about Winnie. I was coming to find you, so he knows he's in charge.' He didn't add that his father had been in charge most of the evening while Archie was out looking for May. Now wasn't the time for all of that.

Together they slipped from the house and hurried down the gaslit street.

'Auntie, it's me, May. Can you hear me?' she asked. Winnie's face was paper white and had an oddly waxen look.

There was no response.

'I've missed you so much and I've realised that I was wrong to judge you about what you did when I was born,' May went on, her voice ragged with emotion. 'I know you did it for my sake. I was lucky I had you to turn to when the same thing happened to me. If I hadn't, God only knows what would have become of Connie and me.' She was speaking quickly because time was of the essence, but every so often she had to break off because she was crying so much and had to wipe the tears that were soaking her face and blurring her vision. 'You were fifteen and you had to do what your sister told you. I've been selfish and I'm so ashamed. I understand now that you had to go along with her plan because you had no choice; you didn't have the support that I had from you all those years later. You more than made up for it when I needed you. My only regret is that I missed growing up as your daughter, and I am deeply sorry for the time we lost together more recently because of my selfishness.'

She held Winnie's hand and raised it to her lips. 'I'm so sorry,' she wept.

She felt the tiniest movement of Winnie's hand.

'Auntie, are you hearing me?' she asked, staring at Winnie, whose eyes were flickering slightly. 'Oh Auntie, please . . . please say that you can.'

'May. You've come,' Winnie said, her voice barely audible before she slipped back into unconsciousness.

'I think you'd better take a break now, May,' suggested Archie, putting his hand on her shoulder. Albert nodded in agreement.

'Let's go and see if we can find a cup o' tea and let Albert have some time on his own with his wife.'

Outside in the corridor, May said to Archie, 'Do you think she heard me when I said all that just now?'

'From the way she spoke I think she must have known you were there,' he suggested hopefully. 'But whether or not what you said registered, I don't know.'

'Oh I do hope it did, Archie,' she told him ardently. 'I so want to put things right. I've missed her so much. I can't believe how stupid I've been.'

'We all get things wrong at times.'

'I messed up in a really big way.' She paused, looking worried. 'The doctors don't seem to think there's much chance of her recovering, do they?'

'No, they don't seem to. But doctors never like to give false hope. They have to make sure that relatives are prepared for the worst, just in case,' he pointed out. 'But where there's life there's hope, that's the way I look at it.'

'I shall certainly be praying for a miracle,' she told him.

'You sit down and I'll go and see if I can produce a miracle and get us a cup o' tea at this late hour,' he said, in such a matter-of-fact manner that she could never have guessed at the turmoil he was in over losing her to Marriot.

May's thoughts were all of Winnie. Her own personal problems could wait.

Unaware that her aunt was desperately ill, Bessie was also praying for a miracle. She was standing at the deserted Tideway quays in the bitterly cold small hours, experiencing something she had lived through many times before; for her father, her brothers and boys from the village she had grown up with.

This time it was Bob who was missing, feared drowned in rough weather in the North Sea. How many times had she waited and hoped like this? Sometimes it was good news; other times, as with her elder brother, it was the worst.

'We ought to go home for a while, sis,' suggested Sam, who was with her. 'Staying here in the cold isn't going to bring him back. All it's doing is freezing us to death.'

'I know,' she said, staring down the river as though willing Bob's boat to come into sight. The night was dry, the cruel wind howling through the village beneath a clear sky sprinkled with stars that created a false impression of tranquillity. 'I suppose I feel closer to him here somehow.'

'I think we should go home and have a hot drink and come back later if he still hasn't appeared. Dad will be on edge at home and it's best if we all wait together,' he said. 'Bob will come to our place first. He knows we'll all be worried.'

'Yeah, I suppose you're right.' As they made their way home up the hill, Bessie said, 'It's my own silly fault. I knew I shouldn't have got involved with a seaman. I always said I wouldn't because I knew I would have to go through this sooner or later. You don't get this with men who have land-based jobs.'

'That's a bit of a selfish attitude, isn't it?' Sam said, surprising her with his sharpness. 'Worrying about how you feel when he's the one in trouble. I'm surprised at you, Bessie.'

'I'm worried about *him*, not me,' she explained. 'That's why I'm in such a state.'

'Jim couldn't have had a safer job but you lost him just the same,' he pointed out. 'I'm no expert, but surely if you love someone you take the risk and all the pain that comes with it. The only way to guard against it is not to care about anyone at all. And that's no way to live your life.'

'I didn't realise you'd become such an expert on human nature,' she said.

'I haven't, but I'm a seaman myself so I see it from a different perspective to you. I'd hate to think that going to sea would put a girl off me,' said Sam, who was still seeing the girl he had met when they went to see the crashed Zeppelin. 'If it did I would think she was a selfish cow and not worth bothering with.'

'So you think that about me?'

'You're not normally a selfish person,' he told her. 'But over this, yes, you are, and if I was your boyfriend I would probably think that too. I mean, the poor chap is out there doing his best to earn a living in the only way he knows how, and to put food on people's plates, and all you can think about is the worry he's putting you through. Your pain; how you feel.'

Shocked by this point of view, Bessie said, 'His pain is my pain. I am frightened for him, imagining him stranded somewhere, cold and alone. I am in fear and dread that he has perished at sea. I admit I don't want to feel like this; I hate feeling like this. I've had enough of waiting for men to come back from sea to last me a lifetime and I'm still having it with you and Dad. I thought I had a choice as regards other men, but I don't as far as Bob is concerned because he means the world to me. I'm involved whether I like it or not, so being permanently afraid is how it is going to be.'

'You've always said you would never marry a seaman,' Sam reminded her.

'It was a silly thing to say. You can't choose who you fall in love with, and I would marry Bob tomorrow if he asked me.' As she spoke, she realised the truth of her words. It had taken this crisis to make her realise that Bob had become much more than a friend to her. Perversely, the situation that she had never wanted to go through again, that could have sent her scurrying in the opposite direction, had clarified her feelings for him. More than anything, she wanted to share her life with him and there wasn't a thing she could do about it, even though it would mean feeling vulnerable on a permanent basis.

'I'm sure he'll be tickled pink about that,' said Sam. 'He's obviously nuts about you.'

'I'm so worried. I want him to come home more than anything, Sam,' she said with a sob in her voice.

'I know, sis,' he said, putting a comforting arm around her as they walked up to the cottage door. 'All we can do is to wait and hope and pray.'

As the pale light of dawn crept slowly over the village, Bessie sat by the bedroom window looking down the hill towards the river, her body cold and her muscles aching with tension. The house was silent at this hour, everyone in bed. She had tried to sleep, but realising that she was fighting a losing battle, she'd wrapped the eiderdown around herself and now sat here, watching and longing to see that tall burly figure come into view.

Her eyes ached and her lids drooped as weariness finally prevailed, and her head fell on to her chest, until a sound woke her with a start. There was a noise downstairs. It was probably Dad or Sam up for work, she thought, but she slipped quietly from the room and down the stairs.

'Bob,' she cried, seeing him sitting at the kitchen table in a thick pullover, his oilskins over a chair. 'Oh Bob, thank God. Am I pleased to see you.'

'I came straight here because I knew you'd be anxious,' he explained. 'It's lucky we don't have to lock our doors at night here in Tideway.'

'Anxious doesn't come anywhere near to how I've been feeling,' Bessie told him, throwing her arms around him, smelling the ocean and the fish and the cold salty air on his skin. 'I've been sitting at the bedroom window looking out for you and I must have nodded off.'

'The boat got damaged in the gales and I thought she was going down, but I managed to get her ashore and get the repairs done,' he explained. 'Sorry I couldn't get word to you. There were no other boats around to bring a message.'

'Oh Bob, you couldn't know how pleased I am to see you,' she told him, tears of relief welling up and brimming over. 'There aren't the words to describe it.'

His face full of tiredness and strain, eyes red and shadowed, lit up as he smiled. 'Perhaps I should give you a fright more often, then, if this is the result.'

'Don't you dare,' she said, wrapping her arms around him, tasting the sea on his lips and knowing that he was right for her.

After Bessie had given him a hot drink and some bread and cheese, Bob went home to sleep and she went back to bed and slept peacefully. In fact she slept so deeply the others were already up and about when she went downstairs. Jimmy was at the kitchen table with his grandfather, who was cutting a loaf of bread. The fire in the parlour was roaring and Sam was sitting by it with a thick chunk of bread on the end of a toasting fork.

'I'll get the porridge on,' she said. 'You should have woken me. I must have slept through the alarm.'

'We thought you'd need some sleep as you've been awake half the night,' said her father. 'Good news about Bob. We heard him come in so knew he was back.'

'Yeah, it's the best news.' She paused, listening to the wind rattling the windows and roaring around the cottage, and looked at the clock, which told her it was eight o'clock. 'You're not taking the boat out today then.'

'No point in this weather,' said her father. 'We'll do some maintenance work on her later. We'll go over and see Bob when he's had time to catch up on his sleep.'

'Can I go to the boat with you?' asked Jimmy.

'If your mother says you can,' said his grandfather.

'Yeah, of course you can go, so long as you wrap up well. It's very cold out there for a little boy.'

There was an air of celebration in the house over breakfast. The communal relief that Bob was safe was palpable. It was cosy in the parlour and Bessie was imbued with a deep sense of well-being. The conversation was interrupted by a knock at the door. Smiling, Bessie went to answer it.

'Telegram for Mrs Minter,' said the boy.

'Oh,' she said, taking the envelope. 'Thank you.'

Trembling with apprehension she opened it, and thought her legs would give in.

'What is it, Bessie?' asked her father when she re-entered the room, pale and trembling. 'You look as though you've had a shock.'

'I have,' she said, her voice breaking with emotion. 'It's Aunt Winnie. Oh Dad, it's so awful.'

Unable to say any more, she handed him the telegram.

★ ★ ★

The screens were around Winnie's bed in the ward and the whole family – who had been told to prepare themselves for the worst – was gathered, though Archie had taken Connie and Jimmy outside, as the bedside of a dying woman was no place for children in his opinion. The fact that she was in hospital added drama to the occasion, because only the most serious of cases were admitted on to the wards. Most ailments were treated at home.

Albert was holding Winnie's hand. May was sitting at her bedside looking at her face, willing her not to die. The doctors couldn't bring her back to consciousness. They suspected that she had sustained brain damage and there was nothing more they could do for her except make her comfortable. May could feel hysteria rising but she knew she must keep calm for the sake of everybody else, especially poor Uncle Albert, who was beside himself. At least Bessie and the others had got here in time; May was glad about that.

The area inside the screens was silent and tense, the normal noise of the hospital ward going on around them: the chink of crockery as food was taken round; someone coughing with an awful chesty rattling; another shouting out in agony. But no one in the gathering around Winnie's bed seemed to notice.

Suddenly there was another sound.

'Good grief,' said Winnie weakly. 'Woss goin' on? Why are you all here? Blimey, I must be about to peg out.'

The silence was electric; then May emitted a nervous giggle, which infected the others and they all began to laugh. Winnie soon went back to sleep and they called the nurse, who called the doctor, whose reaction was cautious: he said it could be a good sign but they mustn't get their hopes up too high because patients did sometimes seem to rally just before the end.

'Just let nature take its course,' he advised them.

It was disappointing but May refused to be negative. When Winnie came to again later on, for longer this time, even the doctor began to become hopeful.

'She does seem to be coming out of it,' he muttered, though he still seemed somewhat circumspect.

By the end of that day, Winnie was awake for longer periods of time, though with consciousness came pain. She had sustained some nasty injuries and they were hurting.

'Getting knocked down by a bus is a painful way of getting you all together at the same time,' she said in her old dry way. 'I don't think I'll bother again.'

'Oh Auntie, you are a card,' said May, planting a kiss on her forehead.

She took May's hand, and the look that passed between them made words unnecessary. All was forgiven and they were friends again; that was what mattered.

It turned into a bit of a celebration after that, because everyone was so happy and relieved. It had been arranged that Bessie and the others would stay overnight with Uncle Albert because there was more room there than at the Motts'. Bessie said she would cook a roast dinner to make a special occasion of it.

It was late that night when May and Archie finally got home. May put Connie straight to bed and Bill turned in. Archie made some cocoa, and he and May sat by the dying embers of the fire to drink it. May felt truly blessed that Winnie had come through the accident and they were friends again. Everything was more bearable with her in her life.

But there was an important matter she needed to deal with right away.

'Now that the crisis is over and we're on our own, I have something to tell you, Archie,' she said.

Archie froze. This was the moment when she told him she was leaving him for William Marriot.

'Not now, May.' He was keen to deter her because he couldn't bear it. 'We're both absolutely worn out. Let's leave it until the morning, shall we?'

'No, it can't wait, I'm afraid,' she said determinedly. 'It's far too important.'

'You'd better get on with it then,' he told her gloomily.

'When you thought I had gone to visit Constance when Auntie was run over, I was actually with William Marriot.'

'Yes, I thought you probably were.' He explained how he had come to that conclusion.

'You didn't say anything.'

'It was hardly the time, was it?' he said.

'Oh Archie, you're so good.'

'Enough of the soft soap,' he said gravely. 'Where exactly does that leave us?'

'That depends on you.'

'This might seem negative but I have to be realistic. I can't compete with him,' he admitted sadly. 'He's always been the love of your life. You were honest with me from the start about that.' He paused, hardly able to utter his next words. 'How long has it been going on, you and him?'

'Nothing has been going on,' she was quick to explain. 'I ran into him a while ago and he gave me his calling card. I admit I have been tempted to go there but I resisted the urge, until last night. I intended to go to see Constance. I even got to her door. But I had a sudden change of mind and went to William's instead.'

'And . . .'

'Nothing happened,' she told him. 'We had a bit of a kiss and a cuddle when I arrived but there was nothing more than that. I wasn't just being dutiful and good, Archie. I didn't *want* anything more to happen.'

'Not for want of trying on his part, I bet.'

'I won't lie to you about that,' she said. 'But the important thing is that things didn't develop.'

'What were you doing all evening, then?'

'Talking.'

'Not about the weather, I presume.'

'That's true. The fact is, Archie, he wants me back,' she informed him. 'Both of us, Connie as well, and he spent the time trying to persuade me.'

'Oh.' It was like a knife in his chest. 'So you're leaving me?'

'Is that all you've got to say, Archie Mott?' she said, her voice rising angrily. 'Is that what you think of me? That I would do something like that?'

'Why else are you telling me?'

'Because I want to be straight with you. I always have been and I intend it to stay that way. If I had slept with William I would have told you. I am telling you that he wants me back because I want to put you in the picture. Our marriage has always been based on honesty. Until, that is, you came back from the war and chose to shut yourself off from me. God knows I've been patient because I know you went through a lot. But you've been home for months and there is no sign of things getting back to normal. I'm only human.'

'I'm . . . I'm sorry.'

'*Are* you sorry, though, Archie? Are you really? Only to me you seem prepared to sit back and let me walk out of your life with another man without lifting a finger to stop me. In fact you seem to be encouraging it. Be glad to be rid of me, will you, so that you don't have to make any effort?'

'How can you say a terrible thing like that?' he asked, looking wounded.

'Quite easily, given the way you've been behaving lately,' she came back at him, her cheeks flaming and eyes full of angry tears. 'For your information, I have no intention of going off with William Marriot or anyone else for that matter, but you are not making it easy for me to stay here.'

'Oh.' His eyes never left her face. 'Why did you go and see him, then?'

'Because I thought I still wanted him. He was my first love and the father of my child; naturally I haven't been able to cast him out of my mind completely over the years,' she explained. 'I don't suppose many women could.'

'Probably not.'

'You have been cold and distant towards me and he made it clear that he wanted me,' she went on. 'I'm a human being, Archie, not some unfeeling apology for one. I honestly intended to go to see Constance but I had this sudden compulsion to see William instead. Maybe it had something to do with the fact that you practically threw me out of the house, probably because you can't bear the atmosphere between us any more than I can. Anyway, I had to know what it would feel like to be with him again. As soon as he touched me I knew that the magic had gone. It had just been a thing of youth, swept away by the passing years.'

'Oh, May . . .'

'I admit that I was still a little in love with him when I married you, and I have harboured some feelings for him all this time. I suppose I'll always have special memories of him. But that's all they are now, just memories. He spent the evening trying to tempt me with what he could give Connie and me in material terms if I left you and went with him. Looking back on it, I'm not sure if I believed any of it. I think it might just have been that he can't resist a challenge. Once he'd won me over he would probably have lost interest. I never really knew what sort of a person he was; I still don't.'

Archie's head was bowed and he was shaking. With a shock May realised that he was crying.

'Archie . . . love,' she said going to him and putting her arms around him.

She had never seen a man cry like this before. His sobs were guttural, his body heaving. She didn't ask why he was weeping. She just held him close, stroking his hair, sensing that this was something he had needed to do for a long time.

'Some man, eh?' he said when he was finally cried out. 'What must you think of me now?'

'Don't be daft,' she said tenderly. 'Shedding a few tears doesn't make you any less of a man, and whoever came up with the idea that it does has a lot to answer for.'

'I'm sorry about how I've been since I got back,' he said thickly. 'I can't tell you why or describe the feeling exactly because I don't understand it

309

myself. I'd longed to come home, but when I got here I felt alone; isolated and out of place. I know it sounds weird, as I was back with people who cared about me. But that's what I've been feeling like. I lost all my confidence.'

'The war sucked it out of you.'

'Yeah, I suppose it must be something like that. It must have done the same to all of us who had been in the trenches. I doubt if I'm the only one. I miss the blokes, those who were left,' he said sadly. 'I'll never have mates like them again.'

'You shared the same experiences.'

'And it made us close.'

'Would it help to talk about what it was like out there in France?' May asked tentatively.

'Absolutely not!' he said quickly in a way that defied persuasion. 'That's enough about all of that.'

'All right, love, I won't press you.'

'You must have been really disappointed in me when I got back and I was such a cold fish,' he suggested.

'I was hurt that you were so distant towards me, and yes, I was disappointed, but not in you as a man,' she made clear. 'Never that! How could I be when you have served your country in the front line? You're a good man, Archie.'

'Things will be better between us from now on, I promise.' He smiled at her and she caught a glimpse of the old Archie for the first time since he'd been back. 'I shall try really hard to make sure that they are. I'll bloomin' well have to with that William Marriot waiting to pounce and take you off me.'

She smiled. 'A bit of competition never did anyone any harm,' she chuckled.

Then he kissed her properly for the first time since before he went away to war.

A year and a half later, in a church in Hammersmith, a christening was in progress: the baptism of three-month-old Henry Mott, son of May and Archie.

Bessie and Bob were godparents, with Sam as another godfather. They were all standing at the font while May, Archie, Connie and Jimmy were in the front pews with Winnie and Albert, Bill, George Bow and some invited guests.

All in all, it had been a good eighteen months, May reflected. It hadn't

310

exactly been 'happy ever after' since the night she and Archie had made that initial breakthrough, but with a great deal of tenderness and patience she had helped him regain his confidence in himself. Gradually the cracks in their marriage had healed and it had re-emerged stronger than before, especially with romantic thoughts of William Marriot no longer an issue for May. What had begun as a marriage of convenience for her had become one of true love.

She accepted that the scars of war would stay with Archie and she must be tolerant of those times when he went to that dark place in his head. Those few awful months following his homecoming had made them both realise just how much they had to lose. When she fell pregnant with Henry they had become even closer. They both wanted him so much.

There had been changes at Tideway too. Bessie and Bob had got married quietly soon after Winnie's accident, and no one was more pleased about it than Jimmy, who thought it was great fun to have a dad, especially a seagoing one.

More recently, Bob had bought a larger boat and George had sold his own smack and now worked for him, which meant that George had a steady income without the worry and expense of maintaining his own boat. This had also allowed Sam to change his job without upsetting his father too much, and he now worked with Bessie, who had a small photographic shop in Tideway and a growing reputation in that part of Essex.

Bessie was passing on to Sam everything that Digby Parsons had taught her, so he was getting the finest grounding in the art of photography. A small village like Tideway wasn't perhaps the ideal place to have a photographic studio, as there was very little passing trade, but there was the benefit of lower overheads than a town shop, and with travel becoming easier, people were inclined to come from further away with their business as her reputation spread. Bessie and Sam did more outside work too, as they had both learned to drive and Bessie had bought a small van.

Here in London, Connie was still as bright and lively as ever. She was absolutely thrilled with her new baby brother and made a great fuss of him. May was aware of the fact that at some time in the future she would have to tell her daughter the truth about her parentage, when she was old enough to cope with such a thing. Later on, perhaps, she could choose for herself if she wanted to get to know her father.

William had made no move to see May or Connie since May had turned him down. The location she lived in had come out in conversation the evening she had spent with him, so he could easily have found her. Maybe he was being unselfish and didn't want to unsettle his daughter.

Or could it be, perhaps, that he was preoccupied with other things at the moment? A new love, maybe?

May caught Bessie's eye and a surge of warmth filled her. She was so grateful to have a sister like her, and sad that Edie wasn't there to share the occasion with them.

But now Henry was objecting noisily to having water splashed on him by the vicar. His shrieks filled the church. Archie took May's hand and squeezed it reassuringly. Connie looked at her mother, covering her mouth with her hand as she erupted into a fit of the giggles, infecting her cousin Jimmy.

Everything was so comfortingly normal, thought May. Babies cried at christenings and children giggled inappropriately wherever they were. That was real life. That was what she valued now: her life with Archie and all the family gathered together at a very special occasion like this.